Refinald Francis Douce Palgrave

Oliver Cromwell

The Protector

Refinald Francis Douce Palgrave

Oliver Cromwell
The Protector

ISBN/EAN: 9783743687196

Printed in Europe, USA, Canada, Australia, Japan

Cover: Foto ©Raphael Reischuk / pixelio.de

More available books at **www.hansebooks.com**

OLIVER CROMWELL

THE PROTECTOR

AN APPRECIATION BASED ON CONTEMPORARY EVIDENCE

BY

REGINALD F. D. PALGRAVE, C.B.

" Turn, Fortune, turn thy wheel "

LONDON
SAMPSON LOW, MARSTON, SEARLE & RIVINGTON
Limited
St. Dunstan's House
FETTER LANE, FLEET STREET, E.C.
1890

THE

Rev. MANDELL CREIGHTON, M.A., LL.D.,

DIXIE PROFESSOR OF ECCLESIASTICAL HISTORY IN THE
UNIVERSITY OF CAMBRIDGE.

Dear Sir,

The encouragement which I received from you, as Editor of the " English Historical Review," enheartened me to attempt this book ; and you cheered me onward, during its progress, by the kind reception of a request that your name might be associated with these pages.

Unworthy as they may be of so high a distinction, you will not feel that your generous consideration has been thrown away, if this essay assists, however slightly, towards a just appreciation of the character of Oliver Cromwell, or leads to a thorough investigation into the Rebellion of 1640-1660, which it is the fashion to regard with much complacency.

REGINALD F. D. PALGRAVE.

Speaker's Court, the Palace of Westminster.
December, 1889.

"The truth of History is simply the truth of the interpretation of an infinitude of details contemplated together."—WESTCOTT.

TABLE OF CONTENTS.

INTRODUCTORY.

The Beginning of the Great Rebellion.

CHAPTER I.

Some Characteristics of Oliver Cromwell's Protectorate.

CHAPTER II.

The Protector and Major Henshaw.

CHAPTER III.

The Protector and the Conspiracies of the Winter, 1654-5.

CHAPTER IV.

The Protector and Major-General Overton.

CHAPTER V.

The Preparations for the Insurrection and Rebellion of March, 1655.

CHAPTER VI.

The Insurrection and Rebellion of March, 1655.

CHAPTER VII.

The Protector and his gainsaying Subjects.

CHAPTER VIII.

The Major-Generals and the Protector.

CHAPTER IX.

The Major-Generals call the Protector's last Parliament.

CHAPTER X.

Parliament, the Protector, and the Major-Generals.

CHAPTER XI.

Parliament, the Protector, and the Crown.

CHAPTER XII.

Parliament, the Protector, and the " Other House."

CHAPTER XIII.

The Protector, Major Wildman, and Colonel Sexby.

CHAPTER XIV.

The conclusion of the whole matter.

PRE-INTRODUCTORY.

An account of the principal sources of contemporary evidence on which the following appreciation of Oliver Cromwell, the Protector, is based.

" A COLLECTION of the State Papers of John Thurloe, Esquire, Secretary, First to the Council of State, and afterwards to the Two Protectors, Oliver and Richard Cromwell, in Seven Volumes, containing authentic Memorials of English affairs from the year 1638, to the Restoration of Charles II. Published from the originals, formerly in the library of John, Lord Somers, Lord High Chancellor of England, and since in that of Sir Joseph Jekyll, Knight, late Master of the Rolls. Including also a considerable number of Original Letters and Papers communicated by His Grace the Archbishop of Canterbury, from the Library at Lambeth, the Right Honourable the Earl of Shelburn, and other hands.

The whole digested into an exact Order of Time. With a complete Index to each Volume ; by Thomas Birch, M.A., F.R.S. 1742."

" The principal part of this collection consists of a series of papers, discovered in the reign of King William, in a false ceiling in the garrets belonging to Secretary Thurloe's chambers, No. XIII., near the Chapel in Lincoln's Inn, by a clergyman, who had borrowed those chambers, during the long vacation, of his friend Mr. Tomlinson, the owner of them." (Extract from Preface.)

" The Correspondence of Sir Edward Nicholas, Secretary of State to King Charles II. during the years 1654-62." British Museum, Egerton MSS. 2533—2562.

These MSS. are being printed by the Camden Society, Mr. George F. Warner, the Editor. Vol. I. 1641—1652. 1886.

By gifts and by bequests, ranging between the years 1759 and 1860, Lord Clarendon's correspondence, and the papers he collected as historian of the Great Rebellion, have been lodged in the Bodleian Library. The most important of these documents were printed "at the Clarendon Printing House," in three folio volumes, issued in the years 1767, 1773, and 1786, by Dr. Scrope and Mr. Monkhouse, the Editors.

Under the direction of the Rev. H. O. Coxe, Bodley's Librarian, calendars have been published, by the Clarendon Press authorities, of these papers, edited, Vol. I. by the Rev. O. Ogle and Mr. W. H. Bliss, and Vols. II. and III. by the Rev. W. Dunn Macray, 1872-76. These calendars extend up to December, 1657, and it is to be hoped that Mr. Macray's MS. calendar of the remaining papers will receive publication.

" A collection of original letters and papers concerning the affairs of England from the year 1641 to 1660, found among the Duke of Ormond's papers, in two volumes, by Thomas Carte, M.A. Printed by James Bettenham, at the expense of the Society for the Encouragement of LEARNING, 1739."

" Letters wrote on the scene and at the time of actions and negotiations, especially when wrote by persons present at those actions, and employed in those negotiations, are with reason deemed the most proper means of obtaining, and conveying down to posterity, just and authentic accounts of the transactions to which they relate;" and "are often as entertaining as any poetical descriptions . . . with this advantage, that they have truth on their side." (Extract from Carte's Preface.)

Calendar of State Papers, Domestic Series, 1653-58, preserved in the State Paper Department of Her Majesty's Public Record Office. Edited by Mary Anne Everett

Green, author of "The Lives of the Princesses of England," &c.

The Leveson Correspondence, 1642—1660, drawn from the MSS. of his Grace the Duke of Sutherland, and the Bradshaw-Wainright Letters, 1650-58, from the MSS. of Miss ffarington, of Worden Hall, calendared by Mr. Alfred J. Horwood, and published in the appendices to the fifth and sixth Reports issued by the Historical MSS. Commission.

"Diary of Thomas Burton, Esq., Member (for Westmoreland) in the Parliaments of Oliver and Richard Cromwell, from 1656 to 1659, now first published from the original autograph manuscript. With an introduction containing an account of the Parliament of 1654, from the Journal of Guibon Goddard, Esq., M.P., now also first printed. Edited and illustrated, with notes historical and biographical, by John Towill Rutt. In four volumes. London: Henry Colburn, 1828."

The original correspondence of Captain Adam Baynes, M.P. for Leeds, 1641—1666. British Museum, Add. MSS. 21417-26.

The catalogues compiled by Mr. Alfred Hackman and the Rev. W. Dunn Macray of the MSS. and the 450 volumes of papers given by Richard Rawlinson and by Bishop Tanner to the Bodleian Library, during the first half of the last century, will indicate the documents relating to the Protectorate era which these grand collections contain. The MSS., from which the seven volumes of the Thurloe Papers were drawn, exist among the Rawlinson Papers.

A few words must be permitted, to meet Carlyle's attempt to decry and to depreciate the evidences of the Protectorate history.

The pother that he makes over that "shoreless chaos" of illegible documents and records, is not the outburst of a perverse imagination, or the off-scourings of dyspeptic irritability. Carlyle's denunciations of those " waste lumber mountains " are elaborated with skilful ingenuity; his reiterated outcries vibrate with a ring of seeming honest indignation. This exhibition of art and artifice had a purpose; and the purpose was descried by no unworthy critic. With the humorous sagacity that goes to make up a true poet, Keble—Cromwell, then newly whitewashed into the Puritan Hero, was under discussion—remarked that " The worst of this whitewashing is that to be successful in it, one must blackwash such a number of other people." (" Life of John Allen, Archdeacon," p. 99.)

Keble had hit the mark. Carlyle sought to obscure the " shot-rubbish " of the Protectorate era with " lurid twilight," to enhance the whiteness of his own " amorphous " creation. The showman blackened the background, to render the phosphorated face of his " Brave One " the more conspicuous. Yet in the fuss he made over that " avalanche of Human Stupidities," Carlyle showed great confidence withal in human stupidity. The unreality of these outcries is made easily apparent by a mere description of the objects of his sophistical wrath.

The papers, which Thurloe so opportunely ceiled up in his garret, were the letters and documents, formal and familiar, official and private, which were swept out of Cromwell's Home Office when the Restoration revolutionized the Revolution. The papers hid away in that false ceiling are therefore of the truest quality. No opportunity occurred for judicious selection, for the smuggling of awkward disclosures out of sight. The notes supplied by Cromwell's trepanner lay alongside the depositions of his victim; the letters from Cromwell's servants, indicating the method whereby he invented conspiracies, were not destroyed.

As for the Clarendon and Nicholas documents, they were dictated by the anxieties and hopes of Charles's needy and factious Court, provoked, day after day, by their coinless pockets, foodless larders, and fruitless expectations. From this source alone can be acquired a glimpse of the thoughts and fears of Cromwell's subjects. During those dangerous days, when Englishmen were afraid to speak to each other, and the Government stifled the newspapers and controlled the printing presses, criticism upon English affairs existed nowhere save on paper intended for exportation across the Channel.

The Baynes collection affords an amusing picture of social life in Leeds under the Protectorate, and of the strife and jealousy which raged between the rival parties of conformists and dissidents who had alike thrown in their lot with the Protector.

The false and virulent depreciation that Carlyle bestows on "this poor Burton" and his parliamentary diary, suggests the notion that, in truth, "this editor has faithfully read it," and discerned that this "book filled with mere dim inanity and moaning wind," revealed a Cromwell quite other than the editor's Cromwell. Next to D'Ewes's Diary of the Long Parliament (alas! still in MS.), Burton's Diary is the most valuable record of the thoughts that governed Englishmen of the seventeenth century. Burton, with admirable fidelity, caught the tone of each debate and of each debater. Every man speaks his own words, and not the words of the note-taker. The soldiers, the lawyers, the courtiers, the radicals, talk in character; they all show up the sham Commonwealth; some indulge in fond retrospects of days when radicalism was in the ascendant; and many speak the language of honest men about Oliver Cromwell, mostly, of course, after his death. The pages that occur hereafter, which are based on Burton's notes, show, I trust, that their worth and vitality are fairly estimated. If that be. so, surely Carlyle gibed and snarled at that Diary of malice prepense, to play up to that large stock of credulity and conceit, which he instinctively recognized among his followers.

According to the modern standard of veracity, Ludlow's and Mrs. Hutchinson's Memoirs, and Heath's Chronicle are to be despised, because they are written by Cromwell haters. Why a hater should be deemed a more untrustworthy witness than a lover, I wot not; but, anyhow, nought has been drawn from those authorities, save what is supported by a mass of concurrent testimony. Mrs. Hutchinson undoubtedly doted more on the "mortal excellencies" of her

Colonel than on the immortal excellency of Justice, and Heath was unwise, and somewhat scurrilous; but Ludlow was a straightforward soldier, who preferred risk and obscurity to place and profit, and if his abhorrence of the Protector biassed his opinions, it did not pervert his statement of facts. The continuation of Baker's Chronicle, from the death of James I., to 1660, was written by E. Phillips, Milton's nephew: the narrative is temperate and impartial, though prepared to suit the Restoration market. Clarendon's inaccuracy as a historian comes not here in question. He is very outspoken, considering his temptations as man, writer, and royalist, anent Charles I.'s ill-advised efforts to rid himself of the Long Parliament, and can certainly be accepted as the narrator of Charles II.'s indolent, pleasure-seeking ways, and of the cautious treatment he accorded to his deluded followers' incitements into action.

A strong sense of indebtedness, prompted by hours of keen interest enjoyed during many years, to the men of the last century who collected and edited the principal memorials of Cromwell's Protectorate, may excuse an expression of indignation at the unjust and disgraceful treatment they received from Carlyle. When he wrote, foremost among those men were the editors of the Thurloe and Clarendon papers. The Clarendon letters are carefully selected, arranged, and indexed; and, with the Thurloe collections, form ten goodly folios. Though few may study those ten folios, all must admire the devotion, the enthusiasm that put those volumes into being. There were giants in those days—collecting giants, Richard Rawlinson and Bishop Tanner—and the editorial giant, Dr. Birch. He obtained the support of over 400 subscribers to the publication of the Thurloe Papers, and he presented them, in return, with some six thousand closely printed folio pages, supervised with skill and care, and indexed with the minute precision that springs from zeal and intimate knowledge. And yet, of these noble monuments of bygone industry and insight, the reviler of the men whose work he misused, asserts that "not one of these monstrous volumes has so much as an available index."

Keble, in that talk over the modern Oliver Cromwell, drolled upon the art of "whitewashing." "It is," he said, "a very good trade, and it ought to have clever men in it, as well as other trades." But, in this instance, clever as he was, the prime artist in the black and white business smudged his own face, and not the "monstrous" folios which he so ill-advisedly vilified.

In one respect Carlyle was at a disadvantage. The activity in the publication of historical material which distinguished the last century, had not been renewed when he published Cromwell's speeches. Had he been brought into contact with the Calendars of the State, and of the Clarendon papers, which Mrs. Everett Green and Mr. Macray have produced, admirably compiled, prefaced, noted, and indexed, he could not have treated their worthy Georgian predecessors so despitefully.*

* An article in the *National Review*, Vol. VIII. 588, deals with "Carlyle as Editor of Cromwell's Speeches."

INTRODUCTORY.

THE BEGINNING OF THE GREAT REBELLION.

On the 10th of September, 1640, England was in this position. Our northern counties were occupied and held down by the army of the Scotch Covenanters. They had routed our troops, exacted 850*l.* a day, and were on the advance to London. King Charles stood face to face with the invader. The Yorkshire trained bands had mustered; and their comrades throughout central England were rallying round the royal standard. The King reviewed "a gallant army with horse and foot sufficient;" he could have met the Covenanters in the field. Nothing had occurred in England to mar this hopeful aspect of affairs, when, twelve days later, on the 22nd September, the King threw up his arms and sank

Note.—This introductory chapter is based on the writer's articles, "Pym and Shaftesbury: Two Popish Plots," and "The Fall of the Monarchy of Charles I." *Quarterly Review*, Vol. 147, No. 294; Vol. 154, No. 307.

The story of the outbreak of the Great Rebellion lies hid away in the MSS. Department of the British Museum, in D'Ewes' Diary of the Long Parliament. Its publication is a national duty. If a company of patriots would furnish the money, and the able and accomplished Deputy-Keeper of the Rolls the supervision, between them they would raise to themselves an enduring monument, and make to English literature a priceless addition.

down. He submitted to the Covenanters : he consented to the Long Parliament. His subjects had deserted him.

Three London citizens, not without risk to life and fortune, came between the King and his army, and laid before him a petition, signed by some 10,000 of their fellow-subjects, informing him, in effect, that they would not fight for him, and that he must yield to the invader.

Nations, however abject, rarely commit abject, instantaneous surrender, unless their conqueror be held in much love, or in much fear. Those Scottish conquerors, Englishmen of 1640 certainly did not love, and perhaps despised. Nor as a nation do we naturally turn our cheek to the smiter. A craving after peace at any price is not our habitual impulse ; yet peace at any price was the demand of the citizens of London.   .

The utter collapse of patriotic and dutiful feeling which overcame England during September, 1640, was not produced by violent antipathy to the King. Upon the action of the three London citizens, therefore, must be charged the disgrace of that national surrender.

Those message-bearers had not undertaken a light or indifferent task. They bore to the King, in the presence of victorious enemies, a declaration from his subjects that they sided with the enemy. Such a message savoured of high treason ; it brought those messengers within the grasp of martial law ; and Strafford, the " thorough," was at hand. They must have been driven onward by strong conviction. Even if it did not imperil their necks, that errand was stamped with grave result to King and country. Their demand, that the King would " compose this present war without effusion of blood," was a demand that Charles should submit to the Scotch, who for two years had been in open revolt, who, having completed their work in their own land, had conquered northern England, and were on the way to conquer all England. Nominal sovereignty, practical abdication, was to the King the result of that demand.

To England equally that message was fraught with disaster. Conquerors, especially Scotch conquerors, make the war business a paying business. To the 850*l.* levied each day for their subsistence, the Covenanters would add a large money ransom : they would not return home until they were satisfied. The Covenanters also were enthusiastic for their religious notions. They might compel us to accept catechisms of singular complexity, and most unpalatable ceremonies.

The fear of a danger which far exceeded the injury caused by submission to the Scotch invader, must therefore have hounded on those message-bearers. If so, their message will disclose terrors of an urgent and appalling nature.

The prayers of the London petitioners are prefaced by a description of the evils of warfare,—peril to H.M.'s sacred person,—possible annoyance to his subjects. Then they bewail sundry innovations in matters of religion,—the great increase of Popery,—the urging of Ship Money,—the imposition of Monopolies and of charges upon Merchandise,—the long intermission of Parliament. These complaints do not ring with a note of despair. These troubles would not send any London citizen, endowed with civic common sense, on an errand disastrous to England and risky to himself.

But among these subdued and moderate griefs, occurs this suggestion. " The great mischief which may fall upon this Kingdom, if the Intention, which hath been credibly reported, of bringing in Irish and foreign Forces, should take effect," is offered " unto the King's most princely wisdom," as a " great danger now threatening " England. Here, then, is the cause of the national catastrophe of September, 1640. Strafford's exclamation, addressed to the King in Council upon the previous 5th of May, " You have an army in Ireland, you may employ here to reduce this Kingdom," is re-echoed by thousands of the King's subjects.

What will not men do to save life, and to save all that makes life precious? Whether the Kingdom which Strafford proposed to reduce was the Scotch Kingdom, or the English Kingdom, that was an ugly suggestion. From such a menace a nation might well seize on any mode of deliverance, however hazardous, however humiliating; and the Covenanters, in their turn, repeated back to us Strafford's words. They told us, by their " national " Manifesto, that they crossed the Border to save England from " the yoke of bondage that was to be laid upon our brethren," the English people, " by the help of such an army as was pretended to be gathered against us," that is to say, by Strafford's Irish army.

With so terrible an outlook before us, a national refusal to resist the Scottish invader was naturally inevitable.

Englishmen, in general, are not a submissive race. Nor, if I may speak for my brethren, are we prone to accept " atrocity " notions. We do not readily believe that those in authority over us are plotting our destruction, or are more depraved and heartless than the rest of mankind.

Yet in 1640 we were compelled by fear to yield to our Scotch conquerors; and in 1641 we became the slaves of a ghastly idea, of a terror that shook us through and through.

The belief that the King plotted our subjection by the Irish army, was in itself sufficiently disturbing; but to the King's opponents that rumour was not sufficient, they coupled with it another belief far more appalling.

England was taught that a vast conspiracy was on foot,

headed by the Pope of Rome, the Queen, and therefore by the King, and therefore by every person connected with the King, the Church, and the Government, to inflict upon us Popery and tyranny. Thus taught, we felt, in everything that the King did, or left undone, the touch of the "Jesuited Papists." This was his motive in the creation of monopolies, in dissolving Parliaments, in driving the Scotch into rebellion; that was why he plotted our ruin by the Irish army.

To the contagion of terror, society was then especially exposed. The strength of rumour was at its utmost. We were a non-reading community, acted upon by the rising power of the printing press. Newspapers were not, as yet, substitutes for talk; they ministered to the fluency of the tongue. The "Diurnals" and "Flying Sheets" fanned the great flame which the "little member" kindleth, nursed and fed rumour, and stamped on rumour undeserved authenticity. Belief that "the Priests and Jesuits, and other adherents to the see of Rome," and every authority over the land, from the King to the parish clerk, were undermining our religion and our laws was truly a "strong delusion." It shocked, enraged, demoralized the nation; it steeped us in a flood of hatred and distrust. Based on tradition, in accord with popular fancy, vague, all-embracing, portentous, that belief enthralled the land. And it was inextinguishable. The plot could not be proved: neither could it be disproved; for the plot never existed. Yet so long as the Queen was in Whitehall, the scarlet spectre hovered over England.

Her persuasive charm, the common fancy that a wife influences a husband, endowed that spectral illusion with reality and energy. She herself unconsciously came within its mischief, and contributed to its potency. The spectre caused terror and danger to her household and to her Roman Catholic subjects. Provoked and alarmed by calumny, threats, and persecution, they reacted on Henrietta Maria. They drove her, and with her, the King, into dangerous courses, which in their turn endowed the apparition with renewed vigour.

Nor was the spectre an honest spectre, the product of unbiassed English intellect. It was the creature of the political agitator, used to serve his ends. Borne aloft by every possible device, the Great Papal Conspiracy was, with malicious craft, kept ever in view, when it might have been effaced by the obliterating touch of time. The months of 1641 rolled on; Parliament met, and Parliament was made perpetual; Strafford was sacrificed; the Irish Army disbanded; but the red spectre was kept afloat, high in air; it grew the vaster as the country grew more tranquil. The men who should have laid the red terror asleep, inflated the monster into a bigger and bigger being. As soon as Parliament appeared in Westminster, the apparition appeared there, and took possession of the House of Commons; and the inspirer, manager, and advertiser of the show was Mr. Pym, the Leader of the House. No more effective exhibition gallery, nor a Barnum more brilliant ever existed. Furnished by nature and by position with manifold resources, Pym intoxicated the people by a perpetual representation of the Popish Plot, under ever-changing effects of form, time, and scenery.

Whatever happened, whatever subject was before the House of Commons, the scarlet spectre came to the front, and was saluted by speeches, motions, and resolutions. The Papist and his devices were thus dragged constantly before the Speaker's chair. Hardly a week passed by, throughout the session of 1641, but some excuse arose for the formation of committees of " religion," for " inquiry after Papists," or into " the Popish hierarchy in England." These proposals provoked statements of the widest and wildest nature; and excited auditors in the House and its precincts gave rapid circulation to the alarm.

The floor of the House of Commons formed, in 1641, an advertising medium quite as effective as it is now-a-days. The not infrequent accident of " strangers " being " told " among members in a Division, proves that the lobby and the space below the bar were habitually crowded with spectators. And a significant hint is given, both of the presence of eager listeners in the committee-rooms, and of the use to which those rooms were put. A motion for the exclusion of " strangers," made by a steady adherent to the King, was " quashed " at the instance of a zealous preacher of the Popish Plot.

Nor did parliamentary news rest dormant in Westminster Hall, or among the talkers in London streets : it was rapidly dispersed throughout England by " Flying Sheets." " Husband's Daily Proceedings in this Great and Happy Parliament " quite fulfils the promise of its title ; and the source of its inspiration is marked by many a paragraph, such as, —that an archdeacon had cursed the Parliament as " a company of puritanical, factious fellows ;"—that a clergyman had affirmed that the " Puritans were all knaves, and Papists all honest men ;"—or that a letter, written in the Queen's name, directing good Catholics to pray for the success of a great design, had been laid before the House.

Every committee was a fresh centre for the circulation of the Papal panic. Every inquiry about the Papists tended to establish its own necessity ; and every inquirer, inspired by the importance of his task, became a minor prophet in the mission of which Pym was the hierophant.

What can convert a nothing into a something, or give vitality to a hobby, more effectively than a parliamentary Committee ? Pym knew this quite as well as we do. So day by day the reports from these Committees were read aloud at the table of the House. Day after day, the Members and the public were thereby warned that thousands of recusants were collected in London ; that they swarmed in Lancashire and Wales ; that "nineteen earls and two countesses" were Papists ; and that sixty Jesuits were, at that very moment, celebrating the Mass, even in sacred Westminster. From the committee-rooms also circulated stories that priests had openly threatened to kill the King, or had boasted that he and the Pope "were all one;" that cartloads of armour were being brought to the houses of Popish noblemen, who were collecting pickaxes and shovels, "there being a great design on foot." And, in confirmation of that design, stores of "popish stuff, black wooden crosses, trinkets, and cords for whipping," were exhibited in the committee-rooms.

These committees, also, justified an aspect of activity. Upon their reports were founded repeated resolutions directing the Officers of Parliament, or the Sheriffs of London and Middlesex, to apprehend, disarm, and fine Papists, to expel them from the Court, or to confine them to their houses. Repeated proposals, also, were made of addresses to the King, and of conferences with the House of Lords touching the Great Papal Conspiracy.

Thus worked upon, many an honest man was convinced that the Papists "had arms enough to draw together 40,000 or 50,000 men;" and "that there was a great design projected for our destruction." Resentment also was stirred up against the Church of England ; for a company of 2000 horsemen, equipped by clerical funds, was added to the Popish Army that rumour set marching upon London. These methods, the perpetual repetition of this ghastly tune, taught the House of Commons, as well as the common people, to pipe in harmony with Pym's whistle. By motions for the "speedy disarming of Papists," for the arrest of suspected persons, and for the detention of the mails, because the House of Commons finds "every day new discoveries of secret counsels, and meetings of Jesuits and others, and of several plots and designs to disturb the peace of this Kingdom," he rehearsed his brother Members in the part of convinced believers in the Popish Plot. And by the resolutions they voted, declaring that, to save England, the country should be "put in a posture of defence," and that all the royal fortresses and arsenals, Portsmouth, Carlisle, Hull, and even the Tower of London, must be placed under the control of Parliament, he prepared the House of Commons to pass from motions into actions, and to snatch from the Crown civil and military government.

Full justice to the skill and craft of Pym cannot be done here; but three of the most exciting scenes in his spectacle play—"England in the jaws of the Grim Wolf of Rome,"—must be described. The first scene, when we were glad and hopeful at the opening of the Long Parliament, exhibited our Catholic friends and neighbours a-sharpening their knives to cut the national throat. The second scene renewed and reinforced that terrible spectacle. The object of the third scene was to play out the King, the Queen, the Government, and the Church, as accomplices in the great Irish Massacre of October, 1641.

Scene the First.—On the 21st of November, 1640, a young Romanist, by name John James, struck with a "long dagger" Mr. Justice Heywood, as he carried through Westminster Hall a list of the Westminster recusants to lay before a committee. The attack occurred on a Saturday, and on the Monday the incident was brought before the House. The Commons, therefore, could not have been overcome by sudden terror. That James was a crazy youth of no special note, and that his attempt was an isolated affair, arising perhaps out of private spite, was known at once. Yet the assault on Mr. Justice Heywood was not so treated. It provoked a long and excited debate. The cry was raised that " a general assassination " would immediately take place; and the Commons were assured that the citizens of London were " ready to hazard their lives for the safety of this House; " and that their Trained Bands would furnish "three hundred men, at a time, for a Guard." The proposal was accepted: it was " Resolved, upon the question, ' that it is expedient for this House to accept of this Guard, so kindly offered for the safety of this House.' "

That kindly offer was a preconcerted move. That it was so is not merely the fancy of to-day: a contemporary observer was of that opinion. Giustiniani, the Venetian ambassador, reported to his Government, that the attack on Heywood had been used " to goad the lukewarm " in Parliament " against the Roman Catholics; " and that, " under this pretext," it had been " sought to further the project of an armed guard of 300 musketeers."

The resolution of the 23rd of November remained inoperative for about twelve months; but its import is unmistakable. Under it a strong outpost, drawn from the best-drilled force in England, would be stationed in Westminster; a daily march of 300 soldiers through London would be maintained. These men would take their orders from the House of Commons; they, therefore, were exempt from the control which the law placed in the hands of the Sovereign. And against whom were they to act ? They were to protect Parliament against the Popish conspirator :

that is to say, against the King, for he, according to Pym, was the head of that conspiracy, and his palace was its head-quarters. That resolution also shows that the "project of an armed guard" dated from the opening of the Long Parliament.

Scene the Second.—" 12th May, 1631, House of Commons. This day Mr. Pym discovered a letter to Lady Shelly which had miscarried, and which, being read, contained words to this effect : ' Madam, though there be some discovery of our design, yet we are sure. You must disburse 20,000*l.* more : keep your counsel, and no danger. We shall destroy the wicked brood before they are aware.' "

No signature, save what a "Diurnal" describes as "characters," the "undecipherable hieroglyphics of a clown," was affixed to this letter; and to us its purport may seem equally undecipherable, unless the scrawl was a malicious device. To Pym the meaning was obvious. Lady Shelly was a Papist " of a violent nature ;" the " wicked brood" were all the Protestants in England ; and the " we " who " shall destroy them," their Papist neighbours. Pym's coadjutors in Parliament declared that " the paper was of great weight," and its discovery in the street " providential." A committee was appointed to search the lady's house ; and an immediate conference was proposed between both Houses to arrange " that the prime persons of the Romish religion may be seized, and delivered as public hostages into the custody of the power of the Country," and for a com-mission "for the disarming of Papists."

Scene the Third.—On the 15th of November, 1641, a breath-less fugitive from popish murderers stood at the door of the House of Commons. He bore the credentials of a horror-struck face, and of sword-cuts, if not upon his body, at least right through his cloak. This witness was "Mr. Thomas Beale, a tailor dwelling in White Cross Street." Mr. Pym introduced him, telling the House that "there was one attending without, who had somewhat to reveal." After a preliminary examination before a select committee, Beale was taken up to the House of Lords, where, standing at the bar, "he made relation of the whole business; viz. that this day, at twelve of the clock at noon, he went into the fields near the Pest House, and walking on a private bank, he heard some talking; and going nearer heard them say, that it was a wicked thing that the last plot did not take; but that if this go on as it is in hand, they all will be made; and also heard them say that there was 108 men appointed to kill 108 persons of the Parliament, every one his man. Some were Lords, and the others were Members of the House of Commons, all Puritans; and the Sacrament was to be administered to the men for performing of this; and those that killed the Lords were to have 10*l.*, and those that were to kill the Members of the House of Commons, 40*s.*"

The conspirators then went into particulars. Mr. Beale thus learnt that "one Philip" was the 108th man, and that he "received his charge in my lord's chamber, where were Father Jones and Father Andrewes;" that "Dick Jones was appointed to kill that rascally Puritan, Pym;" and that "on the same day, being the 18th of this month, there shall be risings in Warwickshire and other counties." Those "that were to kill the Lords," were described as "gallants in their scarlet cloaks, who had received every man his 10*l.* a piece;" and the relation ended with a statement that the project was "Father Andrewes's wit," to prevent sending succour to the Protestants in Ireland.

His story told, Mr. Beale withdrew, and modestly left it

to others to describe the occasion "of his being in the fields," which was "the mending the notes he had taken of a sermon," and his escape from the swords of the conspirators, who, "overtaking him, ran him through his cloathes and cloke in four or five several places, and so left him, as he thought, dead."

The Commons followed, in Beale's case, the precedents supplied by the attack on Mr. Justice Heywood and by the Shelly letter, but with considerable additions. Directions were given for securing the persons of the prime Papists, lists were prepared of their names, and of the popish Lords in Parliament; and it was ordered that musketeers and guards be stationed "near the stairs coming out of Westminster Hall, to-morrow being the day of the conspiracy." Proposals were also made to the Lords to desire their co-operation in placing "the forts and castles of this kingdom" and the trained bands in "good hands," that is to say, under the control of Parliament.

Success was ensured to scene the third, by the season of its production. Mr. Pym's dishevelled tailor could reckon on a sympathetic audience for his shrieks and cries. The Great Irish Massacre of October-November, 1641, was on the rage. Hundreds, thousands, of our fellow-Protestants were at the mercy of those who showed no mercy. The catastrophe, which, to our fancy, was imminent over us, was in Ireland a reality. England "was moved, as the trees of the wood are moved with the wind," "as the corn-fields sway before the breeze."

Beale the tailor and the murderers in Ireland had crowned King Pym. At any moment he could oust King Charles from the Tower of London and the royal fortresses. At any moment Pym could make of Westminster an armed camp. The 300 musketeers promised in February last were forthcoming at his call. Six hours might place London, from the Royal Exchange to New Palace Yard, in his power; whilst the King had not a single soldier within call. The swords and halberds of his personal attendants were his sole defence.

The House of Lords was paralyzed. The arrest the Commons ordered of the Roman Catholic peers, the search through their houses for arms, the list of their names, reaching to sixty in number, drawn up publicly upon the table of the House of Commons, terrified them. They were marked out for proscription; they fled from Parliament; but the roar of "Hang up the popish Lords! No rotten-hearted Lords! No Bishops!" did not cease to resound through Old Palace Yard.

As the storm of slander and abuse rolled on, as it increased in blackness, its purpose revealed itself. Ever more and more it was worked up against Henrietta Maria. Every Protestation or Remonstrance, by which the House of Commons shook the land, was directed against the Queen. Every appeal they made to the people charged all our miseries, and all the misery to come, upon the "wicked plots, counsels, and conspiracies" of the "adherents to the See of Rome;" and she was a "Popish Woman." The Queen was within the mischief of every resolution voted by the House denouncing "Papists of eminence:" for of the English Roman Catholics she was the most eminent.

No pains were spared to exhibit her as the patroness of the Great Papal Conspiracy. The House of Commons repeatedly informed the public that it was by her direction that the Papists were fasting, praying, and collecting arms; and to clench such statements, an impeachment was trumped up against her confessor. Her letter of 1639, desiring contributions from the Catholics towards the assistance of the Government, was laid before Parliament, and the officers of her household appointed to carry out that service were cited as criminals at the bar of Parliament, although perfectly innocent of any legal offence.

These indirect attacks upon the Queen's reputation were but "the beginning of sorrows." First, vague distrust, was roused against her, then fierce resentment, and now detestation. During the tribulation caused by the massacres in Ireland, when, in that Day of Judgment, the "distress of nations with perplexity" was upon us, and "men's hearts were failing them for fear," the English people were informed by the House of Commons that the Irish murderers openly declared that the Queen was "their nursing mother," and that our bishops and the King's advisers were their accomplices. With all the authority of a parliamentary debate, it was proclaimed that the leaders of the Irish rebellion seized forts and towns "for His Majesty's use;" that they acted under a commission sealed with the Broad Seal of England, and gave free passes in the King's name.

The net was wrapped, fold after fold, around the King and Queen. At last the net was thrown over their heads. Upon the 13th of December, 1641, Pym moved, and the House voted, an address to the King praying him "to vindicate the Queen's honour, that she neither had, nor would encourage the rebels in Ireland, nor mediate for them." And this was the mode by which that vindication was to be effected. The King, upon the petition of both Houses, was, "to procure from the Queen her public declaration, that she 'doth abhor and detest the perfidious and traitorous proceedings of the rebels in Ireland.'"

The mischief of this proposal is obvious, even had we been ignorant of its source. In no way could the King or Queen escape from the snare of that resolution. If Charles was pliant,—then he admitted that nought but a disclaimer from the Queen herself, extorted from her by the action of Parliament, could quench "scandalous reports and apprehensions" that she "had, or would, secretly favour and encourage the Irish rebels;" for that was the assigned motive of the Commons. If he resisted,—then their conjoint guilt was proved. A husband and a wife were thus compelled to humiliate or to incriminate each other.

Nor could the savage purpose of that resolution miss its aim, even though it remained inoperative upon the Commons' journal,—as it did. For the mere proposal by the House to approach the Crown with such a suggestion, established it to be a fact that the Commons felt constrained to warn her Majesty from venturing further in the course she had commenced,—from conspiring with the Irish conspirators.

Then came the blow of which these detestable artifices were the prelude, though "the end is not yet." Pym and his associates "resolved to impeach the Queen as having conspired against public liberties, and as having hold intelligence with the Irish rebels."

To impeach the Queen was to throw her among the lions. The cry "overturn, overturn, overturn," with which Pym had maddened the people, denied her, not a fair trial but any trial at all. White hot with anger and dismay, insurgent crowds roamed to and fro between London and Westminster. The Abbey was attacked; the House of Lords was mobbed; Whitehall was threatened. The most powerful of tribunals, fenced about with physical and moral strength, might have bowed before such a storm. For his own defence, or for the defence of the House of Lords,—the Queen's judges upon an impeachment,—the King had not a soldier at his command. The Commons, whilst they infuriated the people, were the masters of the Trained Bands.

And what moral power was left in the House of Lords? Not a very fibrous body, decimated by the arrests of the Bishops, and by the proscription of the Romanist peers, the Lords were already reduced to a state of pulp. But it was not enough merely to threaten, mob, and imprison the Bishops and the popish, rotten-hearted peers. Against the whole House of Lords must be aroused the anger and abhorrence of the nation.

On Pym's motion, the House of Commons, by their " Declaration for the Safety of the King and Kingdom," made " before God and the whole People," charged against the House of Lords that, by " their delays and interruptions," they were accomplices in the Irish Massacre, and in " the plots of the cruel and bloody Papists."

Pym had done his work. The end had come, when he read aloud that Declaration at the bar of the House of Lords, on the 24th Dec., 1641. The Queen's judges were handed over to the fury of the people ; and as for Henrietta Maria, held up before her subjects as the " nursing mother " of the Irish murderers, her fate would have been the fate of any one, whether Queen or scullion, who during the autumn of 1857 was pointed at, in the streets of Calcutta, as a friend of the Sepoys, or an associate with Nana Sahib. Charles would not have been a man, if he had not struck back. He did so ; he impeached " the Five Members," Pym, Hampden, Haselrig, Holles, Strode ; and up flared the Great Rebellion.

Example is better than precept. Lucius Cary, Lord Falkland, worked with the King's opponents from November, 1640, to November, 1641 ; but when Pym began to denounce the King, the Queen, the Bishops, the House of

Lords, and all the English Roman Catholics, as abettors of the Irish massacre, Falkland ranged himself upon the side of the accused. Because he had been persuaded "to believe many things, which he had since found to be untrue," he refused to act further with Pym and Hampden.

Falkland's "great refusal," attests the malignant falsity of the Great Papal Conspiracy of 1641 ; and, as became "a severe adorer of the truth," he bore witness by his death against the many untrue things to which he had consented at Pym's dictation.

Oliver Cromwell, also one of Pym's associates, took the contrary part. When the Lord Protector, he imitated Pym the plot-driver and met, as the following pages disclose, with due reward.

OLIVER CROMWELL THE PROTECTOR.

CHAPTER I.

SOME CHARACTERISTICS OF OLIVER CROMWELL'S PROTECTORATE.

THE due use of labour is one of the rights of labour. Even the hewer and the drawer may justly complain if the wood be left to rot, or the water be thrown into the gutter. Far more may the worker for the mind claim that best recognition of his mental work, its employment.

If this be so, an attempt to deal afresh with those "old, unhappy, far-off things," Oliver Cromwell's character, and the quality of his government, is a matter of duty. The Calendars that are published by Mrs. Everett Green, the Rev. W. Dunn Macray, and Mr. George F. Warner, of the State Papers, 1653-59, of the Rawlinson, Tanner, Clarendon,* and

---

* It is regrettable that the Clarendon Press authorities withhold from publication the conclusion of Mr. Macray's valuable Calendar of the Clarendon MSS. Its completion would be a mark of respect due to him and to his work, and a great gain to the student.

Nicholas MSS., and the Reports of the Historical MSS. Commission impart to the history of Cromwell's Protectorate a fulness of detail as yet unattainable, and as yet unused.

Hence arises our justification for this essay. The exertions of these literary altruists, who work so disinterestedly for others rather than for themselves, demand an effort in return.

But here we must part company. This investigation discloses a Protector so utterly unlike the Image which modern fancy has set up,—a creature who " comes in such a questionable shape,"—that he will deservedly be put to his purgation. With such an innovation the immediate concurrence of my honoured fellow-labourers cannot be assumed.

They may, however, rest assured that it was not " to peer with 'skew eyes into the deeds of heroes," that this inquiry was begun; and that the feelings of Cromwell-worshippers will receive soft handling. If the Protector be likened to the Devil, the comparison will be effected in parabolic fashion. His cruel shuffling ways are set down without malice; and the fact that his subjects regarded him as a man in whom there was no truth, who set snares to entrap them, shall be published, as far as possible, in his own words. Nor are the names or the imaginations of the creators of the ideal Cromwell even mentioned here; although this attempt thereby will lose a certain kind of attractiveness.

Pert contradictions directed against noted writers, are effective counters in the literary game, ring roundly on the board, and attract the heedless by-standers ; and a smart contrast between the pitiable Protector of 1653-58, and Cromwell, the Great and Good of 1845-89, might have afforded some diversion. Contradiction, however, is but an ill mode of telling the truth. He takes the better part who relates his own story, placing demure reliance on the authorities that he cites.

Failure was ordained for Oliver Cromwell's Protectorate from the 16th December, 1653—the day when he entered Westminster Hall to be installed The Lord Protector of the Commonwealth of England, Scotland, and Ireland,—until the 3rd September, 1658. It could not be otherwise. From the day of his installation until the day of his death, Oliver Cromwell never could rise above the source of his authority. The Lord Protector was the creature of some half a dozen Major-Generals.[1] They drew up the "Instrument of Government," the " Articles " which vested supreme legislative authority " in one Person, and in the People assembled in Parliament."[1] And Major-General Lambert, in behalf of those officers, desired the Lord General Cromwell to become that "one Person," and kneeling presented to him the Sword of State.

[1] Ludlow, 202. Burton, I. 363 ; IV. 77. Old Parl. Hist., XX. 247. Baker, 550.

That very act, the words Lambert used, foretold the fate of Oliver Cromwell. His supremacy was founded on a lie, for Lambert led him to the Protector's Chair, " in the name of the Army and of the Three Nations." In so doing, Lambert took in vain the name of the Three Nations and of the Army. The rank and file, the officers, as a body, had not been consulted; many amongst them repudiated government by " a single person." With Cromwell's installation the Three Nations, powerless, voiceless, had nought to do.

Cromwell's associate in power, the " People assembled in Parliament " also was a mockery. The Instrument contained a clause which placed Parliament at the mercy of the Protector's Council, that is to say, of the Military Party.*

Cromwell mocked his subjects, when " His Excellency " accepted " the Civil Sword," and " put off his own, thereby to intimate that he would no longer rule by the Military one." A sword offered to the Commander-in-Chief by his General could not be a " Civil Sword." A scheme of government framed by soldiers, and enforced by the Protector whom they had chosen, was government by the " Military Sword," and not by one sword only, but by many swords, by the swords of the Major-Generals.[2]

Such a Protector was not the Protector of a

. 178, 199.
. 382 ; III. 568. Ludlow, 202, 207, 246. Thurloe, 33.

Commonwealth. He was not a ruler, he was hardly an anything. This was Henry Cromwell's version of the Protectorate. He told Ludlow that though in appearance his father " had power," the Army Officers made " a very kickshaw of him." [2] And Cromwell assigned to himself an even lower position ; he was their " drudge." This was the bargain struck between Cromwell and the Military Party. That bargain is attested by the occasion which forced from him that avowal.

That occasion arose when England, by miserable experience, had learnt the true meaning of " The Instrument of Government." In the year 1655 the Military Party, not content with ruling through Cromwell, undertook rulership themselves. To use his words, they " thought it was necessary to have Major-Generals." England was accordingly parcelled out into military cantons, and over each canton was placed a Major-General as its Governor.* They made themselves intolerable ; government by military magistrates was intolerable. To save ourselves, and to save Cromwell from his associates, Parliament offered Cromwell the Crown.

That offer the Military Party resolved to frustrate : their first move was the noted Address of the Hundred Officers. On 27th February, 1657, they appeared before him ; they insisted, " that His Highness would not hearken to the Title (king), because it was not pleasing to the Army." Crom-

* See Chap. VIII.

well received the Hundred Officers with flouts and jeers. He told them truly that "the time was, when they boggled not at the word 'king';" that the "Title was but a Feather in a Hat." And then out of the fulness of his angered, mortified heart, the Protector made this remarkable description of his lot since the time when the King's death set the Military Party free.

He had been, he declared, their cat's-paw, "they had made him their drudge, upon all occasions." They had compelled him "to dissolve the Long Parliament; to call a Parliament, or Convention of their naming; who met, and what did they? Fly at liberty and property." The Convention disappeared, and then "a Parliament was afterwards called; they sat five months; it is true we hardly heard of them in all that time. They took 'The Instrument' into debate, and" so "they" also "must needs be dissolved." "Some time after that, you thought it was necessary to have Major-Generals; and the first rise to that motion (then was the late general insurrections) was justifiable; and you Major-Generals did your parts well. You might have gone on. Who bid you go to the House with a Bill, and there receive a foil? After you had exercised this power a while, impatient were you till a Parliament was called. I gave my vote against it; but you [were] confident, by your own strength and interest, to get men chosen to your heart's desire. How you have failed therein, and how much the country has been disobliged, is well known." [2]

Cromwell was justly enraged. He and the Military Party had acted in concert throughout. What right had these barefaced hypocrites to come whining to him that a crowned ruler was "a scandal to the People of God," a return to the old servitude, when they had seriously considered the making him into a king? [2] Those zealoters for the "Good old Cause" and free Parliaments had set at nought and degraded parliamentary Government, they had done their utmost to stifle the free voice of England, both in the choice and the return of our representatives. They had avowed openly that they governed us, and that they governed us by the Sword. When their misdeeds were called in question, they declared that their swords should be their indemnity.* Nor were they denying Cromwell the Crown for the sake of England. They were interfering for their own selfish interests, that they might establish the rule of the Sword, that they might perpetuate a succession of "kickshaw" Protectors.

On their side also, the Military Party were justly angered. The man they had made was seeking to break loose from his makers ; the drudge was trying to become master.

The lesson conveyed by the quarrel between Cromwell and the "Hundred Officers" interprets

* See p. 208.

the history of the Protectorate. "When thieves fall out, then wise men can come" not always "by their own," but at least by a knowledge of their position. Cromwell and the "Hundred Officers" had between them stript all disguise from off the Protectorate. It was government by a military syndicate, and Cromwell was its drudge.

Force of habit, the working of the imagination, stamps incredulity upon the notion that Oliver Cromwell could sink so low. That notion, however, ceases to be a fancy, if we regard Cromwell not with the eyes of to-day, but with the eyes of his fellows. That he should be their drudge to them seemed in no way prodigious, for he seemed to them no prodigy. Whilst we esteem him the tallest of the tall, his associates, General Lambert, General Fleetwood, and Major-General Disbrowe did not see this absolute pre-eminence. Not that Lambert, Fleetwood, and Disbrowe, "the three great ones," whose ways Thurloe watched with constant apprehension, ever thought, save once, perhaps, of unmaking their creature; * but they certainly thought that, if death removed Cromwell, they could keep going the governing concern, and could repeat, after his death, the nomination of the Chief Magistrate.†

Nor in popular esteem and effective influence was the comparison between Cromwell and Lambert out of the question. Lambert stood out conspicuous as Lord Protector The Second. This was the opinion of

* See p. 224.   † See p. 170.

Sagredo, the Venetian Ambassador, who spent in England about five months (September, 1655, to February, 1656). Sagredo was an unbiassed, competent observer, and he reported to his Government, that "the first man, and enjoying more than any other the confidence of the Army, is General Lambert. They say of him that inwardly he loves not Cromwell ; but with him, outwardly, Lambert professes the strictest union, being won over by distinguished State employments and by the reward of transcendental emolument. At all events, no one would be more capable than Lambert of effecting changes in the State, or of forming a party." [3]

Sagredo's opinion was fully justified. Lambert was undeniably the second man in England. He was considerably the youngest of the three great ones. This was to his advantage. The contrast between the unworn Lambert and the worn-out Protector, whose uncertain health kept both his masters and his servants on the tenter-hooks, was much to Lambert's advantage. He was also "a gentleman born, learned, and well qualified." [4]

Popular regard apparently Lambert never sought : an unarmed Englishman was not then worth a thought. Over the sole source of authority during the Protectorate, the Army, Lambert possessed a hold. He appealed to the imagination of the soldiery. As Cromwell led his Ironsides, Lambert's

Barozzi, Relatione, European States, Series IV., 339.
[4] Cal. Clarendon MSS., II. 206, 376, 380 ; III. 239, 415.

regiment was renowned as the " Brazen Wall." [4]
Nor did he neglect to obtain adherents among the
officers. When Cromwell purged the Army of
malcontents, Lambert, " as fast as the officers were
put out, gets a friend put in his place." [4] He was
styled " the darling of the Army," possessing
" fourfold Fleetwood's, and almost equalling Cromwell's," influence. [4]

How closely popular fancy evened him with the
Protector appears in the letters of the time, where
Lambert is styled Cromwell's " demy-colleague,"
as his successor, who carries all before him in the
Council, holds " Cromwell in a string," and excites
" his jealousy and discontent." [4] When Lambert
was cashiered into nothingness, the remark of
Henry Cromwell to Thurloe that " now Lambert is
removed, the odium of contra-legal ways of raising
money will fall nearer His Highness," [4] incidentally
proves how close in public esteem the two men
stood together. Evidently, if judiciously exploited,
Lambert, as Sagredo remarked, might have " formed
a party, and made changes in the State."

The unease caused by greedy associates on the
watch for inheritance, formed but a portion of the
burthen borne by Cromwell as Chairman of the
Military Directorate. What would happen after
him might bide its day : their demand for present
profit was urgent, perpetual. It was not Lambert

Carte Letters, II. 89, 92. Thurloe, IV. 676; VI. 101, 820. Cal.
State Papers, 1655-56, 236, 264.

only who was quieted by " transcendental emolument." All the Military Party had likewise to be quieted.

This feature in the Protectorate shall be exemplified by taking the " three great ones " as representatives of their associate money-suckers. Estimating their yearly income at our money value, Fleetwood and Lambert received over 19,000*l.* and 24,000*l.* apiece. Thus, following that mode of calculation, and adding to that sum Major-General Disbrowe's modest yearly gains of over 9000*l.*, the " three great ones " were to England a financial burthen of more than 50,000*l.* a year.[5]

[5] The items forming Lambert's income of 7811*l.*, and Disbrowe's of 3230*l.*, are illustrated by the particulars of Fleetwood's yearly income, as the pay to Fleetwood, as Lord Deputy of Ireland, is the 10*l.* a day allotted to Generals Lambert and Monk.

	£	s.	d.
Member of H.H.'s Council	1000	0	0
Lord Deputy	3640	0	0
Colonel (Horse) Ireland	474	10	0
„ (Foot) „	365	0	0
Colonel (Horse) England	474	10	0
Pay as Major-General of the County Militia	666	13	4
	£6620	13	4

To this amount must be added an estate of 1300*l.* a year, which the Long Parliament bestowed on Lambert. Harl. Miscel., III. 452. Com. Journ., VI. 174 ; VII. 14. Cal. State Papers, 1655, p. 260. Ludlow, 251. Uncertainty must attend attempts to compare the coin value of to-day with the coin value of the past. Mrs. Everett Green, and Dr. Gardiner, who has kindly given me his opinion, endow the 1*l.* of 1650 with four times the purchasing powers of the 1*l.* of 1889. Their lifelong study of the accounts and

The cost of the Protectorate Government is beyond the object of this essay; yet a doubt may be expressed whether we did find it a cheap substitute for Monarchy. Cromwell, besides the cost of his lifeguard, the yearly pay for his civil officers, such as a cofferer at 4500*l.*, a surveyor of H.H.'s houses at 2000*l.*, drew for his annual maintenance first 64,000*l.*, and then 100,000*l.*, sums equal to with us, of 192,000*l.*—and 300,000*l.* Each of the sixteen members of his Council also drew 1000*l.* a year, and created a cost that would have been upon us an annual charge of 48,000*l.*[6]

This practical upshot of republicanism drew from Sir Arthur Haselrig, the "tribune of the people," speaking in Richard's Parliament of 1659, a rueful comparison. Haselrig thus bewailed the financial burthens of the Commonwealth: "We have an Army and a Navy which must be maintained: a Court also, and a Council. We have a Dowager too," Oliver's widow, "some say 20,000*l.* a year, others that 40,000*l.* will not serve her. All the

documents of 1630-58, has insensed them with those social circumstances which must be considered, as well as that more tangible basis for this kind of calculation, a price-comparison of the cost of life necessaries. Following strictly this mode of estimate, Mr. Seebohm, who most obligingly considered the subject, observes that "I would rather put the purchasing power of money, temp. Cromwell, at one and a half of what it is now, than higher." Many years ago I arrived at Dr. Gardiner's conclusion; still when the learned differ, a meek unlearned one had better "hedge." So I have taken the Cromwellian 1*l.* as being equal to three Victorians.

[6] Burton, III. 259. Thurloe, VII. 264. Cal. State Papers,

king's tables heretofore, were maintained at the king's charge; but now they must be borne by the people, and out of their purses." [6]

The cost of the Army and Navy, and the salaries of Henry Cromwell and General Monk, for their services in Ireland and Scotland, are excluded from this estimate; for " 'tis reason a man, that will have a wife, should pay all the scores she sets on him ;" and the nation that will have a Revolution must bear the charge.

It is to the political significance of the yearly 50,000*l.* enjoyed by the " three great ones " that attention must be called. Odious, mischievous as is a job, the money and the commands heaped by Cromwell on Fleetwood, Lambert, and Disbrowe formed an ugly symptom far beyond the misuse of public money. Cromwell, a practical soldier, knew that one officer could not control three or four regiments; and to his five regiments Fleetwood added the Lord Deputyship of Ireland. That post was, however, an absolute sinecure; and Fleetwood was one of the Cromwell family. This excuse did not apply to Lambert. That ambitious, aspiring man, almost an effective rival, was endowed by Cromwell with five military commands. He made him also an Admiralty Commissioner, a Lord of the Cinque Ports, the Military and Civil Governor over the Northern Counties, and placed him on H.H's Council.

1656-57, 237, 304, 321. Cal. State Papers, 1657-58, Preface, p. xiii.

These transactions were not done in a corner. The fortunes the " three great ones " had amassed, and many a minor " great one " also, were notorious. Equally notorious was it that Cromwell staggered under the weight of military and naval expenditure. His liberality to his military associates formed a standing witness that the Protector was their drudge.

Heavy as was the burthen borne by Cromwell, England's burthen was still heavier. He was subject to his comrades ; we were subject not only to him and to the Major-Generals, but also to the source whence they derived their power, the Army. That Army, the best drilled, most effective war-machine of that era, was an apparition, to Europe startling, to us appalling. Nor could England hope to see that apparition laid; no power existed that could conjure it out of sight. Cromwell might exile the Army to the remotest corners of our islands, but he could do no more.

The return home of the man-at-arms was an attractive incident in a peace triumph of the Middle Ages. The soldier was welcomed for his own sake, let us trust : certainly he was welcomed as a sign, not only of the cessation of bloodshed, but also of an army. That glad sight England could not hope for. So long as the Lord Protector existed, his Army must exist. Nor could his tax-gatherer demean himself as an ordinary " publican." He was the exactor for our 40,000 conquerors ;[7] he drew their 100,000*l.* or 60,000*l.* a month for our daily ransom. If his pouch was not filled, England would be filled with angry armed men demanding free quarter; they would have made us envy the days of civil war.

From such painful forebodings Cromwell possessed escape denied his subjects. Death would give him his quittance. But his release would double our danger. Then the " three great ones " would be, not a portent, but a reality. They would make Lambert, Protector The Second; to us a sorry prospect. Cromwell showed in war demonic force ; yet he was the " drudge " of his military associates. If so, how could Lambert deny the Army anything ?

Thus in Cromwell's taxation was a note of despair. We rendered tribute to maintain government by the Sword, and by a sword wielded perhaps by feeble hands. Conquered nations paid ransom to their conqueror. The exaction was renewed from time to time; but the ransom dwindled by degrees; at last it disappeared. England's tribute to the Army seemed ceaseless; from it there was but one mode of relief. We felt with Henry Cromwell that our peace " depended on the Protector's

[7] 40,000 is mentioned in parliamentary debate as the normal strength of the army. Burton, II. 27. See also p. 76.

life, and upon his peculiar skill and faculty and personal interest in the Army."[8] To him, therefore, we turned: we sought to place him, as king, above the reach of his military associates. And Cromwell agreed with his subjects. He had purged out of the Army the malcontents: his peculiar skill, and his alone, kept order in the ranks: he alone could disband them.

But here, as always, the Army officers stood between their drudge and his people. He could not shake off the odium created by the Army, by the cost, by the dread of the Army. The soldiers were, in popular view, Cromwell's red-coats. The tax-gatherer who collected their pay was his extortioner. He could not endear himself to his subjects by proving to them that he placed their interests above the interest of the Army. If Parliament, in the vaguest way, touched the existence of the Army, Parliament must be silenced.[8] It was to protect the interests of the Military Party that the Protector dissolved his first Parliament; and Cromwell openly assured his military associates, after his last dispersal of Parliament, that he was now set free to devote himself wholly to their service. That pitiful address to the Hundred Officers, its angry banter, querulous re-crimination, and base submission, contains the lesson of Cromwell's Protectorate. " The old saying may

[8] Thurloe, VII. 218. Cal. State Papers, 1655, 341.

be applied to him, 'Other folks' burthens break the ass's back.'"

Every way, at every turn, the Army stood between the Protector and his people. This expedient accordingly occurred to him, whereby he could prop up his Government and justify the cost of the military syndicate. The expedient was terrorism. Cromwell sought to convince his subjects that their safety depended upon his safety. His watchfulness, he assured them, alone preserved England from anarchy, from another civil war, from the bloody designs of the Royalists and the Levellers. That Cromwell himself devised the plots and seeming dangers, whereon he attitudinized as saviour of England, was notorious. Even he avows that men said, " Would not the Lord Protector make himself great, and his family great ? Doth he not make these Necessities ?"* What was meant by " these Necessities " is interpreted to us by Sagredo, the Venetian Ambassador.

On his return home, Sagredo according to custom read in the Senate an account of his embassy. He described the past history and the present resources of the Commonwealth. He recognizes Cromwell's courage, and " his talents to persuade and to act ; " notices that he was more feared than loved, his dread of insurrection and assassination, and concludes the subject thus : " Some plots have even been discovered. It is true, however, that the

* See p. 145.

Government often invents conspiracies to afford a pretext against the Royalists, and therefore to increase the Army, and the Guards." [9]

The truth of the Ambassador's statement will be upheld hereafter: though at the outset this general confirmation thereof may be noticed. A congruity of circumstance will be found in each design against Cromwell, that bespeaks a common origin and a single inventor. Similarity of outline attends almost every conspiracy. Whenever the initiation of the plot is the work of one or two men, they always escape scot-free. No plot threatened imminent danger to the Protector, so completely were the conspirators in his grasp. They plied their task within his sight uninterruptedly for months, even for years. Two noted conspiracies were superintended by his agents.

On the plains of ancient Egypt monumental avenues of statue after statue, bearing alike the same portentous and uncanny aspect, led up to a colossal repetition of the same form. So during the Protectorate plot after plot, bearing alike the impress of craft, fatuity, and treachery arose in grim repetition, until Cromwell revealed himself in the last and typical example of his statecraft, the death of Sir Henry Slingsby.

These occurrences will be dealt with in due course. At this moment, an effort will be made to show that the moral and political influence which Crom-

[9] Venetian Studies by Mr. Horatio Brown, p. 393.

well and his Government wrought upon his subjects diffused over England the contagion of systematic fraud.

Mr. Hamerton wisely remarks, that "the most demoralizing of all governments is a government that is really one thing, whilst it professes to be another." Cromwell was the figure-head of such a government. He claimed to be the protector of the "Good old Cause," of free Parliaments, of taxation voted by the people, of a real Commonwealth. To use his own words, he was the maintainer of "the old Puritan, or rather Primitive simplicity, self-denial, uprightness, and justice." He swore that he would govern according to "the Laws, Statutes, and Customs of the Land, seeking the Peace of his subjects." In reality, Cromwell sought their peace by tempting them into conspiracies, by stifling Parliament, by taxing England at his will, by filling the prisons with men detained illegally and on false pretexts.

As for the so-called Commonwealth, "we stayed not long there ;" [10] it promptly became an acknowledged mockery. Thurloe wrote its epitaph, during the closing months of Cromwell's Protectorate, in the expression of an earnest hope that "we," his master's Government, " shall be secured against a Commonwealth." [10]

[10] Burton, I. 331 ; III. 267, 567. Thurloe, VII. 192. Clarendon State Papers, III. 632 ; Harl. Miscel., III. 452.

To the vulgar eye the Lord Protector acted thus to gain the yearly reward of 100,000*l.*, that he might live in regal splendour at Whitehall and Hampton Court. A still more painful interpretation could be put upon his conduct. He sold himself to do evil, that the Lord Lambert, the Lord Disbrowe, the Lord Barkstead might enjoy with him the spoil.

Such a Protector could not stay a moral plague, the plague then rife in England. The spirit of plunder, engendered by the Civil Wars, was keen, universal. Cromwell, and the Major-Generals who stood around him, by example and precept spread abroad the infection. Though the more austere might condemn their ways, saying of them, " is not Gold their God, is not Silver the 'Good old Cause' ? " [10] to the lax majority their 19,000*l.* or 24,000*l.* a year said, go and do likewise. It was to some purpose that men " observed " that " Captain Philip Jones, who has now 7000*l.*," *i.e.* 21,000*l.*, " a year, was born to but 8*l.* or 10*l.* a year," and that the Lord Barkstead, a " thimble-maker," drew, according to our value, 12,000*l.* in yearly income. [10]

The efficiency of Cromwell's army of spies excites the ecstasy of his admirers. They do not exult over his army of trepanners ; wretched men who converted credulous neighbours into a cash profit, by first tempting them into sedition, and then betraying them. Under Cromwell " there was such a devilish practice of trepanning grown in fashion, that it was not safe to speak to any man in those treacherous days."[11] Another contemporary witness asserts "that the art of trepanning began at the time the Protector began his Government."[11] It would be well for our national character if that remark were true. If the art of trepanning was not invented by Cromwell, his devices engendered those artists in depravity.

Another miserable creature was active under his Protectorate. Men made a trade of hunting out the relics of property that Royalists had screened from the sequestrator.[11] This profession, though not the creation of Cromwell's Government, was fostered by the promise of payments and rewards out of "concealed estates." Cromwell himself also, by powers given to the Major-Generals, in their vocation of military magistrates, placed the Royalists at the mercy of their own households, and thus converted them into a nursery-ground for knaves and traitors.[11]

The needy Cavalier took his cue from the world around him. Thurloe's boasted "Black Book," which, if disclosed, "should hang half of them that went for Cavaliers,"[12] was a very likely record. So mixed up were sham Royalists, sham Republicans, and sham Cromwellians, that Thurloe's informants admitted that they could not distinguish

[11] Symond's MSS., Harl. MSS., No. 991, p. 57. Hutchinson, Bohn's Ed., 326, 374. Cal. State Papers, 1655-56, 290, 308, 364. Thurloe, IV. 595. See p.

[12] Hist. MSS. Com., 5th Report, 208. Thurloe, V. 595.

between the genuine devices of the Royalists, and
the royalist plots begun at Whitehall, that is to
say, by Thurloe himself.   Of a Mr. Dobson, the perplexed spy reports that, " if he be not now employed
by you, he is certainly engaged in a business of
great consequence against you." [12]   Rascals such
as Mr. Dobson, products of the Protectorate
atmosphere, were fellow-workers with Cromwell
in his invented conspiracies.   His good fame was at
the mercy of such men.   They put him to shame :
they brought shame upon themselves.   What
self-respect was possible to an Englishman whose
ruler and whose fellows played such dirty tricks ?

Even the popular recognition that those artifices
received, illustrates our national abasement.   That
Cromwell enticed the Royalists into sedition, and
then put them to death, is mentioned by contemporary historians with no lively expression of abhorrence, though Sir H. Slingsby's miserable fate does
excite compassionate remark.   To the man of the
time, a sham plot was a ruler's natural, not so very
reprehensible resource.   Historians of 200 years ago
were chroniclers, not preachers.   An even more
signal example of deadened sensibility is shown by
writers of familiar letters, who might have seen
Gerard or Penruddock on the scaffold, and yet
comment on Cromwell's use of " decoy ducks " to
ensnare those men without horror or disgust. [13]

[13] Baker's Chronicle, 551, 561.   Heath, 403.   Hist. MSS.
Com., 5th Report, 192.

The utter disbelief in honesty felt by Cromwell's subjects is shown conspicuously by the solicitations to which Colonel Hutchinson was exposed, when attempting to procure justice to his neighbour. The sinners must indeed have been in high spirits, who sought to entice that follower of true wisdom from his path, to "lurk privily" with them for the innocent. And the rascals had good cause for high spirits; for if that green stick of respectability could have been put to use, what work they must have made with the gnarled knotted stocks of dry aged iniquity.

Deceit, subornation, injustice, were a good investment, whilst Cromwell ruled the market. He played the part of "Mr. Gripeman, a schoolmaster in Love-gain, which is near the market-town in the County of Coveting, in the North. This schoolmaster taught the art of getting, either by violence, cozenage, flattery, lying, or by putting on à guise of religion;" and scholars such as Mr. Hold-the-World, Mr. Money-love, Mr. Save-all, and Mr. By-ends strenuously followed his "harmless and profitable" instructions.

The triumph given to the profane, the zest imparted to immorality by the "putting on the guise of religion," by the abuse of sacred words and aspirations, even then termed "cant language," [14] undoubtedly aggravated the demoralization wrought by Cromwell; but apparently it was not furthered

[14] Burton, III. 288. Thurloe, I. 240. "Several Proceedings,'

by spiritual oppression or puritanic interference
with private life. Contented with the suppression
of the Church of England, Nonconformists in high
place betook themselves to quarrels among themselves, and left the sons of Belial to their cakes and
ale.

Take, for instance, the outward aspect of London
life. During the spring of 1653 it was reported,
that " everybody here is very fine, and Hyde Park
every night is very full." [14] Society on the 1st of
May, next year, presented an aspect even more un-
chastened.   A " Diurnal " reports that " more a
Maying " had taken place on that day " than for
years past : that much sin was committed by wicked
meetings with fiddlers, drunkenness, ribaldry and the
like.   Great resort came to Hyde Park, many hundreds of rich coaches, and gallants in rich attire ;"
the men adorned with " most shameful powdered
hair," and accompanied by " painted and spotted
women.   Some men played with a silver ball, and
some took other recreation.   But H.H. the Lord
Protector went not thither, nor any of his Council,
but were busy about the great affairs of the Commonwealth." [14]

In 1657, so wholly was Puritanism out of court,
that, under the patronage of H.H. the Lord Protector, to the music of " 48 violins and 50 trumpets,
and much mirth with frolics," the inmates, male and

&c., 27 April—4th May, 1654. Hist. MSS. Com., 5th Report 177.
Guizot, II. 625.

female, of Whitehall Palace, danced together,—
" mixed dancing," [14] as the offence was called ;—
whilst the Cavaliers kept Christmas, if not by religious rites, by devotion to mince pies and bottle worship.[14]

Alehouses were closed, not to maintain sobriety, but to keep the Royalists apart. Horse races also were forbidden, not because " it was His Highness's intention to abridge gentlemen of that sport, but to prevent great confluences of irreconcileable enemies." [15] And the Chester folk being denied a horse race, substituted, unhindered, a competition for " the belt," by " footmen," who ran " three times about the Roodee." [15]

The quiet freedom of private life was, under the Protectorate, apparently undisturbed. Mr. Pepys enjoyed himself ; his devotion to music was unrestrained. Mrs. Dorothy Osborne tended her ailing father and wrote her charming love-letters, unannoyed by intrusion from the crop-haired ones. Whilst subject to the " Usurper," Evelyn delighted his eyes and ears with " curios," rope-dancers, the " hairy woman," and " the incomparable Lubicer on the violin," and kept the " holy festivals " unhindered in Dr. Wild's lodging. Even when the licence enjoyed by the Protector's Court, during 1657, tempted Evelyn into a semi-public celebration of Christmas Day in Exeter Chapel, the soldiers,

---

[15] Thurloe, IV. 607. Hist. Coll. Chester, Harl. MSS., 1929, fo. 55.

who interfered, suffered the congregation " to finish the Office of Communion," and he " got home late the next day."

It was the disregard not the enforcement of piety that dulled the consciences of Cromwell's subjects. Even the army of Saints, his Ironsides, were no longer " a body of well-governed citizens:" they had lost that "order, and discipline, and a face of gravity and piety," which amazed Burnet in his youth.[16] Still more would he have been amazed by the sight exhibited near Ipswich, during March, 1657. He would have found himself " in the midst of soldiers quartered all along the road, filled with insolence, swearing, quarrelling, and all the rudeness in the world." [16]   And when these ruffians reached their destination, France, they ran away in such numbers, that it was suggested that " two or three officers whose troops are weakest by desertion, ought to be cashiered." [16]

But the degradation of a whole army is as nothing compared with the corruption of a man of refined and noble nature into a pestilent reviler. As advocate for the Protector, Milton likened the dead King to Nero, declared that " Charles killed his Father and King by poison," and bespattered that " comely head " with filthy lies.[17]

To those who were not thus seduced by Cromwell's

[16] Burnet's Own Time, I. 107.   Baker, 563.   Tanner MSS., 52, 206 ; MS. Cal. Clarendon MSS., fo. 27.
[17] Masson's Milton, IV. 260.

" deceitful glories," to the mass of the nation, the
Protector was as Giant Despair. We sank under
the apathy of the slave, the prostration of fear, the
faithlessness of friends, the breach of oaths " that
made the land mourn," [18] but most of all under the
infecting touch of him who was accused of deceiving
his subjects, whose word was not believed, whose
crooked ways were before all men, who, pretending
to govern England that " God's own law " might be
" made good in this land," governed by the sword,
and for the sword.

No good could come from such a Protector. In
his way he aimed to be " the repairer of the breach,
the restorer of paths to dwell in," but his ways
were the ways of death.

His apparent success impressed the Venetian
Ambassador. Yet he thus foretold the end, " The
machine is strong, but I do not deem it durable,
for it is violent." [18] What was durable were the
immoral influences of the Protectorate. The kindly
fruits of unrighteousness that ripened under the
Restoration sprang from the crop that was sown
while the Curse of Cromwell rested upon England.
A son of Belial is none other than a Mr. Hold-the-
World on the loose.

[18] Burton, II. 276. Guizot, II. 240.

CHAPTER II.

THE PROTECTOR AND MAJOR HENSHAW.

THE first year of the Protectorate disclosed no overt sign of its disastrous close. The year 1654 was a season of prosperity. Cromwell possessed a well-stored treasury ; his Army was fully paid ; his Fleet was powerful at sea ; Ireland and Scotland were subdued. He negotiated as an equal with the leading European powers. Continental observers felt that, since the King's death, England "had never been in a more secure condition ; so that Cromwell may well claim the throne in reality as well as in name, aided by the discovery of his enemies' plots, the applause of his friends, the friendship of foreign states, and his own military power."[1]

The Army, for a time, threatened danger. Government by "a single Person" caused offence to many, and indignation among the ranks. The soldiers murmured that "they did not fight to make Cromwell a monarch."[1] Against this peril he was ever on the watch. Before the call to supreme authority he weeded out and dispersed "the religious

[1] Cal. Clarendon MSS., II. 367 ; III. 42. Hutchinson's Mem.,

soldiers." [1]   As Protector, he effectually remodelled the Army.   So successful was he, that in December, 1654, Thurloe asserts unhesitatingly, that the Army would "live and die" for Cromwell.[1]

The grip Cromwell kept upon his soldiers had this influence over his policy.   It left him free, if he chose, to pursue a persistent course of terrorism, and to provide the means.   That abiding grasp secured him from external danger.   The Levellers, the extremist Republicans, were a scanty isolated band of men.   The King's adherents were powerless, disarmed, without military leaders, or military training.   That Army of 40,000 men, if their England be compared with our England, represented a force of over 285,000 strong.   The most utter Wildrake, however reckless, trembled before those thousands of thorough soldiers.   Nor would foreign troops serve the King's turn ; they were Papists.   If Charles had embarked for England accompanied by such allies, all England would have risen as one man.   When kingship was coming to the front, Cromwell's courtiers craved for such an invasion, as it would confer on him the crown.[1]

The strength of such opponents, and the weakness of such followers, no one felt more keenly than Charles II.   He never forgot, throughout his continental sojourn, David Lesley's "melancholic conclusion, formed at Warrington, that those men,"

355, 370.   Vaughan's Protectorate, 1, 87.   Thurloe, VI. 255. Cal. Clarendon MSS., III. 258.   Clarendon State Papers, III. 390.

the ordinary Englishman, "would never fight." [2]
The King, as Clarendon repeatedly observes, was
"in nothing more" earnest than in suppressing the
warlike inclinations of his followers.

During the spring of 1654, a year when undoubtedly the Cavaliers were somewhat on the
move, Mr. John Gerard, a young man of good royalist
family, on his return home from the Court at Paris,
asked of the King his instructions; and Gerard
would gladly have received exhortation to be up and
doing. On the contrary, he was directed to charge
his friends, in the King's name, "that they should
be quiet, and not engage themselves in any plots
which must prove ruinous to them, and not do the
King any good;" for, as Clarendon explains, "His
Majesty had observed at his being at Worcester,
and his concealment afterwards, the temper of the
people, the fear they were under, and how fruitless
any insurrection must be." [2]

Again, during September, 1657, when the more
restless English Royalists were planning a general
rising, Clarendon, writing in the King's behalf,
warned a zealous adherent that his associates had
such little confidence in each other, and were so
despairing and "heart-broken," that "if the King
should land to-morrow with as good an army
as could reasonably be hoped for, he would be
overpowered as he was at Worcester, whilst all

<hr>

[2] Clarendon Hist. Ed., 1839, 845, 866. Clarendon State Papers,
III. 364, 410.

men sit still, and look for the effect of the first battle." Even after Cromwell's death, Charles desired his friends, " not to stir at all, till they have some advantage given them from other parties rising and declaring." [2]

The King's determination not to stir at all, unless his efforts were supported by simultaneous action among the Levellers, affords the key to Cromwell's plot devices.

With the King's decided bias towards inactivity most Englishmen were in complete accord. They were fully persuaded not to fight, either for King, or for Cromwell, or for themselves. Their single wish was to avoid another civil war.[3] The prompt collapse of Sir George Booth's rising during 1659, made when the Protectorate Government was crumbling away, and seconded by concurrent efforts, shows the national determination to keep the peace at any price, and that it was not Oliver Cromwell but the Army that we feared.

Yet, while every impulse during the first six months of the Protectorate tended towards tranquillity, evidently some underhand movement was on foot. Between January and June, 1654, occurred two attempts at insurrection, the one following hard after the other. The first was a contemptible affair. The second, a more elaborate attempt, ensnared young Gerard, despite the King's warning, and is known as the Gerard and Vowel conspiracy.

[3] Guizot, II. 632. Clarendon State Papers, III. 324.

Cromwell had not occupied the Protector's chair above six or seven weeks, when the "Diurnals" of February, 1654, startled London by the following vigorous pull at the alarm-bell. According to the Diurnals, an army 30,000 strong was to fall on all parts of England at once. · The Lord Protector, his life-guard, and his councillors were to be murdered, the Tower surprised, all the garrisons throughout England taken; and the King was in London.

This big affair, on examination, shrivels into nothing. The plot was got up by one Pritchard, otherwise Captain Dutton. He tempted about a dozen obscure men to form a royalist committee at various taverns, in fancied subordination to a supreme council of "persons of honour, that did act in a design far above them, who should list men to seize on the Parliament, Whitehall, James's, and the Tower, and raise insurrections in other parts of the kingdom."   Oaths of secrecy were administered; the conspirators drank a quart or two of wine, ate "some sawceages," and agreed to promote, "according to their ability," the restoration of King, Church, and Law.

Their first step towards action was also their last. They decided to send two envoys to the King; and the effort broke up the conspiracy. "The charges of them that were to go to C.S." were 60*l.*, i.e. about 200*l.* of present value, a suspiciously large sum; and the demand produced the natural result. A

call of 3*l.* per plotter was made. Some responded to
the call, and their contributions disappeared into the
pocket of the receiver. Their associates refused to
follow suit, declaring "that they were cheated:"
they resolved "not to send any person to C.S., nor
to raise any money." Finally they were called together "by a noate," sent apparently to collect them
for their arrest; and then they were carried off,
eleven in number, "one or two very penitent, who
cried, and took on lamentably." The captives were
never tried; their detention doubtless was of no
long duration; and so the tears of the penitents, and
the wine and "sawceages" of the plotters, form
the most substantial features of this conspiracy.[4]

As an exhibition of knavery and dupery, the
"Sawceage" Conspiracy forms a fitting precursor
to its successors under Cromwell's rule; and no
sooner had these, the proto-plotters of the Protectorate, been released, than another swindle of the
same kind was commenced, though, in result, far
more tragical.[5]

---

[4] "Several Proceedings," &c., 16—23 Feb., 1654. Thurloe, II.
95, 105, 115.

[5] The State Trials, V. 518—531, and "A True Account of the
late Bloody Conspiracy," &c, 1654, are the authorities touching
the Gerard and Vowel Conspiracy.

It has been supposed that concurrently with Henshaw's conspiracy, the King issued a Proclamation offering reward for Cromwell's assassination. As Mr. Macray has observed, the Proclamation on which this notion is based, exists only in a copy made
by "J. O.," obtained by him from "Mr. H. P.," and forwarded
to Thurloe. No evidence therefore exists which connects that
document with the King or his followers. The wording

During March, 1654, a certain Major Henshaw, with the authority of one "who had served in the French army" and was familiar with the English Court, advertised with exceeding publicity in the streets of London, that he was on the start for Paris, to "discuss some business with the King." Henshaw was setting his snares. He went to Paris, returned, and immediately passed to and fro among the Royalists, announcing that he had held confidential talk with Charles and with Prince Rupert; and that the King had expressly directed him, both by word and in writing, to undertake with his friends in London the assassination of Cromwell, and to offer them large rewards, in cash down or

of the Proclamation, which is addressed to "all rational and unbiassed men," is of a fancy character. It promises to "our loving subjects, peace and prosperity," but it gives them only six days for a renunciation of their rebel courses. Singular, also, are the exceptions which it makes from Our royal Mercy. "Our pardon" is withheld from Lenthall, Bradshaw, and Haselrig; leaving free to make their peace, Lambert and Disbrowe, foremost men under the Protectorate, besides Fleetwood, Goffe, Hacker, and Barkstead, who signed the Death Warrant. That Charles II. had ought to do with this Proclamation, dated 3rd May, 1654, is unproved and improbable.

Positive evidence does exist which implicates Cromwell and his Government with incitement to assassination. On the day following the date assigned to that most doubtful royal proclamation, the 4th of May, acting under "the authority to me given by H.H. and Council," Monk by Proclamation made at the High Cross of Edinburgh, declared "that what person shall kill" Major-General Middleton, the Earl of Athol, Viscount Kenmure, "shall receive 200*l.* sterling for every person so killed." Hyde remarks on "the infamy" of that Proclamation, and cn the probability that it might provoke retaliation on Monk. Cal. Clarendon MSS., II. 365; III. xi. Thurloe, II. 248, 261, 322. Life of R. Blair, 314.

in future profit, as royal " equerries, or pensioners."
To impart a touch of conviction to his words,
Henshaw assured one of his hearers, that when his
name was mentioned, Prince Rupert remarked
with kindly recognition that " he had once given
him a dog." Nothing could be more certain
than Henshaw's intimacy with the King and his
Court.

Henshaw's murderous projects were shaped, by a
lively imagination, to suit his hearers. The forces
that he could muster, " at two hours' warning,"
gathered bulk in discourse, rising from " divers
men," to " a large party," to 3000 insurgents.
When " the onset was given," an army of 10,000
horse and foot would instantly appear " in a
posture" around London, whilst foreign soldiers,
headed by Prince Rupert, simultaneously descended
upon the Sussex coast.

To the more adventurous Henshaw sketched out
brisker methods of despatch. As for the Tower of
London, he could surprise that stronghold with the
aid of five picked men. With what ease, he observed,
the Horse Guards at Charing Cross might be put " in
a maze :" a pistol would do it, " the men being at
nine pins." Equally as though it were a matter of
course, he would suggest that a conspirator might
" ride civilly " up to the Protector, " with a letter
in one hand, and a pistol in the other, and pistol
him."

In talk also Henshaw held large store of money,

even 200,000*l.*, *i.e.* 600,000*l.* of our money. Where
that supply was lodged, or whence it came, he
would not, or could not tell; nor did he give a
penny to a brother plotter, "who had not wherewithal to feed." And Henshaw's audacity equalled
his vast resources. With no heed to ordinary prudence, making no attempt at secrecy, requiring from
his hearers no oath, he went about through London
scattering treason and murder broadcast. Active
on his legs, and prompt in talk, Henshaw infected
with insurrectionary contagion about twenty dupes.
They included two officers of Cromwell's horse
guard, Captain Alexander, and Colonel Aldrich; of
the Royalists, a Colonel Finch, several city appren-
tices, a butcher, young Gerard, and a schoolmaster
named Vowel.

Henshaw's reckless talk gave ample publicity to
the project. Cromwell, however, did not need any
warning. His Council "had one among" the
plotters " daily," who disclosed their doings during
" three months," whilst a " couple of decoy-ducks
drew in the rest." [6] Out of the ensnared ones,
these three were placed at the bar of the High Court
of Justice, an apprentice, Somerset Fox, Gerard, and
Vowel, the schoolmaster. Fox made an ingenuous
confession, and was sold as a slave under " O.P.'s "
warrant.[6] Gerard and Vowel were executed. They
had yielded to Henshaw's influence, they had listened
to his proposals. No written documents were pro-

[6] Hist. MSS. Com., 5th Report, 192. Thurloe, III. 453.

duced against them, no muster-rolls, no commissions or instructions from the King. All the evidence brought out by the trial was talk, either Henshaw's talk, or the comments his talk produced.

Even when Cromwell came to the front and began the arrests, Henshaw, heedless of consequences, would not cease. He went about London declaring " that the business might go on, for all it was discovered," that many regiments were ready to rise, and that Prince Rupert was expected on the Sussex coast with a large army.

At last Henshaw despaired. He was met in Holborn, cursing Gerard, " in much passion," for having hindered the design, and declaring that he would " be gone, and leave them to destruction ;" and so he did. After a temporary retirement in the Tower, under Cromwell's protection, Henshaw reappeared in Paris.

Suspicion, from the beginning to the end of the business, fastened on Henshaw. His schemes were obviously absurd. Gerard, when Henshaw's project for the destruction of the Lord Protector was described at the trial, exclaimed, " How should this be done. With a company of geese?" and Colonel Aldrich ironically asked if the attacking party was to " drop out of the skies?" It was noticed that Henshaw's proposals " did not flavour like truth;" and that, though he boasted of his 200,000*l*., he was himself " very wanting, having no money in his purse." He was told to his face that he was "an idle fellow," and that he had been "set on by the Protector."

Nor did the High Court of Justice enhance the sincerity of the conspiracy. That tribunal was in itself a national offence. Created by Cromwell's "Ordinance," it was revolutionary, unwarranted,—a breach of the Protector's oath. Mr. Justice Atkins withdrew from the Court, declaring that he had sworn as a judge "to do nothing contrary to the Laws of England;" that by those laws men "indicted for Treason ought to be tried by a jury," whereas "by this Ordinance it is otherwise."[7] And the odium brought on Cromwell by the Court was increased by the trial. It revealed, beyond doubt, that complicity did exist between Henshaw and Cromwell. Henshaw was the creator and inspirer of the conspiracy. The Attorney-General charged against him "the first hatching of the plot," but Henshaw was not placed in the dock. Obviously he was unproducible, whilst that he could be produced was notorious. Gerard exclaimed upon the scaffold that "he confidently believed that Henshaw is in their hands;" and we may hold the same confident belief. Major Henshaw's name is entered among the plotters who were imprisoned and examined in the Tower.[8]

Henshaw, then, and Wiseman, his partner in the

[7] Cal. State Papers, 1654, 233.

[8] Thurloe, II. 416, 512, 533. Baker's Hist., 551. Cal. Clarendon MSS., II. 387.

fraud, were the " couple of decoy-ducks who were employed" to "draw in the rest." And their employer was well known. So notorious was it that the Protector was seeking to ensnare "some honest, credulous persons of the Royalist Party to their destruction," that warning was sent to the King, who refused to see Henshaw because " he was employed out of England, from the King's enemies to betray him." [8]

Gerard was executed in July; and in the following August Henshaw wrote a " Vindication" of himself against " several senseless pamphlets, which named him as a chief contriver" of the late conspiracy. That charge Henshaw declared could not be true, because " his alleged discourse with the King is entirely false;" and as Cromwell subsequently confirmed that statement, its correctness may be accepted. Henshaw also denied that he had received money from Cromwell for the journey to Paris, or for the betrayal of the conspirators ; and charged one of Cromwell's officers with the invention of the " pretended plot," in return for 100*l.* down, and the promise of a pension. [x]

The use of a decoy-duck to thwart the purposes of an anarchist would not smirch the purity of the whitest soul. But complicity with a duck who leads his brethren, not along, but into the channel of crime is rather a grimy deed. With what shade of blackness Cromwell begrimed himself by the employment of Henshaw shall not here be estimated ; nor shall I attempt to solve the nicer problem, whether generous tenderness for the dead should at all hamper action by a Chief Magistrate. That question, Cromwell himself places before us. He felt constrained, having ensnared Gerard to death, to bring him again before his fellows, and to condemn him a second time. This necessity had arisen. The Gerard and Vowel conspiracy was tainted with suspicion. In London "few believed anything of it."[9] The same notion spread to the Continent. A report came from Brussels that "none would believe that there was anything of it real."[9] The reality of the conspiracy must therefore be bolstered up; belief that the Protector had "set on" Henshaw must be stifled.

Regardless of the evidence given at the trial, Cromwell thought fit, about fifteen months after Gerard's death, to defame him, to give the lie to his assertion, made before God and in death's presence, that "I know no more about any such design, but only what I have often acknowledged, that it was motioned to me by Henshaw," that "I debated it twice or thrice when I was with him; but I never entertained it at all, and at the last flatly disowned it."[9] Gerard's solemn declaration of his innocence Cromwell contradicted in a proclamation which he published in October, 1655, "upon the occasion of the late Rebellion," *i.e.* the Insurrection of the pre-

[9] Hist. MSS. Com., 5th Report, 193. Thurloe, II. 358. State Trials, V. 354. Old Parl. Hist., XX. 443.

vious March. He stated therein that, although " it is true that the King refused to speak with Major Henshaw " concerning the design of the Gerard and Vowel plot, still it has " come to Our knowledge " that the King " himself spoke to Gerard concerning " the projected assassination with complete approval.[9]

Strong compulsion must have driven Cromwell to make that return upon the unpleasant past. It might charitably be supposed that his attempt to shift the crime from Henshaw to young Gerard, was provoked by the conviction that the truth of the matter was reached at last, that evidence, which effectually rebutted the sworn charges against Henshaw, testified by every witness at the trial, could and ought to be produced.

Cromwell possessed no such evidence. He had utilized the unsupported word of a man who had no personal knowledge of the King's actions, for Charles had expelled the informer from his Court. Bampfield, the spy, a notorious liar, had furnished " Us " with that statement regarding the King, compiled for " Our " benefit about twelve months after Gerard's death.[10] It was therefore on the word of Bampfield, a scoundrel dismissed from his presence by Charles, and subsequently by Cromwell from England, that he gave the lie to Gerard's dying declaration and stultified the decision of the Court of Justice. The solemn Declaration, based on " Our knowledgè," was an attempt to turn the

----

[10] Thurloe, II. 512, 533.

tables on Henshaw, who had rounded upon the Protector, and had, by that pamphlet, advertised that the Gerard and Vowel conspiracy was a fraud. At the most, Cromwell, by his avowal that it was " true that the King refused to speak with Henshaw," gave publicity to the fact that the Protector had been duped by the criminal that "We" had screened from punishment.

That the Gerard and Vowel conspiracy was the sole creation of Henshaw's arts, and was wholly unknown to the King, appears in another way. All the hopes, fears, and projects of Charles and his Continental associates, Clarendon, Ormond, and Nicholas, during the year 1654, are reflected in the letters that passed between them and the Council known as " The Sealed Knot," who represented the leading English Royalists. They were not inactive during 1654. The indignation aroused by the sham Commonwealth, established by " The Instrument of Government," seemed to promise them their sole chance of success,—insurrection by the Levellers, and mutiny in Cromwell's army.

Not only is no reference made to Henshaw's assassination plot in the correspondence between the King and " The Sealed Knot," but its existence is wholly inconsistent with the projects they entertained. An outline of those projects must be given, because, in a fashion, they influenced the Insurrection of March, 1655; and they show effectively the capabilities of the Cavaliers.

During April, 1654, Major Armorer, an active, rather impulsive intriguer, journeyed through England on a royalist mission. He reported to the King that if their friends in the towns of Shrewsbury, Ludlow, and Worcester played their part, " it may prove of great advantage," and that he had hopes regarding Tynemouth and Yorkshire. Nothing could be vaguer than Armorer's assurances. Clarendon commented severely on his associates, and remarked that he " has the report of a very honest and loyal man," but that " his present business is somewhat above his reach."

The movement, however, such as it was, continued. In May Charles sent instructions to " The Sealed Knot," in whom alone " he put entire confidence," defining a course of action for the Royalists. These instructions ran in general terms, recommending care and caution, and that " the attempts should be made at the same time, in all places of the kingdom." The only point touched with certainty is that, " the King will have no General, but himself."

During the summer, Clarendon supplied commissions to various Colonels in the imaginary royal army ; and in July the Cavaliers sent the King " a particular account of our business and desires," which did look rather like real business. They proposed to rise in August, and furnished promising details regarding their readiness to appear in arms throughout England, from Tynemouth to Kent.[11]

This information, however, drew from Charles no enthusiastic response. He told his friends that " he will no longer restrain their affections," and promised due reward. Still, whilst the King assures them that he " is ready himself to bear any part they would wish," he warns them that " he is not willing to embark them in any desperate undertaking," and insists on concerted action, as affording the only chance of success.[11]

The King knew of what stuff his friends were made. November came, but their " desires " had not turned to " business," or towards the way of business. He expresses his sorrow " that the cause is not so ready for hearing as was expected," and commands a zealous Royalist not to " stir," till all were prepared to act together.[11]   Such an emergency had never been in sight. When the zeal of the Royalists touched the top of the tide, during July, 1654, they were still far below any definite scheme of action.

This futile restlessness, this lack of combination and preparation, was the more remarkable, because up to December the King's Continental advisers thought " that things go on in England as well as could be wished ;" and they believed " that the Army will begin the work for us, and even do the work for us." [12]   Hopes soon utterly dispelled. But even those hopes did not spur the English

[11] Cal. Clarendon MSS., II. 334, 356, 369, 383, 384, 413.
[12] Clarendon State Papers, III. 259.

Royalists into action.   They never rose above futile restlessness.   Except in that abortive delusion, the Insurrection of 1655, from 1654 to 1658 the utmost achievement attained by the most zealous Royalist was talk.   In out-of-the-way regions they concealed pistols in their stables; they handed to and fro commissions signed " C. R. ;" they disputed over the command of visionary battalions.   Even when egged on by false assurances of co-operation from Levellers and Republicans, they could do no more.

Cromwell might safely play with such feeble creatures ; the most daring Cavalier was in his hands a harmless puppet.   The Protector acted on Lesley's " melancholic conclusion " that the Royalists "would never fight."   Why should they ? what could they do against Cromwell's 40,000 soldiers ?

CHAPTER III.

THE PROTECTOR AND THE CONSPIRACIES OF THE WINTER, 1654-5.

THE general tranquillity which pervaded England during the year 1654, passed at its close, if Cromwell is to be believed, into a ferment of treason and sedition. The state of the country, he declared, when he dissolved Parliament in January, 1655, was terrifying. All the mischief-working forces in society were on the move, fomented by the example and demeanour of Parliament, which had then been sitting since the foregoing September.

Cromwell's alarming statement entails upon us the necessity of ascertaining, if possible, the actual condition of English society at the close of the year 1654. The following account may be used towards that object, written during September, 1654, by Mr. Greene, a subject of " our admired Protector," to reassure a timid friend, who contemplated a return to England with his family :—" The number of the Levellers and Anabaptists is very small, and the people's hatred of them very great. At the late election for Parliament they proposed candidates in most places and had meetings," to canvass votes " aforehand, so long ago as June last, but very few of them were elected. The Cavalier party is the most numerous, but least considerable; the generality (some few only excepted) are men of such monstrous intemperance as renders them incapable of any secret, and therefore unfit for any design above a ball at a tavern, or the common sequel of it, a duel. This makes them impatient of any action or service that leads them beyond the ken of a wine bush, and so false and perfidious that you scarce find one that dares trust another with an ordinary secret. No conjunction of the Cavaliers with any other party can with reason be imagined. The Presbyterians are now fully reconciled to the Government, greatly favoured by the Protector, and walk hand in hand with the true-hearted Independents." *

Mr. Greene's satisfactory description of English society during the autumn of 1654, is upheld by much co-existent evidence. The Royalists during this season, according to the advices Charles received from England, were incapable of immediate action, or of any action, unless supported by a concurrent mutiny in Cromwell's Army; and events during December, 1654, stifled all such hope. Disturbance by the Cavaliers need not then be feared ; and, as I have mentioned, both the Nation and the King were resolved to keep quiet. In other ways, also, Charles was a peace maintainer. He

* Cal. Clarendon MSS., II. 396.

was himself distasteful to the generality of Englishmen, indolent, licentious, the son of a popish mother, surrounded by popish influences, presumably a papist himself. He was also most unfitted for our need. The need of the moment was a ruler who could control and disband the Army; and Charles decidedly was not such a ruler.

So far as outward appearance went, 1655, as viewed from 1654, promised to Cromwell assured prosperity. He apparently thought otherwise. The presence of Parliament undoubtedly disquieted him. He had stationed soldiers round the House, and excluded about one hundred Members. Still Parliament would not conform. They sought to place his Government on a parliamentary basis. They sought also, and here they touched him close, to prevent his defying Parliament by the illegal levy of taxation under his Ordinance. On the table of the House lay a draft resolution declaring that " after the dissolution of this Parliament, no person shall presume to levy any sum of money for excise, or new impost, or any other tax whatsoever, other than such as shall be agreed upon by this present Parliament ; and that every person, who shall presume to do contrary to this Vote, shall be reputed a betrayer of the rights and liberty of the people, and a Capital Enemy to the Commonwealth." [1]

---

[1] Rawlinson MSS., A. 31, fo. 364. This document is undated, but it belongs to Cromwell's first Parliament, as Sir A. Ashley

Cromwell was, of necessity, that " Capital Enemy to the Commonwealth." He must find the wherewithal to satisfy, not the Army only, and the Navy, but his creators also, and the heavy drafts they made on the Treasury. With such a motion in the air, as he truly remarked to the " One Hundred Officers," Parliament " must needs be dissolved." He could not, however, give the reason. Accordingly Cromwell charged that Dissolution upon "your delays, your sittings and proceedings." Parliament, as he asserted, had demoralized England. " Dissettlement and division, discontent and dissatisfaction, together with real dangers to the whole Nation, have been more multiplied within these five months of your sitting than in some years before !" These were the accusations that formed the key-note of the speech he made, when he dissolved Parliament on the 22nd January, 1655.

The admiring subject, Mr. Greene, and his Protector evidently were at variance, especially as Cromwell felt able to assure his hearers that those " real dangers " were as obvious and as " true as any mathematical demonstrations are or can be."

This was his description of the doings of the Royalists. " I say unto you, whilst you have been in the midst of these Transactions, that Party, that Cavalier Party . . . have been designing and preparing to put this Nation in blood again, with a

Cooper's name is connected with the proceeding, and he was excluded from Cromwell's second Parliament.

E

witness. They have been making great preparations of arms; and I do believe it will be made evident to you that they have raked out many thousands of arms, even all that this City could afford, for divers months last past. But it will be said, 'May we not arm ourselves for the defence of our houses? Will anybody find fault for that?' Not for that. But the reason for *their* doing so hath been as explicit, and under as clear proof, as the fact of doing so. For which I hope, by the justice of the land, some will, in the face of the Nation answer it with their lives : and then the business will be pretty well out of doubt. Banks of money have been framing, for these and other such like uses. Letters have been issued with Privy-seals, to as great Persons as most are in the Nation for the advance of money,—which 'Letters' have been discovered to us by the Persons themselves. Commissions for Regiments of horse and foot, and command of Castles have been likewise given from Charles Stuart, since your sitting."[2]

"Mathematical demonstrations" are, I suppose, incontestable proofs. What evidence could Cromwell produce to prove that Royalists, under commissions from Charles II., were preparing to

---

[2] 22 Jan., 1655. Carlyle, III. 426. Cromwell's description of the Royalist Bank of London, containing over 100,000*l*., and a statement, supported by an appeal to "God, Angels, and Men," that his Army "is now upon free quarter" (Speech, 22nd Jan., 1655), have been examined and found wanting in truth. English Hist. Review, Nos. Oct., 1888, p. 728, Jan., 1889, p. 112.

put England into blood ?   He could produce two
commissions for regiments of horse and foot, and
one commission to hold a castle in Wales ; and he
could call the holders of those commissions, two
Welsh gentlemen, prisoners in St. James's Palace.
The head conspirator was Mr. Nicholas Bayley, and
the accessory, his kinsman Mr. Bagnal. Their
depositions were most straightforward. Bagnal
declared that during the autumn of the past year
Mr. Bayley " did acquaint him that there was a
design for bringing in the King, meaning Charles
Stuart, and that an army would very speedily be
landed from France on behalf of the said King."
Bagnal, thereupon, accepted a commission from
Bayley, signed " Charles Stuart," to command a
regiment of 1000 horsemen ; though, as no occasion
arose for using the commission, he buried it " near
his house, in a box, in the ground."

And this is the outline of Bayley's story.   Being
called to London, during the previous November, by
" some private occasion of his own," as he was " one
morning walking in Gray's Inn Walks," he fell
into discourse with an unknown gentleman.   Their
conjoint royalist sympathies soon inspired a wish
for further acquaintance.   Mr. Thomas Hart (that
was the tempter's name) and Mr. Bayley accordingly
met " at the Castle Tavern in the Strand."   They
" had not sat long," when Hart " drew out a paper "
which, as he told his companion, he would not show
to any one but " a gentleman, and a very honest

man." The paper was a letter, " uppon the top whereof was written C. R.," authorizing the bearer to act in " C. R.'s " behalf. And " from that time " Bayley " took " Hart " for an agent."

These artless conspirators, who trusted each other at first sight, and plotted together in a tavern, next day committed an act of high treason in as public a place as they could select, " the Piazza." They met there, and Hart, assuring Bayley that they " should be in action shortly," handed over to him .a royal commission for himself, and another for his kinsman Bagnal, to command regiments of horse and foot, and a document appointing Bayley governor of Denbigh Castle, " of which " fortress he had undertaken " to give a good account." Hart then disappeared. As he seemed " somewhat shy " in answering an inquiry " where his lodging was," Bayley " pressed him no farther." Nor was more heard from or about the " agent," except by a letter warning Bayley " not to stir," because " that business " " was put off for three months."

Bayley took the hint, " and did not stir." Bagnal, however, was more enterprising. During their sojourn in St. James's Palace, Thurloe received a letter from the Governor of Beaumaris Castle, announcing that " I have discovered a Plott, that was to surprise both these garrisons "—the garrisons, it may be presumed, of the town and castle of Beaumaris—" which if I had not been carefull in preventing by lyeing in the castle myself, it would have been effected ere this." And the Governor warned Thurloe that "he that was to surprise mee, is secured in London, one Mr. Nicholas Bagnal." [3]

Though Mr. Bayley was the chief among this brace of conspirators, Cromwell treated him very leniently. After a few weeks' detention he "returned home amongst his neighbours," to the surprise of the Governor of Conway Castle, who wonders that one "so far engaged in this inhuman business" should have been "so soon cleared;" though the reason for that course, as the Governor remarks, is "best known to his Highness." That was just the case. Mr. Bayley had served the turn that his Highness required, and was therefore dismissed from attendance in St. James's Palace. And Mr. Bagnal also returned safely home amongst his neighbours, having received the Protector's pardon, granted in return for a revelation of "the whole truth concerning the design of the King's party to rise in England." [3]

We have rather kept down than heightened the absurdities of Messrs. Bayley and Bagnal's revelations; but still, ludicrous as it may seem, these two gentlemen were the only Cavaliers Cromwell had in custody during January, 1655, authorized by "C. R.'s" commission to put England "into blood again, with a witness."

[3] Thurloe, III. 125, 127, 128. Rawlinson, MSS. A. 34, fo. 567. Bagnal ascribes the gift of the commissions to a Col. Stephens; and a Stephens is mentioned as a Cromwellian agent, Cal. Clarendon, MSS. III. 81.

The " many thousands of arms " which, according to Cromwell, the Royalists had raked together must now be proved and tested. Thus far his statement is correct. Arms were bought during December, 1654, by royalist agents, and in a very cavalier fashion, for an observer remarked that they took into their confidence " a large number of persons, many mean in parts and condition, and many drunk,"[4] and many an informer also. Every person engaged in the transaction seems to have come before Thurloe: the men that sold and bought the arms, the porters who piled the arm-chests upon the carriers' carts, and the countrymen who unladed them. Full reports were received from the soldiers who accompanied the chests to their destination, and broke open the boxes as soon as they touched the ground.

Careful analysis of this mass of evidence has yielded the following result. The " many thousands of arms, even all that this City could afford," were purchased at two gunsmiths, by four men, Major Norwood, Mr. Rowland Thomas, and Messrs. Custice and Glover, and were deposited in a warehouse in Lime Street. Chests containing arms were forwarded thence to the houses of three country gentlemen, in the counties of Worcester, Stafford, and Derby, to Sir H. Littleton of Hagley, Mr. Walter Vernon of Stokely Park, and Mr. Browne of Hungry Bentley. And those chests yielded to

[4] Clarendon Papers, Cal. III. 20. Thurloe, III. 65, 68, 72, 78, 82, 89, 90, 91, 96, 104, 129. See also Heath, 367.

the soldiers who broke them open, cases or holsters
containing fifty-six pair of pistols and seven blunderbusses. Forty brace of pistols were also found
in Sir H. Litttleton's study, lying " in a place easy
enough to be seen." They were bought " to ac-
commodate" the escort that he was bound to provide
for the judges, " being then Sheriff of Worcestershire." And to these, the only weapons actually
handled by the Government searchers, should,
perhaps, be added seventy carbines, bought by
Custice and Glover, which may have been in five
chests and two trunks, found in the Lime Street
warehouse.

Sir H. Littleton justified himself very fairly
regarding his forty brace of pistols : but Mr. Vernon
and Mr. Browne needed no justification at all regarding the weapons seized at their doors. Not the slightest responsibility in the matter was brought home
to them. They never even saw the seven blunderbusses and the pistols. They were not present when
the soldiers, who accompanied the carriers' carts,
opened, closed, and carried off the arm-chests. No
attempt, even, was made to implicate those gentlemen in the purchase of the pistols and blunderbusses.
The senders, " P. Green " and " T. Taylor," admitted in their accompanying letters that they
were strangers, who had made bold to send Mr.
Vernon and Mr Browne " some things." Had they
expected such a dangerous consignment, surely
Messrs. Vernon and Browne would have been at

home to stow it quickly out of sight? The carts, on the contrary, pulled up at the front door.

A distinct link, however, did appear, which connected the transaction with a person whose name, at least, was well known to those gentlemen, and that was their Protector. He sent a military convoy to attend the carts. This most significant circumstance was brought to light by Thomas Allen, the carrier's man, who brought Mr. Browne's arm-chest from London to Ashburn. To prove his innocence regarding its contents, Allen deposed that it was only after he had left London that he learnt from the " soldiers, as he supposes them," who " went along with him " throughout the journey, that the trunk was " full of arms." And soldiers also " went along " with the consignment directed to Stokely Park.

What was the purpose of those escorts? Highway robbery was barely possible. Nor was that precaution needed to ensure discovery. He who sent the soldiers, and ordered that they should be " dressed as countrymen," knew where they were to go, for the messenger who summoned the guards to meet the chests must have passed the convoy on the road. That being so, no other object can be assigned to that disguised military escort, save to secure that the seizure of those weapons should take place in the shires rather than in Lime Street, to satisfy " good people's minds in the evil design intended by the malignants." [4]

Those who are unversed in the contents of the Thurloe papers may be surprised at the marked discrepancy between the results disclosed by Cromwell's documents and the statements made in his speech. It seems almost impossible to believe that the Protector's " mathematical demonstrations " should prove so contemptible, that the " many thousands of arms, even all that this city could afford," should turn out to be only seven blunderbusses, ninety-six brace of pistols, and perhaps seventy carbines; and that the only proof he possessed of a Cavalier conspiracy were Messrs. Bayley and Bagnal's artless depositions.

Nor is there any reason to suppose that we have not before us all the evidence that Cromwell possessed against the Royalists. The arms-purchase of the winter of 1654 was mentioned during a debate in Parliament, March, 1659, and Lambert's description keeps quite within the account afforded by the Thurloe papers.[5] And, as regards the bloodthirsty Cavalier, Ludlow attributed Cromwell's knowledge of the royalist intrigues of this season to the revelations of " one Bayley, a Jesuit, who discovered his kinsman Mr. Bagnal, together with his own brother, Nicholas Bayley." [5] The " News Letters," also, of the time contain repeated accounts of these designs; and those de-

[5] Burton, IV. 261, 303. Ludlow, 217. Thurloe, III. 125,

scriptions contain, almost without exception, no names other than those which we have mentioned. The arrest is announced of Major Norwood and his associates, Rowland Thomas, Custice, and Glover; of the Vernons, Littletons, and Sir J. Packington. And those doughty conspirators, Messrs. Bayley and Bagnal, are thus referred to. " Wales.— Mr. B—— a gentleman of great fortune. And Mr. Bayley, son to the late Bishop of Bangor, which B—— is a notorious papist. Prisoners at Jameses."[5]

So complete is the harmony between these events as recorded by the weekly journals and by the Thurloe papers, that it is obvious that Thurloe himself supplied the news. If more startling information wherewith to serve his patron and to terrify England had been at hand, the Secretary would have used it. And, as regards the weapons of war in the hands of the Royalists, Cromwell himself may be cited to prove that we possess the whole of his story. If those stores of arms had approached the dimensions that he pictured to Parliament, the arm-chests would not have needed their convoy of pretended countrymen.

One form of proof, however, that the " Cavalier Party " had been designing " to put this Nation in blood again," Cromwell lacked. He expressed a hope that " by the justice of the land some will, in the face of the Nation, answer it with their lives;

453. " Several Proceedings," &c. News Letter, 4 Jan.—11 Jan., 1654-5.

and then the business will be pretty well out of doubt." Not a single Royalist on this occasion suffered more than imprisonment, save Rowland Thomas, who, priced at 100*l.*, was sold " into the Barbadoes " by Mr. Secretary Thurloe.[5]

What purpose, it may be asked, is served by this exposure of Cromwell's exaggerative artifices ? In one respect, it is needless. He could not be an honest man. He had made a covenant with falsehood. He consented to play the Protector's part in that acted lie, the Installation of December, 1653. " The step straightforward and sure, the proud, bright, bearing of truth," [6] could not be looked for in Cromwell. The return he made into the knavish ways of the unjust steward, who took the accounts supplied him by his servants and multiplied them by " four score," serves as an index to his contrivances.

It is obvious, for instance, that the Royalists, as a body, were in the winter of 1654-5 peaceful and quiescent, else Cromwell would not have accused them of designing " to put this Nation in blood " upon such miserable pretexts. It is obvious that he used the grossest deception to convince his subjects that in the Protector alone was their refuge from the " old enemy." Mr. Bayley also introduces us for the first time to one of those gentlemen, who " quickly knits a friendship " with a gullible

<hr>

[6] " The Visions of England," Cassell's Edition, p. 48.

Cavalier, and assures him that the King and his army will speedily be on our coast, and hands over a paper, upon the top whereof is writ " C. R."

Fraud evidently is in the air; and fraud of this kind follows after fraud throughout the Protectorate, framed in like fashion, tending to the same end. And now, as always, Cromwell laded himself with the thick clay of deception to no purpose. He lied in vain. In vain he raised the cry of wolf: it might serve as an excuse for the dispersal of Parliament, but not as an alarum to the Nation. Of that tale of "real dangers," as Cromwell himself tells us, "nothing was believed!"*

Sensitiveness to failure was not Cromwell's weakness. Within three months the wolf was no longer at the door: he was in the fold. Real Cavaliers, who did not hide their commissions in a box, were seen careering sword in hand across England. And again Cromwell's gainsaying subjects hardened their hearts. They did not believe in Messrs. Bayley and Bagnal's efforts to put the Nation into blood; they rejected their Protector's historical retrospect of " the late Insurrection and Rebellion " of March, 1655.* But before that occurrence can be reached, the case of Major-General Overton, and the doings of the Levellers during the months December—February, 1654-5, must be considered.

* See pp. 148, 151.

CHAPTER IV.

THE PROTECTOR AND MAJOR-GENERAL OVERTON.

THE budget of imminent disaster that Cromwell, on the 22nd January, 1655, laid before Parliament, contained a cause for alarm truly formidable. He asserted that the Anabaptist Levellers had leagued with the Royalists, a most threatening combination, and that, to cap the coming catastrophe, an upheaval within the Army was actually at work. Here was indeed a "real danger;" it was thus enlarged upon by Cromwell. He declared that the Levellers, in union with the Royalists, "have been, and yet are endeavouring to put us into blood and confusion, more desperate and dangerous confusion than England ever saw."

This was to be accomplished by debauching and dividing the English Army—by causing "a common rising"—and by inciting the Anabaptists among the troops stationed in Scotland to invade England, leaving their comrades "to have their throats cut there."[1]

At the outset of our inquiry it may be observed that our sagacious informant, Mr. Greene, described

[1] Carlyle, III. 428 ; IV. 113, 114.

the Levellers as being "few in number;" and he pictured thus the inevitable result of the utmost that they could do by their unassisted sword-arms. "Suppose that the Anabaptists could produce 5000 really valiant fighting-men, yet being for the most part untrained, and without arms, horses, or able commanders, what would they do against an old, well-disciplined Army, led with excellent conductors, and accustomed to conquer? And as the Government has many watchful eyes set over them, it would be impossible for them to arm, horse, and embody themselves without discovery." *

The materials shall now be examined on which Cromwell founded his alarming statement. As he subsequently denied the existence of any combination between the Levellers and the Royalists, that source of panic is disposed of.[1] He stated, however, that "We are possessed" of Declarations framed for the purpose of creating "a common rising" by the Levellers, and "the confession of themselves now in custody;" and as those confessions are in our possession also, the story they disclose is easily ascertainable.

The confessors themselves were two in number, Dallington, the suborner, and Prior, his subornee, who for his part retorted against Dallington that he was the first to broach seditious suggestions. That return charge seems probable. Dallington was, according to his own story, a missioner for the

* Cal. Clarendon MSS. II., 398.

Levellers, a blue-jacket in the *Constant Warwick*, who had been dropt ashore at Harwich, to see "how the Country stood affected." He had visited Cornwall and the Scotch army, apparently without special results, for Prior was the only delinquent he denounced to the Government.

Dallington, according to his tale, met Prior casually, "within four miles of his home." After "some conference about public affairs, Prior told him, that there were several in the Army who were resolved to stand to their first principles in ' the Good old Cause,' in opposition to the Government, and that he had a Declaration in his pocket to that purpose, which Declaration the said Prior read to this examinant, and said it should, as soon as they had gathered to their rendezvous, be in print, and put in every market-place. Their rendezvous (Prior said) was to be in January, at several places; and named Salisbury Plain, and Marston Moor; and other places, he said, were also agreed upon, and their colours should be white tape, and white ribbons. He said also, that the Lord Grey should be for them, and so would Colonel Saunders, and Colonel Okey, but did not know what Sir Arthur Haselrig would do. And further that there were agitators sent into the army in Scotland and Ireland, and that many of them should draw unto their assistance in January, when their rendezvous should be."

Dallington was also informed by Prior that he

had distributed that Declaration widely throughout England; and he begged Dallington, "for his further satisfaction," to visit Colonel Eyres, a noted anabaptist officer in London. That satisfaction, however, Dallington failed to obtain, for the Colonel proved to be "timorous, and not willing to speak with him about any such business," *i.e.* seditious business.

Dallington does not look like a true man. Colonel Okey asserted, on his own experience as an anabaptist leader, that at this season "there came several trepanners from Whitehall" among the soldiers in the North;[2] and features in Dallington's tale tend to show that he may have been one of those trepanners. He was regarded with suspicion by "timorous" Colonel Eyres, who was so stout a republican that Cromwell thought it best to lock him up. And Dallington's tale received such slight attention from Cromwell, so unimportant did that "rendezvous" of disaffected soldiers "at several places" appear to him, that it would seem as if it was entirely overlooked when he examined Prior. The slightest hint of a "common rising" in his Army must have caught Cromwell's attention, and Prior was most anxious to clear his character; yet he does not mention that subject in the "full and perfect reply" which he addressed to the Protector in answer "to the questions you asked me."[2]

Those Declarations, and that talk between

2 Thurloe, III. 35, 146. Burton, IV. 157.

Dallington and Prior about the "rendezvous" of soldiers decked with white tape, formed the only approach to proof possessed by Cromwell of "a common rising" by the Levellers in England, when he addressed Parliament on the 22nd January,1655.

Though significance does attach to the fact that Prior, or Dallington, placed that "rendezvous" on Salisbury Plain and Marston Moor, Cromwell's "common rising" needs no further notice. And, in accord with Cromwell, we may suffer the attempt by the Levellers to debauch and divide the Army in England, to pass out of sight. Protracted consideration, however, must be given to that alleged mutiny among the soldiers stationed in Scotland, for on it was based Cromwell's charge against Major-General Overton. With intentional publicity and solemnity, Cromwell declared that "by the designs of some in the Army, who are now in custody, it was designed to get as many of them as possible, to march for England out of Scotland; and in discontent to seize their General there [General Monk], a faithful and honest man, so that another might head the Army;" and Cromwell specified that "another" to be Major-General Overton.[3] There lay the object of that statement.

Who, then, was that Major-General Overton, thus

---

[3] Speech, 22nd Jan., 1655. Carlyle, III. 447. Declaration regarding "the late Insurrection," 31st Oct., 1655. Old Parl. Hist., XX. 434.

accused by Cromwell of the basest crime that a soldier can commit ?

He was deservedly most eminent among the Republican party. A true Puritan, he hated monarchy and episcopal Government, and held that all authority, civil and religious, ought to be in the hands of the people. For that cause Overton fought throughout the Civil Wars with skill and courage. He was also Milton's friend, bound to him "these many years past in a friendship of more than brotherly closeness and affection;" and, with unconscious irony, Milton exhorted Cromwell, "the tutelary God of Liberty," to make "Liberty safe, and even to enlarge it," by taking as a partner in his counsels, such a man as Overton, "of the highest modesty, integrity, and valour." Cromwell, on the contrary, as soon as he could, made "Liberty safe" by making Overton safe. He was removed from active service, and was detained as a suspect during the summer of 1654.[4]

During the following September Cromwell changed his tactics. He sent for Overton, and offered to place him second in command, under General Monk, over the Scottish army. That offer was accepted by Overton on this condition, namely, that, when he was convinced that Cromwell " did only design the setting up of himself, and not the good of these Nations," he should receive notice from Overton, " that he could no longer serve him;" and Crom-

[4] Thurloe, II. 414 ; III 110.

well replied, " Thou were't a knave, if thou wouldest." [4]

On these terms Overton discharged his military duties in Scotland for about two months, October and November, until, during December, Monk, acting on Cromwell's instructions, directed Overton to appear before him at the headquarters. Overton, after about a fortnight's delay, obeyed, was arrested, sent to London, and on 16th January, 1655, he was committed to the Tower. Three years later, January, 1658, Cromwell transferred Overton to Jersey, where he remained until his release by Parliament.[5]

The evidence must be considered on which Cromwell imprisoned " a companion of his labours and trials," and exhibited him to his fellows as a traitor of the most repulsive type.

To ascertain the basis of the charge that Cromwell made against Overton, we must look not to Scotland, where the scene of the crime was laid, but to London. During the autumn and winter of 1654, anabaptist agitators held meetings at the " Blew Boar " in King Street, or the " Dolphin " in Tower Street, under the leadership of Colonel Sexby and Major Wildman, those conspicuous political busy-bodies, assisted by another notorious Leveller, Colonel Richard Overton.

Various forms of attack upon Cromwell's Government were discussed, and the names and resources of

[5] Thurloe, III. 46, 55. Cal. State Papers, 1657-58, 508, 522.

men upon whom the conspirators could " build," such
as Bradshaw, Sir A. Haselrig, and Colonel Birch,
were canvassed.   The leading notion of the conspirators was a combined outbreak among the armies
of England and Scotland.   This project was discussed ; the regiments on which the agitators could
rely, were mentioned ; and it is apparent that, whilst
from the English regiments but little help could be
expected, some co-operation was deemed possible
from troops stationed in Scotland.

The conspirators were suffered to plot unhindered
for about three months, when, in January, 1655,
Sexby and Wildman felt it expedient to quit London.
Sexby then fled to the Continent, and Wildman was
arrested and committed, first to Chepstow Castle,
and then to the Tower.

The only document that approaches the confines
of evidence in support of the charge that Cromwell
brought against Major-General Overton, is a somewhat fragmentary writing headed, " Notes of Major
Wildman's Plot, by Secretary Thurloe," consisting
of his summary, drawn from an informer's statement, of the debates held by the conspirators at the
" Blew Boar " or the " Dolphin."

The passages that seem to incriminate Overton
run thus :—" Overton and Wildman spake together,
before Overton's going, of their dislike of things ;
but no design laid, the . . . of the army not being
known ; but after he was there, he writ letters to
let them know, that there was a party which would

stand right for a Commonwealth. Then Breme sent to them. And a meeting at Overton's quarters, M. Knight, Oates. . . . The Regiments that they relied on, Riche's, Tomlinson's, Okey's, Pride's, Sterling Castle, Alured's, Overton's : some of the General's regiment. Begin with a mutiny, and then his person (Monk's) seized, and put in Edinburgh Castle, which they were sure of ; forced Overton to command. He writ up hither, and their declaration ready, which was drawn by the meeting here, and sent G. Br—and printed there. Spoke as if they should have Berwick. Sure of Hull by Overton's means, and the townsmen, and Overton's correspondence." [6]

At the time of Major-General Overton's arrest Cromwell may also have held an anonymous, undated letter, addressed to General Monk. The letter is to the following effect. The writer, presumably an army Officer, states that he was " lately solicited to act in the following design. Your person was first to be secured by one Captain Lieutenant Crest; then Major-General Overton to have given out orders, and to have drawn 3000 foot, besides horse, into the field, and soon after to have marcht for England, where the Lord Bradshaw, and Sir A. Haselrig was to have joined with them very considerable forces ;" that " Vice-Admiral Lawson was engaged in this design, with a squadron of the Fleet ;" and that Colonel Pride, " and several others were also en-

[6] Thurloe, III. 147, 185 The quotation from Thurloe's notes has been kindly collated by Mr. Macray.

gaged in this plot;" and the writer adds that "this design was to break forth some ten days since." [6]

Put it at the most, the hearsay evidence Cromwell possessed does not bring the charge home to Major-General Overton. When the mutiny took place, then he is either to be " forced to command," or " to have given out orders."

Moreover the Thurloe Notes show that the conspirators never passed from talk into action, nor even towards an approach to action. That this was so is confirmed by further evidence regarding Sexby's intrigues, subsequently acquired by the Government, namely two depositions made by " Samuel Dyer, late servant to Colonel Sexby," who was apprehended and examined in February, 1657. Dyer, in one deposition, described his master's doings from the year 1653 to the close of the year 1656, including the schemes of the winter of 1654, with much detail; the other deposition is more fragmentary.

What we learn from Dyer is the somewhat important fact that Colonel Richard Overton was an active associate in " Major Wildman's Plot." Dyer also proves that Major-General Overton never appeared at the " Blew Boar "or the " Dolphin," and that his supposed complicity rests solely on Colonel Sexby's talk, for it was "the said Sexby" who "acquainted" Dyer "that Colonel Overton, who was in Scotland, was to seize on General Monk, and the headquarters."

Even this statement Dyer himself contradicts. In the other deposition he dropped all reference to Major-General Overton, and gave this description of the mutiny project. "The persons engaged are as follows, a Lieutenant Bemont, this was the man that carried and distributed all the Declarations against His Highness that were published in Scotland; this was the man, likewise, who joined with Richard Overton to cut off the headquarters in Scotland, and to deliver up Hull."[7] Major-General Overton's Christian name is "Robert." Dyer, therefore, evidently refers to that Colonel Richard Overton, who was an active partner in "Major Wildman's Plot."

The last-mentioned deposition consists of notes of Dyer's evidence, taken down at Southampton. The other deposition, which contains the words "Colonel Overton who was in Scotland," is a more formal document, bearing Dyer's signature. This circumstance does not enlarge its evidential value. Preference, indeed, might be given to the informal record of Dyer's own words, made at a distance from Whitehall, where proof against the Major-General was sorely needed.

Dyer also disposes, by his Southampton deposition, of the sentence in Thurloe's notes, "Sure of Hull by Overton's means, and the townsmen, and Overton's correspondence." As the Major-General was, or had been, Governor of Hull, mischief seems to lurk in that allegation; yet on the face of it, if

[7] Thurloe, VI. 831, 832.

Thurloe's notes be read together, a man who must be " forced " into the mutiny, cannot be the man who was " sure " to betray his trust at Hull. And to which of the two Overtons that sentence referred, is explained by Dyer, who deposed that " Richard Overton," with Lieutenant Bemont, undertook " to deliver up Hull."

Besides, the Major-General was in Scotland, whilst Richard Overton was in England ; and though he was apparently no near relation of the Major-General's, still the Overton family was connected with Hull. So that Richard Overton might fairly claim to be " sure of Hull."[7] Richard Overton also was a working partner with Major Wildman and Colonel Sexby, being even trusted with " two sheepskins quite full of Spanish pistoles," some of Sexby's blood-money. That Richard Overton figured effectively in the discussions at the " Blew Boar," and undertook to seize Monk and the head-quarters, is likely enough.

All the evidence against Major-General Overton, contained in the Thurloe papers, has been set forth : and all the certainty to which we have attained is that his namesake may have been the conspirator, and that the Major-General's name was freely used behind his back at seditious meetings, where undoubtedly he was never present.

That the efforts of the London plotters remained in the regions of talk is also evident. Even the supposed support promised them by leading Republicans, such as Lord Grey and Sir Arthur Haselrig, proves exceeding shadowy. An offer made by Lord Grey to raise 5000 Somersetshire men arose, "soon after His Highness was made Lord Protector," and not in the winter of 1654-5; and Sir A. Haselrig's noted saying "that he was loth to begin the business; but as soon as he saw the candle lighted, the Bishoprick of Durham should set it up," was based apparently on Lord Grey's undertaking.[8]

The futility of the Sexby and Wildman intrigues during the autumn and winter of 1654, harmonizes with the unreality of their conspiracy. Those noted firebrands, during three or four months, held meetings in London, distributed inflammatory pamphlets, travelled through the country, and visited the leaders of their party; but they produced no tangible result. In the end, when Cromwell put a stop to their intrigues, Sexby fled; and Wildman was seized without attempting resistance or popular appeal. Even when that distinguished Anabaptist, Lord Grey, taken on his own ground and among his own people, was arrested by Colonel Hacker, he reported to the Protector that there was "no appearance of danger" in the district, "except by those called Quakers, who will not return home, but say they stand in the counsel of the Lord, and not in the will of man."[8]

Thus much, at present, about the English branch of Major Wildman's Plot. And how did Monk and

[8] Thurloe, VI. 829, 832; III. 148.

Cromwell deal with the supposed mutiny in the Scotch army? Monk was informed by that anonymous letter, that "this design was to break forth some ten days since;" and Cromwell knew that the Levellers assumed that they could reckon on almost every regiment in Scotland, that they were sure of Hull, of Edinburgh Castle, and of Monk's head-quarters at Dalkeith.

This "large order" in sedition was met by Cromwell in very leisurely fashion. During the first or second week of December, 1654, Cromwell directed Monk, as commander-in-chief of the Scottish army, to desire Overton by letter, giving no special reason, to quit his military duty at Aberdeen and present himself at Dalkeith. On the 26th December Monk reported to Cromwell that he had sent an officer to arrest Overton, as he had not obeyed Monk's directions. Cromwell was also informed that, under the pretence of his instructions, Monk had ordered Majors Bramston and Holmes, and Lieutenant Keamer, to appear before the Protector at Whitehall, they being "men who are not so well affected to the Government as I could wish them;" and because, "if there were any such design as your intelligence is of, I am sure Colonel Overton could do nothing in it, without the assistance of these two Majors."

As Cromwell's accusation against Major-General Overton was complicity in a mutinous outbreak among the soldiers in Scotland, the "design" that

Cromwell communicated to Monk must have been that projected mutiny. Hence, it is evident that the " design," even from the first, never presented itself to Cromwell, or to Monk, as a definite project needing summary and immediate stamping out. Had prompt action been needed—and what needs prompter action than imminent military revolt?—Overton's arrest would hardly have been made by letters of recall. Had any proof of Majors Bramston and Holmes's complicity in the mutiny existed, Monk would not have arrested them under feigned orders from Cromwell; and the tenor of Monk's letters show that he never felt the touch of mutiny. Even before Overton was shipped for London, Monk wrote to Cromwell that " I hope by the blessing of God, there will be no danger of disaffected persons in Scotland, for I find the Commanders so generally well affected, that I doubt not we shall be able to command any person, both great and small, here." And Monk continued to report " that all things are quiet in these parts," until the close of the following February.[9]

These were all the precautions taken by Monk and Cromwell to stifle a widespread military revolt, which was on the eve of immediate outbreak. Proof that the Scotch mutiny was wholly a London concocted affair, if further evidence of its unreality be needed, Cromwell himself supplies.

The following opening towards some discovery

[9] Thurloe, III. 46, 55, 99, 179.

against Overton seemed to present itself. During December, 1654, a movement took place in the Scottish army among those who resented the mockery Commonwealth that Cromwell had set up. In furtherance of their object, a letter, dated Aberdeen, 18th December, 1654, was addressed to "Major Holmes, to be communicated to our Christian friends in General Monk's regiment," signed by one captain, by six subordinate officers, one private soldier, and army chaplain Otes. The object of the letter was a proposal, made rather hesitatingly, to their Christian friends, that they should meet in Edinburgh, " at the Green Dragon in Cannygate," to consider whether " as God hath called us forth to assert the freedoms of the people in the privileges of Parliament, we may justly sit down satisfied in the present state of public affairs, or whether, except we do somewhat more, the guilt of the blood of so many thousands . . . and the hipocracy of our professions will not lie heavy on our consciences, till we return to our duty."

Whether that " somewhat more " which " we " intended, was only an " address to General Monk, and so to the Lord Protector," for free Parliamentary government, as Chaplain Otes explained to Corporal Parkinson, or hostile concerted action, will never be known; but that the " somewhat more " meant " Major Wildman's Plot " was entirely disproved.[10] The letter was shown to

[10] Thurloe, III. 29, 205. Milton State Papers, 132. Burton, IV. 158. Cal. State Papers. 1657-8. 508.

Major-General Overton ; he discountenanced it, and obtained an undertaking for its abandonment, if not approved by General Monk.   The undertaking was not observed ; the letter was sent to Major Holmes, who handed it to Monk, and similar letters were circulated.[10]   The letter-signers were arrested ; they were tried by a court-martial, and their letter was adjudged to be an incitement to mutiny and sedition.

It occurred to Cromwell that something might have arisen in this affair to incriminate Major-General Overton.   He was a leader among the Anabaptists ; Major Holmes was one of his set ; and the movement was an Anabaptist movement.   So, early in March, 1655, Judge Advocate Whalley was sent to Edinburgh to collect evidence against Overton by the examination of his papers and of those implicated in that letter.   Whalley was quite unsuccessful.   He could make no discoveries among Overton's papers.   Nothing could be wrung from the soldiers, save that they had prepared and signed that letter, and had not laid it before General Monk. So Whalley was forced to report that " though he had much trouble with the officers to obtain their depositions," and had omitted nothing " of his duty to the uttermost of his mean ability," still he was compelled to inform the Protector that he could obtain no information against Major-General Overton, except, as indeed he always admitted, that he saw the letter before it was put in circulation.[10]

This unquestionable advantage belongs to the " Thurloe Papers ; " they tell us exactly what Cromwell knew. That report from Whalley therefore proves that when, in the Declaration of the 31st October, 1655, " on the occasion of the late Insurrection," Cromwell accused Overton of complicity in the mutiny plot, he was aware not only of its actual unreality, but also that his law-officer's careful examination in Scotland had failed to bring to light aught that confirmed that charge.

Is it necessary to give further proof that Cromwell never possessed the slightest legal or quasi-legal evidence against Major-General Overton ?

If further proof be asked for, again to the Protector we can go. When it became obvious that his last Parliament must be dissolved, when his Government was crumbling under his feet, believing that Overton intended to apply for a writ of Habeas Corpus, Cromwell, to avoid exposure, transferred him from the Tower to Jersey, 28th January, 1658, and thus placed him beyond the jurisdiction of the Court.[10]

Still this plea may be urged for Cromwell. He may have been deceived by the " spies, of which he had plenty," who, as Clarendon remarks, watched " Wildman very narrowly." He might have been misled by the similarity of name, and have confounded Colonel Richard Overton with Robert Overton, the Major-General. The Protector naturally enough did not like a sincere and simple Republican, he may have caught too readily at the notion that the Major-General was conspiring against him.

But was it chance or design that brought the Major-General's name into the London-Scotch mutiny scheme? Could Cromwell have mixed the two Overtons? Certainly Thurloe knew which was which. At the very outset of Wildman and Sexby's career in the Blew Boar and other City taverns, Richard Overton, their friend, sent a letter from his lodging in Bedford Street, 6th September, 1654, to Secretary Thurloe, warning him "that there will be attempts and endeavours, by persons of great ability and interests, against the Government," and assuring him that "I shall be glad, if I may be an instrument in the prevention of disturbance," and that "I may happily be capable of doing some considerable service therein." And Richard Overton concludes his letter "with all due acknowledgment of other favours, I received from you." [11]

Would Thurloe reject so welcome an offer coming from a friend in the centre of the Levellers' party? That he did not, Richard Overton's conduct tends to prove. During the remainder of the Protectorate he flitted to and fro between England and the Continent, holding a commission from the King, but acting with Cromwell's agents in that "service" which he profferred in September, 1654. Safe with the Protector, Overton could take a prominent part in Major Wildman's Plot; and thus

[11] Thurloe, II. 590.

the probability is increased that, as Dyer deposed, Richard Overton did undertake to seize on General Monk and to make sure of Hull.

We may now, most gladly, allow Major Wildman's Plot to depart out of our sight.

That Robert Overton, the Major-General, was wholly innocent of any seditious design whatever, may now be proved by Cromwell's own witness, Whalley, his Judge Advocate. Of all men save his master and Thurloe, Whalley by position and training was the most qualified to speak with authority on state offences. The investigation of political crime formed part of his official duty; and, as Whalley conducted that Scottish inquiry, he had thorough knowledge of Overton's case. What that knowledge was, and what it was worth, we can test, with precision, as Whalley twice used it on critical occasions in parliamentary debate.

This was the first occasion. During January, 1657, Parliament was voting a national thanksgiving for Cromwell's deliverance from assassination by Sindercombe. Thurloe acquainted the House with the particulars of "the late heinous plot." Similar attempts were described, and Overton's name was mentioned, though what aroused the lying spirit in Whalley does not appear. He felt that it was his duty, as he asserted, "hearing the names of some of the plotters,—as Colonel Overton,—to say what I know of my knowledge, and to affirm that when General Monk and several officers with myself went to search Colonel Overton's chamber, we found a sealed paper, wherein was expressed that 600*l.* was distributed to several persons, who should have murdered the Lord Protector. I thought good to acquaint you." [12] Whalley's story passed unchallenged, though some of his hearers, as well as ourselves and Mr. Secretary Thurloe, may have known that it gave the lie direct to Whalley's Edinburgh report of March, 1655.

The motive which prompted his second attempt to blacken Overton's character, made some two years later, is apparent enough. On the 16th March, 1659, Whalley had to defend himself. He was regarded by Parliament as a man implicated in the unjust and cruel imprisonment of a fellow-subject, seemingly of an honest man. The treatment of Overton by the late Protector had been brought before Parliament; his warrant transferring his prisoner to Jersey Castle lay on the table.

Former things had, indeed, then passed away. Overton, " who was brought so weak by four years' imprisonment, that he could scarce go over the floor," had been heard at the bar of the House. That he had been brought there, he recognized as a great mercy of God; he raised no accusation against any one; he only made earnest entreaty that he might hear the charge brought against him, which he hoped he could answer thoroughly. He also expressed a hope that he had not done any-

[12] Burton, I. 356, 19th Jan., 1657 ; IV. 155, 16th March, 1659.

thing contrary to what he at first engaged for and fought for, and "he desired, one way or other, to receive according as he had done." His hearers were much moved; their indignation was barely restrained by the feeling that the late Protector, who "had fought them into their liberties," was taken away from this world's judgment. A warm debate ensued, and it was moved "that Judge Advocate Whalley may declare the original ground of Overton's imprisonment."

Whalley, at first, tried to shirk out of the difficulty before him. He sought to frighten the House by assuring them that a revelation of Overton's crime might be "of dangerous conse-quence;" that he was imprisoned for a military offence; that they durst not set forth the grounds of his imprisonment; and he finally warned Par-liament "to take heed how they discouraged the Army." Whatever that warning implied, the "dangerous consequence" argument was unavailing. The Speaker rose ·to put the Motion, declaring Overton's "commitment and detainer" to be "illegal and unjust." Whalley saw that he must, if possible, defend himself, if he could not defend his late master. Silence was then no longer a necessity. The whole fabric of Oliver's state policy, his organized spy system, his agency of traitors "in the very bosom of our enemies," had passed away. Whalley without fear might have produced all the evidence which provoked Overton's arrest. But he did not attempt to prove the mutiny charge, " the original ground " upon which Cromwell based the guilt of Overton. Whalley resorted to his lie, altered and improved, of January, 1657.

This was his statement. " Seeing the Question is about to be put, I think myself bound to say further, as to matter of fact. His late Highness sent me into Scotland. I found divers officers in prison, amongst the rest, Major-General Overton. It was considered at the Council of War. There was a letter showing dissatisfaction to the Government, desiring all the officers to meet together. It was at an unseasonable time. We were in no good frame then. It was when Wagstaff and Wildman's businesses were in hand. I have brought the letter in my pocket. We cashiered several of them, and sent some prisoners, as Major Bramston, for fear they should go abroad to infect the army. Upon examination of this matter, it was proved that Major-General Overton—I must do him right as well as wrong—(*altum risum*).· He saw the letter and approved of it as a good letter, and a godly letter. Major-General Monk saw the letter. I was commanded to peruse his papers. I found one letter sealed with silk and silver ribbon. It had no hand to it. The contents were, that there was an attempt to murder the Protector and Lord Lambert and six others. I was sorry to find it." And the reporter adds : " Lord Lambert smiled." [12]

Lord Lambert's smile was unneeded. The letter

sealed with silk and silver ribbon, that " had no hand to it," condemned itself ; and the Motion was agreed to, resolving that the Protector had acted illegally and unjustly towards Major-General Overton ; and he was set free.

How, then, in conclusion, does the account stand between Cromwell and his prisoner? That Overton was innocent of the precise charge brought against him is unquestionable. In other respects, however, his conduct towards Cromwell may have been blameworthy. As holder of the Protector's commission, Overton undoubtedly committed a fault. He did not report to Monk the Aberdeen letter of the 18th December, 1654, addressed by the republican soldiers to their anabaptist brethren. This the Major-General was bound to do. Whalley scored that point. He suggested to Cromwell that Overton's privity to a letter condemned in severe terms by a court-martial might form " a considerable charge, and article against him."

Cromwell, however, did not avail himself of his Judge Advocate's suggestion. That letter was not the provocation to Overton's arrest. Before Monk had received it, he had been instructed by Cromwell to send Overton a prisoner to London. A court-martial was held on the writers of the letter. Richard Overton, or Wildman himself, might have been produced against the Major-General, but he was not placed before that court. On the contrary, Cromwell did all he could to baffle inquiry into Overton's guilt. For that very purpose, though arrested on a supposed military charge, he was, as a civilian, re-mitted by the Protector's warrant beyond " the reach of the law."

This, however, is certain regarding Overton. He had no great respect or love for Cromwell. " Several unhandsome verses " were found in Overton's letter-case, in which His Highness is described as " an ape," the " counterfeit effigies " of a king, with " a copper nose."[13] And whether these verses were " a trial of " Overton's " wit," or only the song of a " fiddler's boy," Cromwell, it may be urged, knew that these verses were but a symptom showing that the Major-General, in his heart, imagined mischief against him. It therefore might be contended that Cromwell, the righteous ruler, who bore the weight of Government, did right in putting Overton out of the way of mischief. Nor is it impossible that some may argue that, even though Cromwell knew that no mutinous plot in the Scottish army existed, still his distinct and positive assertion of Overton's guilt, should be accepted without question. To establish such a claim upon our confidence Cromwell must show that his conduct towards Overton had been void of offence, absolutely free from taint of malice.

In the spring of 1649, efforts were made to obtain for the service of the state the co-operation of Colonel Hutchinson. In the course of these

[13] Thurloe, III. 75, 111, 197. Hutchinson, Bohn's Ed., 341.

negotiations, " the Lieutenant-General, Cromwell, desired the Colonel to meet him one afternoon at a committee; where, when he came, a malicious accusation against the Governor of Hull was violently prosecuted by a fierce faction in that town. To this the Governor had sent up a very fair and honest defence ; yet most of the committee, more favouring the adverse faction, were labouring to cast out the Governor. Colonel Hutchinson, though he knew him not, was very earnest in his defence; whereupon Cromwell drew him aside, and asked him what he meant by contending to keep in that Governor ? (It was Overton). The Colonel told him, because he saw nothing proved against him worthy of his being ejected.

" But," said Cromwell, " we like him not."

Then said the Colonel, " Do it on that account; and blemish not a man that is innocent, upon false accusations, because you like him not."

" But," said Cromwell, " we would have him out, because the government is designed for you, and except you put him out, you cannot have the place."

At this the Colonel was very angry, and with great indignation told him, that " if there was no way of bringing him into their army, but by casting out others unjustly, he would rather fall naked before his enemies, than so seek to put himself into a posture of defence." [13]

Mr. Live-loose never could endure Faithful, " for

he would always be condemning my way." "We
like him not," said Cromwell of Robert Overton;
" he is not for our turn, and he is clean contrary to
our doings; we are esteemed of him as counterfeits ;
he is grievous unto us even to behold." And so the
Protector, " the great one " of that " lusty fair " of
place and profit that was set up in Whitehall, took
Overton and besmeared him with calumny and
put him in the cage, that he might be a gazing-stock,
for an example and a terror to others.

Parliament, by their Resolution, 16th March, 1659,
assigned the illegality of Major-General Overton's
imprisonment to the technical aspect of Cromwell's
conduct, to a detention by warrant issued under
the hand of the chief magistrate alone, wherein no
cause was expressed ; but the tone of the debate
bespoke the feeling that Overton was an innocent
man, who had suffered unjust and cruel treatment.
Nor could it have been indignation aroused by
mere technical injustice that drew together in
procession " about 500 horsemen, 40 coaches, and
2 or 3000 of the rabble," to welcome Overton when,
on his return from Jersey, he entered London on
his way to freedom.[14]

How similar was that scene, that gathering of
sympathetic admirers, that expression of popular
wrath, to the triumphant reception given to
Prynne, Burton, and Bastwick, when they also
were liberated from " far-distant dungeons," by

[14] MS. Cal. Clarendon MSS, fo. 630, March, 1659.

the order of the House of Commons, 13th of November, 1640. Between the event of March, 1659, and the event of November, 1640, there existed, however, an essential difference. Prynne and his comrades were Puritans punished by Church and State. Overton was a Puritan, evil entreated by the Puritan of Puritans. They had suffered imprisonment according to the law, for proved offences. Overton had been falsely accused and imprisoned by Cromwell, because—" We like him not." *

* The King to Col. Ov.[erton], Cal. Clarendon, MSS., II. 344. A draft letter, thus addressed, exists among the Clarendon documents of April, 1654. The letter states that the King has received information of Overton's affection ; that he has it in his power to redeem what he has heretofore done amiss, and that he should be rewarded if he would assist in the King's restoration.

Whether that letter was addressed to Major-General Robert Overton, or to Col. Richard Overton, who subsequently did accept the King's commission, must remain undetermined ; but this draft letter in no way proves that the intended recipient was unfaithful to the Commonwealth. A similar kind of letter, 12th Aug., 1655, was sent by the King to Monk, (Calendar, Clarendon MSS., III. 53) ; but that therefore Monk had offered his services to Charles has never been supposed. Comment on two letters from Government informers (Thurloe, III. 217, 280), stating that Major-General Overton had made alliance with Charles Stuart, is needless.

CHAPTER V.

THE PREPARATIONS FOR THE "INSURRECTION AND REBELLION" OF MARCH, 1655.

As Cromwell's hand appears when the Insurrection was in progress, it is not improbable that the working of those fingers may also be traceable whilst it was being set in motion. The direction in which those fingers would work is manifest. It is obvious that the Protectorate would receive strength and impetus, if Charles could be enticed into assuming the aspect of an invader. Enthusiasm would thereby be aroused for Cromwell, as our defender against popery, prelacy, and tyranny. The King's determined inaction was the main hindrance that debarred the Protector from putting such a scheme in operation. The only way to overcome that hindrance was to persuade Charles that the Levellers were not only projecting but prepared for an immediate explosion. Charles was so persuaded; how that was accomplished must be explained.

Cromwell knew, through the traitor, Sir R. Willis, all the King's counsels during the latter portion

of the Protectorate;[1] and, during its first years,
he was kept equally well acquainted with the
thoughts and intentions of Charles and his advisers.
In June, 1654, they were warned from England,
that "you have yet more knaves about the King;
find them out; you do nothing but is known here in
ten days."[2]　Neither Hyde nor Nicholas found out
that spy : nor did they know, during the following
November, that Massonet, the King's writing-clerk,
was forwarding to Cromwell copies of the King's
letters.　In this service Massonet was active during
February, 1655, whilst the Insurrection was in
birth ; nor apparently was his treachery ever
discovered. Sir John Henderson, a pretended
Royalist, resident at Cologne from January to
March, 1655, who had access to the King and was
on friendly terms with those around him, kept
Thurloe, during that critical season, in touch with

---

[1] The time when Sir R. Willis began his espial must remain
at present undetermined.　Mr. Macray, our most eminent authority regarding the MSS. history of the Protectorate, identifies
letters to Thurloe, signed Edwards, or Barrett, dated Aug., 1656,
as being in Willis's handwriting; and those letters contain offers
to supply Thurloe with royalist information made evidently for
the first time.　Echard, who could have acquired information
about Willis from his comrades, in a full account of his career,
states that he devoted himself to Cromwell's service in the year
1652 ; and I have exhibited indications of a belief that " Willis
hath betrayed the King all along " throughout Cromwell's Protectorate ; but willing deference is due to the master of all the
manuscripts.　Hist. MSS. Com. Report, V. 153.　Echard, II.
727.　English Hist. Review, July, 1888, p. 523.

[2] Thurloe, II. 594, 610; III. 190.　Cal. Clarendon MSS., II.
379 ; III. 10—15.

the thoughts of the Royal Court; and Manning was entering on his course of espial, to close before long so disastrously in a wood near Cologne.[2]

Thus Cromwell could, hour by hour, feel the royal pulse, and bring influences to bear which might set it beating higher.

There was but one method by which Charles could be roused out of stagnation. On land, Cromwell's 40,000 soldiers were unassailable. At sea, his fleet would make short work of a transport flotilla. If the King could be set in motion, he must be led on by the hope that a sudden rush might be made into an English seaport, open, and prepared to receive him, and by the hope, also, that he would find Cromwell struggling vainly against his Army and the Levellers.

The concoction of this deceptive potion was beset by this difficulty: the ingredients would not blend together. If the Levellers hated a King disguised as a Protector, that they would fight for a real King was most improbable. It was not their game to ensnare to his destruction an unpopular young man, in order that they might poise firmly on his throne Cromwell the apostate. Major Norwood, indeed, when purchasing arms, during the winter of 1654, was gulled into the belief that "the greater part of the Army was for King Charles;"[2] but so absurd a notion would not suit shrewder men like Hyde

---

[3] Thurloe, III. 83.

and Ormond.   Accordingly the bait of January, 1655, took the form of an assurance that the Levellers were ripe for action, and that, though they would not assist the King, he could utilize their assault.   The more alluring bait of an offer from the Levellers to place Charles upon the throne, was reserved for a future occasion.

Faithful followers, if misled by irrational hope, may occasionally mislead their leader.   The persistent creation of false hope betrays an enemy.   The Levellers never had the wherewithal to perform the feats assigned to them, or the promises made in their name.   The imposture of Major Wildman's plot and its mutiny has been exposed.   The Army was thoroughly purged of fervid Republicans.   Of the civilian Levellers, never does Thurloe in his correspondence betray the slightest anxiety.   With apparent truth Mr. Greene characterized them, during the winter of 1654, as a small much-hated party ; and their power was, during the following June, described as " much decreasing." [4]   Thus if to amuse the King by false hopes of aid from the Levellers was Cromwell's object, he could play that game without fear of playing also the part of biter bit.

When the Insurrection scheme of March, 1655, first arose to view, Charles felt especially inert.   He had sought " rest and quiet " at Cologne, a

[4] Clarendon State Papers, III. 274. Cal. Clarendon MSS., III. 380, 396.

" necessitated retreat " from trouble-working Paris. But he sought rest in vain. The tranquillity he " proposed to himself " was uprooted. Charles found himself amidst the strife of tongues, among tormenting, contradictory advisers.[5]

In this strife, Hyde and Ormond at first sided with Charles. They imitated the " Sealed Knot." Influenced by the warnings of these well-advised counsellors, Hyde and Ormond were convinced that " since no rising of the Army is now to be hoped for, any rising of the King's party would only be to their own destruction." The exhilarating notion they had entertained during December, that Cromwell's soldiers " would begin the work for us, and even do the work for us," was replaced in January by despair.   Hyde and Ormond became immersed in " melancholy consultations," over the " broken business " of their projects. They determined that all action must cease until the enterprise could be " cast in a new mould." Not to stir, was the resolution of the King and his ministers, until the beginning of February, 1655.

Then came a rush of outside influence. " Expresses " reached Cologne " every day " from England, imploring, requiring the King to sanction an immediate rising. Those messengers warned Charles that if he neglected this opportunity, the confidence of his adherents would be extinguished :

[5] Clarendon State Papers, III. 263, 265. Clarendon Hist., Ed. 1839, 871.

that they had arms and ammunition : men listed : that they only desired the King to fix the day. Charles, on the contrary, " knew well enough " that his English friends were " deceived ; " that those who sent the messengers " were very honest men, and had served well in the war ;" but that " they were not equal to so great a work."

The contest between the party of action and of inaction became so fierce, that " they grew to reproach and revile one another ;" nor " could the King reconcile this distemper," nor even preserve himself intact.   To escape annoyance, he " thought fit, often to seem to think better of ˌmany things promised, than in truth he did."[5]

Thus was Charles forced on.   The messengers continued to besiege him ; they promised " many things," and much ; that " a place " would be " provided where His Majesty might land in safety ; that the rising would be general, and many places seized upon, and some declare for the King, which were in the hands of the Army.   For they still pretended and believed that a part of the Army would declare against Cromwell, at least, though not for the King." They assured Charles also, " that Kent was united to a man ; and that Dover Castle would be possessed, and the whole country in arms," upon the appointed day.

Those messengers, however, would promise nothing, if Charles did not, before all things, approve the reality of the plot, by stationing himself near the sea coast, that he might " quickly put himself into the head of the Army, which would be ready to receive him."   And he was warned that this was his last chance, and that " if he neglected that opportunity " his followers would desert him, as one hopelessly inert.   Besides these threats, the agitators in England resorted to other means to force Charles into the enterprise.   They fixed the day for the outbreak ; he was not able " to send orders to contradict it."   So he felt constrained, " with little noise," to quit Cologne for Middleburg, to await there the summons to England.[5]

Had the enterprise reached in the slightest degree the dimensions which Charles was led to expect, and which Cromwell described,—that 30,000 armed Cavaliers were ready to confront his 40,000 men, to seize London, and overthrow his cities, garrisons, and strongholds,[6]—agents must have traversed England appointing leaders, summoning the rank and file, prescribing the course of action.[6] That nothing of the kind took place is shown by the evidence which Thurloe collected, hoping to obtain proof to the contrary.*   The only Royalists who appeared in arms,—at Salisbury,—were a " company of mean fellows," of 200 husbandmen, weavers, and curriers.   The leading Cavaliers had obeyed the advice of the King's ablest English advisers, " the Sealed Knot," and held utterly aloof.

---

[6] Declaration, 31st Oct. 1655.   Old Parl. Hist., XX. 434.
* See p. 135.

Of the gallant promises which lured Charles into the enterprise, not one was fulfilled. The warning sent him by an independent friend " against coming as he purposed to England," [7] for if he did, he would certainly be captured, was fully justified. When Insurrection Day came, Kent was united as one man to keep the peace. The only difficulty that Dover Castle caused Cromwell, was the difficulty of getting the conspirators out of its cells. And as for the Royalists, they had no arms or ammunition ready, or men enlisted; " a failing " that, in loyal Cornwall, " disgusted many eminent persons." The preparations for that " general rising " were, as Clarendon states, "weakly and improbably adjusted."

Undoubtedly a belief that a general insurrection was on the anvil, pervaded England during January and February, 1655, from Cumberland to Cornwall. But this belief was accompanied by a feeling that some deluder was at work, or Clarendon would not have asserted, twice over, that those messengers who plagued the King, " I say, still, were honest men, and sent from those who were such." [8] So they might be, but their honesty did not prevent their being dupes.

The delusion that the Levellers were ready, sword in hand, to strike down Cromwell and his sham Commonwealth, was not founded on chance rumour. The pretence was elaborately prepared.

[7] Cal. Clarendon MSS., III. 16.
[8] Clarendon Hist., 871.

Skilfully taught agents, appearing to come from Sexby's Levellers and the army Anabaptists, and from the Presbyterians, were sent among the Royalists. They were induced to believe that Wildman, although he was in hiding, and Major-General Overton, although he was in the Tower, had combined with Fairfax, and were on the eve of a new civil war. So far was Fairfax from such courses, that he wrote to the Protector from Yorkshire, giving him timely notice of that abortive Royalist meeting upon Marston Moor, which was a noted incident in the abortive Insurrection.[9]

A couple of these agents can be exhibited, Colonel Werden and Mr. Douthwaite.

Werden, apparently a zealous Cavalier, makes his first appearance, during February, 1655, as the promoter of an attempt to seize Liverpool for the King;[10] and again on the 3rd of March, just on the eve of the Insurrection, he comes to the front as the assailant of Chester Castle. Werden was held in " a marvellous ill opinion " by his Royalist associates,[10] and that their opinion of him was correct, is confirmed by the following description of his doings, given by himself and by Mr. Francis Pickering, " an exceeding poor " Royalist.

After enticing Pickering into the plot by assurances of a general rising against the Protector, to take place

---

[9] Rawlinson MSS., A. 34, fo. 565.

[10] Thurloe, IV. 315; III. 337, 350, 348. Cal. Clarendon MSS., II. 218, 361, 365; III. 59.

on the night of the 8th of March, Werden announced that his part in the design " was principally to surprise the Castle of Chester." How Werden played his part in this design is recorded by Pickering. He and the Colonel remained quietly at home whilst, at Werden's command, " three or four men," on the night of the 8th of March, " went to seize the Castle." They were inhabitants of Chester, and one of them was commonly known by the name of Alexander the tobacco-pipe-maker. The attacking party returned, and brought back word to Colonel Werden that, at the place where they intended to raise a ladder to surprise the Castle, they heard a sentinel walk and cough. At which report Colonel Werden was very much startled! and sent Messrs. Alexander and Co. to renew the attempt at any other convenient place; 'and then they brought back word that wherever they went they heard sentinels walking.

No third attempt was made by Mr. Alexander and his friends; and next day Pickering was told by Werden " that he was much troubled, for that he could not contrive how to take the said Castle;" and in due course, Pickering found himself in custody.[10]

What manner of man Werden was, if that is not revealed by this narrative, he himself discloses.

During the following April, being taken prisoner, as a Royalist plotter, by General Lambert, this appeal was made to Thurloe by Werden. As an intimate and injured friend, he wrote to the Secre-

tary, who knew Werden " better than any Englishman does," protesting, " in the presence of Almighty
God," his " absolute ignorance of any design or plot
that was afoot" in the preceding March.   The
Cavaliers at Liverpool, and Pickering, could have
told a very different tale.

That blasphemous lying appeal to God was evidently held by Werden in slight regard: he forgot
it altogether.   In the ensuing December he again
got into trouble.   He again resorts to Thurloe,
and regardless of that solemn protestation of his
innocence, Werden urges that if he is implicated
in Royalist intrigues, " his accusers had nothing
to charge me with, but what must have come
through your " (Thurloe's) " hands :" that is to say,
from the letters that Thurloe had received from
Werden as trepanner and informer.[10]

Werden may now stand aside; and Mr
Douthwaite shall take his place.   He is an important historical character.

Douthwaite was one of the chief promoters
of the sole actual outbreak which distinguished
the Insurrection of March, 1655, the surprise
of Salisbury by Wagstaff and Penruddock.*
This fact is thus established.   A Government
agent, resident in the West of England, and
both from local and official position a well-
qualified informant, reported to Whitehall, that the
Salisbury insurgents were "the residue of the

* See p. 119.

plotters discovered by Stradling:"[11] and Douthwaite, who had tempted Stradling into the plot, is described by Major Butler as "the very principal verb" in the enterprise.[11]

Thus in the opinion of capable witnesses, for Butler was military superintendent over the West of England, the Wagstaff-Penruddock rising originated in a movement in which Douthwaite and Stradling took a leading part. Stradling therefore becomes of some importance; but the account he gives of Douthwaite is of still more importance.

We must deal with Stradling first. He is described by Major Butler as being "a poor, but most desperate gentleman," who may "for a small reward, and promise of pardon, make a notable discovery;" and the Major expressess his hopeful confidence that "the Lord will bring more of these youths to our knowledge."

The story told by this youth will show what he and his fellows were like. Stradling, on the 8th of February, at his home, Chedzoy, county Somerset, was desired by Douthwaite to meet him "without fail, as he tendered his full happiness." Thus adjured, Stradling obeyed, and Douthwaite addressed him, "Cousin John, there is a private design intended, which I am not to disclose to you as yet; but as you tender your good, provide yourself horse and arms, and meet me again this evening, at a place where others are to meet me, according to

[11] Thurloe, III. 176, 181, 183, 242.

their appointment." These "others" did not keep their appointment; but Stradling did, and rode throughout the night with Douthwaite. When "within two miles of Frome, in Wilts," they reached the house of Mr. John Bayley, a sequestered minister, who came down hastily, stockings in hand, and bade them very welcome. Douthwaite and Stradling sat down by the kitchen fire, where they were joined by some "more of these youths;" and, curiously enough, Douthwaite created by his talk such an unsatisfactory impression that a wary youth exclaimed, that he felt "confident that this was a plot of my Lord Protector's own devising, and that he had some of his own agents in it, to discover such as had a hand in the business."

About two hours had elapsed, when a Major Leveridge appeared, and told them that they were all undone, betrayed, discovered. The Major vaunted that, having nineteen soldiers at his back, they would have been a strong party, and that they should have rendezvoused near Salisbury, and that they would have fallen upon Major Butler's horsemen at Marlborough. These would-have-beens and should-have-beens were, however, all over. Major Leveridge advised Douthwaite to speed home. Stradling also acted on that advice; and it was in a Chedzoy alehouse that his incautious talk brought that youth to Butler's knowledge.

And what was the "private design" which Douthwaite commanded Stradling to join, "as he tendered his full happiness," and which was to make him a man among the Cavaliers? It was the old story. The design was "first put on foot by the Levellers, who were to be aiding and assisting the Cavaliers, and the Londoners were to fall on the Lord Protector. The King was waiting at sea for an opportunity, and Hull was to be delivered to him." The King did not start for the Dutch coast until the 4th of March,* and Douthwaite gave that assurance on the 9th of February.

Douthwaite's lies and foreknowledge were remarkable; and when asked, very naturally, why, "if the design was such a general rising," instead of conspiring in Wiltshire, "so far from home," he did not raise his friends in Somersetshire, Douthwaite answered, "that he had rather go farther from home, if he should do any mischief, or kill anybody, choosing rather to do it amongst strangers, where he was not known!" [11] This was a very lame excuse. No wonder that Douthwaite provoked the suspicion that my Lord Protector's hand was not far off. Yet such was the man who "drew Stradling into the design;" who was the "principal verb" in calling the Wiltshire Royalists to arms.

The hint supplied by that sceptical Wiltshire yeoman, regarding the originator of the Insurrection, receives some confirmation from the cast of Douthwaite's bait, which indicates Whitehall influences.

* See p. 105.

The King's course and counsels were revealed to Cromwell step by step, and thought after thought. He therefore knew that the King was then hesitating over a cautious move to the coast; and Cromwell and Thurloe must have been the only men in England cognisant of the King's intention. That Whitehall was the source of Douthwaite's information, may also be traced in this way. The London Journals were Cromwell's news agents, and " The Perfect Diurnal " of the 26th February—5th March, was equally well primed about the King's movements, and was also instructed that he intended to land at Hull.

That the men who sought to lure on the Royalists shared in information possessed· by Cromwell, is traceable in another way. That agitator and informer, Dallington, conjured up, in vision, Marston Moor and Salisbury Plain, covered with thousands of mutineers arrayed in " white tape and white ribbon." He imparted that vision to Cromwell: and to the Royalists also the same vision must have been exhibited. For the only spots where the Insurrection of March, 1655, took visible shape were Salisbury Plain and Marston Moor.

Men of the Douthwaite-Dallington type had evidently gulled Wagstaff's companions, for they assured him " that the Levelling party in the Army would join with them, and make disturbance in the Army." [12] They declared during their flight into

[12] Thurloe, III. 344. Perfect Proceedings, &c., News Letter 8th March to 15th March, 1655. Cal. State Papers, 1655, 98.

Devonshire also, " that the discontented Presbyters and Levellers had set them on this work, or else they had not attempted this action ; one of them vowing that if he did suffer for this, he would destroy some of them." [12] And Wagstaff himself was similarly deceived. He must have envisioned crowds of white-taped mutineers on Salisbury Plain. He was something of a soldier. He knew that the Wiltshire squires and their ill-armed levies could not for one moment stand before Cromwell's invincibles, and that in mutiny among those invincibles lay the sole chance for the Royalists.

Lord Rochester, the other leader of the project, was also subjected to the same kind of deceit, when he led his comrades to the rendezvous on Marston Moor. He ascribed the absolute failure of the enterprise to fraud. " He expected four thousand in arms on Marston Moor, with a design upon York ; but, he said, some one had deceived him." [13] He had been deceived; and a distinct clue exists to the deceiver.

Secretary Nicholas, in the course of the autumn of 1655, received, presumably from a Colonel Price, who shared in Rochester's expedition, an anonymous letter, intended to warn the King of the traitors in his cabinet-room ; and, in proof, Price states that Colonel Cromwell, a cousin of the Protector, asserted " that Cromwell hath notice of all we do

[13] Burton, I. 231. Egerton MSS., 2535, fo. 637.

at Cologne; that my Lord of Rochester was known to Cromwell to be in England, as soon as he landed, and that he was permitted to make those essays on purpose to make him have greater confidence in those persons he communicated with, as he would intimate of the Army, whereby Cromwell would learn always what was to be done, those being his friends really, ours in show."[13]

That Cromwell knew "always what was to be done" to stimulate the coming Insurrection needs no revelation by Colonel Price. Even the Royalists themselves knew that they were working in his sight. Henderson the informer describes to Thurloe the sorrow created in the Court by "the first news of the discovery of the plot;" and the party of action used that discovery to force on the design.[14] Colonel Price also, in that warning letter, relates "that Watt Vane" had told him, "with a countenance serious, and pretending great kindness to the King, that all the King's business was betrayed to Cromwell from Cologne;" that he knew the day when the intended Insurrection was to break out, and "also about the King's going to the Coast," to ship for the friendly port, "on $\frac{4}{14}$ March, ten days before he did stir."[14]

Proof that Cromwell watched his enemies at Cologne whilst they formed their plans and started for England, is, however, needless. He boasted

<hr>

[14] Clarendon State Papers, III. 265. Cal. Clarendon MSS., III. 13, 16. Egerton MSS., 2535, fo. 637. Declaration, 31st Oct., 1655.

that he possessed "a full intelligence of these things;" and he made clear that "these things" were the first movements of the enterprise, by taking credit for his precaution in bringing troops across from Ireland to Liverpool; which he did about four weeks before the first conspirator landed at Dover.[14]

But Cromwell did not avail himself of that "full intelligence" in the way that common prudence suggests. Fully forewarned as he was, of the attempt, "soit hazard, soit dessein, Cromwell ne fit rien d'efficace pour la prévenir." And Guizot adds, that he arrested some Royalists, "mais non pas ceux qui préparaient effectivement la prochaine exécution du complot."[14] "Guards were set at every street's end in London;" but the conspirators, when in London, met their friends "with great freedom."

The most conspicuous precaution taken by Cromwell was the moving troops from Ireland to Liverpool; but he cannot have supposed that they would be wanted there, because the only effort to raise the Royalists of Liverpool was encouraged by Colonel Werden, Thurloe's agent,[14] and it was a failure. Yet there the troops remained, far away from the points of disturbance.

Suspected persons at sea-ports were detained;

Old Parl. Hist., XX. 434. Carlyle, IV. 103. Guizot, II. 128. Thurloe, IV. 245. Guizot's quoted remarks were unknown to the writer when he first published comments almost precisely similar.

but the courtiers at Cologne were " cheered by letters which assured them that none of their particular friends at the sea-ports were known ; " [14] and undoubtedly, whether known or not, the King's emissaries found at his post their " particular friend," Mr. Day, the Clerk of the Passage.

Direct evidence that Cromwell promoted the Insurrection of March, 1655, of course there is none.

Here, however, at the outset of the affair, are several indications radiating from various points, but all tending in one direction. The pretended allies who greeted Lord Rochester, the lying messages that tempted on the King, the Werdens and Douthwaites who beguiled the poor and desperate Royalists, could have come only from one source. No one save Cromwell could direct against the King such a stream of false encouragement ; no one else could ensure safety to the men who plied the Royalists with seditious suggestions. And to whose advantage were they thus misled ? No true Republicans would have played such tricks for the benefit of their Lord Protector.

Still the foregoing symptoms might be deemed of slight account, had not kindred circumstances, in which Cromwell himself appears, arisen subsequently, which reinforce the presumption that the Insurrec-

This is mentioned merely to show that two inquirers came to the same conclusion.

tion of March, 1655, ranks among those conspiracies that he so " often invented."   And Sagredo formed that opinion during the autumn of 1655, when the Insurrection, the last occurrence of the kind, was fairly recent.

CHAPTER VI.

THE INSURRECTION AND REBELLION OF MARCH, 1655.

THE Insurrection Day was fixed; the King could not " send orders to contradict it ; " and so, " with little noise," though not unheard by Cromwell, Charles left Cologne for Middleburg on the 14th of March ; and there he remained some weeks, vainly awaiting that destruction of Cromwell and the Commonwealth of which he had received such confident assurances.

The band of insurgents who took the route for England to aid in that catastrophe, were about fourteen in number. They were not mighty men, even according to the low standard of the King's Court. The Marquis of Ormond shrank from heading the expedition ; and the men who took his place were as their flock. Sir Joseph Wagstaff was " so simple, and of so mean an interest that he was not worth valuing." [1] Lord Rochester, vain, irresolute, and cowardly, thrust himself into the enterprise.

[1] Cal. Clarendon MSS., III. 17, 66. The landing of Wagstaff and Rochester at Margate is noticed by Mr. Firth, English Hist. Review, xiv. 314. Could Rochester have ridden round to Dover ? His escape from Dover is mentioned by Manning, the

Their associates were the ordinary type of adventurous Royalists.

Rochester and Wagstaff crossed the Channel together, Rochester freely communicating "his purpose to anybody." They landed at Margate ;[1] the others chose Dover. The conspirators began their journey on the 8th of February, and within a fortnight they all reached London safely. The security these men enjoyed is remarkable. They disregarded a conspirator's precautions. Wagstaff and Rochester did not seek the obscurity of ordinary passengers. They hired a vessel to carry them over, and to return, after a two days' detention, with their messages to the King.[2] The party that selected Dover arrived in quick succession, almost in a body, although it was the most public port and the best guarded on the Southern Coast.

The publicity they courted took effect. Such an influx of pretended traders from France and Holland excited suspicion. Lord Rochester, when he touched our shore, was twice detained, examined, and set free. Of his comrades, four were arrested at Dover, and among them Major Armorer and Mr. Daniel O'Neill.[2] These men were "two of the chiefest complotters in the design."[2] Their capture was considered by Ormond " a considerable defeat,"[2] and that to free them would require " a general

spy, as a proof of the Governor's culpable negligence. Thurloe, III. 190.

[2] Cal. Clarendon MSS., III. 21, 22, 23. Thurloe, III. 198.

rising." No rising raged round Dover Castle, yet Armorer and O'Neill, and their two fellows in captivity, became free men easily.

Not so easy, however, is it to describe the manœuvre by which Armorer was set at liberty. He was arrested on Tuesday, the 13th February, or Wednesday, the 14th, under a government order, styled, "The old Commission for the Passe," which enjoined the detention of suspects, and the notification to Whitehall of persons so "staid and secured." Of Armorer's detention no official report was made. Indirectly, however, Thurloe acquired ample notification of the event, for he received, on Thursday, the 15th, a letter which Armorer had addressed to a supposed friend, Sir Robert Stone. The letter which was so promptly forwarded to Thurloe, runs thus :—

"Dover Castle, 14th February.

"Sir Robert Stone,—Kind salutes. I had the convenience of a passage from Dunkirk in the same boat with your man Morris, but here we found a restraint upon all the passengers from H.H. the Lord Protector. By this means your servant is made prisoner in the town of Dover and I in the Castell, till we can send to our friends. . . . I beseech you do me the favour to prevail with some of your friends near H.H. the Lord Protector to get me leave either to come to London, or to return to Rotterdam. . . . I know you will not forget friends in trouble : worthy Sir,

Your humble Servant, N. Wright. Pray direct your letter to Mr. Robert Day, Clarke of the Passage." [3]

As this letter bears an official endorsement, " Nicholas Armorer to Sir Robert Stone," Cromwell knew that Mr. Wright in Dover Castle was Major Armorer that " chief complotter." The letter moreover, warned Cromwell that Mr. Day, his Clerk of the Passage, was also a complotter with the Royalists. Yet, knowing who Wright was, and what Day was, Cromwell deliberately played into Day's hands, and enabled him to obtain Armorer's freedom.

Cromwell acted in this way. On Thursday, the 15th, or Friday, the 16th February, he sent to the Dover Port Commissioners a new " Commission " or Order, superseding, for the nonce, " the old Commission for the Passe." The Commissioners acted on the new Commission forthwith. On Friday, the 16th,[4] they released Armorer,—Mr. Day " engaging for him, and signifying to the Commissioners his knowledge " that Armorer, *alias* Wright, was, in reality and not in show, a Rotterdam merchant. And then, when the new Commission had served its turn, it was immediately cancelled. By letter written the

---

[3] Thurloe, III. 137.

[4] As Sir R. Stone reported to Thurloe, evidently from London, on Sunday, 18th February, that Armorer was in town, the action of the Port Commissioners took place, in all probability, on Friday, the 16th. Thurloe, III. 162.

next day, Thurloe withdrew the new, and revived the old Commission for the Passe.

The evidence of these transactions is as follows. Thurloe, by a letter written on Saturday, the 17th February, rebuked Wilson, the Deputy-Governor of Dover Castle, for neglect in failing to report Armorer's detention to the Government, commented severely on Armorer's escape, and directed Wilson to inform the Port Commissioners that the Commission under which they had released Armorer was revoked.

Thurloe's letter is not extant; but its tenor is disclosed by Wilson's reply.[6] The reply is dated Wednesday, the 21st; Wilson wrote to Thurloe that he was " much troubled." He had not credited Armorer's assertion that he was a Rotterdam merchant, and feeling "just ground for suspicion," he had secured him in the Castle. And then Wilson proceeded to clear himself. The notification of Armorer's detention had been left to the care of Colonel Kelsey, the Governor of the Castle ; and with Armorer's release Wilson had nothing to do at all.   He regretted " with all his heart," that he had not been present when it took place ; " but there was a cross-providence therein." It was in his absence that the Port Commissioners, immediately upon their "receipt of that Commission from H.H. the Lord Protector," had set free Armorer, with Trelawny, his supposed servant.

[6] Thurloe, III. 164.

Regarding the future, and Thurloe's instructions, Wilson assures him that, "I shall let the gentlemen," the Commissioners, " understand what H.H.'s pleasure is, in relation to the revoking of his last Order to them, and I shall improve my utmost care and diligence to observe the contents of the former Order," *i.e.* the Old Commission for the Passe, under which Wilson exercised control over suspects like Armorer.

If these sentences are read together, it becomes obvious that the "last Order" was the Commission under which the Port Commissioners released Armorer on the Friday, and that it superseded, for that day, "the former Order," the old Commission for the Passe. That being so, "the last Order" was in force only on that Friday; and, as on that day Armorer and Trelawny were set free, that "the last Order" was designed by Cromwell to obtain their liberation, is no violent presumption; especially as Mr. Day, the Clerk of the Passage and Royalist go-between, was so freely allowed to vouch for the supposed merchant from Rotterdam.

Wilson closed his letter by an undertaking which proved beyond his powers. He assured Thurloe that " those persons yet in custody here, of which I have given you an account by the Governor, shall be safely kept, until I know your pleasure concerning them." A vain boast; somebody was again at work behind Wilson's back. Within the next seven days he was forced to inform Thurloe of a second

" cross-providence," as provoking as Armorer's escape.

Among the prisoners at Dover was a Mr. Broughton. Thurloe expressly charged Wilson to take care of Broughton : he was accordingly lodged in the sergeant's house and watched over by a " good guard." On the 27th February Wilson received Thurloe's directions to send Broughton to Whitehall. Wilson immediately ordered out the escort, and desired the sergeant to produce his prisoner. The sergeant came, without the prisoner, but with this story. " Mr. Mayor of Dover, about ten o'clock that morning had given him a pass, and let him go; and about eleven o'clock, he rode towards London." Broughton had disappeared.

" Whereupon, immediately," Wilson, " exceedingly troubled, went down upon Mr. Mayor," and dealt roundly with him. The Mayor attempted no defence ; he could offer no excuse for that " rash and inconsiderate act." He had received from the Protector no " Commission " such as that which set free Armorer. " H.H's. former Order," the old Commission for the Passe, was in force, and the Mayor " had no authority at all to intermeddle " between the Castle authorities and their prisoners.[6]

Then came the third " cross-providence," O'Neill's escape. The " weak and heady " Mayor was outdone by Col. Kelsey, the Governor of the Castle. Two

[6] Thurloe, III. 180, 190. Cal. Clarendon MSS., III. 23.

or three days after the Broughton episode, O'Neill, who had been seized and committed to the Castle with Armorer, released himself. Col. Kelsey had "so carelessly restrained" his prisoner, "as if it were on purpose for him to escape."

This description of the Governor's conduct came to Cromwell on the best authority. Manning the spy, who knew all that the King's Court knew, wrote to Thurloe, 13th March, 1655, that "there is something of concernment now, that I cannot omit to tell you, namely, that the Governor of Dover must be either knave or fool. He hath lately let pass Wilmot, and Philipps, Armorer, Halsey, and Daniel O'Neill. Some of them he restrained so carelessly, as if it were on purpose for them to escape, especially the last," O'Neill. Manning also warned Thurloe that the Governor "or the searchers have connived at many coming over of late, all employed in the capital enemy's service, who are now all in England again, acting their bloody parts by his commands." [6]

O'Neill's escape from Dover Castle was welcomed by the Cavaliers as a presage of victory. Ormond rejoiced, believing "from so many escapes" that Cromwell was badly served, or that the Royalists were "well befriended." And so they were. That single day Commission for the Passe was surely the work of a friend? and certainly those who befriended Armorer and his comrades were treated by Cromwell in most friendly fashion. He was "an ill man to cross," yet he acted as though the prosperity of those fools or knaves, the Governor and the Clerk, was pleasant in his sight.

Within a fortnight after the receipt of Manning's timely notice, the Protector wrote to Governor Kelsey with congratulations on the suppression of the Insurrection, and thanked him for "his zeal and forwardness" therein. In May, Kelsey was specially awarded a yearly salary of 400*l.*, as Admiralty Commissioner; and in August he was appointed Major-General of Kent and Surrey, bringing him in 666*l.* 13*s.* 4*d.* a year, in addition to 474*l.* 10*s.*, his pay as Colonel. If these sums are combined together, and estimated at our rate of value, they amount to 4623*l.* 10*s.* a year.[7]

Handsome as was Kelsey's reward, the favour shown to Mr. Day was even more signal. In O'Neill's escape Kelsey may have acted the fool. Day assuredly was a traitor. That he was an accomplice of the Royalists was evidenced by his conduct, and by that postscript to Armorer's letter. Massonet, the King's Secretary, warned Cromwell that "one Day, the Clerk of the Passage, hath permitted many dangerous persons to pass into England."[8] Yet Day was not sent to the gallows or the Barbadoes. He was retained in his post; he received its profits, and the gratuities of grateful Royalists, until, during the following summer, all

---

[7] Cal. State Papers, 1655, 93, 152, 155, 275.
[8] Thurloe, III. 198.

the conspirators from abroad had returned in safety to the Continent.

If this lengthy, too lengthy introduction leads to nothing, to no "blood and confusion" worth mentioning, that is not my fault. Even Cromwell, with all his amplifying arts, could not magnify " The late Insurrection and Rebellion " into anything that seemed real or credible to his subjects. Such as it was, it must be described. The two leaders of the expedition, Sir Joseph Wagstaff and Lord Rochester, chose, as has been mentioned, for the scene of their rebellion, Salisbury Plain and Hessey, or Marston Moor.†

The events that took place on Marston Moor were thus described by the "Perfect Proceedings" News Letter of March, 1655 :—" York. The 8th of March instant, there was a meeting appointed by the Malignants in Yorkshire to surprise York City. To that end a party was to come on the west side of the City, where Sir Richard Malleverer, with divers others, was on their march. About 100 horse came with a cart-load of arms and ammunition to Hessey (*i.e.* Marston) Moor. And at the wynd-mill upon the Moor, there came some intelligence, that a party, that should have come on the other side of the City, was not ready that night. And more company failing, which they expected to meet them that night upon the Moor, they suddenly and

* See p. 151.   † See p. 104.

disorderly retreated ; some Pistols were scattered, and found next morning, and a led horse, with a velvet saddle, left in Skipbrig Lane, which was found next day."

Lord Rochester " saw danger at a distance with great courage, and looked upon it less resolutely when it was nearer ;" but Marston Moor that night might have convinced the most resolute of men that he had been sent on a sleeveless errand. Rochester " resolved to stay no longer" in Yorkshire. His friends there were " much troubled that he had come at all. They parted with little good-will to each other; the Earl returning through byeways to London, which was the securest place, from whence he gave the King notice of the hopelessness of affairs." [9]

" Sir Joseph Wagstaff appointed his rendezvous to be within two miles of Salisbury; and as soon as the day was fixed, he left London, and went to some of his friends' houses near the place, that he might assist the preparation as much as possible." [9] Those preparations cannot have troubled much his jovial nature : he must have believed that somebody else would do the work for him, as he took the field with about 200 raw recruits, farmers, curriers, and tapsters, headed by two undistinguished country gentlemen, Colonel Penruddock and Captain Grove. The King's call to action had received but a beggarly response.

[9] Clarendon, Hist., Ed. 1839, 873, 875.

With these followers Wagstaff dashed into Salisbury during the night of Sunday, 11th March. They occupied the town till next day; when, being utterly unsupported, they drifted to Blandford. There again they found no resting-place. With dwindling numbers they fled towards Devonshire, hoping to find shelter in Cornwall. South Molton was reached on Wednesday, the 14th. Soon after their arrival they were attacked by Captain Unton Crook, and a troop of horse, sent after the insurgents from Weymouth. A brief street fight ensued: Penruddock, Grove, and about fifty of their followers were taken: Wagstaff escaped.—The Insurrection is over.

England was, during the Protectorate, under military watch and ward. Yet that contemptible outbreak, which began in Wiltshire, lasted from Sunday till Wednesday evening, and circled over 130 miles of ground, undisturbed, through Dorsetshire, Somersetshire, into Devonshire. This woeful spectacle of Royalists flying across England was, at the time, regarded with suspicion, and it provoked a remarkable letter from Major Butler to the Protector. The circumstances which called forth that letter are as follows.

The headquarters of the Cavalry in charge of the west centre of England were at Marlborough, under Major Butler's command. Marlborough and Salisbury are separated by about thirty miles;

between Bristol and Salisbury the distance is some sixty miles. Butler, who had been sent to Bristol because the citizens were restless, reported to Cromwell that Bristol was peaceful, and that he intended to return to his headquarters. Acting on those reports, Butler was on the march for Marlborough, on the 28th February, when Cromwell interfered, and ordered him back to Bristol.[10] To what purpose was that order ?

Cromwell had received warning from Salisbury "that it would be convenient for some horse to be quartered hereabouts," because it was thought that the Cavaliers were after mischief. Cromwell knew also that the Royalists were on the move, and that they reckoned on co-operation from the Levellers, and that a meeting of mutinous soldiers on Salisbury Plain had been talked about. And he knew that whatever uneasiness might prevail in Bristol, it arose from internal squabbles, and that any threatened disorder there was not disturbance by "the enemy," but by his own soldiers; for the commanding officer in Bristol informed Thurloe, that our "distractions" were "increased since" Butler's "troops came hither."[10]

Thus Cromwell was aware that soldiers might be wanted in Wiltshire, and were not wanted at Bristol; and that he possessed intimate knowledge

[10] Thurloe, III. 162, 172, 177, 178, 182, 191, 243. Cal State Papers, 1655, 73, 80. Col. Dove was sheriff of Wiltshire. The insurgents took him with them, and " discharged him upon his

of the designs and movements of Rochester and Wagstaff, is no conjecture. On the very Sunday when Wagstaff broke forth, Cromwell occupied Chichester by horsemen, sent there at daybreak; and he despatched a warning to Portsmouth that "some desperate design was on foot:" but he did not send soldiers Salisbury way.

Butler of course obeyed his commander and returned straightway to Bristol. When he arrived there, he found that there was "no fear of disturbances" in the city; and he made the like report to Cromwell on 3rd March.[10] On the 11th, the Salisbury affair took place. Butler heard of it. Though distanced from the scene of action by Cromwell's unseasonable interference, he sought to do his best; he collected four troops of horsemen and started on the instant against the enemy.

Again Butler was stayed. Whilst on the march he received orders to hold his hand, to avoid an action. Hence arose the following appeal to the Protector.

"May it please your Highness,—This morning Colonel Dove is come hither from the enemy upon his parole. He left them near Evill [*i.e.* Yeovil] and saith, he thinks them to be above 300 in number.[10]

"Now my Lord, though I know it would be of sad consequence, if we assaulting them should be worsted, yet, my Lord, I hope your Highness will

parole," apparently about one o'clock in the morning of Wednesday, 14th March. "Several Proceedings," &c., 15—22 March, 1655.

easily pardon me, being I shall freely adventure my-self upon the good Providence of the Lord, who I know will own us, and I am persuaded succeed us in the business.

"And indeed, my Lord, I cannot with any confidence stay here, nor look the country in the face, and let them alone. I doubt not but to give your Highness a speedy good account of this matter. I shall be this night in Shaftesbury, and then send to your Highness again. The judges I have set at liberty here, and they were like men that dreamt, to see us so suddenly here. . . . I am my Lord, your Highness' most dutiful Servant,

W. Boteler.

"From Salisbury, upon my march towards Shaftesbury,
14 March, 9 a'clock in the morning.

"If I hear any of our friends coming towards us, I shall delay falling upon [the rebels], unless I see a very favourable opportunity." [10]

The tone of this letter shows that restraint had been put upon Butler, and that his plans had been upset, that he had obeyed instructions, and that in consequence he was twenty-four hours too late.

The critical point in Butler's course was the first halt in his march from Bristol. He reached Devizes on the night of Monday, the 12th of March, the night which the insurgents spent at Blandford. He started from Devizes at seven o'clock on Tuesday morning, the 13th. At that moment the enemy were at Blandford or in its vicinity, nor did they, in their flight towards Devonshire, leave Yeovil till the next morning.[11] All that time they were within striking distance. If Butler had been left unhindered during his march from Devizes, instead of writing a despairing letter from Salisbury, at "9 a'clock in the morning," he might have been charging the enemy in the neighbourhood of Yeovil. On the contrary, we find him and his four troops of horsemen, during Thursday, still detained at Salisbury, with orders " not to engage " the enemy.[11] He and his men were not wanted. Captain Crook's single troop of horse had made short work of Penruddock and his followers, though entrenched in the streets and houses of South Molton.

That Major Butler did not promptly do away with that " company of mean fellows " was charged against him. It was supposed that he kept his troopers " at a distance in the rear " of the Royalists, " to give them opportunity of increasing." [11] That surmise was thus far inaccurate. Butler kept at a distance, but it was against his will. Of that we can be certain. Equally certain is it that Cromwell must have known that the insurgents could bring to the front none but untrained, ill-armed countrymen, and that Butler had at his back real soldiers, superior in number to the enemy, and immeasurably superior in well-disciplined, well-armed strength.

Yet, by directions from Whitehall, Butler was left

[11] Thurloe, III. 242, 243. " Several Proceedings " News Letter, 15—22 March, 1655. Heath, 367. Cal. State Papers, 1655, 80.

no discretion ; he was forced into inaction, on the plea of fear lest he " should be worsted : " and in consequence he " could not look the country in the face." Such a remarkable conflict between a trusted officer and his commander-in-chief, when in the presence of actual rebellion, proves that as the enemy were suffered to pass unhindered over more than a hundred miles, through the most disaffected districts of England, Cromwell did not consider that, at all hazard, the Insurrection needed extinction.

As the Insurrection is now over, we must dispose of the insurrectionists. Wagstaff promptly disappeared. The Earl of Rochester, led by his taste " for all places where there was good eating and drinking," made, on one occasion at least, a transient return upon the scene.

He and Major Armorer, who accompanied him, did not, after the Marston Moor fiasco, fly to the coast, or seek separate hiding-places. They journeyed together, with two servants, leisurely through England towards London: nor, to guard his safety, would Rochester disturb his bed-time or his dinner-hour. After the outbreak, people were naturally anxious to pick up what they could, by arresting " the great ones." Of these, Rochester and Armorer were among the greatest; and they were arrested at Aylesbury. The resident magistrate gave a warrant to the constable, desiring him to keep safely the bodies of the Earl and his companion, " in the name of my Lord Protector."

The warrant was acted upon : the prisoners evidently were "persons of great quality." Yet somehow, both magistrate and constable left the Earl and the Major in charge of the innkeeper, "where they lay;" and naturally enough, "when the constable came in the morning, he found that the innkeeper had let the two chiefs escape," taking with them "all their rich apparel." [12]

Had this been merely a sample of Aylesbury carelessness, the incident need not have been noticed. But the example of the magistrate and constable was followed by Cromwell. Although the escape of Rochester and Armorer was promptly known, and their course was closely tracked, and though Cromwell was informed where they might be found, they "wrote very comfortably from London," and endeavoured "to lay the foundation of some new design." [12]

At last, as if he were an ordinary traveller, sending his servants before him, Rochester left England for the Continent, having been a resident here for about five months; and the latter part of his stay in England was a season of extraordinary severity against the Royalists. In like manner every one of his thirteen comrades returned "weekly without difficulty" to their King's presence, apparently at their pleasure; whilst Cromwell's continental informers repeated their warnings that "Day, the Clerk of the Passage,"

[12] Cal. State Papers, 1655, 193, 235. Thurloe, I. 695, III. 358, 428, 530, 532, 561, 659. Clarendon Hist., Ed. 1839 875.

is " a rogue," and that if the Protector had " been ruled " by them " all these had not escaped." [12]

The complete immunity these men experienced is noteworthy. However it may be explained, those enemies, without danger to the State, could remain for months in England, concocting new projects for revolt.

Cromwell's endeavour, the exhibition to his subjects of Royalists in arms and then upon the scaffold, was not a complete success. His power of creating an actual Insurrection was limited: he could not allow the project to become too real. This necessity stood in his way. Of the " hidden works " throughout England, which he attributed to the Royalists, but one actually exploded; one nearly went off; the rest remained dormant. Still to a certain extent he reaped the harvest he sought, the fruits of the judge and of the hangman.

Cromwell would not have felt squeamish over the use of that word, harvest. The exhibition of Royalists in the grasp of the executioner was according to his wish. Thurloe,—and Thurloe and Cromwell were of one mind—rejoiced over the Insurrection because it would prove that his master " hath not made a noise about plots to get money from people's purses ;" [13] and another of Cromwell's servants exulted at being able to prove " that the Plot was real," as " the persons were real," who, in

[13] Vaughan's Protectorate, 16th March, 1654-5. Hist. MSS. Com., 6th Report, 438. Carlyle, III. 426.

consequence, lost their lives or their freedom. In kindred fashion Cromwell expressed a hope, when palming off on Parliament the sham Royalist conspiracies of the winter of 1654, that "by the justice of the land, some will in the face of the Nation answer it with their lives." [13] It was impossible to hang Messrs. Bayley and Bagnal, or the squires at whose doors Cromwell's soldiers had laid the arm-chests; but the Insurrection of March, 1655, did furnish some occupation to the executioner.

As regards the Yorkshiremen, Cromwell's intentions were foiled. He could not bring down a head out of the covey of Royalists who flitted across Marston Moor. To gain that end he did his best. He sent the Judges for that purpose to York, Baron Thorpe, Justice Newdigate, and Sergeant Hutton; but they refused to obey his bidding. They declined to try, upon a capital charge, men who had been arrested neither in arms nor on horseback, nor even on the highway, but in their own houses. The judges were doubtful "whether in point of law" a possible midnight ride could be declared by them "to be treason." It was in vain that Colonel Lilbourn used "diligence" to "pick up such as are right," to serve on the jury. The judges put a complete stopper on the intended trial. They left York, objecting that due notice, under which they could try that "great affair," had not been given.

Pressure was renewed, in vain, upon Newdigate and Hutton. Orders were made directing them to reappear in York to try the Marston Moor prisoners. Cromwell's law officer found them at Doncaster, bent on a return to London, and in a most contrary state of mind. They again refused to act; and they based their refusal on an objection which touched the root of Cromwell's jurisdiction. They asserted, evidently reckoning on Baron Thorpe's concurrence, that they could not, as judges, put in force the Ordinance by which Cromwell had converted high treason against a king into high treason against himself, because that Ordinance was of no validity! They thus anticipated, in the most unpleasant way, Mr. Coney's refusal to pay taxes imposed, not by an Act of Parliament, but by an "Ordinance." * Cromwell was forced to yield; the Yorkshiremen preserved their lives, but not their liberty or their estates; and almost immediately, "Judges Thorpe and Newdigate were put out of their places, for not observing the Protector's pleasure in all his commands." [14]

Cromwell's "pleasure" was, however, served in the West of England by the Lord Lisle, Mr. Sergeant Glyn, and Mr. Recorder Steele, and by the jurymen, "such as were right," over whom they presided. The trial of the Salisbury insurgents was a success. Those poor dupes adopted what

* See p. 165.
[14] Whitelock, 625. Thurloe, III. 359, 376, 385, 391.

may be termed Baron Thorpe's plea.. They argued that their indictment was not founded on an Act of Parliament, and that "there can be no treason by an Ordinance." They urged that a sentence pronounced by the Sergeant and the Recorder, who were mere "pleaders, servants to the Lord Protector," would be illegal; and they asserted their right to be tried by Baron Thorpe, "a sworn judge." They pleaded in vain. The prisoners, who could not be convicted of high treason, were condemned to death as horse-stealers. Their defence, fruitless, but just, was that to requisition a horse for a warlike enterprise was not felony; that they had acted "as the soldiers did now at London, and elsewhere, who came against us;" that "the country knew that we did not intend to steal."[14]

Penruddock, Grove, and about fourteen of those poor fellows were put to death, and seventy were subsequently sold by the Major-Generals into West Indian slavery: doubtless a profitable transaction. About 300*l.* of our money was the market value of an Englishman during Cromwell's Protectorate.

Those who may resent the idea that the Protector deliberately enticed his subjects into treason, and on to the scaffold, are asked to restrain their feelings until they have read how he acted towards Sir Henry Slingsoy. In that case there was no disguise: there was no outsider in the affair, save poor

Slingsby. Indirect action was necessary in the Insurrection of March, 1655. All-powerful as was the Protector, he could not show his hand. He was suspected of such devices ; he could not afford to convert suspicion into certainty. Yet surely Cromwell's hand is seen in the immunity enjoyed by the leaders of the attempt ? Those "friends in show" who met Rochester àt Margate, that "new Commission" which set Armorer free, the remuneration given to the fool Kelsey, the favour to the knave Day, and Major Butler's inability to look the country in the face, may unquestionably be credited to Cromwell.

Yet with what dexterity the Protector worked behind the curtain ! Prince of wire-pullers, he made his puppets perform what part he chose. Some jerked the royal doll, against his liking, from Cologne to Middleburg, and some warned him to keep quiet ; whilst other puppets seemed to fight against the manager of the show, though in reality they fought in his behalf. All played Cromwell's game, though they thought they were playing their own ; and even the most innocent outsiders were pressed into his service. With what cruel craft, yet seeming indifference, the artful old showman treated his mannikins ! He cut off the heads of some amongst those who responded most vigorously to his touch, whilst others, not less free upon the wire, were carefully packed up and sent home safe. By seizing and boxing up in the Tower mere bystanders, wholly unconcerned in the sport, he made his "little tin soldiers" fancy that he did not see their antics. The only hitch in his knavish piece of work arose when, too assured, he placed upon the boards a real live judge, who refused to take the bench in the manager's sham Court of Justice.

In every other respect the play was a complete success. All the world was puzzled, players, spectators, and the gentlemen of the press. Not one even guessed at the true meaning of the performance. Though "men of wicked spirits" would, when Cromwell preached up that spectacle as a solemn reality, assert that it was a sham, they never wholly found him out. They danced to his tune, unconscious that the pipe they heard was in his mouth : they never guessed that the Protector devised the Insurrection and Rebellion of March, 1655, from the beginning to the end.

CHAPTER VII.

THE PROTECTOR AND HIS GAINSAYING SUBJECTS.

THE Insurrection of March, 1655, suggests these three subjects for consideration. The first is what Cromwell did and said about that event, and the second is what he said that people said and thought about it. The third subject, the use that the Major-Generals made of the Insurrection, is dealt with in the ensuing chapter.

Cromwell began, most promptly, to convince his people that they must say and think that the Insurrection was a solemn and terrible national danger.

On the 14th March, 1655, within three days after the rising at Salisbury, Cromwell issued Commissions and Instructions nominating and appointing Militia Commissioners throughout England, because "the enemies are raising new troubles and are now robbing and plundering the people." Those officers were directed to guard the public peace, raise troops, disarm papists, examine and detain strangers, and to charge "the malignant and disaffected," according to their estate, with the cost of providing the militia troops with horses and arms.[1]

Protectorship and " second sight " must have gone together. The Insurrection found the Protector provided with a full-fledged militia scheme stretching all over England, involving in the formation much thought and penmanship, and the consideration and selection of more than three hundred officials charged with important trusts. To find a trustworthy man in those days was no rapid task. The scheme also anticipated that malignant taxation of the Malignants, the decimation of their estates, which Cromwell subsequently exacted, and was based on " new troubles " by the Royalists, long before those disturbances had begun. Such a prophetic gift can only be explained, according to the laws of nature, by seeing, in the organizer of the Militia, the organizer of those " new troubles."

Ten days later, 24th March, the Protector addressed seventy letters to the Militia Commissioners and the Justices of the Peace, informing them that " We doubt not but you have heard of the good hand of God in defeating this Insurrection," that " We hear from all parts, that risings are everywhere suppressed ; hundreds of prisoners in custody, and more daily discovered, and secured." The Protector then acknowledged that the services of " the honest people " had much " encouraged Us, and discouraged the enemy ;" and he promised that

[1] Cal. State Papers, 1655, 77, 92—94.

"the efforts of the enemy shall not inflict any increase of burthen on England." He also warned all in authority to "keep diligent watch," and to take strict account of strangers, "especially on the coast," and to apprehend those "who come from abroad to kindle fires."

One object of those Commissions and Letters may have been to pave the way for the coming event, Government by Major-Generals, of which more anon. Another object certainly was to place the Insurrection before England in a proper official light. The stir thus created throughout the country, and the multiplication of the feeble explosion at Salisbury into "risings in all parts," were needed, if the Insurrection was to be held in lively remembrance. It flickered for a moment, then it died out. The Major-Generals and other officers sent to the area of disturbance, for the purpose of establishing the "general plot of the malignants," utterly failed. Their reports, without exception, tended in the opposite direction.

Even in March, immediately after the Insurrection, Major-General Disbrowe could find no signs, in Devonshire, of "new or late acting" by rebellious Royalists. Writing from Bristol, 15th March, the Militia Commissioners told Cromwell, "that we are quiet here, so is Wales, so far as we can hear, as also Gloucester, Hereford, and Worcester." Dr. Owen reports, 20th March, from Oxford, that "we are here in a quiet condition." Similar assurances were forwarded to the Protector by his officers from all parts of England, telling him that all was well both before, during, and after the Insurrection. In common with Thurloe, they unanimously declare "that the Nation was much more ready to rise against, than for Charles Stuart;" that in the town of Leeds, "not thirty men were disaffected to the present Government;" and that "there was no design on foot," even in "the most corrupt, and rotten places of the Nation," such as Hampshire, Dorsetshire, Kent, and the Eastern Counties. From Bristol to York all were at peace, or wished to be so, during February, March, and April, 1655.[2]

So vexed was Commissary-General Reynolds, because malignant Shropshire yielded him no "complotters," because "so little fruit of our pains doth yet appear," that he begged Thurloe to sanction his making the Royalists "speak forcibly, by tying matches, or some kind of pain, whereby they may be made to discover the plot;" and as Reynolds re-urged that charitable wish of his, the first proposal to use the thumbscrew, or the match, had not drawn from the Secretary prompt rebuke.[3]

The Commissary-General and the Protector were of one mind in that matter. If a conviction that the malignant Royalists had plotted and were plotting

---

[2] Thurloe, III. 223, 246, 248, 253, 265, 281, 290, 308. Cal. State Papers, 1655, 84, 87, 88, 99. Vaughan's Protectorate, March, 1655. Baynes, Coll. Add. MSS., 21,423, fo. 56, 74.

[3] Thurloe, III. 298, 356. The match was used upon three Portuguese at Plymouth. Cal. State Papers, 1657-58, 247.

against England " blood and violence " could not be squeezed or burnt into his subjects, he must terrorize and subdue their minds. Cromwell accordingly issued, " The Declaration of His Highness, by the advice of his Council, showing the Reasons of their Proceedings for Securing the Peace of the Commonwealth, upon occasion of the late Insurrection and Rebellion, October 31, 1655." [4]

The Insurrection of March, 1655, was the most elaborate, in some respects the most successful of the plots which Cromwell so often invented ; and " The Declaration " of October, 1655, was worthy of the occasion. The Protector therein pleads earnestly with his People ; he addresses words of tenderness to the Nation, of just severity to his Malignant subjects, and of piety throughout.

He begins with a justificatory recital of the general position held between the Protector, the English people, and the Royalists. As God, " by His gracious dispensation," had " subjected " the Royalists " to the power of those whom they had designed to enslave and ruin," " the Parliament's party " might, Cromwell asserts, have " extirpated those men, with designs of possessing their Estates and Fortunes." Their conquerors, however, refrained themselves from cutting the throats and seizing the goods of the Royalists, because it " pleased God, in His providence, so to order

[4] Old Parl. Hist., XX. 434.

things." The Royalists, accordingly, were allowed to live and " enjoy their freedom, and have equal protection in their persons and estates, with the rest of the Nation."

But what return, the Protector demands, has been made by the Malignants for the lenity thus extended to them ? " The actings of that party " prove that " neither the dispensations of God, nor kindness of men, would work upon them ;" that " they were implacable in their malice and revenge ;" and he cites the late Insurrection and Rebellion, " as the greatest and most dangerous" of all " their hidden works of darkness."

His Highness then thus summarized that project. He asserted that the " cruel and bloody Enemy " intended to surprise and seize London and all the principal ports and cities throughout England, and that they reckoned on the support of more than 30,000 armed men. This description of the projects and the resources of the Royalists may be at once set aside ; it is contradicted by the abortive and petty nature of the Insurrection, by the complete refusal of England to join therein, and by the conduct of the Protector himself. For he would not have sent that " new Commission" to the Dover Port authorities, or have permitted the performances of his " Passage clerk," if Wagstaff and Rochester and their companions could have summoned 30,000 men to arms, and have seized every important town from London to York.

Having thus dealt out fiction by wholesale, and ascribed the overthrow of that "great and general design" to "The Lord," Cromwell proceeds, according to his method, to show how that overthrow was accomplished. Beginning with the rising at Salisbury, he declares that "the Insurrection in the West was bold and dangerous in itself, and had in all likelihood increased to great Numbers of Horse and Foot, by the conjunction of others of their own Party, besides such Foreign forces, as in case of their success, and seizing upon some place of strength, were to have landed in those parts, had they not been prevented by the motion of some troops, and the diligence of the officers in apprehending divers of that Party a few days before ; and also been closely pursued by some of our Forces, and in the conclusion supprest, by a handful of men, through the great goodness of God."

As Charles had not, in 1655, at his disposal a single ship, or a single foreign soldier, the possibility of an invasion needs no disproof. The description of the overthrow of the Salisbury insurgents needs some review. With Major Butler unable to look the Country in the face, and the suspicion afloat that the pursuers were intentionally "kept at a distance" from the pursued, even Cromwell felt that to ascribe the suppression of Wagstaff's rising to a close pursuit "by some of Our Forces," would hardly suffice. He therefore attributes that happy result "to the great goodness of God," and to "the diligence of the officers in apprehending some of the Party." In the last statement Cromwell made an approach to the truth. Butler had been diligent; and though he failed to seize Douthwaite, that mysterious "principal verb," still, during the last two weeks of February, he did arrest suspects in the West of England; but he left Wagstaff and his comrades undisturbed, whilst preparing for their attempt.[5] Nor is it an unfounded assumption, if their security is attributed to the same influence which admitted them into England, and which protected them from Major Butler's horsemen.[5]

Having thus dealt with that "bold and dangerous insurrection in the West," Cromwell turned northward, and took in hand that rather vague affair at Marston Moor, on which, as he asserted, "the enemy most relied." His account of that event was, that the Royalists who met there dispersed and ran away in confusion, partly because of a failure among the plotters, but also, "in respect that Our Forces, by their marching up and down in the country, and some of them providentially, at that time, removing their Quarters, near to the place of Rendezvous, gave them no opportunity to reassemble." Again Cromwell is to a certain extent correct. Divided counsels did keep some of the principal Yorkshire Royalists from the meeting; and others were stayed, when on the march, by a timely warning that they were on a fool's errand.

[5] Thurloe, III. 176, 181, 191.

But the assertion that the Royalists were dispersed by a providential movement of troops, and by " Our Forces marching up and down" Yorkshire, is utterly false.   And, again, the witness against Cromwell is one of Cromwell's servants.   An officer, responsible for the peace of Yorkshire, reported to his chief in London regarding himself and his comrades, that " notwithstanding all our frequent alarums from London of the certainty of this plot, carried on with such secrecy on the traitor's part, though we were upon duty, and in close quarters, we had no positive notice of it till the day was past." [6]   And no other soldiers were in that neighbourhood, during the night of the 8th of March.   The only military movement which the occasion called forth, was the march of two troops of horsemen into York about three or four days subsequently ; and the officer in command reported, that if more men were wanted, they must be drawn from Durham, Newark, or Hull.[6]

Thus it was that Cromwell dealt with " the Northern Insurrection."   If the Royalists there had, in truth, " reckoned on 8000 " insurgents, or if York had been in danger, Yorkshire would have been filled, not with " alarums," but with soldiers. That " the enemy most relied " on that attempt is a correct assertion.   That darkling ride over the Moor might therefore be taken as a conclusive, and the

---

[6] Baynes, Coll. Add. MSS., 21,424, fo. 50.   Thurloe, III. 226. Cal. State Papers, 1655, 216.

concluding illustration of the unreality of the Insurrection.

Some minor symptoms must, however, be examined. Besides the Cavalier's parade over Marston Moor, other efforts were made to tempt the Royalists into action, on the 8th of March, with results even more trivial. These incidents Cromwell was forced to utilize to justify his assertion that " the Design was great and general." He accordingly declared that " the coming of 300 foot from Berwick " dispersed " those who had rendezvoused near Morpeth to surprise Newcastle:"— that in North Wales and Shropshire, where they intended to surprise Shrewsbury, " some of the chief persons being apprehended, the rest fled :"— and that " at Rufford Abbey, Notts, was another rendezvous, where about 500 horse met, and had with them a cart-load of horse-arms, to arm such as should come to them; but upon a sudden, a great Fear fell upon them," and they also dispersed themselves, and " cast their arms into the pond." Nor did the unabashed Protector forget the assault upon Chester Castle projected by his agent Colonel Werden, and carried out by Alexander, the tobacco-pipe maker. " And thus by the goodness of God, these hidden works of darkness " were discovered. " Fear " was " put into the hearts " of the cruel and bloody enemy, and their great and most dangerous design was " defeated and brought to nothing."

The surprise of Shrewsbury subsided of itself. The conspirators imitated their recruiter-general, who, whilst he urged them to ride out, declared that he should stay at home "because his wife was not well." As for the "rendezvous" of Royalists "to surprise Newcastle;" if Cromwell's spies are to be believed, on the 8th of March, "about three score and ten horsemen armed with swords and pistols" met by night "at a place called Duddo," and then vanished; because the conspirators were warned "that there were 300 sail of ships come into Newcastle, for fear of whom they durst not fall upon Newcastle at that time." And when the "rendezvous" at the New Inn on Rufford Abbey Green, "of 500 horse" accompanied by a cart-load of arms, is tested by the Thurloe Papers, the cart alone remains intact. The conspirators dwindle down to some twenty or thirty; and the Protector's 500 Cavaliers must be eked out by the possible presence in the Inn stables of " horses to the number of about 200." [7]

Notably, in 1655, as Guizot observes, Cromwell made a lying use of that " apparition faible et fugitive," [7] the late Insurrection and Rebellion; and the " Declaration " was a notable attempt to compel his subjects to accept the Protector's estimate of that event. That they absolutely refused

[7] Thurloe, III. 210, 222, 223, 241, 253 ; VII. 302.   Guizot, II. 133.

to learn that lesson and that they did not agree with him over the Insurrection, Cromwell himself tells us most emphatically.

In so delicate a matter as the respect paid by subjects to their ruler's word, we gladly avail ourselves of Cromwell's view of that matter. In our use, however, of the painful avowals he makes, that he was held in utter disbelief, there is no desire to condemn a man fixed in the grip of untoward circumstance. For leaders of men in " this present evil world " much allowance must be made. The higher the seat among the uppermost rooms of society, the further is the seat-holder distanced from those irresponsible ones who, having nothing to hide, can freely speak their minds. Diplomatic fallacy must occasionally veil unsightly truth; profane curiosity compels the just and necessary lie. For such a lie a statesman is not esteemed a liar, if he be in the main honest, if the truth be in him, and if he rests habitually in truth. Cromwell, every way singular in his fate, stands forth among the great men of affairs, the men of renown, as the only potentate who throughout his reign assures his subjects, appealing to God, Angels, and Men, that " I do not lie," and who, in the end, confesses that the just incredulity of his subjects is too much for him. This was Cromwell's wretched position; he thus bore witness against himself, both before his first and his last Parliament.

When he addressed the House on the 22nd of January, 1655, he posed as a justly indignant ruler, who had come suddenly to disperse a factious band of men ; but the lofty position of a Chief Magistrate filled with righteous wrath gave Cromwell no assurance, no confidence in himself. The tissues of his mind are on the quiver; a fierce note of resentment vibrates through his speech. He knew that his subjects accused him of foul play, that those who heard him suspected that "the cunning of the Lord Protector" created "necessities," i.e. conspiracies, to justify unparliamentary taxation, and to secure his government.

The appeals made by Cromwell to God, as the witness that he was telling the truth, shall not be reproduced. All will agree with him that such an appeal is a "tender thing;" and it may be hoped that he did not "know what conscience is," and what it is "to lie before the Lord." Nor can I quite place my readers in the position of those who listened to the "large and subtle speech" of the 22nd of January. Cromwell's tedious repetition, his see-saw sentences, answered his purpose, but defy condensation. This, however, is the upshot of his words. As if constrained against his will, he takes up, then drops, and then recurs to the charge, that "it is an easy thing to talk of Necessities, when men create Necessities; would not the Lord Protector make himself great and his family great ? Doth he not make these Necessities ? And

then he will come upon the People with his argument of Necessity."[8]

This charge against himself, thus shaped by himself, Cromwell persistently renews and contradicts.
Forgetting, doubtless, his decoy-duck Henshaw, the
disguised soldiers who accompanied those arm-chests,
and the Scottish mutiny in which his devoted
servant, Richard Overton, was a leading spirit,
Cromwell asserts that he never " ministered any
occasion" for the plotter to ply his task; and
having declared that in all he had to say about
conspiracies, such as Messrs. Bayley and Bagnal's
efforts to put the Nation into blood, "you will take
it, that I have no reservation in my mind to mingle
things of guess, and suspicion, with things of fact,"
he confidently reasserts that " I have not known
what it is to make Necessities."   On the contrary, he
claims that the " great Revolutions " England had
undergone were " the things of God," and that he,
the very being and personification of those Revolutions, could " speak for God."

That claim was made in vain. He was not
believed.   Faith in " the cunning of the Lord Protector" put his subjects from their faith in his
honesty.   Do all he could, Cromwell knew that
his hearers knew, that he had unjustly disparaged
Parliament, falsely accused the Royalists, and had
palmed off on the nation " feigned Necessities."
He could not, in January, 1655, disperse the dark

[8] Carlyle, III. 379, 443.

cloud of suspicion. Far less could Cromwell clear himself after the "Insurrection and Rebellion" had taken place; when he opened his last Parliament, 17th of September, 1656.

The pitiful position of a Ruler compelled to assure his subjects that "I do not lie," surely, at that moment, was not forced upon him? Cromwell stood before Parliament as their true Protector. Since their last meeting he had, if he spoke the truth, saved England from civil war. By his "Declaration upon" that "Occasion" he impressed upon his subjects its reality. The consequences of that Rebellion had been felt throughout England. As "nothing but the sword would restrain the late King's party from blood and violence," the Major-Generals had been appointed; English local life had been placed under military rule.

No event could be of more seeming "genuine veracity" than the Insurrection of March, 1655. But all the same, Cromwell did not comport himself as our Defender, as "the bold Protector of a conquered land," when he met Parliament in September, 1656. He knew that even the "late Insurrection and Rebellion" had not made his just dealing clear as the noonday. The cloud of suspicion still rested on him. The opening of his speech showed what was on his mind: he stood on the defensive. He commenced by claiming that he did "not pretend" to any affinity with "Rhetoricians," that he did not deal in "words;" and he at once dealt out a most rhetorical assortment of words to establish that papists, Jesuits, Spaniards, and above all the English Royalists, were " out of doubt " seeking " the destruction of the Being and Subsistence of these Nations."

In proof of this dire conspiracy, Cromwell was proceeding to refer to the Rebellion of the last year. But his very words seemed to baffle him. The mere mention of that event set him all in a blaze. His injured honesty fired up at the general distrust that met his statements, at the disbelief aroused by the previous conspiracies against the Protectorate. Passing back from 1656 to the year 1654, he assured his hearers that the Gerard and Vowel plot " was no fable." As real persons were arraigned for it, tried, and " upon proof condemned," that reminder would seem needless.

Then assuring his hearers that he gave them " an account of the things as they arose to him," Cromwell complained that " under what fame We lay, I know not," his description of the " woeful distempers " of the winter of 1654-5, such as the doings of Messrs. Bayley and Bagnal, had been reckoned at its true value ; and that " it was conceived, We had things which rather intended to persuade agreement and consent, and bring money out of the people's purses, or I know not what :—in short, nothing was believed ! " [9]

Having thus avowed that nothing was believed

[9] Carlyle, IV. 106, 107. Thurloe, IV. 133.

of the statements he made, when he dissolved the Parliament of 1654, Cromwell returned to the Insurrection of 1655. But that notorious event gives him no comfort; it does but provoke his wrath, his hot indignation, at the incredulity with which that "bold and dangerous" attempt was received. Cromwell never mentions "the late Insurrection and Rebellion," save "with vehemency." He thus expostulates with his hearers; "Certain it is, there was, not long since, an endeavour to make an Insurrection in England;" the attempt was "as evident as day." "That it was a general Design, I think all the World must know and acknowledge."

These protestations were futile. The Insurrection was regarded as a sham. Cromwell was forced to play the witness against himself. He turned fiercely against "the men of wicked spirits who traduce us in that matter," who, most truly, asserted that Wagstaff's followers "were a company of mean fellows; not a lord, nor a gentleman, nor a man of fortune, nor a this nor that, amongst them; but it was a poor headstrong people who were at the undertaking of this" Insurrection. Anyhow these traducers were not "mean fellows." They were the representatives of England. Cromwell admits that they were men "once well affected to him," but now so lost to honour and conscience as to comply with the Malignants, and to assert that he "dealt treacherously" with the Royalists, and that, to conceal his devices, he "took refuge in lies."

This was why Cromwell protested to those who sat before him, "Give me leave to tell you—we know it—we are able to prove, whether these things were true or no. If men will not believe, we are satisfied, we do our duty," and, as to those "men of wicked spirits,"—"I leave it!" Cromwell, however, again began "to speak now of the very time when there was an Insurrection at Salisbury." It was his final effort. Stung into passion, he exclaimed, "I doubt whether it be believed there ever was any rising in North Wales; at Shrewsbury, Rufford Abbey, where were about five hundred horse, at Marston Moor, or in Northumberland, and the other places where all these Insurrections were at the very time!"[10]   Here he dropped the subject: at last he left it.

A defence bespeaks an accusation. Englishmen are not devoid of honour; they can recognize an honest man when they see him. Yet Cromwell, our "Pattern Man," was forced to scold, to argue, to entreat his subjects to recognize his honesty, and to believe with him that a bold and dangerous Insurrection had actually taken place amongst them. And the "Englishman of Englishmen" broke down in the attempt.

Such indications of a disordered mind would in any case be a touching revelation. But it is Cromwell who is thus on the heave, torn and distended by the yeasty ferment of vexation, anger, and uneasi-

[10] Carlyle, IV. 105—111.

ness.   It was H.H. the Lord Protector, the Colossus of the hour, represented by obsequious artists as trampling down conquered nations, the man to whom the Kings of the earth made obeisance in caricature and in reality, who startled his subjects by these humiliating outcries.

Cromwell never spoke out of the fulness of the heart, merely because his heart was full.   Rage and mortification could make him speak at large, could force from him the painful avowal that he had been and was the drudge of the Military Party.   But then they had driven him out of his subtle self : they were thwarting him, exasperating him.   The Parliament before whom he lashed himself into fury was not a disobedient, gainsaying Parliament ; for it was then on its first day of trial.   It was not therefore wrath, nor infirmity of weakness, which provoked that attack on those " men of wicked spirits " who " traduce us."   This exhibition of unseemly heat was a desperate attempt to bolster up that stale, discredited thing, " the late Insurrection and Rebellion."

Cromwell took refuge in lies to no profit.   His crooked ways and their cruel results, the splashes of blood on the houses of South Molton, the dying men in the streets, the files of prisoners passing into the jails, before the judges, and on to the scaffold, were to no purpose.   All that misery was inflicted in vain.   All that crime was undertaken in vain.

His subjects still remained "incredulous of" the Insurrection, "jealous that it was not real," and that it was his "own devising." Nor could he make that event seem real, though he deafened his hearers by appeals to God, Angels, and Men.

CHAPTER VIII.

THE MAJOR-GENERALS AND THE PROTECTOR.

A committee of Scotch Ministers were sent to London in March, 1654, "to settle Kirk affairs." One of them "was called to preach before the Protector at Whitehall, sundry Scotsmen being present. He prayed for the Royal Family thus :—'God be gracious to those whose right it is to rule in this place, and unjustly is thrust from it. Sanctify Thy rod of affliction unto them,' (*i.e.* Charles II.) And for the usurpers he prayed in these terms, 'As for these poor men that now fill their rooms, Lord, be merciful unto them." Some would have had the preacher accused for praying for the King, and for calling them 'poor men.' But the Protector said, "Let him alone, he is a good man, and what are we but Poor Men in comparison of the Kings of England ?' " [1]

This story is not an irrelevance here. The object of this chapter is to show how bitterly Cromwell had occasion to pray, " Lord, be merciful to me ;" how acutely he was made to feel, by the Military Party,

[1] Wm. Row's Life of Robert Blair, 313.

that, compared with a King of England, he was, indeed, a poor man. His fellow-soldiers dealt with him as no Baron or King-maker ever dealt with any Monarch. Nor was it to their strength that he yielded; their power sprang from his own acts, from what he himself had done. He had succeeded: he had created the semblance of an Insurrection, of a Rebellion. Then came the return shock from that feigned explosion: it placed him at the mercy of the Major-Generals; its influence overshadowed him until he was "got cleanly off the stage" of life, on the 3rd September, 1658.

At no period during the Protectorate were we more quiescent than during the year 1655. The general tranquillity, which the Insurrection of March could not upset, returned, when Cromwell's trepanners were called off. He could not, however, remain at rest; the quietude that England enjoyed did not suit his purpose; and within three months after the Insurrection, he renewed the policy of terrorism.

That this was his deliberate purpose, may be taken for granted; for, to use Godwin's words, the Protector during June, 1655, took a "step" that was "unjustifiable and crooked; he determined to excite a false alarm." The Royalists having lost for the present all enterprise and courage, "were in a state of tranquillity and submission," when suddenly "in this period of repose, Cromwell and his Council issued orders for an extensive arrest of persons, who were known to be favourable to the cause of the exiled King."[2] Some fifty Commoners, and about fifteen members of the aristocracy, were committed to the Tower, and to gaol, and rumour went that they were to be sent to the " Plantations."

Cromwell also issued a Proclamation declaring that he had received undoubted "intelligence of designs now in hand for the destruction of the Government," and commanding all Royalists to keep within their "usual dwellings," and to "depart from London and Westminster," under penalty of punishment as " disturbers of the peace."

In September " a further measure of extraordinary import was adopted." An Ordinance directed " that henceforth no newspaper should be published without permission from the Secretary of State." Six out of eight newspapers, then in weekly issue, were thus suppressed.

These actions bespeak Cromwell's subjection to a superior power : they sprang from external compulsion. The newspapers were not worth extinction. Mild banter from the " Faithful Scout," when he announced the Royalist arrests of June, such as " Brave times! blessed are the poor in spirit," or " More I could say, but few words are best," were the most virulent newspaper attacks directed against the Government.

The creation of an impression that his " strictly prohibiting the printing of news, is a sure sign that

---

[2] Godwin, IV. 223—234. Cal. State Papers, 1655, 215, 232, 384, 395. *Weekly Intelligencer*, 24—32, July, 1655.

his affairs at home and abroad go not well,"[2] did
Cromwell injury.   An exhibition of himself as standing firm, commanding the confidence of his subjects,
as every way " well," was essential to his position.
His influence over Continental powers lay solely in
his prestige.   Wholesale arrests, the suppression of
newspapers, were therefore against his interest. The
Government journals sought to correct the feeling
those arrests caused " beyond seas," and scouted
the rumour that " a great part of our ancient nobility is under a cloud."[2]   To appear as a shaky Protector, to make himself odious to aristocratic and
peaceful land-owners, must have been sorely against
his liking.

The directors of Cromwell's will disclosed themselves in the following October. The outbreak of
oppression, during the summer and autumn of 1655,
was the precursor of the " Declaration " of the
31st October, 1655, by which Cromwell announced
that, " for securing the peace of the Commonwealth,"
he had placed his English and Welsh subjects under
the rule of the Major-Generals, had inflicted on the
Royalists the decimation tax, and had established
" a new and standing Militia of Horse in all the
Counties of England."

Ten Major-Generals were, accordingly, instituted
" Deputy Governors," as they were styled by an ob-
sequious Diurnal, over the Counties of England and
Wales, and two over London and Westminster.
Of this institution the " three great ones," of

course, received a large slice. To Fleetwood was committed Mid-England, his territory of seven counties stretched from Oxfordshire to Norfolk; to Disbrowe the West of England; to Lambert the Northern Counties; and he was also appointed Chief Deputy-Governor.

Their authority was most extensive. Infliction of the death penalty was not granted; and from their sentences appeal was given to H.H.'s Council. The powers of those military magistrates were otherwise unlimited. They could fine, imprison, or sell as slaves all adjudged by them to be refractory Royalists; and judging by the tone of their reports, the sale of their fellow-countrymen was a righteous act, to the Major-Generals especially acceptable.[3] As martial authorities they could, on plea of tumult or unlawful assembly, call out their soldiers, or employ them as they chose. As spiritual authorities, the religious and scholastic ministry was subjected to their rule. As magistrates, they dealt with blasphemy, drunkenness, disorder, alehouses and horse-races; and as armed dictators, they superintended municipal and parliamentary elections, purged corporations, manipulated juries. The Major-Generals were also provided with severe inquisitorial methods for the levy of the decimation tax, which " stirred up the good people to inform " against their neighbours.[3]

[3] It has been urged that the sale of Englishmen to West Indian and American Colonists, by the Protector and his associates, was

No award is needed regarding the grant of such powers to the Major-Generals, or on the way they used those powers, or on the propriety of the decimation tax. An institution condemned by its author, and by all it touched, directly or indirectly, needs no criticism. As soon as the Protector and his subjects had it in their power, they destroyed that institution, condemned the conduct of the Major-Generals, and denounced that breach of national faith, the decimation tax.

Interest, however, much interest does attach to the origin of that institution. The most commonplace common sense must have warned Cromwell to say, No—when the Military Party told him that they "thought it was necessary to have Major-Generals."*

Assuming the truth of his Declaration, that " nothing but the Sword will restrain the late King's Party from blood and violence," and that he was therefore " obliged in duty, both towards God, and this Nation, to erect a New and Standing Militia of Horse in all the Counties of England," that Declaration was an abject confession. The man who, in

the mere repetition of a practice in force during the Civil war, and sanctioned by the Long Parliament. This line of defence is untenable. In time of peace, untried men were taken out of prison, and sold as slaves under " O. P.'s " warrant, and by the Major-Generals. The poignant reproach directed by Cowley, Vol. II. 663, against the Protector for selling Englishmen "to be slaves in America," an act more inhuman and unsupportable than murder, or torture, was after Oliver's death re-echoed in debate as fervidly as could be expected of Members of Parliament.—Burton, IV. 255—273. Thurloe, IV. 595.

 * See p. 6.

the opinion of Europe, had raised himself to an almost throne, was forced, within the second year of his reign, by a "company of mean fellows" at Salisbury, to proclaim that he could not govern England. He had subdued every enemy; and yet he and his 40,000 soldiers could not keep down the unarmed Royalists: he must call to his comrades for help. That call Cromwell could hardly have afforded to make, had the Major-Generals been his drudges, had the Royalists been capable of utmost mischief. Just the reverse was the case; the Royalists were, as Godwin tells us, "in a state of tranquillity and submission," and Cromwell tells us that he was "the drudge" of the Army Officers. Even if the Protectorship had been not a pretence, but a reality, their title to rule was as good as his; he and they were on an equality. They had framed the "Instrument of Government," and, under that, General Lambert had made General Cromwell the Lord Protector. His tenure of power was therefore their tenure. They were military adventurers; he was a military adventurer. He could not without supreme danger make his brother swordsmen the "Deputy Governors," Co-Protectors of England. Their grip on the Country was tighter than his own. The Protector was isolated in Whitehall: they were everywhere. In the levy of taxes he was bound by custom. They could shape any new instrument they chose for the extraction of the decimation tax. The sight of the Royalists twitching under the tweezers of these operators taught every Englishman that he, too, might be handled in like fashion ; that he, also, might be unable to call his own, his own. A dozen task-masters was, also, a bitter novelty. England, in past centuries, had suffered much under weak or cruel Monarchs. A single Pharaoh was bad enough ; but he was as of aforetime. Cromwell's twelve Pharaohs were a new and terrible phenomenon ; they excited the hatred, anger, and despair of his brother bond-men, his subjects.

Thus the institution of government by the Major-Generals was to Cromwell not a humiliation only ; it was a source of danger ; and it was a burthen which pressed on him, just where his back was weakest. He had always an empty Treasury in sight. To provide for those taskmasters, and for the 40,000 soldiers, and for a powerful Navy, and for his army of spies, he pushed taxation to the uttermost. The only reserve source he possessed was exaction from the Royalists.

When, in 1658, his Government was paralyzed by bankruptcy, to re-pillage the Royalists was the only remedy present to Cromwell's despairing advisers.[4] He must have foreseen that he might be driven to adopt that course ; yet of that plunder he gave to the Major-Generals first pick. He empowered them to draw therefrom a yearly salary

[4] Thurloe, VII. 192, 218. Harl. Miscell. iii. 452. Thurloe, V. 504.

of 666*l.* 13*s.* 4*d.*,[4] as Deputy Governors, and to justify their salaries he was forced to erect the new Militia standing at 1000*l.* a year per troop.[4] Those troops were in number fifty-four, assigning two to London and Westminster, and one to each of the fifty-two counties of England and Wales. Thus, as 12 times 666*l.* 13*s.* 4*d.* make 8000*l.* —and as 54 times 1000*l.* make 54,000*l.*, the total yearly cost of the Major-Generals amounted, at the money rate of to-day, to 186,000*l.* Nor was it with other people's money that Cromwell made so free. That 186,000*l.* a year might have been his own. He could have decimated the Royalists for his own profit, or have reserved their estates for the political rainy day.

Such an outlay was to Cromwell every way a vexation. It enriched encroaching associates ; and it was wholly unnecessary. Even supposing that the Insurrection of 1655 had been a general affair, still, that brief explosion over, England at once reverted to repose. So safe felt Cromwell that, during that summer, he reduced his Army, beginning with regiments stationed in England ; although the substitution of militia for army soldiers was a step so perilous, that the mere thought of it was forbidden to Henry Cromwell.[5]

That the affair at Salisbury was a mere pretext for the institution of those military Magistrates and

[5] Cal. State Papers, 1655, 107, 229, 251, 260, 265. Thurloe, V. 504.

of a local Militia became notorious. It was not on that account that the Military Party "thought it necessary to have Major-Generals." That demand was part of the bargain they made with Cromwell over "The Instrument of Government." When he was dead, the truth of the matter came to light. Under Richard, parliamentary tongues were free, and when that painful subject, government by the Major-Generals, cropped up in debate, that institution was not charged against the Royalists, but against the Major-Generals themselves. That was why the past experience of those Military Magistrates was so distressingly present to the mind of Richard's Parliament. After Oliver's death fear of " the mischief of the sword " was again upon us. To avert that mischief we were exhorted to support Richard, else again " we must go to the Major-Generals, and to the Instrument of Government " for " upon it " the Major-Generals " came in." [6] The notion that Cromwell had acted freely in the elevation of his comrades into their Co-Protector-ships did not occur to any of the debaters.

Parliament, during March, 1659, felt the impulse which actuated Parliament during the spring of 1657. It was to deliver not England only but also our Protector from the hands of the Military Party, that we strove after a King Oliver.

Thus the Insurrection brought the Crown within

[6] Burton, III. 116, 567, 568 ; IV. 11, 16, 33.

Cromwell's grasp, and then the Major-Generals, the antagonist forces raised to power upon the Insurrection, snatched it away. This sequence of events tells its own lesson.

Penruddock and his companions, cheated as they were into their graves, had no cause to regret the sad result of their simplicity. With that group of men before us, the Protector and those twelve Co-Protectors, it is unnecessary to prate about retribution.

CHAPTER IX.

THE MAJOR-GENERALS CALL THE PROTECTOR'S LAST PARLIAMENT.

IF a story of degradation, mortification, and disaster constitutes a tragedy, then Oliver Cromwell's Protectorate was indeed a tragedy. Yet it produced during its progress a comic interlude, which might be styled " The Catspaw's Revenge."

Six months had not passed by since the Major-Generals had extorted from Cromwell their Co-Protectorate, when they again made him their catspaw. They compelled him, during August, 1656, to convene Parliament for their benefit. As it fell out the reverse was their lot. Parliament, if the conclusion may be thus far anticipated, gave Cromwell his opportunity; it expelled the Major-Generals from their Deputy Governorships. By no other means, save Parliament, could their expulsion have been effected. In that moment of tribulation, when on the 27th February, 1657, " the Hundred Officers " struck in between Cromwell and Kingship, he could not refrain from reminding the Majors of this humorous result of their own device. " You might have gone on" for ever in your Deputy Governorships, he told them, had you not been "impatient till a Parliament was called. Who bid you go to the House with a Bill, and there receive a foil?"

That was the precise truth of the matter. The duration of their office was unlimited, until Cromwell could declare that the state of England was no longer urgent. That declaration he could not make. Sancho's proverb, " He who gives the broken head, can give the plaster," was inapplicable. Terror of civil war, of anarchy, was Cromwell's stock-in-trade, the basis of his authority, of his right to exact taxation. To him therefore the dismissal of the Major-Generals from their Deputy Governorships was impossible.

The Majors, in their impatience for a Parliament, were not without reason. A Statute to perpetuate their Deputy Governorships was to them a prime necessity : still more necessary to them was an indemnity for the past. Government by the sword had its risk. Both Cromwell and the Major-Generals alike, by many a high-handed action, had overridden and broken the Law. That his taxation Ordinances were wholly illegal, he had received an unpleasant and public reminder. A London merchant, Mr. Coney, refused to pay the customs' duties levied by the Protector's fiat. Coney, in return, was imprisoned. He retained counsel to claim his writ of Habeas Corpus ; and they were committed to the Tower. In the end, Coney gave way ; but if some twenty or thirty like-minded city Hampdens had combined with him, those twenty or thirty Coneys would have proved no " feeble folk." In other ways Cromwell was also get-at-able. During the heat of the General Election threats were heard that a reckoning would be sought with " His Highness," not only " for breaking up the Long Parliament," but " for what he hath done since." [1] A threat that might involve a heavy reckoning.

As for the Major-Generals, they dreaded, as Lambert avowed, that " if a Parliament should be chosen according to the general spirit and temper of the Nation, those may creep into this House, who may come to sit as our judges for all that we have done." [2] And not Parliament only, even an ordinary magistrate's court might put them into a quandary. That this could be so, the case of Story . *v.* Randall was an effective warning. Randall, a constable, was directed by my Lord Barkstead to report to him, as Major-General over Middlesex, the names of all mulctable Royalists in Enfield. To keep his name out of that report, a Captain Story offered Randall the bribe of 40*l.* Randall placed the matter before Barkstead. He replied, "Take the bribe : we can convict thereon ; and Story hath a large estate, and only one witness against him."

Randall acted accordingly, took the bribe, rounded on the briber, and then found himself

[1] Thurloe, V. 384.
[2] Cal. State Papers, 1656-57, 384. Burton, I. 281 ; III. 448 ;

prosecuted by Story before the Middlesex Quarter Sessions, as " a trepanner." Story's example was followed, and Randall was confronted by six or seven more writs, merely " for performing his duty." The constable naturally turned to his employers : he appealed to the Protector. But even the Protector could not protect his agent's agent. Cromwell ordered Story to come out of the Magistrate's Court, and to place himself and his complaint before my Lord Barkstead and his Commissioners ; but Cromwell interposed in vain.

Such a tribunal would have suited Randall ; it did not suit Story. Naturally enough a refusal to proceed before Lord Barkstead was Story's reply. He kept his course ; " told his tale " to the Middlesex Magistrates: and they fined Randall. Despite Cromwell's intervention, they decided that H.H.'s constable was a trepanner. Thus an ordinary magistrate, backed by the law, proved himself a stronger man than either the Protector or his Major-Generals.[2]

Some three years later, during the days of Richard, the Lord Barkstead was again " brought upon the stage," the parliamentary stage, on this occasion, for the improper detention in the Tower of Mr. Portman for over twelve months. Although Barkstead had therein obeyed a letter " all writ in H.H.'s own hand," the House resolved that the imprisonment of Mr. Portman by the Lieu-

IV. 257, 403. Thurloe, VII. 620. Clarendon State Papers III. 441, 447.

tenant of the Tower "was and is illegal and unjust,"[2] and Barkstead was thus exposed to any action that might be brought against him "by the malice of particular men."

About the same time, Major-General Butler, that zealous swordsman, was actually, by the vote of Parliament, "disabled" from all his military and Civil offices, for the forcible seizure of an estate; and still further injury and degradation were threatened against him. Nor did Butler's assertion "that we must be governed by the Army" bring him any salvation.[2] That 100*l.* also, which Thurloe made by the sale of Mr. Thomas into the Barbadoes, had like, during those altered times, to have cost the vendor dear.[2]

A parliamentary title to their Deputy Governorships was their sole security from such troubles, and from all troubles. Rooted in office by Statute, they would survive their creator. On the death of the Protector, the Deputy Governors would in due course nominate the chief Governor. That nomination Lambert, the chief Deputy, had in view: and the occasion might promptly arise. Serious illness afflicted Cromwell during the autumn and winter of 1655-56.[3] The "O. P." signatures of that September and October are tremulous as the track of an inky and paralytic spider.[3] H.H. was in February "much and often perplexed with stone;"[3] and Sagredo, then our

<hr>

[3] Cal. State Papers, 1655, 365. Venetian Studies, by Mr.

visitor, noticed that the Protector looked "pulled down," and showed "signs of a health not entirely restored, and that the hand which held his hat trembled."[3]

Expectants occasionally cannot afford to wait. The Majors felt that they must utilize Cromwell when they could; justly "impatient were they." Acting evidently for his fellows, by letter dated 8th February, 1656, notice was sent to Cromwell by Disbrowe, that he intended to wait upon His Highness in London; and that, if the Protector would please to summon all the Major-Generals up to wait on him within a fortnight, somewhat should be propounded to him, "which might be of great use and advantage to this poor Nation."[3]

Disbrowe's directions were followed. The Major-Generals assembled at Whitehall, and then resolved to postpone their "somewhat" for the advantage of our poor Nation till May.

In one matter Cromwell at once obeyed them. He had been sluggish over the appointment of the Major-Generals for London and Westminster. He now forthwith filled up those vacancies, and placed his subjects and neighbours under Co-Protectors Skippon and Barkstead, to the "great distaste" of the City; and the alienation of the citizens was precisely what Cromwell dreaded.[3]

Horatio Brown, 393. Thurloe, IV. 520. Carte Letters, II. 81, 93. Tanner MSS., 52, fo. 135, 197. Clarendon State Papers, III. 327. Cal. Clarendon MSS. III. 415.

On Saturday, the 17th May, took place the conference between Cromwell and the Major-Generals. It formed a highly dramatic situation. Cromwell saw before him a dozen men determined to oppose " successive Government," [3] to be the choosers of the Chief Magistrate, and to root themselves in lordship over England. They were headed by the " three great ones," Lambert, Fleetwood, and Disbrowe; of whom it was said that " they " also " hoped to be what the Protector now is ;" [3] whilst Cromwell, for his part, was equally resolved to unseat the Major-Generals, and to seat himself upon the Throne.

The goings on of the Major-Generals agitated the fancies and the tongues of Londoners. " Great alterations shortly," were expected in February. In May, the sight of the military conclave " sitting close and daily " at Whitehall, gave rise to much " talk of a Parliament intended, and of an enlargement of the Major-Generals' Commission," or that Cromwell would " settle the legislative power in himself," or receive the Crown from his Army officers. [4]

Passing from rumour to the account furnished by our own reporter, Cromwell, of the transactions at Whitehall, this was the result. Whilst the Major-Generals were confident " by their own strength and interest, to get men chosen to their hearts' desire," their hearts' desire and Cromwell's were in direct

[4] Hist. MSS. Com., 5th Report, 152, 180, 6th Report, 440. Thurloe, V. 9. Cal. Clarendon MSS. III. 245. Carte Letters, II. 81, 110. Cal. State Papers, 1656-57, 257, 344.

opposition, and he " gave his vote " against a Parliament.[5] The Majors and all H.H.'s Councillors voted against him; so the general election took place. Cromwell was in the right. Dragooned and silenced England spoke out lustily from Northumberland to the South Foreland. Our cry was "no swordsmen, no redcoats, no decimators, no mercenaries, no salaried men, no courtiers."

Confusion seized the Major-Generals. They were lost "in contendings and strugglings," wrapped in "a black cloud," tried by "a dark dispensation." Their friends were "faint;" perverse spirits rampant. Then the Majors pulled themselves together. By troops round the hustings, by terrorism, by their physical, military, and magisterial power, they forced themselves and many a nominee into Parliament. If the general election went not wholly as they could wish, the upshot did not quite suit their opponents. The Major-Generals were not utterly beaten. Governor Kelsey's proposal to Cromwell, that if England was unconformable, he should "take to his assistance, such as would stand by him, in maintaining the interest of God's people,"[6] i.e. the interest of the Military Party, was needless. Parliament, if not fully moulded, was mouldable.

No apter illustration of the real condition of England could be found, than the general election of

---

[5] See p. 6.
[6] Cal. State Papers, 1656-57, 87.

August, 1656, no clearer proof that Oliver's Protectorate was Revolution in disguise. The electors were without leaders, apparently without concerted action, every way harassed and hampered; the decimated ones had no votes; and yet the verdict of the Nation was "that they will down with Major-Generals, Decimators, and the new Militia."

Escape from Government by the Sword was the desire of the Nation. Where lay the sole possibility of that escape? In one way only, government by a King and government by Major-Generals were incompatible. A King, it was hoped, would not, like the Protector, break the oath that he had taken to govern England according to Law. A King alone could stand between England and the Army. The man upon whose "peculiar skill, and faculty, and interest in the Army our peace depended," must wear the Crown.[7]

This rebound of popular feeling towards himself distinctly influenced Cromwell when Parliament met; and even the French Ambassador foresaw in him not only a King, but the founder of a dynasty.[7]

The Ambassador overrated the Protector. Cromwell's true nature was indicated by his conduct during this conjuncture. He could not throw himself heartily among his subjects. He prefaced the parliamentary session by a return upon his wonted policy. To impress on England the imminence of

[7] Heath, 382. Guizot, II. 272, 273. Hist. MSS. Com. 6th Report, 441.

anarchy, he arrested and imprisoned six or seven leading republicans, such as Sir H. Vane, Major Harrison, and Colonel Rich : and he did the like to a dozen royalists.[8]   Despite his ever-pressing money troubles, having increased his Life Guard and raised the cost to what would be nowadays about 30,000*l*. a year, Cromwell also increased the Army.   During September and October, nine new companies were added to the ranks ; and nine regiments were re-cruited up to 1200 in strength.   Additions were made to the garrisons of Dover and Windsor ; London was guarded as if an enemy was at the gate ; and the soldiers' quarters at Scotland Yard and Charing Cross were enlarged and strengthened.[8]

Cromwell also summoned the principal Army Officers to Whitehall.   He told them that Charles Stuart had round his standard 4000 Spaniards, 4000 Dutch, and 4000 English troops ; that the invader was at hand ; and he exhorted his hearers to be zealous and watchful to defeat the designs of the enemy, both at home and abroad.[9]   The King's army existed solely in Cromwell's inventive mind. His informants from Bruges, the Hague, and Antwerp told him that the royal levies came in "but slowly," that they could not be raised in Flanders, and that "of all sorts," Charles "had not yet above 400 men."[8]

These precautions, as that heedful observer, the French Ambassador, remarked, were "founded on

[8] Cal. State Papers, 1655-56, IX. Godwin, IV. 276. Cal.

the pretext of a royalist conspiracy, and the active malice of the republicans; but many believe, and with good cause, that they are designed to overawe the Army, and stifle sympathy for Cromwell's evil treatment of those who were earnest for the privileges of the people."[8] And as usual the cry of "wolf" failed. Cromwell's alarm was deemed to be "invented and feigned." No wonder that, when he addressed Parliament, he complained so bitterly that nobody believed in him, or in his conspiracy tales of December, 1654, or in his insurrection of March, 1655.

The French Ambassador's vision of the crowned Cromwell was in a measure justified. The general election had completely changed the political outlook. The Protector was no longer that stale old Necessity, a Protector against imaginary anarchists, against plotters who could hardly be got to plot. He was really wanted by his subjects. The same need subsequently drove England towards his incapable successor. During February, 1659, Hyde was informed "that the officers of the Army, having let their intentions be made known of governing by the soldiery, have put all men in such a fright, that they will strive to make Richard, King."

To all, save the Good old Cause-ists, it was obvious that a King was the sole cure for the "mischief

State Papers, 1656-57, 94, 105, 119, 128. Thurloe, V. 407, 427, 431, 449. Guizot, II. 610.

[9] Thurloe, II. 64; III. 302, 303, 317. Massey to Hyde, MS. Cal. Clar. MSS. slip 565. Clarendon, Hist., Ed. 1839, 887.

of the sword." This remedy, the necessity of crowning Cromwell, according to report, suggested itself to the Protector's Council as far back as February, 1654, because to combine government by the " Instrument," and government by established Law, was an impossibility.[9] Terror of the Army made even Royalists perceive that a King Oliver might serve their turn, whilst a King Charles certainly could not.[9]

The possibility of a monarchical turn in the political game had been foreseen by Cromwell during the opening months of 1656. He improved, to his own advantage, the disadvantageous position forced on him by the Major-Generals. He used their help to make friends with the mammon of royalist aristocracy. He adapted to this end a cunningly invented device constructed for the vexation of the Cavaliers.

The Major-Generals could summon before them every Royalist, however quiet and inoffensive, and bind him, under heavy penalties, to the good behaviour of his servants,—that they would not " act against the State," or commit " drunkenness or swearing." [10] This power placed every Royalist householder at the mercy of any fool or rascal whom ill-luck brought under their roof. The nobility and large landowners were obliged to have a great following : custom forced on them troops of Wimbles and Wildrakes. Thus, though the poorer Royalist

[10] Cal. State Papers, 1655-56, p. 83. Egerton MSS. 2534, fo. 580, 9th Dec. 1655 ; 2536, fo. 38, 14th Jan. 1656. Earls North-

suffered much under the decimation-tax, his quantum of exaction was defined.　A large-acred neighbour, by his servants, was constantly exposed to fine and imprisonment.

Some aggrieved Royalists represented to Cromwell the hardship of being responsible for the tongues and throats of their retainers.　At first he would not help them.　Wealthy Cavaliers were the pet prey of the Major-Generals.　He told the royalist deputation that he saw no reason "but that they may be as able each to govern his own family from such disorders, as he doth forty thousand soldiers in his army;" and he added "that most of the inconveniences of the Kingdom do proceed from the forlorn poor Cavaliers, who get into good houses to be gentlemen ushers to ladies, stewards to great persons, companions, hangers-on, hungry fellows, who empoison their masters' and servants' minds, keep up the King of Scots his credit, speak ill of the State, swagger, drink; and therefore, to deter gentlemen from keeping such servants, he will have them to answer for their behaviour." [10]

This interview took place in December, 1655. Cromwell's severity was, however, only in show. Nicholas was, ere long, informed that "some of the Lords, as the Earl of Bedford, Clare, Lindsey, the Marquis of Dorchester, and two or three more, have made such application to Cromwell, that they have

ampton, Middlesex, Dorset, Sussex, Bedford.　Lord Westmoreland, Lord Paulet, Lady Vere, Sir W. Hervey, Sir R. Thorold,

got letters from him to the Major-Generals, or
Commissioners, of the respective counties where they
are concerned, that they proceed not against them
as to the matter of security, nor," as the informant
" took it, about their tenths. " [10]

That information was correct. Major-Generals
Whalley, Butler, and Berry wrote to Cromwell that
" the taking off " of " great estates " in the counties
of Northamptonshire, Bedfordshire, Hunts, and
Rutland was starving the militia troops; that
the Commissioners were much discouraged; and
that odium was brought on the Major-Generals,
because " the chiefest enemies, of the greatest
estates, were cleared off by H.H.," and that, " even
the Royalists cried out against the partiality thus
shown to their great neighbours." [10]

Assistance more direct in a quest after the Crown
the Major-Generals themselves afforded Cromwell.
If they brought some odium on him, they had
brought more odium on themselves. They were
hated of all men. To lovers of the Grand old Cause
of civil and gospel freedom, the Majors were traitors;
they had sold the Cause for place and profit. They
were to the mass of the people both noxious and
obnoxious. Equally odious were they to their Iron-
sided comrades, those armed enthusiasts who bound
Kings with chains. Nor could the Major-Generals
reckon implicitly on the soldiers of the Protectorate

Sir W. Farmor. Cal. State Papers, 1655-56, 89, 182, 214, 288,
323. Thurloe, IV. 189, 324, 409, 411, 509, 511, 515.

leaven, the mercenaries. Their support might be claimed as professional men. They might act together to keep government in their hands ; but the Major-Generals could not break the bond of discipline. Instinctive obedience from the Army, as an Army, Cromwell could ever exact.

The overthrow of those universally hated Military Magistrates was therefore possible. Cromwell, backed by Parliament, could upset the Military Syndicate, might convert the drudge into the master. This danger the Majors foresaw. They perceived that Parliament might become that awkward thing, the third man in a crisis. The roar of national feeling at the general election, the cry of "no swordsmen," rang in their ears: the Major-Generals knew that England longed for their abolition.

Accordingly, while Cromwell was locking up old friends and peaceable enemies ; massing troops round London ; rallying round him the Officers ; crying "wolf at the door" to an unbelieving generation,—the Major-Generals made their preparations also. They were practical in their efforts. Cromwell was but beating the air. They took in hand that third man in the coming duel, the Parliament. The powers that Cromwell had conferred on them were not exhausted. They had terrorized the voters ; and now they could deal with the representatives that England had sent to Westminster. "The Instrument," framed by the

Military Syndicate, prescribed that "no persons should be admitted to Parliament, but what were approved by the major part of the Council." The Council, accordingly, on the day when Parliament met, 17th September, 1656, granted tickets to such Members as they chose, and denied tickets to 105 Members, to more than one-fourth of the English vote in Parliament.[11]

The exclusion of these 105 Members from Parliament has always been reckoned up against the Protector, as one of his most discreditable performances. When it was the fashion to say something like the truth about Cromwell, he received therefore much resonant invective. That his subjects placed this constitutional offence at his door, was to be expected. They had not before them, as we have, the minute-books of his Council. He was their Protector; they naturally supposed that H.H. was master in H.H.'s Council-room. When Parliament met, and for some months afterwards, cleavage between Cromwell and his Major-Generals was invisible. No one supposed that the Protector and the Majors were in direct antagonism; that he absented himself from the Council-room whilst the purgation of Parliament was in hand, and that this proceeding was really directed against him.

[11] Mr. J. Hobart, Member for Norfolk, in his list of " names of such Members as were kept out of theParliament House by armed men," 17th Sept., 1656, makes their number 105. Tanner MSS. 52, fo. 156. Thurloe, V. 453.

That this was the case was partially visible at the time. An acute observer remarked that the Protector's "information of persons was, as many thought, but bad, for he has excluded many who, if not his friends, would not have ventured to be his enemies, and that he had admitted others, who were only restrained by fear." [12] That statement, though tending aright, did not strike home. The exclusion of members from this Parliament acted every way against Cromwell. The Crown was to be offered to him by the three Nations. If Parliament failed him he thought, it is reported, that he could appeal to the English people. A ticket Parliament, a packed, purged, and moulded body of representatives, was therefore, to his purpose, the most unsuitable; and examination shows that the purgation business was not his doing.

The exclusion clause was inserted in the "Instrument of Government" by its draughtsmen for their own protection. As Lambert has told us, the Military Party feared that "if a Parliament should be chosen according to the general spirit and temper of the Nation, and if there should not be a check upon such election, those may creep into the House who may come to sit as our Judges for all we have done in this Parliament, or at any other time or place." [13] And the use the Council made of

---

[12] Cal. Clarendon MSS. III. 189.   [13] Burton, I. 281.

that clause was to effect that very object. Certainly
fierce republicans, lovers of a real Commonwealth,
hostile alike to Cromwell and the Major-Generals,
were kept out, such as Sir Arthur Haselrig, or
Messrs. Scot, Weaver, and St. Nicholas. It was
their admission, in the second session, that wrought
Cromwell's overthrow. But then the wreck of
the Protectorate and the decrepitude of Parliament
gave them such destructive power.

Parliament when new showed no disposition to
dally with republicanism. On the contrary, the
summary rejection of a motion condemning the exclusion process so discouraged the republicans that
" many withdrew from the House, because they
could not have their will in the vote." [14] Exclusion certainly was not specially directed against them.
That company of 105 Members must have included
many besides the irreconcilables, for apparently they
mustered only some thirty votes. The exclusion
also affected the representation of constituencies
wholly unconscious of a Leveller.

The Major-Generals felt instinctively who were
their most bitter enemies. They were chiefly in the
counties, and 77 of the disabled 105 were returned
by the counties. The City of London, more than
any other city, suffered severely at the hands of
the Lord Barkstead, and four of the six City
members were ticketless. No wonder, therefore,
that of the City relicts, one proposed and the other
voted the Crown to Cromwell. The bias shown by the

City showed the bias of the generality. Even the Monarchists began to see that it would be well to get a King anyhow; and undoubtedly highly royalist counties, Wiltshire, Worcestershire, Oxfordshire, Kent, and Sussex received stringent purgation. The whole of the Hertfordshire representation was disabled.

A Monarchist was, of necessity, an anti-Major-Generalist, and thus a double injury was inflicted on Cromwell's interests by one stroke : it knocked over both undoubted enemies of the Majors and the Protector's possible friends. This was the case. Some disabled ones crept into Parliament, and their presence there is proved by the appearance of eight of that band among the voters for the Crown.

Rumour also tends in this direction. When Cromwell had finally refused Kingship, according to Whitehall news, " the excluded members would be called to sit among the rest, and then being a full House, they shall vote a kingly government, and it will be accepted by the Protector." [14]

The guiding spirit which regulated the exclusion is also visible, not only in those who were shut out of Parliament, but in those who were kept in. The sixty so-called representatives from Scotland and Ireland were government nominees : they were beyond the reach of H.H's Council. The Scotch and Irish members were therefore sure of their

[14] Thurloe, V. 453. Hist. MSS. Com. 5th Report, 164. Thurloe, VI. 37.

admission tickets; and they supplied twenty-seven out of the sixty-one votes for monarchy, nearly half the majority. Indeed, but for these votes, and the support of thirty-six independent Englishmen, Cromwell would never have sighted Kingship at all. Had these voters failed him, the numbers in the division would have been sixty for, and sixty-one against the Crown.

To turn from indications to facts. His Highness's Council was Cromwell's only in name : in reality it was the Military Party over again. The working number of the Board, during September, 1656, was fourteen. Of these fourteen votes, nine were at the disposal of the officers, namely the four Majors on the Board, Disbrowe, Fleetwood, Lambert, and Skippon and of the other members, Colonels Sydenham and Jones, Sir Gilbert Pickering, Mr. Strickland, and Lord Lisle were their allies, and supported their Militia Bill.[15]

That the Board was theirs seems to have been recognized by Cromwell : he left the Majors to their devices. This is shown by the attendance table of the Council. As the general election was not completed till the close of August, the returns for the three Nations could not have been laid before the Council until after the 9th or 10th of September. Between the 9th September and the 17th, the opening day of Parliament, the Council held ten

---

[15] Cal. State Papers, 1656-57, p. XX. Burton, I. 233—241.

sittings, meeting on three occasions both in the morning and the afternoon.   At these sittings Cromwell was present only once, on the morning of the 10th September, when the exclusion business was hardly before the Council.[14]   Lambert, on the contrary, the chief Major-General, then in the height of popularity, sat there daily; and Disbrowe's attendance was almost as constant.

Had Cromwell been present every moment whilst the Council held session, he could not have hindered or changed their tactics.   He was powerless.   As the Majors had managed the general election, the Protector could not hinder their using the Council to mould, at their pleasure, the result of the Election. He was still their drudge.   Though England had risen in fury and disgust at his Deputy-Governors, he could not as yet throw them over.   Just the reverse : he was making ready to bless them, to exult, in his opening address to Parliament, over their pious zeal for our welfare : to claim that they were his " little, poor Invention."

The Major-Generals held the Council Table. They would not have been men if they had not striven to hold Parliament also.   Indemnity was essential to them.   They might vapour as they pleased, and assert that their swords were their indemnity,* but they knew that the Nation spoke in the cry " no swordsman, no decimator."   If they could exclude enough of the national party, who

* See p. 208

sought to substitute, for their rule, government by King Oliver, they were safe.

The Major-Generals scored at this turn of the game. In Cromwell's name they granted and they denied parliamentary admission tickets. The gain was theirs; the offence and the reproach went to the Protector. The next turn in the game, the rejection of their Bill, gave the catspaw his revenge upon his tormentors.

CHAPTER X.

PARLIAMENT, THE PROTECTOR, AND THE MAJOR-GENERALS.

To a Nation whose single wish was settlement, government according to Law,—to a Parliament returned, after a fierce struggle, to rid us of military rule,—Cromwell in his opening speech, 17th September, 1656, gave but sorry satisfaction. "The erecting of the Major-Generals" was his own "little, poor Invention." They had "been effectual for the preservation of our Peace," had discountenanced Vice, and settled Religion; and if that "righteous thing," the decimation of the Royalists, was "to be done again, he would do it."

So the Major-Generals were our masters; and Parliament accepted the situation. Putting faith still in Cromwell, seeing in him the sole chance of safety, they proceeded forthwith to consolidate and strengthen his power. A motion to condemn that national wrong, the exclusion of about one-fourth of the representatives of England, attracted only 29 votes against 125. Bills were rapidly passed, to annul "the pretended title of Charles Stuart," and to establish a High Court of Justice for

" the security of H.H. the Lord Protector, his person." It was resolved " *N.C.*,—That the Parliament doth declare that the War against the Spaniard was undertaken upon just and necessary Grounds, and will, by God's blessing, assist His Highness therein." Parliament also directed, significantly, that all Bills " should be tendered to H.H., for his consent to be given in Kingly fashion, in the Painted Chamber." [1]

So free was Parliament from the "spirit of contradiction," that, excepting the brief disturbance over the disabled Members, no Division took place, on any vital question, during the first ten weeks of its existence. Until December, as Thurloe expressed it, Parliament still " jogged on :" nor did he discern mischief in an Order of the House, 31st October, appointing a Committee of fifty-five Members to consider the "great Misdemeanours, and Blasphemies of Joseph Nayler."

If postponement of the coming contest between Parliament and the Majors, and between the Majors and Cromwell, were desired, no apter wherewithal could be devised, than Nayler's blasphemies. Lunacy is contagious; and his freaks aroused that latent eccentricity that ever abides in Parliaments, and in mankind. From the 5th to the 17th December, the House busied itself about Nayler and his claim to be a new Christ, and in discussion over his punishment. Nayler's neck having been saved by a narrow

[1] VII. Com. J. 425, 460. Thurloe, V. 453.

division of ninety-six against eighty-two, it was
resolved that he be pilloried in London and Bristol,
that hot irons be applied to his tongue and forehead,
and scourges upon his back.[2]

Much was involved in that Nayler business.
Cromwell had declared himself for "freedom of
all judgments;" by which "it is supposed he
has aroused a party in the House."[2] He also
warned Parliament that all "who believe in
Jesus Christ, let his form be what it will,"
should "enjoy his liberty, so long as he walked
peaceably."[2] And as Nayler avouched his faith
before the House, "pretty orthodoxly," it was
contended that he could claim the immunity
accorded by the Protector.[3] Throughout their
treatment of Nayler, Parliament recognized that
they were disregarding Cromwell's injunctions.

The Nayler dispute also showed that the Protector-
ists possessed no control over the House. Cromwell's
interests would therefore drift, and to drift is to lose
way, and to lose way is to lose the day, especially
in Parliament. There swiftness is almost success.
Thurloe was not the cunning man in parliamentary
tactics, and outside troubles filled his mind. During
the first ten days of December the Majors began to
be nasty. Thurloe complains that His Highness
had occasion to say, " My familiar friends, in whom

---

[2] Thurloe, V. 453, 472, 672. Cal. State Papers, 1656-57, 113.
VII. Com. J. 465, 468. Burton, I. 24, 48, 1—167. Carlyle, IV. 123.
   [3] Burton, I. 59, 78. Thurloe, V. 708. Burton, I. 192, 190-195,
255.

I trusted, have lift up the heel against me." [3]   They were determined to legalize their Deputy-Governorships.   If they succeeded,—then for Cromwell no Crown.

The kick-off in the game of Sword or Crown, was made by the Major-Generals.   On Saturday, 20th December, Lambert began the sport; Sir W. Strickland, acting in his behalf, moved that the House be called over on Thursday next,—Christmas Day, as it happened.[3]   In itself the proposal for a " Call " was justifiable.   Of a Parliament containing 460 Members, however vital the occasion, the attendance rarely exceeded one hundred.   Two hundred only were attracted together even by an offer of a Crown, or the overthrow of the Major-Generals. This neglect of duty was gross, conspicuous.   " It was reported abroad," as a Member told the House, " that we are but a rag of a Parliament, made of none but soldiers and courtiers." [3]

Meritorious as was the motion, the mover was to blame.   An effective Call needs a preface of several weeks.   The summons to attend is circulated throughout the three kingdoms.   A Call, ordered on a four days' notice, on a Saturday for the next Thursday, was a dodge to obtain a packed House. Even Strickland was puzzled how to justify his proposal.   So he pushed to the front that odious Christmas Day, and attempted to convert the Call into a puritanic test,—" that it might be known who were absent that day," in devotion, either to religion, or to the bottle.　Strickland, the precisian, was met by this reproof.　A yet severer precisian urged that Christmas Day was beneath the attention of Parliament.　" Surely," he asked the House, " you will take no notice of Christmas Day?　You will not call the House, because it is Christmas Day !" [3]

The question of feasts and fasts, however, soon disappeared before a consequence, natural and inevitable, that sprang from Strickland's motion.　If Parliament be called, every Member returned at the General Election must be summoned.　Those Members that H.H.'s Council, i.e. the Major-Generals, had " disabled," would therefore be restored to Parliament.　That was the parliamentary consequence of a Call according to rule.　The presence of those Members was certainly not what Lambert desired. He did not perceive, as will be hereafter explained, that the excluded ones had lost their seats ; accordingly he shaped his motion for the Call, so as to " distinguish between such as are approved, and such as are not." [3]　Lambert was not an old parliamentary hand : he had spoilt his game.

A Resolution of the House so worded, conferred the sanction of Parliament upon the arbitrary exclusion of its Members.　Even that ticket meeting was roused to wrath.　It was felt intolerable that the swordsmen should tamper with the forms of Parliament.　An amendment was moved to leave out the words, " such as are approved."　If the amendment were not accepted, " if all be not admitted," it was proposed that "all should go home"!

This daring suggestion of a dispersal, not a Call, ushered in the storm. Each party tried to silence the other by appeals "to order," and by calls "to the Bar."　"The meekness of the House," as a combatant remarked, "suffered much affront." Lambert saw that he must beat a retreat. He sought to allay the turmoil. He urged that "he never intended the least heat, when he first moved this business;" he begged that it should not "breed further dispute."

Major-Generals Goffe, Whalley, and Butler also interposed. They implored the House not to rise in anger, to remember "what would be said abroad." The Majors evidently feared "the consequence of such a business," i.e. increased publicity to the exclusion business. The "heat" so "soon stirred," was "laid aside." Butler's hope, "that we shall be friends again," was realized, in semblance at least; and the attempted Call of the House on Christmas Day passed out of sight.[3]

Though beaten, the Major-Generals kept to their purpose. When Christmas Day came, and the Members met together, that offensive Festival forced its unwelcome presence upon the House. Those advocates of "gospel liberty" could not purge the 25th of December from its Christian influences. They felt uneasy, out of harmony with the outside world. To rehearten themselves, their celebration of the day began with a Bill "for abolishing, and taking away Festivals." The appearance of the House proved the need of the measure. Its promoter remarked, "the House is thin, much I believe occasioned by observation of this day.[4]" He therefore desired to stifle Christmas Day for ever. His associates chimed in, much to the same tune. Luke Robinson, the Radical, "could get no rest all night, for the preparation of this foolish day's solemnity;" and others declared that Christmas Day was kept stricter than the Lord's Day; that "one may pass from the Tower to Westminster, and not a shop open, or a creature stirring." The Cavaliers also were pictured, as "haply now merry over their Christmas pies, drinking the King of Scots' health, or our confusion." The Bill was accordingly read a first time, that people might not say "abroad, that those superstitious days have favourites in this House." [4]

Had a Cavalier gifted with "second sight" spent that day in Parliament, he would have needed no pie or wine-cup to cheer his heart. For he would have seen the beginning of an end to the Protectorate, when Major Disbrowe stood up and said, "I have a short Bill to offer you, for the continuance of a tax upon some people, for the maintenance of the Militia." This modest proposal, brought forward in this artless manner, contained the supremacy

---

[4] Burton, I. 229—243. VII. Com. J. 475. Hist. Rec. MSS. Com. 6th Report, 441.

of the Major-Generals over England, and over Cromwell.[4]

So far as talk went, that Christmas Day's work was satisfactory to the Majors. Of the debaters, five only spoke against their Bill, and twenty were its hearty supporters. And this twenty included seven members of H.H.'s Council, besides Thurloe, Cromwell's own man. Unpleasant symptoms, however, disclosed themselves. A disposition arose to obstruct the Bill. The House "had much ado to come to the Question;" and the Bill was, in our reporter's belief, "much against the Speaker's mind." The House also was put to a division, by Lord Claypole, Cromwell's son-in-law; and while eighty-eight voted that leave be given to bring in the Bill, they were met by sixty-three opponents.[4] Still, thus far the Majors were successful; their Bill, known as the Militia Bill, was brought in; and they hoped to take the first reading upon the morrow, Friday, the 26th December.

So the House met; when suddenly, "where we least think, there starts the hare." Parliament, from its daily routine, the Major-Generals from their Bill, its opponents from their attack, were all started off in a direction they least thought of when they came down to the House. Protector-baiting, not Bill-debating, turned out to be the unlooked-for sport.

The sport thus began. Some private bills were discussed. The business of the day, the Militia Bill, came to the front, when the Speaker rose and said,—

" Here are five or six up; I cannot hear all together; but I must acquaint you with a Letter from the Lord Protector, to the following effect: 'Having taken notice of a sentence by you, given against one James Nayler, albeit We do abhor such wicked opinions and practices, We, being interested in the Government, desire to know the grounds and reasons how you proceeded herein without Our Consent."

Both in moment and method, the Protector's intervention in Nayler's behalf was singular. Sentenced on Tuesday, the 16th December, whipped from Westminster to the Old Exchange on Thursday, the 18th, Nayler was to be tongue-bored and forehead-branded on Saturday, the 27th; and now, on Friday, the 26th, Cromwell sent that Letter to the Speaker.

A Chief Magistrate, who interferes in behalf of a persecuted subject ten days after the sentence has been passed, eight days after the sentence has been put in operation, and one day before the completion of the punishment, places himself in strange wise before his subjects. They might justly ask, If such interference was necessary, why so tardy? Who was, as he described himself, more " interested in the Government " than the Protector? Did he need ten days wherein to "take notice" of Nayler's sufferings? To the punished one, such tardiness was painfully unsatisfactory. Nayler " had no skin left between his shoulders and hips." The delay was also highly. unsatisfactory to the Parliament, who were responsible for the woeful rawness of Nayler's back.

If the moment of Cromwell's intervention was studiedly perplexing, equally perplexing was the method. His Message to Parliament was in terms most vague and uncertain. Naturally enough, so soon as the Speaker had read the Protector's Letter, there arose a medley of assertions, denials, disputes, debate, that resists condensation. Parliamentary discussion nowadays breaks bounds; in the Protector's day, it was boundless. The course of the word-storm he thus created is untraceable; to follow it is as impossible as to mark time to the hop of a flea.

The following outcries however, were predominant. What did the Message mean? What did His Highness want? Did the stress of the Message lie in the words "without Our Consent"? or did the Protector merely ask to see the evidence whereon Nayler had been condemned? Anyhow, why did he wait until Nayler had been flogged? Why did he interfere, when twenty-four hours would send Nayler to the pillory? Did the Protector purposely delay his Letter, in order that it might arrive too late, —that he might return upon Parliament the punishment which they had inflicted,—in order that, as urged in the debate, he might whip them "for whipping Nayler"?

Parliament could not persuade themselves that the Protector merely craved to know why they had punished Nayler. The Message, if it meant anything, was a challenge of their right to punish. To no purpose did plausible courtiers, such as Major-General Jephson, or the Lord President, assure the House that His Highness had no such desire ; that he only wanted an account of the transaction ; that he would be satisfied if the report of the Committee on Nayler's blasphemies were laid before him.

They contended in vain : they were not believed. No, it was retorted, let us " return this short answer to H.H.'s letter ;—' We had the power to do so ;'—" and an awkward precedent was cited for so rude a reply. When Parliament demanded of H.H.'s Council the " grounds and reason " for their clean sweep-out of the English representatives, H.H.'s Council returned a like " short answer," that " they did it in pursuance of ' The Instrument of Government.' "   But then, if the whole force of the Message rested on the words " without Our Consent," it was naturally asked, Did the Protector thereby intend to pose as Defender of the Faith ? If so, what Faith ? Faith practised by any spiritual free-lance, or Faith agreeable to the Presbyterian, or to the Independent? Nobody, however, would admit that Cromwell's toleration views embraced Nayler's extravagancies. Even the heir-apparent, the Lord Richard, passed his judgment, " that Nayler deserved to be hanged." [5] Parliament would not credit the notion that Nayler's " wicked practices " were acceptable to His

[5] 26 Dec., 1656, Burton, I. 246—257.

Highness, that he had a weakness for blasphemy, that he " pleaded anything for crime."   On the contrary, Parliament stoutly insisted that Nayler's " wicked opinions and practices " were abhorred by the Protector.   If he did not abhor them, Colonel Markham declared that " he would not serve him." Thus, by the process of exhaustion, by weeding out what the letter did not signify, namely, that Cromwell did not want information, that he was no friend to the blasphemer, it became obvious that Cromwell sought to befriend himself, to defend his own jurisdiction.

So, after all, that Letter was, in effect, a denial of the jurisdiction of Parliament.   That was why the Solicitor-General claimed to speak against the sentence passed on Nayler, because " the whole question before you is, Why a judgment without the Lord Protector ? "   Fervid indignation was kindled. The Cavaliers and Sectaries disputed the legality, the very being of a Parliament chosen under " The Instrument of Government."   The Protector was playing their game.   He was trying to compel Parliament to " arraign their own judgment;" to stultify themselves ; to even themselves with " a Parliament called Insanum Parliamentum ;" to make the House a " matter of laughter both to wise men and fools ;" and the Protector was warned that " the dispute " he had raised endangered " sad consequences," that he had best " lay aside the further questioning of this judgment."

Mr. Luke Robinson summed up effectively the opinion of his fellows : " If this House have no judicatory power, I doubt we have no foundation ;" and Mr. Bacon clenched that remark by asserting " that men's lives, liberties, and estates are in the power of Parliament. I would have us assert our own power." [5] Parliament took that advice. The next day, Nayler's re-punishment day, Saturday, the 27th, a Motion, which deferred but slightly to the Protector's will, " That the further punishment of Jas. Nayler shall be respited till this day seven-night," was rejected by 113 noes, against 59 yeas. And Mr. Burton, the reporter to whom we are so much indebted, left the House, and went " to see Nayler's tongue bored through, and him marked on the forehead. He put out his tongue very willingly, but shrinked a little, when the iron came upon his forehead. He was pale when he came out of the pillory, but high-coloured after the tongue-boring." Nayler " embraced his executioner, and behaved himself very handsomely and patiently ;" and so, bidding him farewell, we can part company. [6]

But Parliament had not parted with Cromwell. When the House met again, on Tuesday, 30th December, Major-General Goffe revived the sport of Protector-baiting by this innocent-seeming remark, —" I presume His Highness does expect an answer to his letter." Thus started off, away they went after the Protector. He forgot that if he ques-

[6] 27 Dec., Burton, I. 260—265. VII. Com. J., 476.

tioned the jurisdiction of Parliament, his jurisdiction might be questioned in return. He had slighted the proverbial prudence required from a glass-in-dweller.

Accordingly, when his courtiers contended that Parliament could not judge Nayler without the Protector's concurrence, they were reminded that, if he denied the rights of Parliament, he might be asked by what right he expelled those Members of the last Parliament who would not sign a " recognition " of " The Instrument of Government." By what right, also, was the decimation-tax imposed ? How would the Protector answer those questions ? And his advocates were told that before they touched the jurisdiction of Parliament, the jurisdiction of the Government must be reviewed. For instance, what security did Parliament possess for its very existence ? Under " The Instrument of Government," H.H.'s Council were " the judges of your Members." They could therefore purge them into nothingness, until there " be no Parliament at all." [7]

Thus the House, although entreated " not to ramble into former precedents, nor fall to dispute jurisdictions," tossed to and fro His Highness's Letter, and, in the end, tossed it away unanswered. In vain the Speaker stood up and told the House, " that it is my duty, once a day, to remind you of the business of the day, that is an

30th Dec., Burton, I. 270—232.

answer to the Letter." Whenever the Speaker did his duty, "several stood up to propose other business," or three successive motions to adjourn the House were made; and so the answer to the Protector's Letter was intentionally "jostled out, and nobody said a word to it."[8]

Parliament had reason. The real motive which prompted that Letter rendered reply impossible. That motive was not resentment aroused by the tortures inflicted on Nayler, nor a desire to establish free trade in religious opinions, nor an intention to assert H.H.'s supremacy. Cromwell's move was a crafty revival of a parliamentary precedent. In the year 1621 the House of Commons had condemned a Mr. Floyde to the pillory and the lash, for words deemed an insult to the Royal Family and the Protestant cause.

James I. had brought the House to book for their dealings with Floyde. By an adroit Message the King had reminded them that the punishment of Floyde was beyond their power; and the King had scored. The Commons were forced to stand aside, and to allow the House of Lords to play the part of righteous judge, and to flourish the whip and the branding-iron over Floyde. Cromwell thought that he would go and do likewise, and rival that Solomon, his predecessor. The object of the Letter was to assert that "the Instrument of Government" stood "in need of mend-

2 Jan., 1657, Burton, I. 294—296.

ing;" to cast discredit on the document drawn up by Lambert and some half-dozen Major-Generals; to show to England what a Parliament, unchecked by a House of Lords, could do, and that a King was a necessity.

Cromwell's device was recognized by his courtiers. They urged that an assembly convened under "The Instrument of Government," was not a real old traditional thing; and that as the Constitution "was new," Parliament "was new" also; " that we are now upon another bottom and foundation, than former Parliaments were;" that "we have" not "all the power that was in the House of Lords, now in this Parliament."[9] Cromwell himself took up that parable before the "One Hundred Officers." He pointed out that "by the proceedings of this Parliament, you see they stand in need of a check, or balancing power (meaning the House of Lords, or a House so constituted); for the case of James Nayler might happen to be your own case. By their judicial power they fall upon life and member; and doth 'The Instrument' in being enable me control it?"

Cromwell's little knowledge of history made of him a fool. That dose of Jacobeian statecraft operated disastrously, as must every dose that is thoroughly unsuitable to the patient. The Letter in the first place was needless. Parliament required no historic illustration of the "mischief of the sword," of that,

---

[9] Burton, I. 254, 257, 274, 275.

the reign of the Major-Generals had wrought abundant conviction. Nor did the Army officers care about the balance of the Constitution. A controlling " check " was the last thing they wanted. But that Letter was far worse than useless ; it was poignantly inapplicable. In administering that corrective to Parliament, Cromwell acted like a physician who gives a purge to a patient who has got no stomach ; it was an irritating and humiliating blunder. By that " witty invention " of his, Cromwell exhibited the seamy side of Protectorship and the blessings of Kingship, in a way that destroyed his position and damaged his reputation. The timid, tentative tone of the Message embarrassed his friends ; and its miserable evasiveness provoked malevolent and destructive criticism from his enemies. If interpreted as an effort to protect Nayler, that Letter enabled Parliament to pour contempt on Nayler's would-be protector. If Cromwell sought to check the encroachment of Parliament, Parliament, with unparalleled insolence, shoved him aside as a thing of naught.

Those who wish well to Cromwell must believe that, as pleaded in his defence, the Letter was " wrung from him by importunity." [9] No monarch ever made to Parliament a communication more contemptible. It exceeds in mischievous impotence that wretched message by which Charles I. handed Strafford over to the executioner. The excuse Charles pleaded was not possible to his successor. Cromwell was not driven to ask Parliament to bring him out of a "great strait." He sought to effect—as an advance towards the Crown,—the degradation, the depreciation of Parliament. Parliament in return put him into a "great strait." They showed by their treatment of his Letter that such a deplorable shuffler could no more be turned into a King, than, to use their own phrase, a "bird-bolt" could be shaped "out of a pig's tail."

The slap in the face that Cromwell had thus brought upon himself was not to him wholly comfortless. The Parliament that insulted the Protector could deal with the Major-Generals, could help him by the rejection of their Bill.

This conjuncture the Majors had not forecast. That Cromwell would abet Parliament in their overthrow, that he dared to turn against them, even to the end they could not believe. Nor did Cromwell undeceive them. Though "all men were in great expectation" concerning the fate of the Militia Bill, Cromwell made no sign. He "gave good words" to the officers: he kept them in play; they worked for him and with him in support of the Nayler Message; they chimed in, during the debate, desiring that His Highness should receive satisfaction.[10] So certain were the Major-Generals that Cromwell was their faithful servant, that they could not comprehend why son-in-law Claypole divided the House against the introduction of their Bill,

[10] Ludlow, 245, 246. Thurloe, VI. 20, 37, 38.

and headed their opponents on the first reading. When the Protector's cousin once removed, " honest Harry Cromwell," cast his *tu-quoque* at them,—You claim to punish innocent Royalists because some have done amiss. · If, therefore, some of the Major-Generals have done amiss, all deserve to be punished, —the Major-Generals told Harry that his *tu-quoque* " His Highness would and did take ill."

Even Harry's vote against them, wearing the Protector's " rich cloak and gloves, to the great satisfaction of some and trouble of others," did not fully open their eyes.[10] They could not recognize their position. After " the Bill was cast out," they assured Cromwell that the vote of the House was cast, not against them, but against him, and that Parliament would " pass nothing that might tend to his accommodation : that they would raise him no money." He knew better. He told them that he hoped nicer things of Parliament. His hopes were justified. In spite of the efforts of the Military Party, " the House " promptly, and " with a deal of cheerfulness, voted 400,000*l.* to be forthwith levied to carry on the Spanish war." [10]

Well would it have been for Cromwell, had he remembered that " no man can serve two masters," had he cleaved to Parliament and despised the Majors. On this occasion, he did so ; and they were overthrown. The first reading of their Bill stood upon the Order Book of Wednesday, 7th Jan., 1657. The Bill was called on, and, acting as was recognized at Cromwell's dictation, Lord Claypole rose immediately. He denounced the illegality, the injustice, the cruelty of the decimation-tax : he ended by moving " that this Bill be rejected."

That the contest over the Majors' Bill involved a national crisis, was recognized. A Member, during that sitting, estimated the number present to be " 220 at the least, besides the tobacconists ; " and if his computation be accurate, this was the largest House of that Parliament. " There was," also, " a very mettled and serious debate, and will be, before all be done, for one might perceive by many men's countenances, that they stood full charged for speaking to the business." [11]   The Debate was accordingly adjourned till " to-morrow morning, nothing to intervene."

" To-morrow morning," Thursday, 8th Jan., came, and with it something that did intervene. Mr. Speaker intervened.   The adjournment of the House was moved " in respect of " his " weakness."   The motion was resisted by Lord Lambert and Majors Whalley and Goffe. Nothing, they demanded, should delay their Bill. " The Country " was earnest to know " what testimony we shall show to the old interest of England ;" to see Parliament " scruple at this business " discouraged their friends, and encouraged their enemies. The House, on the contrary, could not see that Government by the Sword was " the old interest of England."   The Speaker's " in-

[11]   Burton, I. 311, 320, 322.   VII. Com. J. 483.

disposition of body" was utilized, and the Majors' Bill was postponed into next week.

During the evening of that same Thursday, Sindercombe, the assassin sent by Colonel Sexby to murder Cromwell, was led, basket in hand, by the Protector's servants to Whitehall Chapel.* Through no fault of theirs, the "firework" was stagnant, and satisfied nobody, not even H.H.'s Council. Still, though the firework did not work, it could not be left stifled among the pews. The greater the failure, the more that faulty advertisement needed nursing by time and manipulation.

Again the Major-Generals' appointed day, Monday, the 12th January, came, but not their Bill. The House waited long. At last Mr. Speaker was brought in a sedan to the lobby door. "With much ado" he was hoisted into the Chair, "but looked most piteously." At once it was proposed to adjourn for a week. Suspicion, however, arose that the sedan and the Speaker's piteous looks were for effect: it was even "doubted his being sick." He was bluntly asked to "deal plainly" with the House: he was directed to declare the cause of his sufferings: he was warned that "the House may think that you are in good health, and able to sit." The Speaker, tormented within and without, "thereupon stood up, and with tears in his eyes," assured the House, that "if you please to go on, I shall sit till twelve o'clock."

* See p. 284.

Mr. Speaker's intentions were obviously beyond his strength. "Very ill he was :" and the House adjourned for a week. Nor did the Majors' Bill re-appear with the re-appearance of the House. When it met, the solemnities over Sindercombe's basket, the rehearsal in Parliament of the "late heinous plot," their congratulations to the Protector, and the "princely entertainment," with "rare music," that he gave in return, swept everything else out of sight.

At length the Major-Generals' Bill re-appeared. Eke it out how you may, by antipathy, resistance, Speaker's illnesses, motions for adjournment, obstruction cannot last for ever. The final tussle came, those two last days so occurrent in our history, when Parliament feels that procrastination must cease, that a national dispute must be closed. "Mettled" debates lasted through the 28th and 29th January; and the Major-Generals lost their Bill by 124 votes, against 88.

Messrs. Lambert, Fleetwood, Disbrowe and Co. were put out of their Deputy-Governorships ; but an end was not put to their power over Cromwell.

CHAPTER XI.

PARLIAMENT, THE PROTECTOR, AND THE CROWN.

So effective a rebuff as the rejection of their own Bill
by a Parliament which they had moulded at the first,
and had manipulated afterwards, was to Messrs. Lambert, Fleetwood, Disbrowe and Co. a thorough defeat,
and a defeat, also, which strengthened the abhorrence felt against them. They had showed during
the contest their true nature. The spirit which inspired Governor Kelsey to suggest, that if Parliament proved unconformable, the Army could do
their work, was reflected in their speeches. Parliament offered them indemnity; that offer was rejected with scorn. They retorted, " It is our swords
that must indemnify us. It is that, must procure
our safety." [1] Such menaces, showing that the
Major-Generals " durst openly avow themselves to
be our lords and masters," stamped reality on prevalent rumours that the Army Officers were planning
" a Heptarchy, and of cantonizing the country :"
and that, if they had their way, they would " at last,
bring all things to be military." [1]

[1] Cal. State Papers, 1655, 375. Burton, I. 313, 315, 317.
Thurloe, VI. 219. Cal. Clarendon MSS., III. 239. Ludlow, 245.

Decisive as was the overthrow of their Bill, the victory over the Major-Generals was to England and to Cromwell neither a final nor an unblemished victory. To England the rejection of the Militia Bill would bring no safety, if Cromwell were not made King ; but he had emerged from the contest in a very blemished condition. The Major-Generals most justly warned him " how much," by the vote against their Bill, " the House had reflected on him." Much indeed! Cromwell had given them authority over England. As military magistrates they had carried out his instructions. They had acted on the straight; whilst he, towards them, had behaved most shabbily. They were not to blame if he " cantonized the Nation, and prostituted our laws and civil peace," [2] by subjecting us to their rule, and by exacting from the Royalists the decimation tax. Nor was it the fault of the Majors, if he maintained this systematic oppression in effective operation for more than a year. It was he who had made them odious ; and then he threw them over. Using his son-in-law as the representative of his opinion and judgment, he declared that system to be " against common justice, nay, against all justice." Just in the same way, having declared before Parliament, in a tone of blustering self-satisfaction, that " We did find out a little poor Invention—the erecting your Major-Generals ; " which had " been more effectual towards the dis-

[2] Burton, I. 314, 315. Carlyle, IV. 116, 131. See p. 6.

couraging Vice, and settling Religion, than anything done these fifty years;" he went in hot
and strong for the destruction of his own "little
poor Invention;" and lastly he denied that he was
its inventor, and retorted against the Army Officers
that it was "you" who "thought it necessary to
have Major-Generals." [2]

This excuse may be urged for Cromwell. The
contempt he thus brought upon himself was not a
voluntary act, as in the Nayler case. He could
not do otherwise. Deception is the most absolute
act of homage that weakness pays to strength.
That tribute of respect Cromwell rendered handsomely and consistently to the Major-Generals.
Whenever they touched him he gave out lies, as
spontaneously as an electric jar gives out sparks.
Nor did his lies spring from a robust indifference to
truth, they were the tremulous lies of servitude.

Yet, at the opening of Parliament, Cromwell must
have deemed that if he could not push aside his
military masters, he might sidle round them, and so
ascend the throne. Thurloe knew his patron's
difficulties; yet "some good measure of establish-
ment" by "this Parliament" was hoped for by the
Secretary, and he assured Henry Cromwell that the
Government would be pleasantly changed in "one
point." Thurloe also was certain that "the body
of this Nation doth desire" [3] King Oliver; and

[3] Thurloe, V. 453, 694; VI. 220. Clarendon State Papers,
III. 327.

Cromwell seems to have thought likewise, and to have boasted that the people would crown him, and of an appeal to them by a dissolution of Parliament.[3]

Nor, until the close of the conflict over Kingship, were the Military Party conscious of their strength. They floundered about between submission and resistance, from violent counsels to a resolve that they would "wait and see what Providence will produce."[4] In their counsels "the resolutions of the morning and the evening, and of the evening and the morning, were as different amongst them as light and darkness."[4] Individually their actions were equally unsteady. Major-General Haynes was first Cromwell's friend, then his enemy. Disbrowe rudely resists, then joins, and lastly opposes his chief. Whalley passed from antagonism to neutrality. Lambert, the greatest one, was first hot against Kingship; then "stood at a distance;" and then was brought to bear on Cromwell, "just in the nick of time." Mrs. Claypole's playful picture of the Ladies Lambert and Disbrowe "washing their dishes at home," was seemingly applicable to their husbands.[4]

The Major-Generals possessed this advantage over Cromwell. They could ply their craft in a corner. He was forced to carry on his artifices in public, in the Protector's Chair. When he did

[4] Clarendon State Papers, III. 326, 327, 333. Cal. State Papers, 1656-57, 307. Thurloe, VI. 74.

try to hide his hand, he failed : it was visible. His plot-inventions, his lies, his shufflings, were seen and known of many, if not of all men. He was sorry stuff to shape into a Monarch : at best he would be but a disloyal King. Still nations in the grasp of a revolutionist cannot be squeamish ; they cannot pick and choose their deliverer. England was in that plight. Parliament felt ready to do anything to blot out " the name Protector ;" that name, " they say, came in by the sword, and not by Parliament, nor will there be a free Parliament so long as that continues." [5] So they clung to Cromwell. By rejecting the Major-Generals' Bill, he was severed from the Military Party. To sever him from them yet further, and to push him onward into Kingship, Parliament by a Resolution, " That no money ought to be levied without common Consent in Parliament," and by an analogous provision in the " Petition and Advice," [5] put an end to taxation by the Protector's " Ordinance." To hold his own, to pay his way, he must obtain the Crown.

The first definite move towards Kingship took place on the 23rd February, 1657. Sir Christopher Pack, the member chosen to bell the cat, to show the Crown to Parliament, was a man of action and of tongue. He had been " elected burgess for the City of London, only for his valour in committing

[5] VII. Com. J., 10th Feb., 1656, 489, 504. Burton, I. 347. Thurloe, VI. 219. Old Parl. Hist., XXI. 135.

four soldiers" to prison.[6] During the session he approved himself as "a man that will speak well."[6] In a Committee of Trade, amidst a severe contention between keenly self-interested disputants, "Sir C. Pack turned in the debate like a horse, and answered every man, he did cleave like a clegg;" and in a conference at Whitehall about the admission of Jews into England, "of all the head pieces that were there, he was thought to give the strongest reasons against their coming in, of any man."[6]

Sir Christopher Pack evidently was up to the mark. He suddenly rose in his place, and offered to the House his notable "Paper," which he declared would tend "to the settlement of the Nation, and of Liberty and of Prosperity," and would free us from "the several inconveniences which this Nation is subject unto, under this present form of Government." And what these "inconveniences" were, he proved by his "exclamation against the Major-Generals, and the decimations brought in by them."[6]

The Motion that Pack's "Paper," *i.e.* the new form of Constitution known as the "Petition and Advice," should be considered, was carried by 144 votes against 54. After stiff obstruction, waged through two sittings, the House began the task; and in about a month's time the title of King was

[6] Cal. Clarendon MSS., III. 190.   Burton, I. 308, 309. Thurloe, VI. 84. VII. Com. J., 496. Carte Letters, II. 94.

conferred on Cromwell by 123 against 62 votes. The new Magna Charta of 1657 was so far completed. On the 31st March, the Petition was presented to Cromwell: on the 3rd April he made the first refusal of the Crown. Parliament next day renewed their offer of Kingship, voting 78 against 65, that "this House doth adhere to the Petition." Cromwell's Kingship majority had dwindled down from 90 to 13.[7]

On the 8th April Cromwell made his second refusal; held five conferences with Parliament, which resulted, 21st April, in the return of the Petition with a "paper of exceptions." His desires were obeyed. The Petition, altered to suit his views, was for the third time tendered to him on Friday, 1st May. On the following Friday, the 8th, Cromwell made his third and last refusal of the Crown.

This slight outline of the struggle over Monarchy must be clothed with light and shade. The course taken by Parliament during this "paroxysm of state," can be learnt from its proceedings. Cromwell and the Major-Generals, those subtle combatants, must, if possible, be made to disclose their tactics. Some indications also may arise of the feelings with which that interested but most outside bystander, England, regarded the contest.

What Parliament did during the spring of 1657 can be ascertained to some extent; what Parlia-

[7] VII. Com. J., 496, 511, 520.

ment underwent is incalculable. Victimized by Cromwell's irresolution, harassed by his selfish shifts, they strove and suffered, submissive, not to him, but to the terror of the sword. Thus driven, Parliament resisted obstruction; worked line by line through the Petition; sat early and late, day by day, from February to the end of March. Committees on the details of the new Constitution met every morning at seven, and the House itself at eight o'clock. And their efforts, stimulated by fear, were carried on in fear. To the end they never knew whether Cromwell was on their side, the side of peaceful government, or on the side of the Army and of government by the Sword.

To keep his adherents at bay seemed the Protector's sole object. He assured them that he loved the Petition and Advice, and "all the things in it;" and yet to make waste paper of the Petition seemed his chief endeavour. When they had tendered the Crown again to him, on the 8th April, all that Parliament received in return, day after day, were messages that H.H. could not, or would not give any answer; replies "which did strongly build up the faith of the contrariants," the sword-wearers. On the 20th April, the envoys between Whitehall and Westminster seemed to touch ground. But they "returned as unsatisfied as before," having received from Cromwell nothing but a "dark, promiscuous" speech. With even graver dissatisfaction, after the visit of next day,

did the envoys pace back to Westminster. Cromwell had inflicted on them not only a speech " as
dark almost as before," but also a long schedule of
his " exceptions " to the beloved Petition.[8]

The difficulties raised by Pack's Paper were
nought compared to the perplexities created by
Cromwell's " paper of exceptions." He thereby
unsettled the being of Parliament, disturbed the
footing of religion, and demanded large annual
supplies of money. To these demands, touching
every Englishman in body, soul, and pocket,
Cromwell added another, to Parliament, most
grievous. Before he felt himself " set free " to
give that final answer, so urgently needed, the
Protector compelled Parliament to share with him
the odium and the responsibility of all those Acts
and Ordinances which he had made " without the
consent of the people assembled in Parliament."
He insisted that Parliament should show that they
did " approve well of what hath been done by Us,"
in that levy of taxation which was " not according
to the fundamental laws of the Nation." [9]

As Thurloe truly remarked, Cromwell required
" too much to have been expected of a Parliament."
Still he was obeyed. Parliament " confirmed "
more than a hundred Acts and Ordinances, " naught
at all " being read " but the titles ; " though the
House was warned that such law-making " in a

---

[8] Burton, II. 7.   Hist. MSS. Com., 5th Report, 163.
[9] Carlyle, IV. 283, 4.   An. 1656, chap. X.   Scobell's Acts, 389.

lump " would create " an earthquake in the Nation,"
and " draw such a scandal upon us, as never was." [9]
Over this task the House struggled and wrangled
from April 24th to April 30th, meeting at eight, and
sitting on till as late as nine o'clock, occasionally
dinnerless. The strain knocked the House out of all
form, and told woefully on the Speaker. A division
produced " a tie;" and he was required to give the
casting vote. He rose up, "and said, I am a Yea,—a
No,—I should say. This caused an alternate laughter
all the House over; and some said the Speaker was
gone." " Much heat " arose out of the luckless slip
from the Chair. The Speaker, having cried " Yea,"
was allowed to explain " that his meaning was, that
he was No." Another member therefore claimed,
" that he also was mistaken in giving his vote,"
and proposed to reverse the Speaker's process, and
to claim that, although he had " gone out " with
the ayes, he should be reckoned among the noes. [10]

This point of practice " bred a great debate."
In the end it was determined, that while to their
weary Speaker some latitude might be permitted,
it should not be further extended; and the House
agreed that, while " it was certain that the other
gentleman could not recall his vote, you may recall
yours." And then, as oft happens when the genius

VII. Com. J., 523-29. Burton, II. 39—85; IV. 195, 316.
Thurloe, VI. 261.

[10] Burton, II. 70, 73, 94, 101. Hist. MSS. Com., 5th Report,
164. The following point of practice, fortunately for the occupants
of the Table of the House, is not now in force :—" 29th May, 1657.

of mischief is in the air, one blunder preludes another. The Speaker again became "gone."[10] He blundered when putting a Question to the House for its decision. He used the wrong form of words; and when the mistake was challenged, he "was at a loss to explain his meaning." The House fell into another "great confusion," which bred "great debate," and propagated yet more confusion.

After these annoying incidents, the exhausted House returned to the swallowing process, and by a rapid digestion converted into statutes all the "several Acts, Ordinances, and Orders relating to the Customs and Excise." That last bolus was a bitter mouthful. "Grievous to the Nation" were those Ordinances; hearty was the hatred of the City merchants, who "stormed highly," enraged by "the destruction of trade," caused by Cromwell's heavy exactions.

At length, after the House had sat through Thursday, 30th April, from eight o'clock in the morning to eight o'clock at night, no dinner interval allowed, the Committee which had so often "formerly attended the Lord Protector," were instructed to desire from His Highness a "positive resolution, and answer to the humble Petition and Advice."

No "positive answer," no answer at all, was forthcoming, when, next day, Friday, 1st May,

---

Mr. Bamfield observed the Speaker speaking to the Clerk, and moved that it was usual with him to do so, while men were the Committee stood before Cromwell, and for the third time offered him the Crown. "He spoke low," and asked them to call again.[10]

No "Ironside," inured to the hip and thigh business, showed more tenacity of purpose than did the disconsolate group of about eighty men, who stood up in Parliament for Cromwell and the Crown, from January to May, 1657. They did not bind any one with "links of iron:" they were themselves bound down to a hopeless task. No soldier ever fought under circumstances more discouraging, or under a more discouraging commander; they strove for a man who was deservedly contemned. The deep drop in their majority, after the first refusal of the Crown, showed that Cromwell's backers despised him.

Another proof of the Protector's low estate, lay in Parliament's contemptuous treatment of Venner's Fifth Monarchy Plot. Though carefully watched by Thurloe, that design in itself was genuine enough. Whilst Parliament was sitting, those men, zealous for the best "old Cause," had prepared a sudden rising. They were seized when ready to strike. They would have given London an effectual "rouse up." Thurloe might justly have anticipated, when he told his story of alarm to the House,

speaking, but it was against the Orders of the House. Mr. Speaker laboured to excuse himself, but could not come off very well. He said, 'I only spoke to be informed about the order of your proceedings.'" Burton, II. 149.

on Saturday, 11th April, an enthusiasm vivid as
the excitement that Sindercombe's " firework " had
kindled. But the Fifth Monarchy sensation would
not work. The House only directed that the affair
should be considered on Monday. Then, though
the " courtiers " reminded Parliament that to disregard that " matter of great consequence, would
not sound well abroad," the affair was stifled by
postponements from Wednesday to Saturday, then
on to Tuesday, and then utterly. And if the first
refusal of the Crown " caused great consternation
in Parliament," the second refusal reduced Cromwell's supporters to despair. The " country gentlemen voters said they were trepanned," and " would
fain be gone into the country." [11]

The gagged newspapers stifled public opinion.
What England felt during the " paroxysm of state,"
that lasted from January to May, can only be
surmised. Parliament's dwindling confidence in
the Protector must have been shared by his
subjects. " The countrymen exclaimed " against
their representatives. " The Presbyterians, encouraged by the feud between Cromwell and his
soldiers, were in hopes that my Lord will use his
interest in their interest." The Cavaliers laughed
" to see us setting up the things we have pulled
down ;" and the Protector is described as sneering at

[11] Burton, II. 3, 6. VII. Com. J., 522. Hist. MSS. Com., 5th
Report, 163. Thurloe, VI. 281. Cal. Clarendon MSS., III. 288.
Cal. State Papers, 1656-57, 328.

everybody, and saying, " O homines ad servitutem nati." [12]

. That picture of Cromwell was drawn more for effect than accuracy. He was in no sneering mood; of all his subjects, he was the most utter subject. Though standing aloft in the forefront of the State, apparently his own master, he was a captive to irresolution, bound down by bands which he could not snap. Uncertainty, irresolution, is to any man misery enough; to the Protector, to the great Commander, it was absolute torment. Protracted anxiety also was his portion, from January to June, 1657. Every day of suspense pulled tighter the tension of affairs; every day his footing became more ticklish. Parliament, by the Resolution forbidding taxation under the Protector's Ordinance, checkmated him completely. As King Charles was bound down by the perpetual Parliament Act, so Cromwell was bound down by that Resolution. His hands could no longer dive into the pockets of his subjects; by a parliamentary vote alone could he get supplies. Parliament therefore was essential to his existence. But the strain, if continued much longer, would break down Parliament; and that catastrophe was placed at the mercy of accident. The overpowering suspicion which dominated us during the Protectorate, had paralyzed the procedure of Parliament. Distrusting

[12] Baynes Add. MSS., 21,434, fo. 224. Clarendon State Papers, III. 335. Cal. Clarendon MSS., III. 288.

themselves, they resolved that, until the whole of the Petition and Advice was agreed to, " no vote that shall be passed " thereon, " shall be binding to this House, until all the particulars thereof shall be resolved."   Thus an enemy by a snatch division, or a friend by a blunder, might make void all their decisions.[13]

Mere exhaustion might produce that result.   Even feeble obstruction would exhaust the weary assembly.   Thus the slightest parliamentary upset would strip Cromwell of governmental power.   He had done all he could, by the Nayler Message, to discredit Parliament and the Instrument of Government, which had created both Parliament and the Protectorate.   No wonder is it that during the crisis of May, his adherents "trembled at the apprehension of his becoming bankrupt."[14]

Nor were Cromwell's military opponents so weak as they seemed.   The Army Officers represented the most corporate body in England.   Parliament might represent England, and England might be passionate for monarchy ; but a Parliament was a very incorporate body ; they might come and go, whereas the Army Officers would hang on for ever.

The Major-Generals had another advantage.   The Protector would be obliged, sooner or later, to act.   Sooner or later he must give his opponents their opportunity.   If he played the waiting game, they

[13] VII. Com. J., 497.
[14] Clarendon State Papers, III. 339.

could securely " stand on the stay," and wait also. And he did play the waiting game. He clung to his position, to the hold he had got above them. They had only to go on from below, shake, shake, shake, and their creature must come down. He clung on ; they continued to shake ; they gave a pull and dropped him into such a hole, that he could neither accept nor refuse the Crown, "save with extreme disadvantage." [15]

That was how the Major-Generals acted. Taking rumour as our guide, early in February, Lambert anticipated the coming kingship by "heightening" army discontent. The London soldiery became "violently displeased." A "violent rising" was expected. Then the Army quieted down : nothing is heard of them, until Pack's Paper was accepted by Parliament. That step produced the Address of the "One Hundred Officers," and Cromwell's invaluable reply.* His frank declaration that he had throughout the Protectorate acted with and for the Army, seems to have served its purpose. Thurloe heard that the Protector's "plain, yet loving and kind expressions," were "very much to their satisfaction ;" and certainly during the first half of March Thurloe was able to report that "the seeming trouble that was in the Army, has vanished." [15]

---

[15] Clarendon State Papers, III. 333, 334, 339. Thurloe, VI. 93, 106. Cal. State Papers, 1656-57, 300, 324.

* See p. 6.

The vote of Wednesday, the 25th of March, which invested Cromwell with royalty, disturbed the calm. Triumphant as was the call of Parliament to the throne, Cromwell was " in a dilemma." [15] Mutiny came again to the front. On the following Friday, Lambert and seventeen malcontent officers met, consulted, and resolved "to bring up six regiments of Horse, to oppose the prevailing party, to assist the Instrument of Government, and to establish the Major-Generals in their just power." Before action, however, Lambert and his friends resolved " to seek the Lord : " [15] and they did no more. During April, the Army Officers remained dormant. Lambert withdrew from active opposition ; he became " daily more contemptible ; " [15] and at the end of the month, Henry Cromwell is informed that " your father's troubled thoughts seem to be over."

Thus the Major-Generals, by their advances into the open, and by their withdrawal, kept Cromwell quivering on the tenter-hooks. The last act of the drama, " Oliver Cromwell a King, or not a King," shows effectively how they befooled him. On the 1st of May he had once more the Crown within grasp. Parliament, having agreed to his demands, had again insisted that he would be pleased to ascend the throne. But what a hopeless business it was! When they offered him the Crown for the second time, on the 8th of April, he sent them back with that " paper of exceptions." Had there been a scrap of backbone about him, he would not have haggled over his indemnity, or a money supply. The title " King " would have absolved him and stocked his treasury with cash. As might therefore be expected, on Friday, the 1st of May, paralysis was still upon him. The parliamentary envoys stood before him, and he stood before them, not like a King, but like an awkward recruit. Unable to step out, not knowing how to march, Cromwell " marked time," and looked like a fool.

And, " as he was," Cromwell remained from that Friday till Wednesday. Then, having stood like a fool, he " spake like a fool." Boldness, boldness, sudden unexpected action was his sole chance of success ; but he acted neither with " celerity " nor with " secrecy." " If resolved to do anything, don't say anything," is a safe rule; Cromwell, on the contrary, sought to stiffen his trembling will by talk. For a moment,—" bold in his own humour,"—" H.H. was pleased to declare to several of the House, that he was resolved to accept " the Crown.[16] He sent word to Parliament by the Committee, which had so often appeared before him, that he would meet the House on the morrow, in the Painted Chamber, the chamber of the House of Lords. There it was that he opened and dissolved Parliaments " in Kingly fashion." To meet Parliament there was to ascend the throne.

Surely Cromwell might have known " what shall be on the morrow." Yet when the morrow became to-day,—Thursday morning—he again assured " several of the House," that his determination to be King was fixed.[16] Those words were hardly uttered, when suddenly the Protector's " countenance changed, his knees smote one against the other." He " cried aloud to bring in " again before him the men from Westminster. He sent hurriedly " for as many of the Committee as could be gotten together, and desired that the meeting of the House might be put off, and that the Committee would meet him again that afternoon at five o'clock;" and when they came, he was " trembling " with " disorder."[16]

Shake, shake, had been renewed. Humpty Dumpty had got his great fall. During the morning of that Thursday, whilst the Members of Parliament were gathering themselves together, crossing New Palace Yard, or passing through the Hall up into the House, that they might at last present themselves before their King, Cromwell received a letter from the " three great ones," Lambert, Fleetwood, and Disbrowe, warning him that upon his acceptance of that title, they must " withdraw from all public employment," and with them " several other Officers of quality, that had been engaged all along in this war." They struck " just in the very nick of time." Hence Cromwell's hurried recall of the Committee, and " his disorder " when he met them. Hence his demand that the

[16] Thurloe, VI. 281. VII. Com. J., 531.

meeting of the House be put off, and his announce-ment that he would receive them on the morrow, not in the Painted Chamber but in the Banqueting House.[17]

Even then the Major-Generals had not quite done with Cromwell. They sent Colonel Mason down to Parliament, with a petition from some of the Officers in London, desiring Parliament " to continue steady to the Good old Cause," and not "to bring the Nation under servitude." The petition met Parlia-ment on the move to Whitehall to meet their Sovereign. Kingship did not rest with them, but with Cromwell. The sole purpose therefore of the petition was to advertise to the world why, when they stood before Cromwell, Parliament would hear him reject the Crown : to make notorious the power of the Army. That this was its object Cromwell himself bears witness. Else why did he blame Fleetwood for the presentation of the petition, because he had known that it was Cromwell's " resolution not to accept the Crown, without the consent of the Army ? " [18]

Cromwell spoke truth. In his quest after the Crown he had followed his own maxim, " No one rises so high, as he who knows not whither he is going." He had started for the throne with no outlook, save some vague hope that he might bribe or divide the Army officers into submission. Cromwell's maxim

[17] Thurloe, VI. 281. Clarendon State Papers, III. 342.
[18] Thurloe, VI. 281. Ludlow, 249.

proved an erring guide. The Major-Generals were justly angered. Towards him they had done their duty; he had meanly turned against them. They had supported his Protectorship. He had tossed them over. Compromise between such opponents was impossible; the nearest approach thereto lies in an absurd report, that Cromwell secretly undertook, if the offer of the Crown was permitted, that " he would content himself with the honour, and refuse it." [19]

That Cromwell was all those months an opportunist, without an opportunity; that he was treading a " darksome way," with no holdfast, no clue, exceeded the belief of those who watched him. One of his agents abroad could " hardly believe that the Protector would have set this business," the Kingship business, " on foot underhand, unless he were sure of the Army, for that is the only thing that can uphold him." [19] Again, when Cromwell showed his hand, and the Major-Generals were overthrown, it was supposed that " there would now be no great opposition why the Protector may not be King." [19] And then, lastly, when that notion was extinguished by the attitude of the Army, he was credited with courage not his own, and with intending to mass round London regiments " that he dares confide in," and to make safe " the dissenters." [20] Such a thought was far from him. The spectacle Cromwell presented when he thrust

[19] Cal. State Papers, 1656-57, 271, 337. Thurloe, VI. 101.

himself upon the company of Disbrowe and Fleetwood, took his dinner with them, attempted to cajole them, and then huffed off, railing at them as "a couple of scrupulous fellows," affords a just measure of the man.[20]

During March, April, May, Cromwell "guided himself from day to day by the immediate occasion." The " northern plebeians wondered at the great silence, and hushness of things above," and "every man without doors wondered at the delay;" they felt that " this conjuncture must soon come to a period, lest it beget an unsettlement." [20] For five months England had been kept on the rack. To the end Cromwell was hesitation itself. His mind was known to his Secretary, and yet, when " Parliament had complied with H.H.'s very hard task, whether, when all is done, H.H. will accept of Kingship," Thurloe "was unable to say." [21] It became obvious that Cromwell was good for nothing. His partial friends confessed that " he was an ill judge of opportunity." His candid friends condemned him as " a wild, and wanton lavisher of his good fortune;" whilst his enemies, " the Major-Generals and Officers of the Army, laughed at his hopes, and despised him for his fears, the effect of a feeble, inconstant mind." [21]

[20] Baynes Add. MSS., 21, 424, fo. 233. Cal. State Papers, 1656-57, 271, 351, 352. Ludlow, 248.

[21] Thurloe, VI. 157, 248, 261. Clarendon State Papers, III. 339.

Nor in his frailties did Cromwell find safety. His refusal of the Crown placed him at the mercy of Parliament. In revenge they could wreck the Government. They had provided for the occasion, by a provision, that if the Protector did not " consent to all the matters and things in the Petition and Advice," then nothing in the same was of " force and binding." To that " thing," the Crown, he did not consent. Parliament therefore was not bound to " The Petition and Advice." [22] That was the bargain. Parliament, if they chose, might throw back the Constitution into the anarchical melting pot ; and if they did, Cromwell, of the two contracting parties, was by far the worst off. He could not dissolve Parliament, for by that Resolution prohibiting unparliamentary taxation, supply was in their hands. The mere collapse of the " Petition and Advice " would bring down chaos again. For by their practical acceptance of the " Petition and Advice," both Parliament and the Protector had virtually abrogated " The Instrument of Government." No Constitution was therefore in existence, neither " Petition " nor " Instrument." Power of extra-legal taxation was gone. If, then, the " Petition and Advice " was wrecked, as Henry Cromwell truly observed to Thurloe, " His Highness with his friends and relations, as also these Nations, will be left more naked and destitute than if the proposal had never been made." [22]

[22] VII. Com. J., 513.　Thurloe, VI. 183.

" Naked and destitute " Cromwell was left by his last rejection of the Crown. His most disinterested adherents, " the country gentlemen," the men who hoped that he would stand between the Nation and the Army, were " under strong discouragement and discontent." Their votes had with difficulty carried Kingship; if they turned restive, he would cease to be Protector. Thurloe's hope for safety was that disgust would make them " begone." [23] That expectation was fulfilled. A feeling seems to have arisen, that if Cromwell was not worth support, he was not worth opposition. The courtiers and salary-men were left to fight the battle of the Protectorate ; and the Resolution that " Your Highness will be pleased, by and under the Name and Style of Protector of the Commonwealth of England, Scotland, and Ireland, to hold and exercise the office of Chief Magistrate of these Nations," was, on the 22nd of May, carried by a neck-and-neck division of 53 yeas, against 50 noes. [23]

A majority of three was a slender thread whereon to hang the dynasty that Cromwell coveted. The votes of 53 members, out of a constituent body of 460, formed but a sandy foundation for our new Magna Charta, the " Petition and Advice." Even Thurloe was in despair. The day after Cromwell had assented to the Petition, his Secretary "did perceive" that the new Constitution " goes

[23] Thurloe, VI. 281, 811. VII. Com. J., 537. Burton, II. 136.

down, with the generality of those who opposed
Kingship, very difficultly, and is much against the
haire. The Lord can bring light out of this darkness, and heal the great divisions which are amongst
us." [23]

In a measure Thurloe's prayer was answered.
Despite strong obstruction,—disputes over the chair
of Committees of Supply,—adjournments of the
House,—through " great and tugging debates,"
waged till " a candle was brought in," even on the
eve of the longest day,—a Supply Bill was passed
assessing England at the rate of £60,000 by the
month ; and on the 24th June, Parliament considered
the inauguration of the new Protectorate. [24]

Cromwell was a capable master of the ceremonies : he made ready for the occasion beforehand.
Parliament resolved " that Westminster Hall be
prepared, suitable to the Solemnity of the Inauguration," with, " at the higher end thereof, a Chair of
State, a Canopy, Table, &c. ;" but as the event took
place within forty-eight hours after Parliament had
passed that motion, neither the " rich cloth of
state," the " chair of state," the " seats raised one
above another, and decently covered for the Members of Parliament," nor " the large bible richly
gilt and bossed," nor " the sceptre being of massy
gold," were of their ordering.

A brief contention, which took place in Parliament over the Inauguration ceremony, is most

[24] Burton, IV. 254—270.

significant. It was proposed "to have it done in the Painted Chamber," a room of no large size and hid from public view; or even in the Chancery Court, a narrow pen boarded off in the south-west corner of Westminster Hall, about 100 feet long and seventy feet wide: a place of ill omen, as the House was reminded, " because there was lately another Government settled there," that is to say, Cromwell's previous Inauguration as Protector under " the Instrument of Government," on Friday, 16th December, 1653.

That the inauguration should be " done not expensively," in a hugger-mugger, unnational, unregal fashion, was sought by the Military Party. A Resolution, " that the Speaker shall show His Highness to the people, and make Acclamation," was negatived. The Protector's decoration with the sword, " the emblem of justice," was opposed. And a comic situation, an opportunity for open derision was obtained by the handsome proposal that, to do him honour, a royal robe of purple velvet should be provided for the Protector. A fancied slip of the tongue converted that royal robe into a cloak for maliciousness. Vainly did the advocate of purple velvet declare, that he had spoken " as plain as he could, a Robe ;"—"some understood it a Rope ; and it caused " altum risum." [25] They laugh who win ; yet that roar of unseemly laughter must not drown the fact that, in appearance, Cromwell had

[25] Burton, II. 302—309.

won somewhat by the new Constitution, by the Royal Protectorship, as it was termed, established under "The Petition and Advice."

Cromwell was now our "Chief Magistrate," nominated, not by a junto of officers, but by Parliament. He was invested with sovereign power. He could summon that "Other House" of Parliament. He could name his successor. And as regards the past he might feel comfortable. For doings such as the imprisonment of men without trial, and illegal taxation, he could not be called to account.

Nor was immediate trouble from the Military Party to be expected. General Lambert was quietly cashiered. The two other "great ones," Disbrowe and Fleetwood, cottoned up to Cromwell. Of the Army, Thurloe wrote fairly cheerfully. Although endeavours were spoken of "to remand H.H. to his former position," the "most suspected officers showed satisfaction rather than otherwise," or were "silent, seeing the stream run so hard" against them. Certainly no "considerable army revolt" was feared.[26]

Apparently also the Nation was satisfied. Neither Cavalier nor Republican made the slightest stir. Yet, despite these seeming advantages and these favourable symptoms, though Cromwell had attained the Royal Protectorship, he had lost everything. He had worsened his position into certain ruin. He

[26] Thurloe, VI. 412, 425. Clarendon State Papers, III. 349.

was still merely a Protector. That title came in with the sword, and with the sword it must remain. But of the sword Cromwell had lost hold; he was no longer Protector under the "Instrument" of the Military Party. He was only a Protector made by three votes in Parliament. If the "Petition and Advice" would not work, down he must go.

The odds were that the "Petition and Advice" would not work. Parliament had no sword; and he had no authority. The right to command obedience, because he was afraid of nobody, because he would be obeyed, he could not claim. There he stood before the world "naked and destitute," the drudge of the Army. His tricks, evasions, his dodges to obtain delay, his abject submission in the end, showed that he was afraid. A trickster may command obedience, but not a coward. Cromwell was utterly discredited: even he seems to have felt that he was discredited. During February, 1657, a boast was attributed to him, that if Parliament failed, the people would crown him King. In June he showed that he feared the people. It was by his direction that Parliament was adjourned till the 20th January, 1658. He dared not risk a General Election.

Timidity again completes Cromwell's downfall. By the adjournment of his Long Parliament he gave the vantage to his opponents. They had made themselves felt during the protracted parliamentary

battle.   They had " given check to the major part of
the House, had affrighted his favourites, and startled
even the Protector himself." [27]   Henry Cromwell
had anticipated the result of keeping Parliament
in being.   He foretold that " the opposite party,
besides the opinion of victory, have had by their
frequent debates and other proceedings, such opportunity to know persons and things, that they,
remaining still in their full power, will be much more
exalted than before." [27]

That exaltation of " the opposite party " was
established ; to them was given not merely " the
opinion of victory," but victory itself, when the
Military Party forced Cromwell away from the
Crown, and when he adjourned the Parliament.
King Oliver, a House of Lords, and a House of
Commons were possible ; but not a crownless Protector, and his " Other House," faced by a mutinous
House of Commons containing his enemies " in full
power."   In that Royal Protectorship " the man
whose hands were mighty had found nothing."

[27] Clarendon State Papers, III. 349.   Thurloe, VI. 183.

CHAPTER XII.

"The happy Inauguration " of the Lord Protector in Westminster Hall on Friday, 26th June, 1657, augured to the Court celebrants most happy issues. " His Highness " stood " adorned in Princely State according to his Merit and Dignity," under a " rich Cloth of State," clad in the Purple Robe, with a Sceptre of massy gold in his hand, the sword of Justice girt about him, looking upward " to the Throne of the Most High ;" and this " comely and glorious sight " foretold a long reign " to his own comfort, and to the comfort of the People of the three Nations."

That " high and happy solemnity " was to less courtly eyes a sign of coming tribulation. The second investiture of Cromwell, as Protector, promised no escape from the government of the Sword, no return of the Law. Failure, not even compromise, was stamped upon that ceremony. To account for " the occasion of this Convention " in Westminster Hall, the Speaker, with felicitous audacity, converted the three votes that conferred on Cromwell the title of Lord Protector, into " the full and unanimous consent of the people of these Three Nations assembled in Parliament," and he absolutely congratulated the Protector on having "no new name" as Chief Magistrate, "but a new date added to the old Name ; the 16th December is now changed to the 26th of June." But with all his dexterity, the Speaker could not juggle away distressing associations from that name, which "came in with the sword," and which was, whether new or old, a standing witness to the domination of the Major-Generals. Nor to them was that "comely sight" wholly satisfactory. The "oblation" of the massy gold sceptre, and the purple velvet robe "lined with ermine, as antiently used at the solemn investiture of Princes," reminded the Military Party that Cromwell had crawled up nearer to the Crown than they liked ; that he was almost a King. Still that "almost" was everything. No one knew better than Cromwell the all to nothing difference between a Protector and a King, and the true significance of the ceremony of the 26th June, 1657.

Even the aspect of the "great Theatre" of that "great Convention," Westminster Hall, showed to "the large chore of people," the spectators, what a hollow peace it was between the Army and the Protector. Of Cromwell's associates in arms, of the men who, in December, 1653, made him Chief Magistrate, Fleetwood alone was present, the feeblest of the "three great ones," the most meagre representative of the Army. Thus interpreted, that august ceremonial was a " pageantry of fear," of future mischief,—a proof that Cromwell and the Military Party were at war. Could it be otherwise ? He had taken away their Co-Protectorships ; he could name his successor. Why should the Major-Generals pretend to do Cromwell honour by their attendance in the Hall ? They could shake him down again when they chose ; they had only to bide till Parliament returned to Westminster. A clause in the Bill, which adjourned Parliament from June to January, made his fall certain ; and to that Bill Cromwell had given his assent. The Petition and Advice was waste paper ; and the Inauguration of the 26th June was a farce.

What he had done, how he had been cozened, Cromwell was, on that " high and happy day," quite unaware. The bliss of ignorance was his, when " the Trumpets sounded, and the People made several great Acclamations, with loud shouts, ' God save the Lord Protector,' " and he, passing under " the Great Gate," entered into his coach, " being in his Robes," and went up King Street attended by " the Horse of Honour with rich Caparisons," by H.H.'s Life Guards and other Guards, by the Lord Mayor, the Judges, the Officers of State " all waiting on H.H. in their Coaches to Whitehall."

Cromwell was unconscious regarding the future ; and of the past most likely he was heedless, though he might have noticed, on the way to Whitehall, that he was passing along the route taken by a former actor in a "great Convention" held in Westminster Hall, to him, as to Cromwell, his last appearance there in high solemnity. King Street, on that previous occasion, was also lined on both sides with soldiers, whilst "with a guard of Halberdiers the King was returned to Whitehall in a close chair." The "soldiers were silent as His Majesty passed; but the shop stalls and windows were full of people, many of whom shed tears, and some, with audible voices, prayed for the King." Had Cromwell known, in that his day of triumph, the things that would ere long befall him, he might have envied the man who was welcomed by tears and prayers, and for whom was awaiting on a scaffold prompt repose.

Assuming again the style of the Court journalist, "On the 1st July, Cromwell was proclaimed Lord Protector, in London, at the usual Places, and with as much magnificence as if he had actually accepted the Crown; and the same was afterwards done at Edinburgh and Dublin, and throughout the Three Nations."

" Being thus possessed of the Sovereign Power, and having insured his own greatness, he thought it necessary to distinguish his Family by Titles of Preferment. Accordingly in pursuance of this Plan, his eldest son Richard was, upon his own Resignation of the office of Chancellor of the University of Oxford, installed therein, with great Solemnity: he was sworn a Privy Counsellor, made a Colonel in the Army, and not long after, the first Lord of the Other House. His younger son Henry was appointed the Lord Deputy of Ireland.

" On the 11th November, the Protector's youngest daughter, Frances, was married to the Hon. Robert Rich, Son of Lord Rich, and Grandson of the Earl of Warwick; and on the 19th of November, the Protector's third daughter, Mary, was married to the Lord Fauconberg at Hampton Court." [1]

The Autumn of 1657 was spent by Cromwell in ostensible comfort. The Army gave no external symptom of discontent. The junto of " the three great ones " had collapsed. Lambert was reduced from the post of demy-Protector to nonentity.

Cromwell seems to have enjoyed high spirits. He indulged in those unseemly antics which must have fascinated his new son-in-law. The Puritan was fast peeling off from the Protector. He transmogrified his household ways. Dancers drove out the preachers who had hitherto held possession of Whitehall.[2] He raised his income from 64,000*l.* to 100,000*l.*, a year. He intimated the intention of clothing himself in royal splendour. He contracted debts to an imperial amount ; and rumour attributed to him a determination to obtain the Crown.[2]

Such an all-round difference exists between

---

[1] Old Parl. Hist., XXI. 152—162.
[2] Guizot, II. 626.

Charles I. and Cromwell in the man, in manners, and environment, that likeness in their lot seems impossible.   Yet thus far they experienced a kindred touch of adversity.   Had Charles been able to rid himself of the Long Parliament, he might have held his own.   That opportunity was denied him.   By statute, that Parliament was made perpetual. Just in the same way, "The Act for the Adjournment of this present Parliament from the 26th of June, 1657, unto the 20th of January next ensuing," debarred Cromwell from dissolving the Parliament.   Had he been his own master, the ignominious fate that was awaiting him, might have been averted.   When Parliament reappeared, the Protector was "talked out."   That was his lot. His royal Protectorate, the New Constitution, his nominal supremacy, were all thrown down by utter jabber, by—the disgusting word must be used— by obstruction, brutal obstruction.

To bring about that fate, Cromwell had worked deliberately.   He provided ample materials for dispute, difficulty, annoyance, by the creation of the "Other House."   Create it how he might, still that assembly was not a House of Lords, nor an accredited recognized body of men ; it must be a mere "kickshaw."   Over the selection of those would-be Peers Cromwell shortened his fast-shortening days, and reduced his dwindling strength.   "The Lord be with him in" that task, is Thurloe's prayer for his distressed patron, for though he "hath the opinion, and deservedly, of knowing men better than any other man," still "H.H. will be tried in that particular now, to the purpose."[3]

At first sight Cromwell's conduct seems inexplicable. So obviously undesirable was the attempt, that he was credited with a resolve not to create the "Other House" until he had established Monarchy, and could, as King, summon genuine Houses of Lords and Commons.[3] That every way was his right course. He was not obliged to summon the "Other House" to meet on the 20th January, 1658. When he called his first Parliament under the Petition and Advice, then alone was the "Other House" a necessity: then alone would that experiment receive fair trial. The two Houses, the Upper and the Lower, would then stand upon the same bottom. A representative House, chosen as a Parliament, having acted as a Parliament, would certainly not cheerfully submit itself to a nominated House, its own creation. But the course of reason Cromwell could not follow. As before, so now, he was the drudge. In the creation of the "Other House," his submission to those taskmasters, to the Military Party, is distinctly visible. And their object is equally visible. They had been dismounted from their military magistracies: they were to be restored to power. That House was to

---

[3] Thurloe, VI. 609. Guizot, II. 626. Burton, IV., 28, 31, 33, 35, 77. Clarendon State Papers, III. 441.

be their citadel whence they could rule the land and control the Protector. Accordingly they appeared in force amidst that company of sham Peers. Cromwell summoned to the "Other House" Generals and Major-Generals Monk, Fleetwood, Skippon, Barkstead, Disbrowe, Whalley, and Colonels Clarke, Cooper, Ingoldsby, Jones, Pride, Berry, Goffe, and Hewson. Amongst them they held " twenty-two or twenty-three regiments, divers garrisons, and the Tower of London." [3]

The men of Cromwell's day recognized that the " Other House," so manned, was, in effect, government by the Sword : that " the House consists of Major-Generals : " that we were again " brought under the Major-Generals." Not less notorious was it that this was their doing. It was observed that " those persons that now sit " in the Other House, " indeed did choose themselves. They chose the Single Person, and he chose them." [3] And they chose themselves effectively. " My Lord Disbrowe offered " H.H. Richard, during the last convulsions of the dying Revolution, March, 1659, " to dissolve this House of Commons, and to govern by the Other House." [3] Was that suggestion drawn from the mind of Oliver ? Disbrowe was somewhat of a dullard.

How salutary is it to watch the contortions, the "wheel-about and turn-about " pranks of a revolutionist ! The first act of Cromwell, " the drudge," was the expulsion of the Long Parliament ; the last, the installation of a sham House of Lords. That task was certainly not for his benefit. The " Other House " could give him no help. His most pressing want was money. A House of Lords could grant him no supply. He could hardly have supposed that men whom he had degraded from being a Parliament into a Lower House, whom he had tried to the uttermost, and who had tried him, and found him wanting, weak, treacherous, would join with that nonentity, his Upper House, to offer him Kingship for the fourth time.

To what purpose, then, did Cromwell call into being that " Other House " ? Was it to endow a select company of men of worth with that mild form of constitutional authority that springs from lordship in " another place " ? A seat in that Upper House was not worth much. The lordship it conferred was a mockery ; it was speedily blown out of sight by the bad breath of a few creatures in the Lower House. Then, after all, the sole governing faculty possessed by Cromwell's " Other House " lay in those ennobled soldiers, in their " twenty-two or twenty-three regiments, divers garrisons, and the Tower of London."

Let us part in charity with Cromwell. It could only have been under compulsion that he sought to cheat his subjects, to convert the new royal Protectorate into government by the Sword, by endowing the Military Party with high position in the State. That it was Cromwell's object thus to bring England again under the Major-Generals, was seen and recognized; and that clause which has been mentioned in the Adjournment of Parliament Act had provided an effectual remedy against such a manœuvre.

In the game of craft his adversaries proved the better men. That statute in itself might have aroused Cromwell's suspicion. It was a surprise, pushed through on the last day of the Session, within an hour or so of its presentation for his acceptance. The Act was quite unnecessary. If Charles the First's Long Parliament adjourned itself from the 9th of September till the 20th of October, 1641,[4] why could not Cromwell's Long Parliament follow that precedent? Unnecessary legislation is mischievous legislation; it was specially so to Cromwell. It gave his enemies their opportunity. They slipped into the Bill a clause whereby "all such persons as have been duly returned to serve in this present Parliament, being qualified according to the qualifications in the humble Petition and Advice, and not disabled thereby, are required to give their attendance," when Parliament reassembled in January.[4]

Cromwell had assented, in "The Petition and Advice," to a provision which enacted that the ancient and undoubted Privileges of Parliament should be observed, and that "those persons who are legally chosen by the free election of the people

[4] II. Com. J., 289; VII. Com. J., 575-6.

to serve in Parliament, may not be excluded from sitting in Parliament, but by the judgment and consent of that House whereof they are members." That provision did not touch Cromwell or the Parliament then sitting : it could not admit the excluded Members. Not only was that provision wholly prospective, contingent upon a general election under the " Petition and Advice; " but it was in effect wholly inapplicable. It could no more restore to Parliament the disabled Members, than a plaster can create a missing leg. Those Members were dismembered. They had lost their seats; they were dead to Parliament. Difficult as it is to restore life or limb to such an unpromising attempt, the political situation added another difficulty. It was the " Instrument of Government " which had dropped the extinguisher over the excluded ones. They had been adjudged according to the qualification it prescribed, and had been found wanting. To recall them, to rehabilitate their election, that disqualification must be cancelled by legislation. But then thereby " The Instrument of Government " would be stultified; the illegality of its provisions would be emphasised. Such an enactment would offend the Major-Generals and H.H.'s Council. To undisable those Members by nullifying " The Instrument " was therefore an impossibility. That is why the clause in the Adjournment Act endowed them with the qualifications to a seat under the " Petition and Advice," although they had been elected long before that document was drawn or thought of.

This tricky device discloses singular ingenuity. The Radicals would gladly destroy " The Instrument." The Courtiers, if they followed their Patron's lead, would do the like. To the Major-Generals every particle of their handiwork "The Instrument" was precious. Thus seemingly their interests were respected. The one person whose interests were not considered was the Protector; and to keep him in ignorance every precaution was taken. Not only was the Adjournment Bill smuggled through with dexterous speed, but the clause was furtively inserted. To hurry forward the Bill, the Committee stage was negatived. To obtain the insertion of that clause, it was read and added to the Bill by the House at the second reading stage,—a monstrous proceeding, tactics truly revolutionary.

The same crafty wiliness is visible in the presentation of the Bill to the Protector. It was his practice to examine, most properly, Bills submitted to him for approval. On a previous occasion he postponed the presentation of a batch of Bills, because " he had read one of those Bills, and if he should rise at four o'clock in the morning, he could not read them in a whole day." [5] The promoters of the Adjournment Bill thwarted that precaution. The last day of the Session, when the Bill was shoved through, was also Cromwell's " high and happy "

[5] Burton, II. 180. VII. Com. J., 575.

Inauguration Day; the pomp and circumstance, the preparations, were enough to divert the attention of the most circumspect. The Bill was being shaped out whilst the Protector was getting ready. Its final engrossment was in hand when he was on the move to Westminster. Of the contents of the Bill he must have been absolutely ignorant.[5]

We learn from Henry Cromwell that, though his father's enemies "found him no fool," still that about this time he had been "cozened."[6] Certainly the Protector was cozened by the Adjournment Bill. He would have been indeed a fool, had he knowingly consented to any clause or provision which gave free admission to the whole batch of the excluded Members. Some of them were not his enemies. Some had slipped into their places in the House, and had voted in favour of Kingship; but among those who remained outside were his bitter opponents, men who hated him and his sham Commonwealth. The slightest adverse change in Parliament would be fatal to his Government. With that ticklesome concoction, the " Other House," in reach of their fingers, three or four malcontents could tickle the most rigid Protector out of his proprieties. And so it happened. Sir Arthur Haselrig, Mr. Scot, Mr. St. Nicholas, and about a dozen like-minded ones, entered the House, in pursuance of that clause; and in fourteen days they accomplished their object. No political avalanche swept Crom-

[6] Thurloe, VII. 72.

well away. A feeble trickle of talk washed from under his Chair its sandy foundations.

The meeting of Parliament, 20th January, 1658, was treated as a new Session. The Protector received the two Houses in the " Lords' House ;" addressed to them a brief and vague speech on civil and gospel liberty, on the 85th Psalm at some length ; and he then referred them to the Lord Commissioner Fiennes, who " would discourse " to them "a little more particularly." Fiennes discoursed to Parliament with large particularity. He likened England to the Patriarch Jacob; the Protector and the Parliament to Joseph, Manasseh, Leah, and Rachel. The new Constitution, the royal Protectorate, Fiennes exalted into an " Eden." He exhorted the inhabiters of that constitutional Paradise to resist the " crafty Devices of the subtle and malicious Serpent," and warned them that " the wild Boars of the Forest " and " the little Foxes " longed to root up the Fences of our Garden, to " spoil the Vines." Uninterrupted allegory is hardly possible. Fiennes was forced to disclose the imminent risk that threatened the Cromwellian Paradise, and to show its weak side to the Boars and to the Foxes. They heard enough when told " that the supplies granted, have fallen short of the Commonwealth's necessities." Is it not easy to talk out supply ?

Parliamentary obstruction in action is nauseating : still more offensive is obstruction in description. Yet " the talk out " administered to Cromwell and his Royal Protectorate saved England from military tyranny, and must therefore be dealt with somehow.

Wednesday, 20th January. No sooner had the Speaker taken the Chair than the House felt the presence of its superior neighbour. Their clerk, Mr. Scobell, being by Act of Parliament " constituted Clerk of the Parliament for his life," had deserted them for the " Other House." A wrangle arose over his successor. Some claimed that the appointment of " our clerk " was " the undoubted right of this House." Others asserted that " our clerk " held his office by patent. At length, after much talk, the House accepted " one Mr. Smyth, who waited at the door." Black Rod then summoned them to appear before H.H. in " The House of Lords." The Speaker, when he repeated the message from the Chair, directed the Members to repair to " the Other House;" but his hearers made him " correct his mistake." The Boars and Foxes had not as yet appeared in force.[7]

Thursday, 21st January. " A great debate " arose about the " Clerk's Oath, which by the entry appeared to be calculated for a Commonwealth, viz., without a King or a House of Lords;" and the matter was referred to a Committee. The House, during the rest of the sitting, was exhorted " to begin to build the House of God." And consideration of the money supply, without which " we," i.e.,

[7] Burton, II. 316.

Thurloe and the Government, "cannot subsist, if Parliament relieves not," was thereby prevented.

Friday, 22nd January. To-day came the grand opportunity for the Boars and Foxes, the first communication from "another Place." The Serjeant reported to Mr. Speaker "that there were two Judges at the door, with a Message from the Lords." The challenge was immediately taken up. The Message was deemed " a trial whether they were a House of Lords." Five of the once excluded ones rose up in succession to insist that their House should "not receive any such Message from them, as the Lords." On went the debate : Cromwell's courtiers besought their associates "not to give their enemies the advantage," "not to stumble at the threshold." Still the debate went on. The House divided : the Judges waited : nor did they, in the end, bear back with them more than this intimation, "We will return an answer by Messengers of our own."[8]

Monday, 25th January, was marked by the first appearance in the House of the chief wild Boar. The coarse fibre of Cromwell's nature made him dull of apprehension, tactless. He absolutely supposed that he could propitiate Major Harrison, the Fifth Monarchist, by inviting him to a Whitehall court dinner, " with rich wine, and eight or ten dishes of meat, and as many gentlemen to attend on him."[9] And in like manner Cromwell tried to efface

[8] Burton, II. 330—346.
[9] Cal. Clarendon MSS., II. 397. Burton, II. 346. Carlyle, IV. 346.

Sir Arthur Haselrig, by a call to the " Other House."
Would Haselrig, one of the notorious " Five," to
whom Cromwell was both an apostate and an
upstart, accept a sham Peerage from an " ape " of
a king ? On the contrary, Haselrig walked into
the House of Commons, and demanded to take the
oath, as representative for the town of Leicester.
He was met, at first, by a formal, I dare not.
The House was aroused; the authorities gave way.
Sir Arthur repeated " the words of the oath very
valiantly and openly;" he passed on, and " sat
close by the Chair."

Cheered by his presence, Haselrig's brother
Boars resumed the pursuit after their " old servant," Mr. Scobell. He had " disowned " them; he
had treated them with contempt; and the House
was warned that " if the servant do so, what will
his masters "—that other House—" do ? " A summons to stand before the Protector interrupted
them, yet even the summons was obstructed. The
House was called upon to remain sitting, till they
had settled the proper title of " the Other House."
A dispute also arose, whether the Serjeant should
bear the mace before the Speaker, because " some of
the Other House " had asserted that when they and
their mace appeared on the scene, the Commons'
Serjeant and his mace were put out of court. The
summons at last took effect.

Both Houses proceeded to the Banqueting
House, and heard " a very long, plain, and serious

speech," Cromwell's last appeal to Parliament.   He demonstrated, "not as a rhetorician," that the Protestant Interest was "quite under foot, trodden down" all over the Continent; that the Dutch were selling arms to Charles Stuart, and lending ships for "the transport upon us" of 4000 foot and 1000 horse; that the Cavaliers were kindling insurrection; that the Army was "five or six months behind in pay," and that, "if we return again to folly,"—"it will be said of this poor Nation,—'it is all over with England.'"   The appeal was made in vain; to his enemies it was foolishness: they saw close at hand the " all over " with Cromwell.

Tuesday, 26th January, was spent by the House in discussing the detention of their Journals by that assertative gentleman, Mr. Scobell, and upon Bills for uniting Parishes in Huntingdon, and regulating the Yorkshire cloth-makers.

Exercises appropriate to " a Day of public Humiliation," " begun at ten o'clock, and held till half an hour past five," occupied the House throughout Wednesday, 27th January.

Thursday, 28th January.   The Speaker's report of the speech of Monday last placed the House and the Protector face to face; and immediately the House turned round, and presented to him its back. First it was proposed to send " Five " members, headed appropriately by Sir A. Haselrig, " to ask for H.H.'s leave for the printing of his Speech." When this mocking mark of respect had afforded sport sufficient, a motion was brought forward to take H.H.'s Speech "into speedy and serious consideration." It was considered,—but without the slightest consideration for H.H. The exclusion of Members of Parliament "by the long sword," afforded a ready means of attack on H.H.'s Council ; and H.H. himself was accused of imprisoning and sending beyond seas "men's persons," by his own Order, or by sentence from his High Court of Justice. The only attempt made by Cromwell's friends to stay the tide of insult and obstruction, was a fruitless effort to persuade their brother Members to consider " the title of the Other House." [10]

Friday and Saturday, 29th and 30th January. The battle over "the title" raged furiously. Obstruction was triumphant. Motions were made that the House should go into a Grand Committee, to adjourn, to rise that Members might " now go to dinner." A farcical vote of thanks was proposed to Sir A. Haselrig for vouchsafing "to sit among the Commons, notwithstanding his call to another place ;" another vote of thanks was suggested " for his long speech " to Mr. Scot, " the person who blew this disturbance into a flame." What was the matter for debate before the House, or whether there was anything at all, provoked lively dispute. It was contended, on the one hand, that as the motion in debate was, " what answer they will return to the Message, brought from the " Other

[10] Burton, II. 343—379.

House," the title and functions of the quasi-House of Lords " comes not now at all in question." It was argued on the other side, that to debate the matter was absurd, that the House was "beating the air," because the "Other House" had no right to send them any Message at all. It was also suggested that, as the House of Lords had been abolished by Act of Parliament, its restoration in any form was impossible.

The spectacle afforded by the House of Commons on the 30th January, 1658,—such a proof that " we did stand in as crazy a time as the people of England were in, at the close of the Barons' Wars,"—formed an appropriate celebration of the ninth anniversary of that day which had rid us of that " Tyrant, the last King " of England, and had replaced our " Liberty Restored." The Scotch nobleman's remark, which the Great Rebellion provoked at its outset, " If this be what you call liberty, God send me the old slavery again," was re-echoed by England at its close.

The debate was worthy the occasion, degraded, chaotic, ungovernable. The execution of Charles I. was extolled, as a just punishment " for his obstinacy and guilt;" but after the exclamation, " So let all the enemies of God perish!" came an admission that "some motion" was on foot "for a day of humiliation for this blood." The Long Parliament was extolled as "victorious;" it was decried as " corrupt." While Haselrig exulted that "We are yet a Commonwealth," the blessings and even the existence of a Commonwealth were disputed; and the House was told, "that we have sad experience of what treasure it cost us, when we were a Commonwealth." All that the House decided by debates that "routed in the very bowels of the whole Petition and Advice," and shook "Government by a single person," was a Resolution "That the first thing to be debated shall be the Appellation of the persons, to whom an Answer shall be made." [11]

Monday, 1st February, was ingeniously devoted to a Call of the House; and the business "appointed to be this day taken up," namely, "what we shall call the Other House," was adjourned until "to-morrow morning at 8 o'clock."

Tuesday, Wednesday, 2nd and 3rd February. On these two days the courtier party made some way. Haselrig felt the turn of the tide. On Saturday he had gloried that we are yet a Commonwealth, on Tuesday he exclaimed, "Well for Pym, Hampden, and Strode, my fellow-traitors, impeached by the late King, that they are dead." Major Beake retorted that "God hath poured contempt upon a Commonwealth;" others chimed in, proposing that "we should agree them to be a House of Lords," and Mr. Gewen moved that "now we are a free Parliament, we should draw up a Bill to invest H.H. in the title and dignity of King, Providence

[11] Burton, II. 379—404.

having cast it upon him." This would not do; that "Other House" must be trotted out again. Hazelrig moved, protesting "on his knees,"—" I do it not for delay, but that we may counsel one another,—that we do debate this matter of the highest concernment," in a Grand Committee. The proposition was justly opposed. It was urged that Committees " destroy the business ;" that " certainly we may understand one another as well by once, as by often speaking." Committee or no Committee, it was all the same to Haselrig, the debate went on.

Thursday, 4th February. Though the Grand Committee dodge was overborne, the torrent of obstruction was irresistible. On it swept, questioning whether the " Other House " should be a House of new Oliverian Lords, or of old and real Lords, and whether they should be able to "put a negative upon the People of England," or be merely a second, inferior House of Commons ; until the debate swerved round to that ancient theme, the exclusion of Members. When suddenly Mr. Speaker announced, " The Black Rod is at the door." Mr. Scot rose up to speak. Haselrig shouted out, " What care I for the Black Rod ? "

The Black Rod delivered his message : " Mr. Speaker, His Highness is in the Lords' House, and desires to speak with you." In retort the House " resolved, that the Debate touching the appellation of the Other House be adjourned, till the House return." They trooped off, and stood before the Protector.

Tormented to the quick by anger and dismay, not a moment too soon, the Protector had hurried down to Westminster. For half an hour he directed against Parliament that strange, wild outburst of self-justification, and invective, which ended with, "I do dissolve this Parliament: let God judge between me and you." * He was met from the Commons by a defiant "Amen:" they dispersed: "the mace was presently clapped under a cloak; the Speaker withdrew; and exit Parliamentum;" — "having caused H.H. more prejudice in fifteen days' session, than all the preceding Parliaments together." [12]

It was most fitting that Parliament should devote some of its last words to the incident that opened its sitting, the exclusion of the Members. Their presence enforced by that clause in the Adjournment Act, had done its work. Dominant as was the Protector, even so poor a creature as Sir Arthur Haselrig was the stronger man. That he was so, Cromwell confessed, when he sneeringly referred to Haselrig, as a "Tribune of the People," for whose sake the House of Commons, that "he might be the man that

---

* This Speech, as printed, is a meagre reflection of Cromwell's words. A report, taken at his elbow, exists in the British Museum, Lansd. MSS., 754, fo. 342.

[12] Burton, II. 406—464. VII. Com. J., 591-2. Thurloe, VI. 778.

might rule all," had uprooted the Government, " to establish a Commonwealth."

Whether or no Haselrig was an accepted leader of the people, undoubtedly he overthrew Cromwell. He forced the Dissolution of the 4th of February, and by that Dissolution Cromwell dissolved himself. " The Petition and Advice," the new Magna Charta, was destroyed. " The Instrument of Government " was annulled. No supply could be obtained, save by Parliament. But if Parliament was recalled, that would recall the " Other House." The leverage that absurdity supplied, made the parliamentary " Boar " irresistible. The " Other House," Parliament and the Protector, would again be at the mercy of the enemy. And what message from the Nation would be brought by Parliament, which, returned under " the Petition and Advice," would be free from purgation ? Though the roar of, " By the living God, I will dissolve the House," which Fleetwood's interference provoked from Cromwell, may not have resounded outside Whitehall, his act of reckless violence astonished and disturbed the Nation, and widened the deep alienation between Cromwell and the City of London. " The unexpectedness " of the stroke, " the ignorance the most knowing were in concerning it," filled Henry Cromwell's heart full of apprehensions," and alarmed H.H's Council.[13] Those apprehensions went abroad. Cromwell's ' doing such desperate things of his own head,

[13] Thurloe, VI. 811. Tanner MSS., 51, p. 2.

against such persuasions, and being secret even of his own Secretary, show him to be at his wits' end." [13]

Men "began to see that they have been fooled under the specious pretence of liberty of conscience, to betray the civil liberty of their own native country." "Some sense" also arose "in the Army, how unworthy a thing it is to take pay to betray and enslave their Country, and that all this oppression, for so many years, is for nothing, but to set up a single and inconsiderable family." [14] Mutinous notions were ripe in Cromwell's own regiment, and the Army was described as "staggering." [14] The Protector also was staggering, his health was breaking down.

The wreck of the royal Protectorate is thus described by a well-informed eye-witness in London : —"The present state of affairs is not to be described. Cromwell himself is yet in suspense whether he shall depend upon 'The Instrument' or 'The Petition and Advice;' and this doubt of his perplexeth the lawyers, with all the sober part of the Nation, beyond measure : there being in the Interim no basis of Government. The Army (as he openly declared in his speech to both Houses), is infected with sedition. His treasure is exhausted. The Army are within one degree of free quarter, owing everywhere for five months' billet ; those

[14] Tanner MSS., 51, p. 2. Thurloe, VI. 810. Clarendon State Papers, III., 388.

quartered in Paul's obtained, with great difficulty, 500*l.* last week of the Common Council; but no persuasion of Cromwell's could procure a larger sum." Yet money "must instantly be raised to satisfy the clamours of victuallers, shopkeepers, and people of all sorts, to whom he and his children are indebted for wages, diet, and apparel. And where he will be timely supplied in this exigence, unless by the seizing the wealth of private citizens, which must cause some commotion, I neither see, nor guess." And he adds that the Confessor to the French Minister, "assured me, that they were full of thought, and that the falling house made guests beware." [14]

" Thus hath the course of justice wheeled about," and made Oliver the Lord Protector " even as this " Charles the First. Whitehall Palace during the winter of 1641-2, and now again in the winter of 1657-8, was confronted by an insurgent City, in league with an insurgent Parliament. The hostile tactics which in January, 1642, drove the King from London into war, were revived in January, 1658. According to report, " the major part of the House resolved to remove into the City, to vote the old Parliament in, make Lord Fairfax General, and establish the Commonwealth as it was formerly." [15] In the creation of that notion Justice did well: it contains a wholesome lesson. Yet even more instinct

[15] MS. Cal. Clarendon MSS., fo. 70. Thurloe, VI. 802.

with retribution was the sole offer of help which Cromwell received in his distress.

On the 13th of February, Lockhart wrote to the Protector from Paris, that " The Cardinal desired me to tell your Highness, that your enemies threaten you with invasions from abroad, and insurrections at home," and that " he offers to assist your Highness at his own expense with 6 or 8000 men, for whose fidelity and zeal for your service he will answer." [15]

Mazarin mimics Strafford, and reminds the Protector that " You have an army in France, you may employ in England, to reduce that nation."

CHAPTER XIII.

THE PROTECTOR, MAJOR WILDMAN, AND COLONEL SEXBY.

CARDINAL MAZARIN offering to prop up the " bold Protector of a conquered land," might have served as an effective tail-piece to this essay, but for a statement made in the opening chapter, that throughout the Protectorate no conspiracy threatened imminent danger to Cromwell, so completely were the actors within his ken.   Some explanation therefore is needed regarding Miles Sindercombe's assassination plot, and the conspiracies which brought Dr. Hewet and Sir Henry Slingsby to the block.   That explanation, much to my regret, must be somewhat intricate, for it drags us down among Cromwell's " hidden works."

The train that led up to Dr. Hewet's execution on the 8th June, 1658, was laid in the spring of 1656, by Major Wildman, and by a Sussex gentleman, Colonel Henry Bishop.   Major Wildman is our old friend, the noted Anabaptist Leveller, whose devices during the winter of 1654, enabled Cromwell to trump up that false charge against Major-General Overton.   Seized, when penning with dramatic effect his Proclamation "against the Tyrant, Oliver Cromwell," 10th February, 1655, Wildman was transferred, having spent three weeks in Chepstow Castle, to the Tower ; and after imprisonment there, for about a year and three months, he was released, 26th June, 1656, giving security for 10,000*l.* " to return in three months, and meantime not to act against the State."[1] Wildman did not return to the Tower till 26th November, 1661, having meanwhile unceasingly acted "against the State."

That Major Wildman should find a colleague in Colonel Bishop was natural enough. He was Wildman's " familiar," his " great confidant," and they acted in such harmony, that, as will become apparent, imprisonment produced on the Colonel and the Major a similar effect. Bishop spent part of the winter of 1655-6 as one of Cromwell's suspects, " strictly kept in a sad prison." He was released ; and he addressed to Thurloe a letter protesting that it was to Thurloe he owed his life, and that "there is nothing I desire more, than to appear faithful to the present Government."[1] That letter was written on the 3rd April, 1656, and a few weeks afterwards Bishop was actively conspiring against Cromwell. But it must not therefore be supposed that Bishop had deserted the Protector. During the following September Thurloe received from Bishop a letter of renewed devotion, stating that "I must ever acknowledge to live by your favour " and " to attend your commands ;" yet all the same he continues to act as if he were ready to die for Charles Steuart.

Bishop, for the enticement of the Royalists, possessed singular advantages. He was a composite politician, half Leveller, half Cavalier. As a Leveller, Bishop in April, 1655, when Cromwell frightened Colonel Sexby out of England, "conveyed" him and Richard Overton "oversea," from the Sussex coast. At the same time, as a Royalist, "all the affairs of C. S., which related to Sussex, since the battle of Worcester, were under his control." Thus it was that whilst he "held a commission from C. S. to treat with the Levelling party," Bishop, as Wildman's partner, held another commission from the Levellers. As an Anabaptist, Bishop was esteemed "the best friend the King had, in dividing the Army;" and as a Cavalier, he sat and acted in the Royalist intrigues and councils. His last appearance in the Thurloe papers proves that, on the eve of the Restoration, Bishop had wholly dropped the Leveller, and figured as a stanch Royalist.[1]

Wildman's intrigues must be first dealt with. He was told off to play decoy duck before the King, whose co-operation was essential to obtain a quasi-genuine royalist conspiracy. After Wildman's captivity in the Tower had lasted about a year, March,

---

[1] Cal. State Papers, 1655-56, 387. "Perfect Proceedings," News Letter, 8—15 March, 1655. Thurloe, IV. 673; V. 442; VII. 66, 98, 109, 866.

1656, Charles received a hint, through a lady, that "a match" was possible between him and Major Wildman. Mrs. Ross, the wife of a Royalist agent, the go-between, was as good as her word. Before long the match was accomplished, the republican in the Tower and his sovereign in exile were joined together.[2] And it is obvious that if Wildman could offer his services to the King, some understanding must have existed that the captive would be set at liberty; for, though, whilst in the Tower, Wildman freely communicated with the King, to be an effective friend, to exert his pretended influence over the Levellers, Wildman must be enfranchised. This is obvious : yet curiously enough, Wildman in the cell was far more direct and plump in his enterprising offers to the King, than Wildman in the street. The information that Wildman supplied out of the Tower was to the King most attractive. According to the Major's report, the republican soldiery were in active and potent agitation : that they intended to insist that Cromwell should place "several ports and garrisons in their hands, and among them Deal Castle," which Wildman "thought he could secure for the King."[3] Wildman also intimated that though the Army agitators "look another way," yet "things will turn out to the King's advantage."[3]

[2] Cal. State Papers, 1655-56, 244, 372.
[3] Cal. Clarendon MSS., III. 135, 142. Clarendon State Papers, III. 300.

Such a communication from Wildman, who assumed leadership over the Levellers, was gladly welcomed. It opened up the sole chance of the King's restoration, disruption from within of Cromwell's Army. Wildman in return was assured that Charles esteemed him "of great value," gave full credit to all he said, and desired him to continue "his advertisements and endeavours for the King's service." [3]

Those endeavours were continued. During July Sir R. Shirley informed the King that "Wildman is very zealous for your interest, and that though he seems to comply with the Canting Party, which he wholly rules, yet he desires to raise himself chiefly by the King's favour," and that, if assured of the King's favour, "he will be highly serviceable, without tying the King too strictly in particulars." [3]

Those "particulars" were soon forthcoming. The King received an Address from "many thousands of Your Majesty's most humble Servants," who "left themselves at the feet of your Mercy." They, the King's humble servants, offered to "hazard our lives and all that is dear to us for the restoring and re-establishing Your Majesty on the throne of your Father." Ten names represented those "many thousands," of whom two only are recognizable, namely, a Mr. William Howard and Major John Wildman.

This address was stuffed with Scriptural phrases,

so extravagant and so incongruous as to seem an
intentional parody of puritan "slang." The source
of the address is vague. Though the King is
assured that "every man's hand is on his loins,"
that "their bowels are troubled," and that "they
fly like hunted partridges," still those who were thus
chastised with scorpions are not specified, nor do
the "we" who disdain "mean thoughts of our own
private safety" explain how we propose "to hazard
our lives for the King." [4]

This deficiency, however, was made good by Mr.
Howard. He accompanied the Address by a busi-
nesslike letter describing the "rage and just
indignation of the people" against Cromwell,
claiming to have gained over "many of the chief
of" those who "suffer under the opprobrious name
of Levellers, to the assistance of Your Majesty's
cause and interest;" and suggesting an "advance of
2000*l.*" [4] And a few weeks later Charles received
a visit from Howard, who was welcomed as a valuable ally. He had been expelled from Cromwell's
Life Guard because of his political opinions; he was
also a young gentleman who, "though an Anabaptist, made himself merry with the extravagancy
and madness of his companions," and "possessed
very extraordinary parts, sharpness of wit, and volu-
bility of tongue." Howard "corresponded with the

[4] Clarendon Hist., Ed. 1839, 903. Cal. Clarendon MSS., III.
145. Thurloe, V. 393 ; VI. 706, 749. Clarendon State Papers, III.
422.

King very faithfully with his professions," until Cromwell interfered, and shut him up in St. James's Palace; whence, upon the Protector's death, that lively young gentleman made to the King a very unpleasant revelation.

Wildman emerged from the Tower in June, 1656; but, as has been observed, his freedom seemed to restrict his power of action. His proposals showed a marked change of front. Money down, and something for the plot-driver, henceforward were Wildman's terms. Deal Castle, which as spoil snatched from Cromwell, Wildman offered gratuitously to Charles, now dropped out of sight. The King received notice from his negotiator with the Levellers, Sir R. Shirley, that they inclined to bribery as the best mode of obtaining for the King "the delivery of some place of strength," and that when the King says what money he will give, and on what security, Wildman will treat with the Deputy Governor of Portsmouth, a man "sufficiently necessitous."[5] And during October the Levellers made a positive offer of Portsmouth. They had agreed on the price: 15,000*l.* was to be paid to the necessitous Deputy Governor; and they threw into the bargain an undertaking "in a short time" to stab Cromwell and Lambert. The names of the Levellers engaged in this transaction do not appear,

[5] Cal. Clarendon MSS., III. 152, 192. Clarendon State Papers, III. 300.

but the moving spirits therein are obvious. The 15,000*l*. was to be handed over to Colonel Bishop, and "one who knows the Levellers well" advised that 1000*l*. should be paid to Major Wildman; money well earned, because, " as they affirm, a large part of the Navy is theirs already." [5] If the bribe be reckoned at half our present money value, 30,000*l*. was a large sum to be raised by a penniless exile.

Up to this point, throughout 1656, the King had only received words from Wildman. In January, 1657, he passed from words to deeds. He superintended the attempt made by that stout trooper, Miles Sindercombe, to assassinate the Protector; * though, after all, the enterprise only drew forth much stout talk from the Major. He assured the King that " if it had not been discovered, Cromwell had not lived that night; " [6] but it was discovered, the attempt was an utter failure. Wildman nevertheless plied Charles with vigorous assurances, declaring that " we are as active as ever," and that " Cromwell must fall, or some thousands of us, for we have gone too far to retreat." [6] Who were the " we " and the " thousands " never transpired : they were in " buckram."

Throughout the summer of 1657, Wildman kept in friendly touch with the King; and, during the following November, he again offered to assassinate Cromwell, if the King would cash up. Charles, for

* See p 284.
[6] Clarendon State Papers, III. 327, 335. Cal. Clarendon MSS.,

his part, naturally declined to pay blood-money "beforehand," and evidently desired to see the Major.[6] That desire, before long, became urgent, imperative. The moment of moments arrived during the opening days of January, 1658. Cromwell was in a critical position. His Government was sinking daily deeper into debt. If he obtained supplies and hearty co-operation from the then approaching Parliament, Cromwell would be secure. If, on the other hand, Parliament forced upon him a Dissolution, ticklish times would ensue, the very season for an agitation. The King accordingly desired to see Wildman face to face, "to discourse with him about the garrisons, and other things," "that is to say about Portsmouth, and that sudden outbreak by the Levellers, which Wildman had for two years been promising. But the ampler the opportunity, the feebler was Wildman's energy. He would not come to the fore. He felt so shy, that even though he came into the King's neighbourhood in Flanders, on a visit to a brother conspirator, Father Peter Talbot, Wildman "could not be persuaded to see the King, Ormond, or Hyde." [6]   So again, when he returned to London, sending his refusal not direct to the King, but through Father Talbot, Wildman respectfully declined to obey the King's desire. The Major had lost heart; he wished that he had been sent for sooner. Now it was too late; a visit to

III. 388, 391. MS. Cal. Clarendon MSS., 12th Jan., 1658, fo. 15.

Bruges would be worse than useless. In fine he warned the King, that he had "slipt the time for the market," that it was "spoiled," because the Cavaliers had filled the Town with reports of the King's preparations.[6]

The tale of Wildman's action on the King is ended. How that partner in the plot business, Colonel Henry Bishop, demeaned himself, must now be exhibited. He undertook the English department of the conspiracy. He imitated closely the tones and attitude of his "great familiar," Wildman, and whilst the Major was devoting himself to the King, Bishop simultaneously tendered his services to the Cavaliers. During May, 1656, he visited Major Smith, a leading Sussex Royalist, and disclosed to him a most cheerful prospect. "Major Wildman," Bishop declared, " and others of the Levelling party had a correspondence with Charles Stuart in order to making an insurrection in the Nation," but that " the royal party need not appear, till they, the said Levellers, had gotten into arms." The Cavaliers were, however, to make themselves ready, for Bishop assured Major Smith that " it would be very shortly a time for the royal Party to show themselves."

Bishop also figured, not only as a captain over the Levellers, but as an ardent Royalist who could speak for his fellow-Cavaliers. In that capacity, he visited Mr. Mills, another royalist agent in the south of England, and sought to engage him in " a design " that was " on foot for raising a party for the King."

T

Mills replied " that he would think about the proposal," and saw Bishop " no more for a twelve-
month."

That must have been at the time when the Sussex
Royalists found Bishop again amongst them, renew-
ing his temptation, though in an altered form.   In
March, 1657, he presented himself to Major Smith.
Reverting to his assurance of the previous year,
Bishop now asserted that " the Levelling party
found themselves not able to do so great a work "
as to rise unassisted against Cromwell, " but did
require 1500 horse to join with them, which Bishop
said would be raised about the City of London,
whereupon there would be some action suddenly."
And at Bishop's suggestion, Major Smith placed
before Colonel Gunter, Lord Clarendon's brother-
in-law, the " proposed conjunction of the Levellers
and the Royalists."   That conjunction, however,
Gunter " did by no means approve, not only because
he feared that the Levellers were but Decoys to
draw the Royal Party in," but also because he had
"lately received intelligence from" his brother-in-law
" that the King hopes very shortly to land a considerable force in England," and because, " to Gunter's knowledge," Portsmouth would be surrendered
to the King. This proof of partner Wildman's decoy-
ing powers, must have interested Bishop.   Nor did
Gunter's suspicions discourage him. Bishop continued to ply his task, to push on the plot business,
assuring the Cavaliers that the King's landing was

nigh, and that the Marquis of Hertford was to be his " generalissimo." [7]

A crisis in the State may work a crisis in a kitchen. A national catastrophe produces unlooked-for results; and among the far-reaching consequences of Cromwell's death, it wrought conviction upon the King, that the men whose " bowels were troubled," every one with " his hand upon his loins," were nowhere, and that their leader was an impostor. As soon as the event of the 3rd of September, 1658, was an ascertained fact, " for Sir Robert Stone hath seen the carcase," Mr William Howard renewed his correspondence with the King, hoping to be the first to tell the welcome news. In his letter Howard mentions that " the old tyrant had boasted that he was acquainted with all my actions," and " that he had this information from one that was my chief confidant." That the confidant must be Wildman, Howard maintains, because the information supplied to Cromwell was known only to Wildman ; and also because, as Howard writes word, " since my confinement, I have had some discourse with one that was implicated in Dr. Hewet's conspiracy, and he, not knowing that Wildman was known to me, made it plain by many circumstances, that Wildman and Colonel Bishop were the first discoverers of the design to Cromwell." [8] What a simple but disagree-

<hr>

[7] Thurloe, VII. 65, 74. 80, 81, 93, 98, 103.
[8] Clarendon State Papers, III. 408.

able interpretation of the dreams and disappoint-
ments of the last two years did Charles receive in
that announcement! He had been gulled all that
time by the man he esteemed as the " author of his
good fortunes," by "the wisest and honestest" of
mankind.

Howard's belief that Major Wildman was Cromwell's trepanner-general, can be confirmed by further
evidence. During the spring of 1657, when Wildman and Bishop were inviting the Sussex Cavaliers to form an armed union with the Levellers, a
warning was sent to them from the Tower by
Major-General Overton, " that Wildman holds secret
correspondency with the Protector;" and Overton,
from past experience, was likely to esteem Wildman
aright. In the following October, a leading English
Royalist was " somewhat troubled " by hearing that
Major Wildman had appeared at Gravesend with " a
pass in the name of John Jones, signed with Cromwell's signet, to go beyond sea; " that an over-
zealous port official, recognizing Wildman, had
committed him to the " block house," and that
Cromwell had sent orders to release Jones-Wildman,
to provide a ship for him, and a skipper who would
" not question him, but to carry him wheresoever
he should direct." [9] And, as has been mentioned,
Wildman did cross over to Flanders on a visit to
his continental agent, Father Talbot, during the

[9] Cal. Clarendon MSS., III. 375. Thurloe, I. 708, 711.
Clarendon State Papers, III. 442, 526.

autumn of 1657. A year and a half later, February, 1659, when political intrigue boiled up under Protector Richard, the Cavaliers were openly taunted by the Levellers for being "once more outwitted" by Wildman, so notorious was the deception that he had continuously practised upon them.[9]

In other ways it can be shown that Cromwell and Wildman were on excellent terms. Though the Protector's grip was never far from Wildman's shoulder, yet he conspired in perfect safety. Though he was actually in that clutch for more than a year, the Major was not tried and condemned. His treason was patent, he would have made a handsome sacrifice to the majesty of the Protectorate; and Cromwell certainly did what he could to procure such offerings. Yet when Wildman's "inevitable death was expected by his friends and others, after a short imprisonment he was unaccountably set free."[10] He did not return to the Tower within three months after his release, according to his solemn engagement. He plotted strenuously against the State; and yet his bond was not enforced; the penalty of 10,000*l.* was not exacted. And as Cromwell treated Mr. Day the traitorous Passage Clerk, and Governor Kelsey the fool or knave, so Cromwell dealt with Wildman : he was rewarded whilst entering into that royal "match." When the union was in its first vigour, the Protector sent orders to release Major Wildman's "great estate" in Lancashire

[10] Echard, II. 713. Thurloe, IV. 179 ; V. 241.

from the sequestration placed upon it by Major-General Worsley.[10]

Not less certain is it that Wildman conspired in Cromwell's sight. He knew that even in the Tower Wildman was leaguing with the King. For Cromwell could have seen and handled Mrs. Ross's letters of March and June, 1656, describing the " match " between the King and Cromwell's prisoner, for her correspondence lay in Cromwell's Home Office ; and he might have read this remark made to her by Pile, a Royalist agent, that, " the underhand dealings of Wildman with the King, will come to nothing, for I am certain Cromwell knows it." [11] Pile was quite correct. Mr. Corker, Charles II.'s "Agent for the East Parts of England," was also Cromwell's agent, and supplied him with a continuous narrative of the intrigues between Wildman, Bishop, and the Cavaliers, and of the various schemes wherewith, as Corker pleasantly remarks, " we," the Royalists, " feed ourselves withal, and animate those fools that will believe us." [11]

Regarding Wildman's radical or moral opinions no delicacy need be felt. He was a thorough Mr. By-Ends. On quitting the Army, about 1650, he " betook himself to civil affairs, in the solicitation of suits depending in Parliament, or before Committees ; " [12] and whilst thus busy, that " cunning person Major Wildman," vexed Colonel Hutchinson's righteous

[11] Cal. State Papers, 1655-56, 395. Thurloe, I., 707—720.
[12] Clarendon Hist., Ed. 1839, 848. Hutchinson, Bohn's

soul, and was " a great manager of papist's interests;" and he had among his agents that Father Talbot of whom mention has been made, a very shady Irish Jesuit. Wildman also, it is reported, devoted his fluent and democratic pen to Cromwell's service; [12] and although it might be urged that his anxiety " to raise himself by the King's favour," and to receive from him 1000*l.*, or " a large estate," may have been only a pretence, still that Wildman utterly deserted the republican idea is proved by his conduct during the crisis when, after Cromwell's death, England was struggling towards monarchy. Wildman then became " as much an enemy to the King as he was before a seeming friend, not on account of a Commonwealth, for he met every day repulses from that Party, but because he hoped to set up the interest of the Duke of York against the King." [12]   And finally Wildman the Radical, the Cromwellian, the Royalist, became a respectable Whig, and Post-Master General to William III.[12]

Colonel Sexby and Major Wildman were partners in conspiracy. Was Sexby, like Wildman, in partnership with Cromwell? The careers of these two men were so blended that seemingly " what is sauce for the" Major, "is sauce" also for the Colonel. To this extent that proverb is applicable. The suspicion with which Wildman was regarded by Major-

Ed., 350.   Cal. Clarendon MSS.,.III. 40, 388.   Noble, I. 299, *n*. Macaulay, IV. 27.   Clarendon State Papers, III. 311, 475.

General Overton was extended to Sexby by another Anabaptist Leader, by Major-General Harrison. He asserted, according to a report of his talk about the winter conspiracy of 1654, that he " thought Sexby only to be a decoy for His Highness, because he observed all those that Sexby had been with, were secured, but he himself at liberty ; and that he knew Sexby to be a treacherous fellow, and would have nothing to do with him." [13] And the close of his career seems to confirm the notion that Sexby was " H.H.'s decoy." He was seized, and committed to the Tower in July, 1657. He died there, cut off by sudden illness, in January, 1658, having been in Cromwell's grasp for about six months. That Miles Sindercombe was Sexby's servant was known and proved. During his residence in the Tower, three months before his death, Sexby's confession was published, stating " that he was guilty of the whole business of Sindercombe, as to the design of killing the Lord Protector." Yet, like Wildman, Sexby was preserved from appearance before a Court of Justice and from the scaffold.

Cromwell wilfully and unjustly put to civil death that " companion of his labours and trials," Major-General Overton. Sir Henry Slingsby was, by Cromwell's express orders, tempted into treason, that he might become food for the executioner. Neither tenderness for a misled Republican nor mercy for an enemy can be claimed for Cromwell.

[13] Thurloe, III. 195.

It was his duty to destroy Sexby, the would-be murderer. That something about Sexby's career would not bear the light is shown by a rumour that he was poisoned by Wildman's associates.[13]

Whether knave for self, or Cromwell's knave, Sexby's ways smack of knavery. During his life of intrigue, despite his perpetual protestations that he would do Cromwell to death, the extraction of money from the King of Spain was Sexby's sole exploit. His other achievements consisted of wordy undertakings that he would open English seaports to the enemy, rouse up the Army, and tear in pieces the sham Commonwealth; and the only approach to action made by Sexby reveals his shifty nature. He kept on, during twelve months, assuring his employers that he would kill Cromwell "in three weeks,"—"before Parliament meets,"—or by "strange engines."[14] Always going to do the deed, just like the mountebank at a fair, Sexby was ever crying out to his dupes, "5l. more, and up goes the donkey." At last, the donkey was positively to soar aloft. Cromwell shall be destroyed. Sexby went over to England, and then he returned, leaving Cromwell in the hands of Sindercombe, that is to say, in the hands of Wildman.

Throughout Sexby conducted his intrigues on Wildman's lines. After some holding aloof, he was converted to royalty by Father Peter Talbot. So effective was Sexby's conversion that he declared

[14] Cal. Clarendon MSS., III. 98, 148, 203.

that his offer " to join His Majesty, and to further his service," was made "out of scruple of conscience : " and the only radical scruple left him, was, that he must " be dispensed withal for not kneeling to His Majesty, for he thought that to be a kind of idolatry." [14] But still Sexby posed as a true Leveller. Ardent republicanism was his stock-in-trade ; thereon, like Wildman, he based his influence. In pretence those two men worked apart. The King was artfully instructed to conceal from the Major and the Colonel that he was in league with both partners in the plot firm. But in reality Sexby's offers were Wildman's offers. The men that Sexby claimed as his followers were Wildman's men. Save through Wildman, Sexby, habitually in exile, could have no authority over the English Levellers. It even seems that they were alike deceivers, and claimed influence over the Levellers which neither of them possessed. A well-informed English Royalist incidentally warned Clarendon, 25th March, 1657, that " applications made to the King from the Commonwealth men will be most probably deceptive, in which Sir A. Haselrig and Sir H. Vane are not particularly interested, for they are the leaders " of their party.[15] That Vane and Haselrig were the true leaders of the Republicans is highly probable. Suspicion of Messrs. Wildman and Sexby must have been widely spread. Major-General Harrison's disbelief in Sexby

[15] Cal. Clarendon MSS., III. 75.

would be known by many; and, if Major-General Overton sent that warning to his opponents, the Royalists, he must have warned his own friends also.

Even if Sexby were a true hater of Cromwell, still Cromwell's agents surrounded him; they managed him throughout his intrigues. As I have mentioned, Wildman had some connection with the Roman Catholics. Peter Talbot, the Jesuit, who introduced Sexby to the King, was a rascal, and a royalistical Leveller. In December, 1654, he offered to the King, that, if he would become a papist, in return, " Sexby, the Independents, Anabaptists, and Harrison's factious endeavours shall be steered by the King's directions;" [15] and Father Talbot acted for Sexby in his negotiations with the Spanish Government. Father Talbot was also on intimate terms with Wildman.

Gilbert Talbot, Peter's brother, a Royalist in Thurloe's pay, was instructed to watch Sexby, and examine his papers.[16] Richard Overton acted in the fourfold capacity of Royalist, Wildman's associate, Cromwell's servant, and Sexby's aide-de-camp. But most of all, by Wildman, was Cromwell's thumb placed on Sexby's head. To his Continental practices the Protector had no objection; any one suited his purpose, who enticed Charles into the semblance of an invader; and, whilst in England, Sexby was in Wildman's hands.

[16] Cal. Clarendon MSS., III. 70.

With these wires under Cromwell's touch, no Sunday-school excursionist was more lovingly and personally conducted than was Miles Sindercombe; though nothing, to all appearance, could be more formidable than his enterprise. Every way it was a business-like affair. The stout trooper was furnished with ample funds. He certainly was not hurried over the murder job, for he was on the quest from the 17th September, 1656, until the following January. He bought horses and arms, and hired houses for his purpose. He did his best, and yet he was constantly baffled. Some show, however, must be made. The personal conductor appears. When Sindercombe had repeatedly ridden forth, in vain, to shoot down Cromwell on the high road and in the park, Wildman turned him aside into the safer way of placing "a basket of wildfire made up of all combustibles, as tar, pitch, tow, gunpowder, &c., in little pieces," in the Chapel of Whitehall Palace; a device which had the advantage of being harmless as regards Cromwell, and useful as a startling advertisement of the "hidden works" of the bloody conspirator. To the "firework" Sexby and his emissaries objected, "there being no reasonable hope that it would succeed;" but "Wildman was opinionated in the business, and his authority prevailed."[17]

[17] Clarendon State Papers, III. 331, 325. Burton, I. 332. Thurloe, V. 774, 776. Tanner MSS., 52, fo. 188. State Trials, Vol. V.

So the day was fixed.   In the morning, Cromwell's informer, who throughout had attended on the conspiracy, warned his employer of the coming event.   In the afternoon, Sindercombe, conducted, it is said, by " people appointed by His Highness," [17] placed the basket in the chapel.   During the evening it smouldered some three hours, and then it was duly smelled out.   Every way the " firework " fully justified Sexby's distrust.   The " wildfire " proved a very tame and fizzenless mixture; it failed to effect even the contriver's purpose, which was to set Whitehall on fire, that " their party " might perceive " that they were at work to accomplish what they had designed."   Nor did the experiment please those who watched it on Cromwell's behalf, his Councillors, who were sent for to inspect the basket in the chapel.   The wretched thing would not work at all.   So they themselves " purposed to have set some seats on fire, and doubled the guard, and so watched the consequence : but this was thought to raise too great a tumult, and call down the City, and make the people believe it was only a purposed plot to try men's spirits;" a notion that had a wide circulation, for the English at Antwerp were " of opinion that the powder-plot is a simple invention of the Protector." [17]

Nor, at its deadliest, was the project intended to compass the Protector's death.   Sindercombe's companion stated that the " firework " was meant as an advertisement, to show that " they were not idle." They left it to take care of itself; they went home, where next day they were arrested. It was only "if the fire did not take," that Sindercombe proposed " to set upon the Protector, to take away his life." [17]   Wildman was acting his part when he "insinuated" to the King that the enterprise was designed " not only to destroy Cromwell, but that if he should chance to escape, the setting Whitehall on fire was to be the watchword to a rising." [17]   Had that been the case, Cromwell's Councillors would certainly not have " purposed " their sensational conflagration in the Chapel and the sudden call to arms.   The guard would have been mustered round Whitehall to a very different purpose.

The existence of latent insincerity in the doings of Wildman and Sexby reveals itself in another way. If, during the two years 1656-58, they had been really able, in the name of the Levellers, to offer to Charles, the King of Spain, and the English Royalists, the ports of Dover, Deal, Portsmouth, Hull, and Yarmouth, to divide Cromwell's Army, and to hand over his Navy, the Protectorate was not worth half an hour's purchase.

The quality of these assurances is appreciable, inasmuch as they were made by Cromwell's agents, Wildman and Bishop, and by Sexby, Wildman's subordinate. That they were thoroughly deceptive is also proved by the tenor of the Protectorate history throughout those years. An army, navy, and people, infected with widespread disaffection, could not have been purged of that humour save by violent and conspicuous remedies. Nothing of the kind took place. Cromwell, in his speech of September, 1656, though he knew that Wildman, acting seemingly for the Levellers, was, at that very time, offering to place Charles upon the throne, expressly exonerated that party from complicity with the King; and in the speech of January, 1658, the "old enemy" appears as the only source of danger. Except during the contest over the Crown, not a trace of uneasy feeling regarding the Army and Navy is found in Thurloe's letters during 1655-57. He mentions in December, 1657, with indifference, that, "to our knowledge," the Royalists were "tinkling with some of our garrisons to obtain one of them for a landing-place;"[19] and he wrote confidently to Lockhart that England was never in a better temper with the Protector.

Meantime the delusion that the Anabaptists were able to overthrow the Protectorate was persistently spread by Wildman and Sexby throughout Europe and England. Had not Charles been screened from its influence by the instinct of good sense and for good living, he might have shared his father's fate. Charles I. was wrecked by the prevalent belief that he had handed England over to Strafford's Irish papist army. Had Charles II. embarked even a single regiment of foreign mercenaries for our shores, all the slumbering hate and fear of the papists would

[19] Thurloe, VI. 628, 806. Cal. Clarendon MSS., III. 258.

have flamed out.   England would have risen against him as one man; here and there a few Cavaliers would have appeared in arms to their destruction; the Royalists would have been re-decimated, and the Protector's dynasty might have been seated on the English throne.   It was remarked, that if he could, Cromwell would have purchased such an invasion.[18]

The great expectations that were spread abroad amongst the Royalists afford another illustration of their real nature.   Were they to be believed, then Cromwell's overthrow was certain.   The Royalists had only to wait, ready to cut in when the Levellers had done the work.   Cavaliers endowed with the slightest pluck would be on the start.   But evidently Wildman and Bishop were not believed : the mass of the English Royalists never moved.   The conspiracy for which Dr. Hewet suffered, extended only over portions of Sussex and Surrey; it was, at the most, a very shadowy affair.   To render the notion, that the King might land at Hull, at all plausible, Cromwell himself overlooked the ensnarement of Sir Henry Slingsby.

Wildman and Bishop, to a certain extent, were successful.   Although their efforts provoked marked symptoms of disbelief, and doubts that there was " a design to ensnare us," [19] the allurements they spread before the English Cavaliers produced some effect among the more excitable of that party.   Cavaliers in Surrey and Sussex met and talked, and sought

[19] Thurloe, VII. 83, 103, 110.

after recruits, and passed to and fro commissions
initialled " C. R." throughout the summer and
winter of 1657 and on into the spring of 1658.
Rumour was set on the run that the King would
invade England with an army " that would be able
to do his business."   Those busy plotters, O'Neil
and Armorer, reported back, that designs were
laid for the surprise of Shrewsbury, Gloucester,
Bristol, and even London;   and urgent messages
were sent to Charles, declaring that " we were in
such a state of universal readiness " that " we would
begin the work ourselves." [20]

Whether those messages sprang from deception or
delusion, they were absolutely untrustworthy.   That
" nothing in England was really ready " for action
was disclosed to the King by Ormond, who visited
England, February, 1658, " to confer with the most
forward " among the Royalists.[20]   The project fell
through.   Then, as usual, disappointment provoked
recrimination.   The English Cavaliers asserted
" senselessly " that " the expectation of the King's
landing had hindered them from falling upon Cromwell and his Parliament;" [20]   they " vented their
discontents " against the King's advisers, because,
" when they knew that they could not come," they
encouraged the Royalists " to make preparations." [20]
And these charges were met by Clarendon with the
retort that " the King had not been able to satisfy

[20] Clarendon Hist., Ed. 1839, 898, 899.   Thurloe, VI. 806,
1st March, 1658, Ormond to Hyde, MS. Cal. Clarendon MSS.,

himself of any one plan laid, that could be depended on in any place in England."[20]

The use that Cromwell made of the lie-begotten conspiracy for which Dr. Hewet suffered will be described in the next chapter.

fo. 74 ; and Hyde to O'Neil, May, 1658, fo. 213. Clarendon State Papers, III. 394. Nicholas MS., 2536, fo. 123.

CHAPTER XIV.

THE CONCLUSION OF THE WHOLE MATTER.

IF an adventurer attempts an upward climb into "good society," and is repulsed, he naturally falls back upon his former habits, and among his former chums. Cromwell, mighty adventurer as he was, could not escape the adventurer's lot. Dispossessed of his sham Royal Protectorate by a mutinous House of Commons, he returned at once to the boon companions he had discarded, and to his wonted method of terrorism. In a moment, down he sank, for the last time, into the drudge. The 4th of February, 1658, when he dissolved Parliament, was a Thursday. On the following Saturday he sneaks up to the Army Officers; he calls them together, speaks to them "familiarly," drinks wine with them "very plenteously," and prostrates himself before them. "Gentlemen," he said, "we have gone along together, and why we should differ, I know not." He then assured them, that the defunct Parliament was summoned against his will, that the last Session was, "in his own judgment, no way seasonable," and that, as Parliament was no more, " it had pleased

God to put Me in a capacity to protect you, and I will protect you." [1]

How had the Protector protected the Army officers ? He had put England under their feet, and the Royalists under their extortion. And if Cromwell had been able, the second dose of his protection would have doubled the first. For in the approaching crisis of despair, not re-decimation of the incomes of the Royalists, but seizure of " a moiety of their estates," was vainly sought by Thurloe and his fellow-councillors, as the only way to save the bankrupt Government. [1]

Having made his submission to his masters, Cromwell turned to his subjects. To the Army officers he said, I will protect you ; to the English people, I will terrorize you. He summoned for that purpose the Lord Mayor and the City authorities. The principal Army officers were also called together. They stood before him on the 12th of March, when he enlarged on " the dangers wherein the City of London, and the whole Nation were involved, by reason of the new designs of the old enemy, Charles Stuart," who had " 8000 horsemen, and twenty-two hired transport ships," in readiness for invasion. And to convince his hearers, he told them, " that the Lord of Ormond, in person, had been lately in England, for three weeks together,

---

[1] Hist. MSS. Com., 5th Report, 166, 177. Tanner MSS., 50, fo. 1. Thurloe, VII. 21, 192. XXI. Old Parl. Hist., 206.

The public notice given by Cromwell of his knowledge that

being come over, on purpose, to promote the design."[1] But Cromwell did not tell his hearers that Ormond had left London because his errand was fruitless, because the Royalists were wholly incapable of action. Nor did he dare to ask from the City the loan he needed so urgently, a self-restraint which was noticed sarcastically by Henry Cromwell.[1]

As usual, the Protector's cry of "wolf" awoke distrust. His subjects heard his "stories of flat-bottomed boats, but we did always esteem of them accordingly."[2] The French Ambassador remarked that the address to the Lord Mayor, made many believe that Cromwell had some bye-motive : that he rang the alarm-bell, to draw the Army and those who hated the Stuarts closer to his side.[2] It was necessary, as Fleetwood expresses it, to "convince all men" that the Government had not "pretended a plot, but that the thing was real."[2]

Yet the wolf of the 12th March was, in truth, a more real beast than he had ever been before. The deep resentment aroused by the session and by the dispersal of Parliament, the renewal of the army terror, the reappearance of the Republican agitator, justified Mazarin's offer of French soldiers to support the tottering Protector; and the stimulants applied by Sexby, Wildman, and Bishop, to the

Ormond was in London, is taken as a generous mode of warning away an enemy. Cromwell could not touch Ormond under the compact with Willis the informer. Lingard, VII. 258, 305.

[2] Burton, III. 123. Guizot, II. 631, 632. Thurloe, VII. 71. Clarendon State Papers, III. 390.

Spanish Government, to Charles, and to his English friends had produced some effect. Although, as Lockhart told Thurloe, 27th February, 1658, the King's levies were not "an army," but "scarce the number of a good regiment," [2] yet, at that very time, the more sanguine of Charles's advisers thought that the moment had come. The Earl of Bristol assured him that, at Ostend, a fortnight would complete the preparations for embarkation, and prepare a seaport to receive the King's fleet. From England, Mordaunt reported that Surrey was ready to appear in arms.[3]

The Royalists were deluded. The better-informed French Ambassador was of opinion that, in reality, no revolution was in sight, and that to escape another civil war, England still would gladly make Cromwell King.[3] The Lord Fleetwood, in the name of the Army, engaged to stand by His Highness with their lives, freely and heartily. The invasion project was stifled. Cromwell blockaded the opposite shores; and from that moment his enemies at home and abroad were powerless. The Spanish Government delayed the promised help; and Hyde withdrew from England those reckless adventurers O'Neil and Armorer,[3] and wrote to Mordaunt, that no invasion could be before next winter.

So far Cromwell was secure; but day by day bankruptcy approached closer and closer. He dared

[3] MS. Cal. Clarendon MSS., 28th Feb., 1st March, 4th April, fo. 67, 88, 149. Guizot, II. 631.

not call a Parliament, even the acquisition of Dunkirk could not encourage him.   He must therefore resort to his standard policy, terrorism, to the devices of the first years of his Protectorate, to the materials that Wildman and Bishop had provided for him.   He took the last public step in his career ; he called together the High Court of Justice ; he proceeded, as related by a contemporary, to make " the most of all plots and designs whatsoever." [4]

" For news," during April, 1658, to use the words of a sympathetic subject, " our Great Plot, that hath long been under the hatches, is now come on the decks, and cries, who is for my Lord Protector ? For, our Malignants will lose their lives, and I hope the rest will pay a good part of their estates towards the Army, by way of decimation.   A Court of Justice is expected, the persons are prepared for it." [4] Cromwell also was preparing for his last human sacrifice ; he had brought up his troops, and stationed them near at hand.   He bisected London from the City to Westminster, with a chain of military outposts; at the Tower, at " Paul's, once more a stable," the Horse Guards, and a regiment at "James's." [5] "Every night the soldiers searched divers houses, and took thence many into prison." Those who were left free, saw and heard " troops of horses trumpetting to and fro, and companies

[4] Baker, 561.   Hist. MSS. Com., 6th Report, 23rd April, 1658, 443.

[5] Hist. MSS. Com., 5th Report, 171, 180, 181, 183.   MS. Cal. Clarendon MSS., fo. 27.   Carte Letters, II. 118, 119.

of foot, grumbling with their drums daily in the streets." [5]

Cromwell also set up his High Court of Justice, though not without difficulty. The judges were cited to appear; but several "boggled," and refused to sit, "conceiving the last Parliament,"—the authors of the High Court of Justice Act—to be "a stained company," i.e. a packed Parliament, and therefore unable "to authorize them safely to undertake the execution thereof against the express provisions of our known laws." [5] And "most men's thoughts were offended" by a tribunal which acted "after the arbitrary way, without a jury, where 'satis est accusare.'" [5]

From among the persons who were "prepared" for the Court, two were condemned and executed, Dr. Hewet and Sir Henry Slingsby. The scanty proof of Hewet's guilt was observed; it was remarked that the evidence was "very slender," "most dubiously delivered," and that "our Great Plot" turned out to be only "discourses tending to a design." [5] Not so regarding Sir Henry Slingsby's treason. Undoubtedly he had "traitorously plotted, and contrived to betray, and yield up the garrison of Hull unto Charles Stuart." He had sought, according to Lisle, the Lord President of the Court, to inflict on "this poor Nation" civil war, to betray to the Papists "the Protestant Interest," and to involve us in "desolation upon desolation." [*]

[*] The city apprentice plot of May, 1658, was, as I have de-

The account of the manner in which Sir Henry
Slingsby was prepared for execution, must be prefaced by a return back, in time, to the 28th June, 1654.
On that day an aged Romish priest, Southworth, was
executed amid a crowd of sympathizing Londoners,
who " all admired his constancy."   Southworth was
arraigned in the year 1654, upon a sentence of banish-
ment passed in the year 1617.   Whilst he maintained
his innocence of treason, Southworth acknowledged
that he held priest's orders.   He knew the consequences of the admission.   He was accordingly
condemned to death, because he was a priest.   The
Portuguese ambassador went to Whitehall and received Cromwell's assurance, in God's name, that his
hand should not " be consenting to the death of any
for religion, and did promise a reprieve."   But with
the scruples of a tender conscience, especially of
Cromwell's conscience, who can reckon?   There
was that oath he had taken, which governed all his
conduct, that he would obey strictly the laws of
England.   Accordingly, the ambassador was informed next evening, that Cromwell's " Council

scribed in the English Historical Review, Oct., 1888, p. 735,
concocted between Col. Manley, a knave, and Col. Dean, a dupe.
Talk about the surprisal of the Lord Mayor, or " a collection of 5*l.*
a piece from the officers, for some person to seize on " the Protector, formed the plotters' nearest approach to action.   The day
of outbreak was named by Manley, but no leaders were told off to
head the enterprise, no horses provided, nor arms, save two boxes
of pistols and some powder horns.   As Corker, the spy, had
Dean in hand, this affair, though it sent three men to the gallows,
was as unreal as the " sawceage plot," which inaugurated the outset
of Cromwell's Protectorate.

advised him that the laws should be executed to which he had swore." So the ambassador had to content himself with buying "the quarters of the priest from the hangman for 40s." Southworth was put to death to revive the popular hatred against the papists.[6] And Slingsby was "ripened," by Cromwell's orders, for the scaffold, to convince England that Charles, "in the great Papist Interest," had almost made good a landing on our shores.

Here is the outline of the story. An incident may be remembered in the Insurrection of March, 1655, namely, a midnight ride taken by some Yorkshire squires over Marston Moor, and their prompt return home, because the Insurrection proved, in vulgar phrase, "a thorough sell." Those gentlemen were thrown into York jail; and if Cromwell could have had his way they would have figured on the scaffold. Cromwell did not have his way. His judges were doubtful "whether in point of law" that midnight ride was an act of treason. The judges were "put out of their places," but the squires saved their lives. Sir Henry Slingsby was, however, detained in jail by the Major-Generals. He was, at the opening of this narrative, December, 1657, a prisoner, lodged in Hull under the custody of an officer of the garrison; he was shortly afterwards transferred to the Castle, and finally, on the 8th June, 1658, to a scaffold on Tower Hill.

[6] Lingard, VII. 163. Thurloe, II. 406. Symond's MSS., Harl. MSS., 991, fo. 22.

Slingsby's crime of High Treason against the Protector, as told in court by Cromwell's witnesses, is positive enough. Those witnesses were three officers of the Hull garrison, Major Waterhouse, Captain John Overton, and Lieutenant Thompson. They proved that, for about three months, from the close of December, 1657, to the opening days of April, 1658, Sir Henry tempted them, with bribes and entreaties, to enter the King's service; and that on 2nd April Slingsby delivered, in Overton's presence, to Major Waterhouse a royal commission, appointing him Governor of Hull Castle. Thereupon Slingsby was sent up to London.

According to Major Waterhouse and Captain Overton, Slingsby persistently, wilfully, and of his own accord, without any incitement on their part, forced upon them his treasonable proposals. So eager was he, that he commenced his persuasions with no previous attempt to ascertain how his overtures would be received. He was so reckless in the game of treason, that he wrote his seditious messages on the open leaves of a table-book, and sent the first of these notes to Major Waterhouse when upon the hunting-field. This was strange conduct on the part of one who was described by Clarendon as a man "of good understanding, but of a very melancholic nature, and of very few words."

Slingsby's conduct, however, is not strange, when explained by the letters about him which passed between Cromwell, Thurloe, and Colonel Smith,

Governor of Hull Castle. During those three months Slingsby was "dancing in a net" spread for him by the Protector and Colonel Smith. Their device was simple enough. The Governor of the Castle pretended that he was an Ardent Royalist, and employed Major Waterhouse as his assistant to trepan their prisoner. At first Waterhouse was unsuccessful. From December to the 1st January, 1658, no written evidence could be drawn from Slingsby against himself, except those notes written on the leaves of his table-book. At this point in the transaction the Protector makes his appearance. Evidently those notes were not enough; he required a delivery by Slingsby, in the presence of two witnesses, of a commission from the King.

Cromwell's instructions can be gathered from the Governor's letters. He reports to the Protector "that, according to your Highness's commands, I have endeavoured by all the ways and means that is possible I could, to get further proof against Sir Henry Slingsby, besides Major Waterhouse, but cannot by any means accomplish it, for the present. I have desired the Major to use all the arguments that he could, to persuade him (Slingsby) to give way to the Major to engage a friend of his in the plot, who should be as a messenger betwixt them, for the better carrying on of the business, but he would not condescend to it, telling the Major it would be dangerous to both of them to have any other made privy to it, till nearer the time of putting things in execution." [7]

Though His Highness's commands received due attention, a letter to Thurloe from the Governor shows that, in his opinion, Cromwell was needlessly slow in taking Slingsby's life. Cromwell's desire, it would seem, had been anticipated by the Governor, for he remarks, " I believe if His Highness had given way to it, the Major might have had a Commission very shortly from " C. S.," by the means of the gentleman formerly mentioned (i.e. Slingsby), which would have been good evidence against him, and have convinced others." [7]

Acting as the Protector desired, the Governor took a step which, if Slingsby had been in the hands of honest men, would have put him put out of reach of temptation, and saved his life. He was removed from lodgings in the town, and remitted to close imprisonment in Hull Castle. But the tighter Cromwell's net was drawn round his victim, the more lively in the meshes did he become. Close imprisonment, an obvious sign that suspicion was rife against him, provoked Slingsby to unwonted activity. With himself and his papers under the immediate supervision of the Governor, he cast aside all hesitation ; and he " had not been many days" in the Castle, when he "manifested his malicious treachery against His Highness, endea-

---

[7] Letters from Colonel Smith, 4th and 5th Feb., 1658. Thurloe papers, VI. 777, 780 ; VII. 123.

vouring to engage Captain Overton, as he had formerly Major Waterhouse." [8]

Cromwell had now got his second witness. Then a hitch occurred in the business of maturing Slingsby for the scaffold. Some five days elapsed, and the Governor had to inform Cromwell that Slingsby "had not proceeded so far with Overton as he did with Major Waterhouse." The Protector's sickle, however, did not pause long when once upon full swing. In about a fortnight he was informed that Slingsby was trapped, "according to H.H.'s commands," and that "the business is ripe." Assuring Cromwell that he had acted "in pursuance of His Highness's instructions," the Governor reports that "this evening Sir Henry delivered the inclosed commission to Major Waterhouse, in the presence of Captain Overton. I do humbly conceive that there is now sufficient evidence against him concerning the whole business."[8] Unquestionably the business was now "ripe" enough. Cromwell's "former commands" and his "instructions" had been obeyed. The net he had woven was drawn over his prisoner's head.

The chain of evidence against the Protector is without a flaw. He instructed his officer, Governor Smith, throughout "the business." [8] Major Waterhouse stated that he never visited the prisoner, save under the Governor's "commis-

[8] Colonel Smith to the Protector, 13th March, 2nd April, 1658. Thurloe, VI. 870; VII. 46. State Trials, V. 879.

sion." Captain Overton was Major Waterhouse's " friend in the plot;" and the third witness, Lieutenant Thompson, who " was not forward in the work," offered this excuse for his appearance in court. " I was desired to go and see Sir Henry Slingsby;" [8] and the prisoner confirmed that statement by a tragi-comic account of the manœuvres whereby he and Thompson had been brought together at dinner, and how Waterhouse had sneered at Slingsby's hesitation in winning Thompson over to Charles Stuart.

With Cromwell and his servants as witnesses, it is hardly necessary to confirm their evidence by the testimony of contemporary historians. They state, however, that those three officers of Cromwell's army " were sent unto Slingsby to make the motion to him, and sift out his mind with purpose to betray him."[9] They did their work well : " the sleight of hand and cunning craftiness " that tricked Slingsby's head off his shoulders were, almost to the end, invisible to him. That Hull Castle should furnish a hiding-place for a commission from Charles II., and serve as an enlistment ground for soldiers to surprise its own ramparts, aroused no suspicion.[9] Slingsby trusted in his friend the Governor. It was not till the trial was drawing to a close that Slingsby's eyes were opened, and he exclaimed, " I see that I am trepanned by

[9] Baker, 561. Heath, 403. Thurloe, VII 111.

those two fellows : I never sought to them, but they to me."

The Attorney-General, at Slingsby's trial, in demand for judgment, declared that " he was sorry that people should be thus seduced, and drawn into designs, which he was confident would never take, for their seducers bring them to the gallows, and then laugh at them." A most just remark. The seducer who triumphed over the prisoner in the dock was His Highness the Lord Protector.

It may be urged that Cromwell lured Slingsby onward, fearing his capacity for mischief, and that it is justifiable to avert peril from the State by luring a dangerous conspirator to his fate. Such an excuse would, on this occasion, be ludicrous. That penniless, melancholic prisoner was not the centre of a vast conspiracy, or of any conspiracy at all. He was perfectly harmless ; he had no adherents, save those that Cromwell provided for him. So resourceless was Slingsby, that three recruits were all that he could offer for the fancied surprise of Hull Castle, and of these three, only one visited him there. So ignorant was he of the outside world, that he gravely asserted that Major-General Overton was engaged to bring six regiments over to the royal cause, and that he was to receive a pardon for what he had done, being quite unconscious that the Major-General was safely under lock and key.

Not an effort was made at the trial to prove the existence of a plot, or of any scheme for the seizure of Hull.   Had even a far-off danger of such an attempt been suspected, Cromwell would not have "lain in wait to deceive," and kept Slingsby on the ply for over three months.   The Protector knew that he could safely wait, whilst the victim was being got ready for the sacrifice.

The Great Rebellion has finely tapered down.   It was begun by the craft of a subject directed against his Sovereign : it ends in the death of an otherwise unknown subject wrought by the craft of his Royal Protector.   Time or opportunity, however, to weave more nets for the ensnarement of Englishmen, Oliver Cromwell did not enjoy.   Faced by these two certainties,—bankruptcy without a supply from Parliament,—overthrow if he summoned Parliament,— hit, hard and sore, by disease and grief, he lingered on, until, within three months of Slingsby's execution day, Cromwell received his dismissal on the 3rd September, 1658.

Though wrecked in mind, body, and estate, until his death, the spell cast by that dark Protector brooded not over England only, it stretched across the Channel.   When the news of the 3rd of September reached Amsterdam, not "the mourners," but dancers "went about the streets," and "the language at every turn " was, " the Devil is dead." [10]
The application of that designation to a Crom-

[10] Clarendon State Papers, III. 412.   J. R. Green, History, II.

well was, at least, no novelty. Taught by bitter
experience, the subjects of Henry VIII. applied
that peculiar name to a man who used high position
in the State to tempt and to deceive, and then accused and destroyed those whom he had ensnared.
It is to Thomas Cromwell that I refer.

He "made himself great and his family great"
by terrorism, by "tales of plots and conspiracies."
He called to his aid a host of trepanners and
informers. By their help he sought to effect the
abolition of the religious houses. To prove the
destruction of the Conventual establishments to be
"no feigned necessity," and that his accusations
were "things of fact, of evident demonstration," it
is "traditioned" that he played the tempter's part,
and sent "gallants with fair faces, flattering tongues,
youth, wit, wantonness," to seduce and to inform
against the nuns. For conduct such as this, Thomas
Cromwell was styled the *Diabolus Monachorum.*

Fortune, however, turns her wheel, and rolls forth
different ideas of right and wrong. In return for
the destruction he wrought upon the Papists, the
Protestants adopted Thomas Cromwell as their
"Pattern Man." They converted the Diabolus
into a Saint.[10]

This simile speaks for itself. "The Father of Lies
is of no party." Misplaced adoration is a weakness
possible alike to a Positivist and to a Protestant.

164. Hook's "Lives of the Archbishops," I., N.S. 115. Fuller's
"Church History," book VI. 318.

Yet it is as well that the hour should come when " the vile person shall be no more called liberal, nor the churl," who by " wicked devices " destroyed "the poor with lying words," be esteemed " bountiful."

Can it be held of those who made Oliver Cromwell's " excellent dissembling look like perfect honour," that they had no cause to consider their ways ? Surely they had warning enough. Had the cry of the Lord Protector, " I do not lie," or of his prisoner, " I see that I am trepanned," been duly heeded, they would have perceived that they were ensnared by a being who calls on " him that wanteth understanding," " Turn in hither ! "—and then leads his " guests " where " the dead are," and among those who " are in the depths of Hell."

INDEX TO INTRODUCTORY CHAPTERS.

GENERAL INDEX.

proposes to torture Royalists, 136.

Rochester, Lord, met by sham friends sent by Cromwell, 101; one of the leaders of the Insurrection, 109; lands in England, 110; delusions practised on, 104, 105; conduct at Marston Moor, 118; at Aylesbury, 125; his escape from England, 126.

Ross, Mrs., the go-between in the match between the King and Wildman, 267.

Royalists, in England, corrupted by the Protectorate, 21; incapable of action, 29; their schemes during 1654, 43; accused by Cromwell of conspiracies in January, 1655, 49; described by Mr. Greene, 47; Cromwell's Royalist Bank, 50, *n.*; purchase of arms by, 54; their action on Charles to sanction the Insurrection of 1655, 93; hold aloof from the Insurrection, 95; deluded regarding the Levellers, 96; proposal to torture, 136; their designs according to Cromwell's " Declaration," 137; arrests of June, 1655, 154; the decimation tax imposed upon them, 156; turn towards King Oliver, 175; power of Major-Generals over their households, *ib.*; acted on by Wildman and Bishop, 264, 273, 288; cast their inaction on King's advisers, 289. *See* Insurrection of March, 1655.

Rufford Abbey, Royalist meeting at, 142.

Sagredo, his remarks on Lambert's position in the State, 9; on Cromwell's plot inventions, 17; on the instability of the Protectorate, 27; on Cromwell's ill-health in 1655-6, 168.

Salisbury, seized by Wagstaff, 119; warning about the Royalists there, 121.

Salisbury Plain, mentioned as a Leveller's rendezvous, 6, 103

" Sawceage " Conspiracy, the, 32.

Scobell, Mr., Clerk of the Parliament, deserts the Lower House, 251; debates thereon, 253.

" Sealed Knot," the Council of English Royalists, 42; warns Charles against the Insurrection of 1655, 93.

Sexby, Colonel, his plots during the winter of 1654, 67; flies from England, 68; Bishop's help, 266; suspicious character of, 279; his intrigues, 281.

Shirley, Sir R., agent for King with Levellers, 268.

Sindercombe, his attempt to murder Cromwell, 206, 281, 284.

Slaves, Englishmen sold as, 36, 59, 157, *n.*

Slingsby, Sir H., mention of his death by contemporaries, 22; how he was ensnared by Cromwell, 298; his trial, 203.

Smith, Colonel, Governor of Hull, ensnares Slingsby, 299.

South Molton, capture at, of Penruddock's followers, 120.

Southworth, priest, executed by Cromwell, 297.

THE END.

PRINTED BY GILBERT AND RIVINGTON, LD., ST. JOHN'S HOUSE, CLERKENWELL ROAD.

A Catalogue of American and Foreign Books Published or Imported by MESSRS. SAMPSON LOW & CO. *can be had on application.*

St. Dunstan's House, Fetter Lane, Fleet Street, London,
October, 1889.

A Selection from the List of Books

PUBLISHED BY

SAMPSON LOW, MARSTON, SEARLE, & RIVINGTON,

LIMITED.

Low's Standard Novels, page 17.
Low's Standard Books for Boys, page 18.
Low's Standard Series, page 19.
Sea Stories, by W. CLARK RUSSELL, page 26.

ALPHABETICAL LIST.

ABBEY and Parsons, Quiet life. From drawings ; the motive
by Au-tin Dobson, 4to.

Abney (W. de W.) and Cunningham. Pioneers of the Alps.
With photogravure portraits of guides. Imp. 8vo, gilt top, 21*s.*

Adam (G. Mercer) and Wetherald. An Algonquin Maiden.
Crown 8vo, 5*s.*

Alcott. Works of the late Miss Louisa May Alcott :—
Aunt Jo's Scrap-bag. Cloth, 2*s.*
Eight Cousins. Illustrated, 2*s.*; cloth gilt, 3*s.* 6*d.*
Jack and Jill. Illustrated, 2*s.*; cloth gilt, 3*s.* 6*d.*
Jo's Boys. 5*s.*
Jimmy's Cruise in the Pinafore, &c. Illustrated, cloth, 2*s.*; gilt edges,
3*s.* 6*d.*
Little Men. Double vol., 2*s.*; cloth, gilt edges, 3*s.* 6*d.*
Little Women. 1*s.*   } 1 vol., cloth, 2*s.* ; larger ed., gilt
Little Women Wedded. 1*s.* }   edges, 3*s.* 6*d.*
Old-fashioned Girl. 2*s.*; cloth, gilt edges, 3*s.* 6*d.*
Rose in Bloom. 2*s.*; cloth gilt, 3*s.* 6*d.*
Shawl Straps. Cloth, 2*s.*
Silver Pitchers. Cloth, gilt edges, 3*s.* 6*d.*
Under the Lilacs. Illustrated, 2*s.*; cloth gilt, 5*s.*
Work : a Story of Experience. 1*s.*   } 1 vol., cloth, gilt
———— Its Sequel, "Beginning Again." 1*s.* }   edges, 3*s.* 6*d.*
———— *Life, Letters and Journals.* By EDNAH D. CHENEY.
Cr. 8vo, 6*s.*
———— See also "Low's Standard Series."

Alden (W. L.) Adventures of Jimmy Brown, written by himself.
Illustrated. Small crown 8vo, cloth, 2*s.*
———— *Trying to find Europe.* Illus., crown 8vo, 5*s.*

Alger (J. G.) Englishmen in the French Revolution, cr. 8vo, 7s. 6d.
Amateur Angler's Days in Dove Dale : Three Weeks' Holiday in 1884. By E. M. 1s. 6d. ; boards, 1s. ; large paper, 5s.
Andersen. Fairy Tales. An entirely new Translation. With over 500 Illustrations by Scandinavian Artists. Small 4to, 6s.
Anderson (W.) Pictorial Arts of Japan. With 80 full-page and other Plates, 16 of them in Colours. Large imp. 4to, £8 8s. (in four folio parts, £2 2s. each) ; Artists' Proofs, £12 12s.
Angling. See Amateur, "Cutcliffe," "Fennell," "Halford," "Hamilton," "Martin," "Orvis," "Pennell," "Pritt," "Senior," "Stevens," "Theakston," "Walton," "Wells," and "Willis-Bund."
Arnold (R.) Ammonia and Ammonium Compounds. Translated, illus., crown 8vo, 5s.
Art Education. See "Biographies," "D'Anvers," "Illustrated Text Books," "Mollett's Dictionary."
Artistic Japan. Illustrated with Coloured Plates. Monthly. Royal 4to, 2s.; vol. I., 15s.; II., roy. 4to., 15s.
Ashe (R. P.) Two Kings of Uganda ; Six Years in E. Equatorial Africa. Crown 8vo, 6s.
Attwell (Prof.) The Italian Masters. Crown 8vo, 3s. 6d.
Audsley (G. A.) Handbook of the Organ. Imperial 8vo, top edge gilt, 31s. 6d.; large paper, 63s.
———— *Ornamental Arts of Japan.* 90 Plates, 74 in Colours and Gold, with General and Descriptive Text. 2 vols., folio, £15 15s.; in specally designed leather, £23 2s.
———— *The Art of Chromo-Lithography.* Coloured Plates and Text. Folio, 63s.

Bacon (Delia) Biography, with Letters of Carlyle, Emerson, &c. Crown 8vo, 10s. 6d.
Baddeley (W. St. Clair) Tchay and Chianti. Small 8vo, 5s.
———— *Travel-tide.* Small post 8vo, 7s. 6d.
Baldwin (James) Story of Siegfried. 6s.
———— *Story of the Golden Age.* Illustrated by Howard Pyle. Crown 8vo, 6s.
———— *Story of Roland.* Crown 8vo, 6s.
Bamford (A. J.) Turbans and Tails. Sketches in the Unromantic East. Crown 8vo, 7s. 6d.
Barlow (Alfred) Weaving by Hand and by Power. With several hundred Illustrations. Third Edition, royal 8vo, £1 5s.
Barlow (P. W.) Kaipara, Experiences of a Settler in N. New Zealand. Illust., crown 8vo, 6s.
Bassett (F. S.) Legends and Superstitions of the Sea. 7s. 6d.

THE BAYARD SERIES.

Edited by the late J. HAIN FRISWELL.

Comprising Pleasure Books of Literature produced in the Choicest Style.

"We can hardly imagine better books for boys to read or for men to ponder over."—*Times.*

Price 2s. 6d. each Volume, complete in itself, flexible cloth extra, gilt edges, with silk Headbands and Registers.

The Story of the Chevalier Bayard.
Joinville's St. Louis of France.
The Essays of Abraham Cowley.
Abdallah. By Edouard Laboullaye.
Napoleon, Table-Talk and Opinions.
Words of Wellington.
Johnson's Rasselas. With Notes.
Hazlitt's Round Table.
The Religio Medici, Hydriotaphia, &c. By Sir Thomas Browne, Knt.
Coleridge's Christabel, &c. With Preface by Algernon C. Swinburne.
Ballad Poetry of the Affections. By Robert Buchanan.

Lord Chesterfield's Letters, Sentences, and Maxims. With Essay by Sainte-Beuve.
The King and the Commons. Cavalier and Puritan Songs.
Vathek. By William Beckford.
Essays in Mosaic. By Ballantyne.
My Uncle Toby ; his Story and his Friends. By P. Fitzgerald.
Reflections of Rochefoucauld.
Socrates : Memoirs for English Readers from Xenophon's Memorabilia. By Edw. Levien.
Prince Albert's Golden Precepts.

A Case containing 12 Volumes, price 31s. 6d.; or the Case separately, price 3s. 6d.

Beaugrand (C.) Walks Abroad of Two Young Naturalists. By D. SHARP. Illust., 8vo, 7s. 6d.

Beecher (H. W.) Authentic Biography, and Diary. Ill. 8vo, 21s.

Behnke and Browne. Child's Voice : its Treatment with regard to After Development. Small 8vo, 3s. 6d.

Bell (H. H. J.) Obeah : Negro Superstition in the West Indies. Crown 8vo, 2s. 6d.

Beyschlag. Female Costume Figures of various Centuries. 12 reproductions of pastel designs in portfolio, imperial. 21s.

Bickerdyke (J.) Irish Midsummer Night's Dream. Illus. by E. M. Cox. Crown 8vo, 1s. 6d.; boards, 1s.

Bickersteth (Bishop E. H.) Clergyman in his Home. 1s.

—————— *Evangelical Churchmanship.* 1s.

—————— *From Year to Year : Original Poetical Pieces.* Small post 8vo, 3s. 6d.; roan, 6s. and 5s.; calf or morocco, 10s. 6d.

—————— *The Master's Home-Call.* N. ed. 32mo, cloth gilt, 1s.

—————— *The Master's Will.* A Funeral Sermon preached on the Death of Mrs. S. Gurney Buxton. Sewn, 6d.; cloth gilt, 1s.

—————— *The Reef, and other Parables.* Crown 8vo, 2s. 6d.

—————— *Shadow of the Rock.* Select Religious Poetry. 2s. 6d.

—————— *Shadowed Home and the Light Beyond.* 5s.

—————— See also " Hymnal Companion."

Biographies of the Great Artists (Illustrated). Crown 8vo, emblematical binding, 3s. 6d. per volume, except where the price is given.

Claude le Lorrain, by Owen J. Dullea.
Correggio, by M. E. Heaton. 2s. 6d.
Della Robbia and Cellini. 2s. 6d.
Albrecht Dürer, by R. F. Heath.
Figure Painters of Holland.
Fra Angelico, Masaccio, and Botticelli.
Fra Bartolommeo, Albertinelli, and Andrea del Sarto.
Gainsborough and Constable.
Ghiberti and Donatello. 2s. 6d.
Giotto, by Harry Quilter.
Hans Holbein, by Joseph Cundall.
Hogarth, by Austin Dobson.
Landseer, by F. G. Stevens.
Lawrence and Romney, by Lord Ronald Gower. 2s. 6d.
Leonardo da Vinci.
Little Masters of Germany, by W. B. Scott.
Mantegna and Francia.
Meissonier, by J. W. Mollett. 2s. 6d.
Michelangelo Buonarotti, by Clément.
Murillo, by Ellen E. Minor. 2s. 6d.
Overbeck, by J. B. Atkinson.
Raphael, by N. D'Anvers.
Rembrandt, by J. W. Mollett.
Reynolds, by F. S. Pulling.
Rubens, by C. W. Kett.
Tintoretto, by W. R. Osler.
Titian, by R. F. Heath.
Turner, by Cosmo Monkhouse.
Vandyck and Hals, by P. R. Head.
Velasquez, by E. Stowe.
Vernet and Delaroche, by J. Rees.
Watteau, by J. W. Mollett. 2s. 6d.
Wilkie, by J. W. Mollett.

IN PREPARATION.

Barbizon School, by J. W. Mollett.
Cox and De Wint. Lives and Works.
George Cruikshank, Life and Works.
Miniature Painters of Eng. School.
Mulready Memorials, by Stephens.
Van de Velde and the Dutch Painters

Bird (F. J.) American Practical Dyer's Companion. 8vo, 42s.

—— *(H. E.) Chess Practice.* 8vo, 2s. 6d.

Black (Robert) Horse Racing in France : a History. 8vo, 14s.

—— See also CICERO.

Black (W.) Penance of John Logan, and other Tales. Crown 8vo, 10s. 6d.

——See also "Low's Standard Library."

Blackburn (Charles F.) Hints on Catalogue Titles and Index Entries, with a Vocabulary of Terms and Abbreviations, chiefly from Foreign Catalogues. Royal 8vo, 14s.

Blackburn (Henry) Art in the Mountains, the Oberammergau Passion Play. New ed., corrected to date, 8vo, 5s.

—— *Breton Folk.* With 171 Illust. by RANDOLPH CALDECOTT Imperial 8vo, gilt edges, 21s.; plainer binding, 10s. 6d.

—— *Pyrenees.* Illustrated by GUSTAVE DORÉ, corrected to 1881. Crown 8vo, 7s. 6d. See also CALDECOTT.

Blackmore (R. D.) Kit and Kitty. A novel. 3 vols., crown 8vo, 31s. 6d.

—— *Lorna Doone. Édition de luxe.* Crown 4to, very numerous Illustrations, cloth, gilt edges, 31s. 6d.; parchment, uncut, top gilt, 35s.; new issue, plainer, 21s.

—— *Novels.* See also "Low's Standard Novels."

Blackmore (*R. D.*) *Springhaven.* Illust. by PARSONS and
BARNARD. Sq. 8vo, 12s.; new edition, 7s. 6d.

Blaikie (*William*) *How to get Strong and how to Stay so.*
Rational, Physical, Gymnastic, &c., Exercises. Illust., sm. post 8vo, 5s.

—————— *Sound Bodies for our Boys and Girls.* 16mo, 2s. 6d.

Bonwick. British Colonies. Asia, 1s.; Africa, 1s.; America,
1s.; Australasia, 1s. One vol., cloth, 5s.

Bosanquet (*Rev. C.*) *Blossoms from the King's Garden : Sermons*
for Children. 2nd Edition, small post 8vo, cloth extra, 6s.

—————— *Jehoshaphat ; or, Sunlight and Clouds.* 1s.

Bowden (*H. ; Miss*) *Witch of the Atlas : a ballooning story,*
Crown 8vo, 6s.

Bower (*G. S.*) *and Spencer, Law of Electric Lighting.* New
edition, crown 8vo, 12s. 6d.

Boyesen (*H. H.*) *Modern Vikings : Stories of Life and Sport*
in Norseland. Cr. 8vo, 6s.

—————— *Story of Norway.* Illustrated, sm. 8vo, 7s. 6d.

Boy's Froissart. King Arthur. Knightly Legends of Wales.
Percy. See LANIER.

Bradshaw (*J.*) *New Zealand as it is.* 8vo, 12s. 6d.

—————— *New Zealand of To-day,* 1884-87. 8vo, 14s.

Brannt (*W. T.*) *Animal and Vegetable Fats and Oils.*
Illust., 8vo, 35s.

—————— *Manufacture of Soap and Candles, with many Formulas.*
Illust., 8vo, 35s.

—————— *Manufacture of Vinegar, Cider, and Fruit Wines.*
Illustrated, 8vo.

—————— *Metallic Alloys. Chiefly from the German of Krupp*
and Wildberger. Crown 8vo, 12s. 6d.

Bright (*John*) *Public Letters.* Crown 8vo, 7s. 6d.

Brisse (*Baron*) *Ménus* (366). A *ménu*, in French and English,
for every Day in the Year. 2nd Edition. Crown 8vo, 5s.

Brittany. See BLACKBURN.

Browne (*G. Lennox*) *Voice Use and Stimulants.* Sm. 8vo, 3s. 6d.

—————— *and Behnke* (*Emil*) *Voice, Song, and Speech.* N. ed., 5s.

Brumm (*C.*) *Bismarck, his Deeds and Aims; reply to* " *Bismarck*
Dynasty." 8vo, 1s.

Bruntie's Diary. A Tour round the World. By C. E. B., 1s. 6d.

Bryant (*W. C.*) *and Gay* (*S. H.*) *History of the United States.*
4 vols., royal 8vo, profusely Illustrated, 60s.

Bryce (*Rev. Professor*) *Manitoba.* Illust. Crown 8vo, 7s. 6d.

—————— *Short History of the Canadian People.* 7s. 6d.

Bulkeley (*Owen T.*) *Lesser Antilles.* Pref. by D. MORRIS.
Illus., crown 8vo, boards, 2s. 6d.

Burnaby (Mrs. F.) High Alps in Winter; or, Mountaineering in Search of Health.   With Illustrations, &c., 14s.   See also MAIN.
Burnley (J.) History of the Silk Trade.
———— *History of Wool and Woolcombing.* Illust. 8vo, 21s.
Burton (Sir R. F.) Early, Public, and Private Life. Edited by F. HITCHMAN.   2 vols., 8vo, 36s.
Butler (Sir W. F.) Campaign of the Cataracts.   Illust., 8vo, 18s.
———— *Invasion of England, told twenty years after.*   2s. 6d.
———— *Red Cloud; or, the Solitary Sioux.*   Imperial 16mo, numerous illustrations, gilt edges, 3s. 6d.; plainer binding, 2s. 6d.
———— *The Great Lone Land; Red River Expedition.*   7s. 6d.
———— *The Wild North Land; the Story of a Winter Journey* with Dogs across Northern North America. 8vo, 18s. Cr. 8vo, 7s. 6d.
Bynner (E. L.) Agnes Surriage.   Crown 8vo, 10s. 6d.

CABLE (G. W.) Bonaventure: A Prose Pastoral of Acadian Louisiana.   Sm. post 8vo, 5s.
Cadogan (Lady A.) Drawing-room Plays.   10s. 6d. ; acting ed., 6d. each.
———— *Illustrated Games of Patience.*   Twenty-four Diagrams in Colours, with Text.   Fcap. 4to, 12s. 6d.
———— *New Games of Patience.*   Coloured Diagrams, 4to, 12s. 6d.
Caldecott (Randolph) Memoir.   By HENRY BLACKBURN.   With 170 Examples of the Artist's Work.   14s.; new edit., 7s. 6d.
———— *Sketches.*   With an Introduction by H. BLACKBURN. 4to, picture boards, 2s. 6d.
California.   See NORDHOFF.
Callan (H.) Wanderings on Wheel and on Foot. Cr. 8vo, 1s. 6d.
Campbell (Lady Colin) Book of the Running Brook: and of Still Waters.   5s.
Canadian People: Short History.   Crown 8vo, 7s. 6d.
Carbutt (Mrs.) Five Months' Fine Weather in Canada, West U.S., and Mexico.   Crown 8vo, 5s.
Carleton, City Legends.   Special Edition, illus., royal 8vo, 12s. 6d. ; ordinary edition, crown 8vo, 1s.
———— *City Ballads.*   Illustrated, 12s. 6d.   New Ed. (Rose Library), 16mo, 1s.
———— *Farm Ballads, Farm Festivals, and Farm Legends.* Paper boards, 1s. each ; 1 vol., small post 8vo, 3s. 6d.
Carnegie (A.) American Four-in-Hand in Britain.   Small 4to, Illustrated, 10s. 6d.   Popular Edition, paper, 1s.
———— *Round the World.*   8vo, 10s. 6d.
———— *Triumphant Democracy.*   6s. ; also 1s. 6d. and 1s.
Chairman's Handbook.   By R. F. D. PALGRAVE.   5th Edit., 2s.

Changed Cross, &c. Religious Poems. 16mo, 2s. 6d.; calf, 6s.

Chess. See BIRD (H. E.).

Children's Praises. Hymns for Sunday-Schools and Services. Compiled by LOUISA H. H. TRISTRAM. 4d.

Choice Editions of Choice Books. 2s. 6d. each. Illustrated by C. W. COPE, R.A., T. CRESWICK, R.A., E. DUNCAN, BIRKET FOSTER, J. C. HORSLEY, A.R.A., G. HICKS, R. REDGRAVE, R.A., C. STONEHOUSE, F. TAYLER, G. THOMAS, H. J. TOWNSHEND, E. H. WEHNERT, HARRISON WEIR, &c.

Bloomfield's Farmer's Boy.	Milton's L'Allegro.
Campbell's Pleasures of Hope.	Poetry of Nature. Harrison Weir.
Coleridge's Ancient Mariner.	Rogers' (Sam.) Pleasures of Memory.
Goldsmith's Deserted Village.	Shakespeare's Songs and Sonnets.
Goldsmith's Vicar of Wakefield.	Tennyson's May Queen.
Gray's Elegy in a Churchyard.	Elizabethan Poets.
Keats' Eve of St. Agnes.	Wordsworth's Pastoral Poems.

" Such works are a glorious beatification for a poet."—*Athenæum.*

Christ in Song. By PHILIP SCHAFF. New Ed., gilt edges, 6s.

Chromo-Lithography. See AUDSLEY.

Cicero, Tusculan Disputation, I. (Death no bane). Translated by R. BLACK. Small crown 8vo.

Clarke (H. P.) See WILLS.

Clarke (P.) Three Diggers: a Tale of the Australian Fifties. Crown 8vo, 6s.

Cochran (W.) Pen and Pencil in Asia Minor. Illust., 8vo, 21s.

Collingwood (Harry) Under the Meteor Flag. The Log of a Midshipman. Illustrated, small post 8vo, gilt, 3s. 6d.; plainer, 2s. 6d.

———— *Voyage of the " Aurora."* Gilt, 3s. 6d.; plainer, 2s. 6d.

Collinson (Sir R.; Adm.) H.M.S. "Enterprise" in search of Sir J. Franklin. 8vo.

Colonial Year-book. Edited and compiled by A. J. R. TRENDELL. Crown 8vo, 6s.

Cook (Dutton) Book of the Play. New Edition. 1 vol., 3s. 6d.

———— *On the Stage: Studies.* 2 vols., 8vo, cloth, 24s.

Cozzens (F.) American Yachts. 27 Plates, 22 × 28 inches. Proofs, £21; Artist's Proofs, £31 10s.

Craddock (C. E.) Despot of Broomsedge Cove. Crown 8vo, 6s.

Crew (B. J.) Practical Treatise on Petroleum. Illust., 8vo, 28s.

Crouch (A.P.) Glimpses of Feverland: a Cruise in West African Waters. Crown 8vo, 6s.

———— *On a Surf-bound Coast.* Crown 8vo, 7s. 6d.

Cumberland (Stuart) Thought Reader's Thoughts. Cr. 8vo., 10s. 6d.

———— *Queen's Highway from Ocean to Ocean.* Ill., 8vo, 18s.; new ed., 7s. 6d.

Cumberland (S.) Vasty deep : a Strange Story of To-day. New Edition, 6s.

Cundall (Joseph). See " Remarkable Bindings."

Cushing (W.) Initials and Pseudonyms. Large 8vo, 25s.; second series, large 8vo, 21s.

Custer (Eliz. B.) Tenting on the Plains; Gen. Custer in Kansas and Texas. Royal 8vo, 18s.

Cutcliffe (H. C.) Trout Fishing in Rapid Streams. Cr. 8vo, 3s. 6d.

*D*ALY *(Mrs. D.) Digging, Squatting, and Pioneering in* Northern South Australia. 8vo, 12s.

D'Anvers. Elementary History of Art. New ed., 360 illus., 2 vols., cr. 8vo. I. Architecture, &c., 5s.; II. Painting, 6s.; 1 vol., 10s. 6d.

—— *Elementary History of Music.* Crown 8vo, 2s. 6d.

Davis (Clement) Modern Whist. 4s.

—— *(C. T.) Bricks, Tiles, Terra-Cotta, &c.* N. ed. 8vo, 25s.

—— *Manufacture of Leather.* With many Illustrations. 52s. 6d.

—— *Manufacture of Paper.* 28s.

—— *(G. B.) Outlines of International Law.* 8vo. 10s. 6d.

Dawidowsky. Glue, Gelatine, Isinglass, Cements, &c. 8vo, 12s. 6d.

Day of My Life at Eton. By an ETON BOY. New ed. 16mo, 1s.

Day's Collacon : an Encyclopædia of Prose Quotations. Imperial 8vo, cloth, 31s. 6d.

De Leon (E.) Under the Stars and under the Crescent. N. ed., 6s.

Dethroning Shakspere. Letters to the Daily Telegraph ; and Editorial Papers. Crown 8vo, 2s. 6d.

Dickinson (Charles M.) The Children, and other Verses. Sm. 8vo, gilt edges, 5s.

Dictionary. See TOLHAUSEN, " Technological."

Diggle (J. W.; Canon) Lancashire Life of Bishop Fraser. 8vo, 12s. 6d.

Donnelly (Ignatius) Atlantis ; or, the Antediluvian World. 7th Edition, crown 8vo, 12s. 6d.

—— *Ragnarok : The Age of Fire and Gravel.* Illustrated, crown 8vo, 12s. 6d.

—— *The Great Cryptogram : Francis Bacon's Cipher in the* so-called Shakspere Plays. With facsimiles. 2 vols., 30s.

Donkin (J. G.) Trooper and Redskin : N.W. Mounted Police, Canada. Crown 8vo, 8s. 6d.

Dougall (James Dalziel) Shooting : its Appliances, Practice, and Purpose. New Edition, revised with additions. Crown 8vo, 7s. 6d.
"The book is admirable in every way. . . . . We wish it every success."—*Globe.*
"A very complete treatise. . . . . Likely to take high rank as an authority on shooting."—*Daily News.*

Doughty (H.M.) Friesland Meres, and through the Netherlands.
Illustrated, crown 8vo, 8*s.* 6*d.*
Dramatic Year: Brief Criticisms of Events in the U.S. By W.
ARCHER. Crown 8vo, 6*s.*
Dunstan Standard Readers. Ed. by A. GILL, of Cheltenham.

EARL (H. P.) Randall Trevor. 2 vols., crown 8vo, 21*s.*

Eastwood (F.) In Satan's Bonds. 2 vols., crown 8vo, 21*s.*
Edmonds (C.) Poetry of the Anti-Jacobin. With Additional
matter. New ed. Illust., crown 8vo, 7*s.* 6*d.* ; large paper, 21*s.*
Educational List and Directory for 1887-88. 5*s.*
Educational Works published in Great Britain. A Classi-
fied Catalogue. Third Edition, 8vo, cloth extra, 6*s.*
Edwards (E.) American Steam Engineer. Illust., 12mo, 12*s.* 6*d.*
Eight Months on the Argentine Gran Chaco. 8vo, 8*s.* 6*d.*
Elliott (H. W.) An Arctic Province : Alaska and the Seal
Islands. Illustrated from Drawings ; also with Maps. 16*s.*
Emerson (Dr. P. H.) English Idylls. Small post 8vo, 2*s.*
———— *Pictures of East Anglian Life.* Ordinary edit., 105*s.* ;
édit. de luxe, 17 × 13½, vellum, morocco back, 147*s.*
———— *Naturalistic Photography for Art Students.* Illustrated.
New edit. 5*s.*
———— *and Goodall. Life and Landscape on the Norfolk*
Broads. Plates 12 × 8 inches, 126*s.*; large paper, 210*s.*
Emerson in Concord: A Memoir written by Edward Waldo
EMERSON. 8vo, 7*s.* 6*d.*
English Catalogue of Books. Vol. III., 1872—1880. Royal
8vo, half-morocco, 42*s.* See also "Index."
English Etchings. Published Quarterly. 3*s.* 6*d.* Vol. VI., 25*s.*
English Philosophers. Edited by E. B. IVAN MÜLLER, M.A.
Crown 8vo volumes of 180 or 200 pp., price 3*s.* 6*d.* each.

Francis Bacon, by Thomas Fowler.	Shaftesbury and Hutcheson.
Hamilton, by W. H. S. Monck.	Adam Smith, by J. A. Farrer.
Hartley and James Mill.	

Esmarch (F.) Handbook of Surgery. Translation from the
last German Edition. With 647 new Illustrations. 8vo, leather, 24*s.*
Eton. About some Fellows. New Edition, 1*s.*
Evelyn. Life of Mrs. Godolphin. By WILLIAM HARCOURT,
of Nuneham. Steel Portrait. Extra binding, gilt top, 7*s.* 6*d.*
Eves (C. W.) West Indies. (Royal Colonial Institute publication.) Crown 8vo, 7*s.* 6*d.*

FARINI (G. A.) Through the Kalahari Desert. 8vo, 21*s.*

Farm Ballads, Festivals, and Legends. See CARLETON.

Fay (T.) Three Germanys ; glimpses into their History.   2 vols.,
    8vo, 35*s.*
Fenn (G. Manville) Off to the Wilds: a Story for Boys.
    Profusely Illustrated.   Crown 8vo, gilt edges, 3*s.* 6*d.*; plainer, 2*s.* 6*d.*
———— *Silver Cañon.*   Illust., gilt ed., 3*s.* 6*d.* ; plainer, 2*s.* 6*d.*
Fennell (Greville) Book of the Roach.   New Edition, 12mo, 2*s.*
Ferns.   See HEATH.
Fitzgerald (P.) Book Fancier.   Cr. 8vo. 5*s.* ; large pap. 12*s.* 6*d.*
Fleming (Sandford) England and Canada : a Tour.   Cr. 8vo, 6*s.*
Florence.   See YRIARTE.
Folkard (R., Jun.) Plant Lore, Legends, and Lyrics.   8vo, 16*s.*
Forbes (H. O.) Naturalist in the Eastern Archipelago.   8vo.
    21*s.*
Foreign Countries and British Colonies.   Cr. 8vo, 3*s.* 6*d.* each.

Australia, by J. F. Vesey Fitzgerald.	Japan, by S. Mossman.
Austria, by D. Kay, F.R.G.S.	Peru, by Clements R. Markham.
Denmark and Iceland, by E. C. Otté.	Russia, by W. R. Morfill, M.A.
Egypt, by S. Lane Poole, B.A.	Spain, by Rev. Wentworth Webster.
France, by Miss M. Roberts.	Sweden and Norway, by Woods.
Germany, by S. Baring-Gould.	West Indies, by C. H. Eden,
Greece, by L. Sergeant, B.A.	F.R.G.S.

Franc (Maud Jeanne).   Small post 8vo, uniform, gilt edges :—

Emily's Choice. 5*s.*	Vermont Vale. 5*s.*
Hall's Vineyard. 4*s.*	Minnie's Mission. 4*s.*
John's Wife : A Story of Life in	Little Mercy. 4*s.*
South Australia. 4*s.*	Beatrice Melton's Discipline. 4*s.*
Marian ; or, The Light of Some	No Longer a Child. 4*s.*
One's Home. 5*s.*	Golden Gifts. 4*s.*
Silken Cords and Iron Fetters. 4*s.*	Two Sides to Every Question. 4*s.*
Into the Light. 4*s.*	Master of Ralston. 4*s.*

        **** There is also a re-issue in cheaper form at 2*s.* 6*d.* per vol.
Frank's Ranche ; or, My Holiday in the Rockies.   A Contri-
    bution to the Inquiry into What we are to Do with our Boys.   5*s.*
Fraser (Bishop).   See DIGGLE.
French.   See JULIEN and PORCHER.
Fresh Woods and Pastures New.   By the Author of " An
    Amateur Angler's Days."   1*s.* 6*d.*; large paper, 5*s.* ; new ed., 1*s.*
Froissart.   See LANIER.
Fuller (Edward) Fellow Travellers.   3*s.* 6*d.*
———— See also " Dramatic Year."

*G*ASPARIN *(Countess A. de) Sunny Fields and Shady Woods.*
    6*s.*
Geary (Grattan) Burma after the Conquest.   7*s.* 6*d.*
Geffcken (F. H.) British Empire.   Translated by S. J. MAC-
    MULLAN.   Crown 8vo, 7*s.* 6*d.*

Gentle Life (Queen Edition).   2 vols. in 1, small 4to, 6s.

THE GENTLE LIFE SERIES.

Price 6s. each ; or in calf extra, price 10s. 6d. ; Smaller Edition, cloth extra, 2s. 6d., except where price is named.

The Gentle Life.   Essays in aid of the Formation of Character.
About in the World.   Essays by Author of " The Gentle Life."
Like unto Christ.   New Translation of Thomas à Kempis.
Familiar Words.   A Quotation Handbook.   6s.; n. ed. 3s.6d.
Essays by Montaigne.   Edited by the Author of " The Gentle Life."
The Gentle Life.   2nd Series.
The Silent Hour.   Essays, Original and Selected.
Half-Length Portraits.   Short Studies of Notable Persons. By J. HAIN FRISWELL.
Essays on English Writers, for Students in English Literature.
Other People's Windows.   By J. HAIN FRISWELL.   6s.; new ed., 3s. 6d.
A Man's Thoughts.   By J. HAIN FRISWELL.
Countess of Pembroke's Arcadia.   By Sir P. SIDNEY.   6s.; new ed., 3s. 6d.

Germany.   By S. BARING-GOULD.   Crown 8vo, 3s. 6d.
Gibbon (C.) Beyond Compare : a Story.   3 vols., cr. 8vo, 31s. 6d.
Giles (E.) Australia twice Traversed : five Expeditions, 1872-76. With Maps and Illust. 2 vols, 8vo, 30s.
Gillespie (W. M.) Surveying.   Revised and enlarged by CADEY STALEY.   8vo, 21s.
Goethe.   Faustus.   Translated in the original rhyme and metre by A. H. HUTH.   Crown 8vo, 5s.
Goldsmith.   She Stoops to Conquer.   Introduction by AUSTIN DOBSON ; the designs by E. A. ABBEY.   Imperial 4to, 42s.
Gordon (J. E. H., B.A. Cantab.) Electric Lighting.   Ill. 8vo, 18s.
—————— *Physical Treatise on Electricity and Magnetism.*   2nd Edition, enlarged, with coloured, full-page, &c., Illust. 2 vols., 8vo, 42s.
—————— *Electricity for Schools.*   Illustrated.   Crown 8vo, 5s.
Gouffé (Jules) Royal Cookery Book.   New Edition, with plates in colours, Woodcuts, &c., 8vo, gilt edges, 42s.
—————— Domestic Edition, half-bound, 10s. 6d.
Grant (General, U.S.) Personal Memoirs.   With Illustrations, Maps, &c.   2 vols., 8vo, 28s.
Great Artists.   See " Biographies."

Great Musicians.   Edited by F. HUEFFER.   A Series of
Biographies, crown 8vo, 3*s.* each :—

Bach.	Handel.	Rossini.
Beethoven.	Haydn.	Schubert.
Berlioz.	Mendelssohn.	Schumann.
English Church Com-	Mozart.	Richard Wagner.
posers. By BARRETT.	Purcell.	Weber.

Groves (J. Percy) Charmouth Grange. Gilt, 5*s.*; plainer, 2*s.* 6*d.*

Guizot's History of France. Translated by R. BLACK.   In
8 vols., super-royal 8vo, cloth extra, gilt, each 24*s.*   In cheaper
binding, 8 vols., at 10*s.* 6*d.* each.

"It supplies a want which has long been felt, and ought to be in the hands of all
students of history."—*Times.*

———————————— *Masson's School Edition.* Abridged
from the Translation by Robert Black, with Chronological Index, Historical and Genealogical Tables, &c.   By Professor GUSTAVE MASSON,
B.A.   With Portraits, Illustrations, &c.   1 vol., 8vo, 600 pp., 5*s.*

Guyon (Mde.) Life. By UPHAM.   6th Edition, crown 8vo, 6*s.*

*H*ALFORD *(F. M.) Floating Flies, and how to Dress them.*
New edit., with Coloured plates.   8vo, 15*s.*

———— *Dry Fly-Fishing, Theory and Practice.*   Col. Plates, 25*s.*

Hall (W. W.) How to Live Long; or, 1408 *Maxims.*   2*s.*

Hamilton (E.) Fly-fishing for Salmon, Trout, and Grayling;
their Habits, Haunts, and History.   Illust., 6*s.*; large paper, 10*s.* 6*d.*

Hands (T.) Numerical Exercises in Chemistry.   Cr. 8vo, 2*s.* 6*d.*
and 2*s.*;   Answers separately, 6*d.*

Hardy (A. S.) Passe-rose : a Romance.   Crown 8vo, 6*s.*

Hardy (Thomas).   See " Low's Standard Novels."

Hare (J. L. Clark) American Constitutional Law.   2 vls., 8vo, 63*s.*

Harper's Magazine.   Monthly.   160 pages, fully illustrated, 1*s.*
Vols., half yearly, I.—XVIII., super-royal 8vo, 8*s.* 6*d.* each.

"'Harper's Magazine' is so thickly sown with excellent illustrations that to count
them would be a work of time ; not that it is a picture magazine, for the engravings
illustrate the text after the manner seen in some of our choicest *éditions de luxe.*"—
St. James's Gazette.

"It is so pretty, so big, and so cheap. . . . An extraordinary shillingsworth—
160 large octavo pages, with over a score of articles, and more than three times as
many illustrations."—*Edinburgh Daily Review.*

"An amazing shillingsworth . . . combining choice literature of both nations."—
Nonconformist.

Harper's Young People.   Vols. I.-V., profusely Illustrated
with woodcuts and coloured plates.   Royal 4to, extra binding, each
7*s.* 6*d.* ; gilt edges, 8*s.* Published Weekly, in wrapper, 1*d.* ; Annual
Subscription, post free, 6*s.* 6*d.* ; Monthly, in wrapper, with coloured
plate, 6*d.* ; Annual Subscription, post free, 7*s.* 6*d.*

Harris (Bishop of Michigan) Dignity of Man : Select Sermons.
Crown 8vo, 8*s.* 6*d.*

Harris (W. B.) Land of African Sultan : Travels in Morocco.
Illust., crown 8vo, 10*s.* 6*d.* ; large paper, 31*s.* 6*d.*

Harrison (Mary) Complete Cookery Book. Crown 8vo.

—— *Skilful Cook.* New edition, crown 8vo, 5*s.*

Harrison (W.) Memorable London Houses: a Guide. Illust. New edition, 18mo, 1*s.* 6*d.*

Hatton (Joseph) Journalistic London: with Engravings and Portraits of Distinguished Writers of the Day. Fcap. 4to, 12*s.* 6*d.*

—— See also LOW'S STANDARD NOVELS.

Haweis (Mrs.) Art of Housekeeping: a Bridal Garland. 2*s.*6*d.*

Hawthorne (Nathaniel) Life. By JOHN R. LOWELL.

Heldmann (B.) Mutiny of the Ship "Leander." Gilt edges, 3*s.* 6*d.*; plainer, 2*s.* 6*d.*

Henty. Winning his Spurs. Cr. 8vo, 3*s.* 6*d.* ; plainer, 2*s.* 6*d.*

—— *Cornet of Horse.* Cr. 8vo, 3*s.* 6*d.*; plainer, 2*s.* 6*d.*

—— *Jack Archer.* Illust. 3*s.* 6*d.* ; plainer, 2*s.* 6*d.*

Henty (Richmond) Australiana: My Early Life. 5*s.*

Herrick (Robert) Poetry. Preface by AUSTIN DOBSON. With numerous Illustrations by E. A. ABBEY. 4to, gilt edges, 42*s.*

Hetley (Mrs. E.) Native Flowers of New Zealand. Chromos from Drawings. Three Parts, 63*s.*; extra binding, 73*s.* 6*d.*

Hicks (E. S.) Our Boys: How to Enter the Merchant Service. 5*s.*

—— *Yachts, Boats and Canoes.* Illustrated. 8vo, 10*s.* 6*d.*

Hinman (R) Eclectic Physical Geography. Crown 8vo, 5*s.*

Hitchman. Public Life of the Earl of Beaconsfield. 3*s.* 6*d.*

Hoey (Mrs. Cashel) See LOW'S STANDARD NOVELS.

Holder (C. F.) Marvels of Animal Life. Illustrated. 8*s.* 6*d.*

—— *Ivory King: Elephant and Allies.* Illustrated. 8*s.* 6*d.*

—— *Living Lights: Phosphorescent Animals and Vegetables.* Illustrated. 8vo, 8*s.* 6*d.*

Holmes (O. W.) Before the Curfew, &c. Occasional Poems. 5*s.*

—— *Last Leaf: a Holiday Volume.* 42*s.*

—— *Mortal Antipathy,* 8*s.* 6*d.* ; also 2*s.* ; paper, 1*s.*

—— *Our Hundred Days in Europe.* 6*s.* Large Paper, 15*s.*

—— *Poetical Works.* 2 vols., 18mo, gilt tops, 10*s.* 6*d.*

—— See also "Rose Library."

Howard (Blanche Willis) Open Door. Crown 8vo, 6*s.*

Howorth (H. H.) Mammoth and the Flood. 8vo, 18*s.*

Hugo (V.) Notre Dame. With coloured etchings and 150 engravings. 2 vols., 8vo, vellum cloth, 30*s.*

Hundred Greatest Men (The). 8 portfolios, 21*s.* each, or 4 vols., half-morocco, gilt edges, 10 guineas. New Ed., 1 vol., royal 8vo, 21*s.*

Hymnal Companion to the Book of Common Prayer. By BISHOP BICKERSTETH. In various styles and bindings from 1*d.* to 31*s.* 6*d. Price List and Prospectus will be forwarded on application.*

ILLUSTRATED Text-Books of Art-Education.   Edited by
EDWARD J. POYNTER, R.A.   Illustrated, and strongly bound, 5s.
Now ready :—

PAINTING.

Classic and Italian.   By HEAD. | **French and Spanish.**
German, Flemish, and Dutch. | **English and American.**

ARCHITECTURE.

Classic and Early Christian.
Gothic and Renaissance.   By T. ROGER SMITH.

SCULPTURE.

Antique : Egyptian and Greek.
Renaissance and Modern.   By LEADER SCOTT.

Inderwick (F. A. ; Q.C.) Side Lights on the Stuarts.   Essays.
Illustrated, 8vo, 18s.

Index to the English Catalogue, Jan., 1874, *to Dec.,* 1880
Royal 8vo, half-morocco, 18s.

Inglis (Hon. James ; " Maori ") Our New Zealand Cousins.
Small post 8vo, 6s.

—— *Tent Life in Tiger Land : Twelve Years a Pioneer*
Planter.   Col. plates, roy 8vo, 18s.

Irving (Washington).   Library Edition of his Works in 27 vols.,
Copyright, with the Author's Latest Revisions.   "Geoffrey Crayon"
Edition, large square 8vo.   12s. 6d. per vol.   *See also* "Little Britain."

JACKSON.   New Style Vertical Writing Copy-Books.
Series 1, Nos. I.—XII., 2d. and 1d. each.

—— *New Series of Vertical Writing Copy-books.*   22 Nos.

—— *Shorthand of Arithmetic : a Companion to all Arithmetics.*
Crown 8vo, 1s. 6d.

Japan.   See ANDERSON, ARTISTIC, AUDSLEY, also MORSE.

Jerdon (Gertrude) Key-hole Country.   Illustrated.   Crown 8vo,
cloth, 2s.

Johnston (H. H.) River Congo, from its Mouth to Bolobo.
New Edition, 8vo, 21s.

Johnstone (D. Lawson) Land of the Mountain Kingdom.
Illust., crown 8vo.   5s.

Julien (F.) English Student's French Examiner.   16mo, 2s.

—— *Conversational French Reader.*   16mo, cloth, 2s. 6d.

—— *French at Home and at School.*   Book I., Accidence.   2s.

—— *First Lessons in Conversational French Grammar.*   1s.

—— *Petites Leçons de Conversation et de Grammaire.*   3s.

—— *Phrases of Daily Use.*   Limp cloth, 6d.

KARR (H. W. Seton) Shores and Alps of Alaska.   8vo,
16s.

Keats.   Endymion.   Illust. by W. ST. JOHN HARPER.   Imp.
4to, gilt top, 42s.

Kempis (Thomas à) Daily Text-Book. Square 16mo, 2s. 6d.; interleaved as a Birthday Book, 3s. 6d.

Kennedy (E. B.) Blacks and Bushrangers, adventures in North Queensland. Illust., crown 8vo, 7s. 6d.

Kent's Commentaries : an Abridgment for Students of American Law. By EDEN F. THOMPSON. 10s. 6d.

Kerr (W. M.) Far Interior : Cape of Good Hope, across the Zambesi, to the Lake Regions. Illustrated from Sketches, 2 vols. 8vo, 32s.

Kershaw (S. W.) Protestants from France in their English Home. Crown 8vo, 6s.

King (Henry) Savage London ; Riverside Characters, &c. Crown 8vo, 6s.

Kingston (W. H. G.) Works. Illustrated, 16mo, gilt edges, 3s. 6d.; plainer binding, plain edges, 2s. 6d. each.

Ben Burton.	Heir of Kilfinnan.
Captain Mugford, or, Our Salt and Fresh Water Tutors.	Snow-Shoes and Canoes.
	Two Supercargoes.
Dick Cheveley.	With Axe and Rifle.

Kingsley (Rose) Children of Westminster Abbey : Studies in English History. 5s.

Knight (E. J.) Cruise of the " Falcon." New Ed. Cr. 8vo, 7s. 6d.

Knox (Col.) Boy Travellers on the Congo. Illus. Cr. 8vo, 7s. 6d.

Kunhardt (C. B.) Small Yachts : Design and Construction. 35s.

—————— *Steam Yachts and Launches.* Illustrated. 4to, 16s.

LANGLEY (S. P.) New Astronomy. Ill. Cr. 8vo. 10s. 6d.

Lanier's Works. Illustrated, crown 8vo, gilt edges, 7s. 6d. each.

Boy's King Arthur.	Boy's Percy: Ballads of Love and
Boy's Froissart.	Adventure, selected from the
Boy's Knightly Legends of Wales.	"Reliques."

Lansdell (H.) Through Siberia. 2 vols., 8vo, 30s.; 1 vol., 10s. 6d.

—————— *Russia in Central Asia.* Illustrated. 2 vols., 42s.

—————— *Through Central Asia ; Russo-Afghan Frontier, &c.* 8vo, 12s.

Larden (W.) School Course on Heat. Third Ed., Illust. 5s.

Laurie (A.) Conquest of the Moon : a Story of the Bayouda. Illust., crown 8vo, 7s. 6d.

Layard (Mrs. Granville) Through the West Indies. Small post 8vo, 2s. 6d.

Lea (H. C.). History of the Inquisition of the Middle Ages. 3 vols., 8vo, 42s.

Lemon (M.) Small House over the Water, and Stories. Illust.
by Cruikshank, &c. Crown 8vo, 6s.

Leo XIII. : Life. By BERNARD O'REILLY. With Steel
Portrait from Photograph, &c. Large 8vo, 18s.; *édit. de luxe,* 63s.

Leonardo da Vinci's Literary Works. Edited by Dr. JEAN
PAUL RICHTER. Containing his Writings on Painting, Sculpture,
and Architecture, his Philosophical Maxims, Humorous Writings, and
Miscellaneous Notes on Personal Events, on his Contemporaries, on
Literature, &c. ; published from Manuscripts. 2 vols., imperial 8vo,
containing about 200 Drawings in Autotype Reproductions, and numerous other Illustrations. Twelve Guineas.

Library of Religious Poetry. Best Poems of all Ages. Edited
by SCHAFF and GILMAN. Royal 8vo, 21s.; cheaper binding, 10s. 6d.

Lindsay (W. S.) History of Merchant Shipping. Over 150
Illustrations, Maps, and Charts. In 4 vols., demy 8vo, cloth extra.
Vols. 1 and 2, 11s. each ; vols. 3 and 4, 14s. each. 4 vols., 50s.

Little (Archibald J.) Through the Yang-tse Gorges : Trade and
Travel in Western China. New Edition. 8vo, 10s. 6d.

Little Britain, The Spectre Bridegroom, and *Legend of Sleepy*
Hollow. By WASHINGTON IRVING. An entirely New *Edition de
luxe.* Illustrated by 120 very fine Engravings on Wood, by Mr.
J. D. COOPER. Designed by Mr. CHARLES O. MURRAY. Re-issue,
square crown 8vo, cloth, 6s.

Lodge (Henry Cabot) George Washington. (American Statesmen.)
2 vols., 12s.

Longfellow. Maidenhood. With Coloured Plates. Oblong
4to, 2s. 6d.; gilt edges, 3s. 6d.

———— *Courtship of Miles Standish.* Illust. by BROUGHTON,
&c. Imp. 4to, 21s.

———— *Nuremberg.* 28 Photogravures. Illum. by M. and A.
COMEGYS. 4to, 31s. 6d.

Lowell (J. R.) Vision of Sir Launfal. Illustrated, royal 4to, 63s.

———— *Life of Nathaniel Hawthorne.* Sm. post 8vo. [*In prep.*

Low's Standard Library of Travel and Adventure. Crown 8vo,
uniform in cloth extra, 7s. 6d., except where price is given.

1. The Great Lone Land. By Major W. F. BUTLER, C.B.
2. The Wild North Land. By Major W. F. BUTLER, C.B.
3. How I found Livingstone. By H. M. STANLEY.
4. Through the Dark Continent. By H. M. STANLEY. 12s. 6d.
5. The Threshold of the Unknown Region. By C. R. MARK-
   HAM. (4th Edition, with Additional Chapters, 10s. 6d.)
6. Cruise of the Challenger. By W. J. J. SPRY, R.N.
7. Burnaby's On Horseback through Asia Minor. 10s. 6d.
8. Schweinfurth's Heart of Africa. 2 vols., 15s.
9. Through America. By W. G. MARSHALL.
10. Through Siberia. Il. and unabridged, 10s.6d. By H. LANSDELL.
11. From Home to Home. By STAVELEY HILL.
12. Cruise of the Falcon. By E. J. KNIGHT.

Low's Standard Library, &c.—continued.
  13. Through Masai Land. By JOSEPH THOMSON.
  14. To the Central African Lakes. By JOSEPH THOMSON.
  15. Queen's Highway. By STUART CUMBERLAND.

Low's Standard Novels. Small post 8vo, cloth extra, 6s. each,
  unless otherwise stated.

JAMES BAKER. John Westacott.
WILLIAM BLACK.
  A Daughter of Heth.—House-Boat.—In Far Lochaber.—In
    Silk Attire.—Kilmeny.—Lady Silverdale's Sweetheart.—
    Sunrise.—Three Feathers.
R. D. BLACKMORE.
  Alice Lorraine.—Christowell, a Dartmoor Tale.—Clara
    Vaughan.—Cradock Nowell.—Cripps the Carrier.—Erema;
    or, My Father's Sin.—Lorna Doone.—Mary Anerley.—
    Tommy Upmore.
G. W. CABLE. Bonaventure. 5s.
Miss COLERIDGE. An English Squire.
C. E. CRADDOCK. Despot of Broomsedge Cove.
Mrs. B. M. CROKER. Some One Else.
STUART CUMBERLAND. Vasty Deep.
E. DE LEON. Under the Stars and Crescent.
Miss BETHAM-EDWARDS. Halfway.
Rev. E. GILLIAT, M.A. Story of the Dragonnades.
THOMAS HARDY.
  A Laodicean.—Far from the Madding Crowd.—Mayor of
    Casterbridge.—Pair of Blue Eyes.—Return of the Native.—
    The Hand of Ethelberta.—The Trumpet Major.—Two on a
    Tower.
JOSEPH HATTON. Old House at Sandwich.—Three Recruits.
Mrs. CASHEL HOEY.
  A Golden Sorrow.—A Stern Chase.—Out of Court.
BLANCHE WILLIS HOWARD. Open Door.
JEAN INGELOW.
  Don John.—John Jerome (5s.).—Sarah de Berenger.
GEORGE MAC DONALD.
  Adela Cathcart.—Guild Court.—Mary Marston.—Stephen
    Archer (New Ed. of "Gifts").—The Vicar's Daughter.—Orts.
    —Weighed and Wanting.
Mrs. MACQUOID. Diane.—Elinor Dryden.
HELEN MATHERS. My Lady Greensleeves.
DUFFIELD OSBORNE. Spell of Ashtaroth (5s.)
Mrs. J. H. RIDDELL.
  Alaric Spenceley.—Daisies and Buttercups.—The Senior
    Partner.—A Struggle for Fame.
W. CLARK RUSSELL.
  Frozen Pirate.—Jack's Courtship.—John Holdsworth.—A
    Sailor's Sweetheart.—Sea Queen.—Watch Below.—Strange
    Voyage.—Wreck of the Grosvenor.—The Lady Maud.—
    Little Loo.

Low's Standard Novels—continued.

FRANK R. STOCKTON.
  Bee-man of Orn.—The Late Mrs. Null.—Hundredth Man.
Mrs. HARRIET B. STOWE.
  My Wife and I.—Old Town Folk.—We and our Neighbours.—
  Poganuc People, their Loves and Lives.
JOSEPH THOMSON. Ulu: an African Romance.
LEW. WALLACE. Ben Hur: a Tale of the Christ.
CONSTANCE FENIMORE WOOLSON.
  Anne.—East Angels.—For the Major (5s.).
French Heiress in her own Chateau.

See also SEA STORIES.

Low's Standard Novels. NEW ISSUE at short intervals. Cr.
  8vo, 2s. 6d.; fancy boards, 2s.
BLACKMORE.
  Clara Vaughan.—Cripps the Carrier.—Lorna Doone.—Mary
  Anerley.
HARDY.
  Madding Crowd.—Mayor of Casterbridge.—Trumpet-Major.
HATTON. Three Recruits.
HOLMES. Guardian Angel.
MAC DONALD. Adela Cathcart.—Guild Court.
RIDDELL. Daisies and Buttercups.—Senior Partner.
STOCKTON. Casting Away of Mrs. Lecks.
STOWE. Dred.
WALFORD. Her Great Idea.

To be followed immediately by

BLACKMORE. Alice Lorraine.—Tommy Upmore.
CABLE. Bonaventure.
CROKER. Some One Else.
DE LEON. Under the Stars.
EDWARDS. Half-Way.
HARDY.
  Hand of Ethelberta.—Pair of Blue Eyes.—Two on a Tower.
HATTON. Old House at Sandwich.
HOEY. Golden Sorrow.—Out of Court.—Stern Chase.
INGELOW. John Jerome.—Sarah de Berenger.
MAC DONALD. Vicar's Daughter.—Stephen Archer.
OLIPHANT. Innocent.
STOCKTON. Bee-Man of Orn.
STOWE. Old Town Folk.—Poganuc People.
THOMSON. Ulu.

Low's Standard Books for Boys. With numerous Illustrations,
  2s. 6d.; gilt edges, 3s. 6d. each.
  Dick Cheveley. By W. H. G. KINGSTON.
  Heir of Kilfinnan. By W. H. G. KINGSTON.
  Off to the Wilds. By G. MANVILLE FENN.
  The Two Supercargoes. By W. H. G. KINGSTON.
  The Silver Cañon. By G. MANVILLE FENN.
  Under the Meteor Flag. By HARRY COLLINGWOOD.
  Jack Archer: a Tale of the Crimea. By G. A. HENTY.

Low's Standard Books for Boys—continued.
The Mutiny on Board the Ship Leander. By B. HELDMANN.
With Axe and Rifle on the Western Prairies. By W. H. G. KINGSTON.
Red Cloud, the Solitary Sioux : a Tale of the Great Prairie. By Col. Sir WM. BUTLER, K.C.B.
The Voyage of the Aurora. By HARRY COLLINGWOOD.
Charmouth Grange : a Tale of the 17th Century. By J. PERCY GROVES.
Snowshoes and Canoes. By W. H. G. KINGSTON.
The Son of the Constable of France. By LOUIS ROUSSELET.
Captain Mugford; or, Our Salt and Fresh Water Tutors. Edited by W. H. G. KINGSTON.
The Cornet of Horse, a Tale of Marlborough's Wars. By G. A. HENTY.
The Adventures of Captain Mago. By LEON CAHUN.
Noble Words and Noble Needs.
The King of the Tigers. By ROUSSELET.
Hans Brinker; or, The Silver Skates. By Mrs. DODGE.
The Drummer-Boy, a Story of the time of Washington. By ROUSSELET.
Adventures in New Guinea : The Narrative of Louis Tregance.
The Crusoes of Guiana. By BOUSSENARD.
The Gold Seekers. A Sequel to the Above. By BOUSSENARD.
Winning His Spurs, a Tale of the Crusades. By G. A. HENTY.
The Blue Banner. By LEON CAHUN.

New Volumes for 1889.

Startling Exploits of the Doctor. CÉLIÈRE.
Brothers Rantzau. ERCKMANN-CHATRIAN.
Young Naturalist. BIART.
Ben Burton; or, Born and Bred at Sea. KINGSTON.
Great Hunting Grounds of the World. MEUNIER.
Ran Away from the Dutch. PERELAER.
My Kalulu, Prince, King, and Slave. STANLEY.

Low's Standard Series of Books by Popular Writers. Sm. cr. 8vo, cloth gilt, 2*s.*; gilt edges, 2*s.* 6*d.* each.
Aunt Jo's Scrap Bag. By Miss ALCOTT.
Shawl Straps. By Miss ALCOTT.
Little Men. By Miss ALCOTT.
Hitherto. By Mrs. WHITNEY.
Forecastle to Cabin. By SAMUELS. Illustrated.
In My Indian Garden. By PHIL ROBINSON.
Little Women and Little Women Wedded. By Miss ALCOTT.
Eric and Ethel. By FRANCIS FRANCIS. Illust.
Keyhole Country. By GERTRUDE JERDON. Illust.
We Girls. By Mrs. WHITNEY.
The Other Girls. A Sequel to "We Girls." By Mrs. WHITNEY.
Adventures of Jimmy Brown. Illust. By W. L. ALDEN.
Under the Lilacs. By Miss ALCOTT. Illust.
Jimmy's Cruise. By Miss ALCOTT.
Under the Punkah. By PHIL ROBINSON.

Low's Standard Series of Books by Popular Writers—continued.
An Old-Fashioned Girl. By Miss ALCOTT.
A Rose in Bloom. By Miss ALCOTT.
Eight Cousins. Illust. By Miss ALCOTT.
Jack and Jill. By Miss ALCOTT.
Lulu's Library. Illust. By Miss ALCOTT.
Silver Pitchers. By Miss ALCOTT.
Work and Beginning Again. Illust. By Miss ALCOTT.
A Summer in Leslie Goldthwaite's Life. By Mrs. WHITNEY.
Faith Gartney's Girlhood. By Mrs. WHITNEY.
Real Folks. By Mrs. WHITNEY.
Dred. By Mrs. STOWE.
My Wife and I. By Mrs. STOWE.
An Only Sister. By Madame DE WITT.
Spinning Wheel Stories. By Miss ALCOTT.
My Summer in a Garden. By C. DUDLEY WARNER.

Low's Pocket Encyclopædia: a Compendium of General Know-
ledge for Ready Reference. Upwards of 25,000 References, with
Plates. New ed., imp. 32mo, cloth, marbled edges, 3*s.* 6*d.*; roan, 4*s.* 6*d.*

Low's Handbook to London Charities. Yearly, cloth, 1*s.* 6*d.*;
paper, 1*s.*

Lusignan (Princess A. de) Twelve years' Reign of Abdul Hamid
II. Crown 8vo, 7*s.* 6*d.*

*M*cCULLOCH (*H.*) *Men and Measures of Half a century.*
Sketches and Comments. 8vo, 18*s.*

Macdonald (D.) Oceania. Linguistic and Anthropological.
Illust., and Tables. Crown 8vo, 6*s.*

Mac Donald (George). See LOW'S STANDARD NOVELS.

Macgregor (John) "Rob Roy" on the Baltic. 3rd Edition,
small post 8vo, 2*s.* 6*d.*; cloth, gilt edges, 3*s.* 6*d.*

———— *A Thousand Miles in the "Rob Roy" Canoe.* 11th
Edition, small post 8vo, 2*s.* 6*d.*; cloth, gilt edges, 3*s.* 6*d.*

———— *Voyage Alone in the Yawl "Rob Roy."* New Edition,
with additions, small post 8vo, 3*s.* 6*d.* and 2*s.* 6*d.*

Mackenzie (Sir Morell) Fatal Illness of Frederick the Noble.
Crown 8vo, limp cloth, 2*s.* 6*d.*

Mackenzie (Rev. John) Austral Africa : Losing it or Ruling it?
Illustrations and Maps. 2 vols., 8vo, 32*s.*

Maclean (H. E.) Maid of the Golden Age. Illust., cr. 8vo, 6*s.*

McLellan's Own Story : The War for the Union. Illust. 18*s.*

Maginn (W.) Miscellanies. Prose and Verse. With Memoir.
2 vols., crown 8vo, 24*s.*

Main (Mrs.; Mrs. Fred Burnaby) High Life and Towers of
Silence. Illustrated, square 8vo, 10*s.* 6*d.*

Malan (C. F. de M.) Eric and Connie's Cruise in the South
Pacific. Crown 8vo, 5*s.*

Manning (E. F.) Delightful Thames. Illustrated. 4to, fancy
boards, 5s.

Markham (Clements R.) The Fighting Veres, Sir F. and Sir H.
8vo, 18s.

———— *War between Peru and Chili,* 1879-1881. Third Ed.
Crown 8vo, with Maps, 10s. 6d.

———— See also "Foreign Countries," MAURY, and VERES.

Marston (W.) Eminent Recent Actors, Reminiscences Critical,
&c. 2 vols. Crown 8vo, 21s.; new edit., 1 vol., 6s.

Martin (F. W.) Float Fishing and Spinning in the Nottingham
Style. New Edition. Crown 8vo, 2s. 6d.

Matthews (J. W., M.D.) Incwadi Yami: Twenty years in
South Africa. With many Engravings, royal 8vo, 14s.

Maury (Commander) Physical Geography of the Sea, and its
Meteorology. New Edition, with Charts and Diagrams, cr. 8vo, 6s.

———— *Life.* By his Daughter. Edited by Mr. CLEMENTS R.
MARKHAM. With portrait of Maury. 8vo, 12s. 6d.

Melio (G. L.) Manual of Swedish Drill for Teachers and
Students. Cr. 8vo, 1s. 6d.

Men of Mark: Portraits of the most Eminent Men of the Day.
Complete in 7 Vols., 4to, handsomely bound, gilt edges, 25s. each.

Mendelssohn Family (The), 1729—1847. From Letters and
Journals. Translated. New Edition, 2 vols., 8vo, 30s.

Mendelssohn. See also "Great Musicians."

Merrifield's Nautical Astronomy. Crown 8vo, 7s. 6d.

Mills (J.) Alternative Elementary Chemistry. Ill., cr.8vo, 1s.6d.

Mitford (Mary Russell) Our Village. With 12 full-page and 157
smaller Cuts. Cr. 4to, cloth, gilt edges, 21s.; cheaper binding, 10s.6d.

Mody (Mrs.) Outlines of German Literature. 18mo, 1s.

Moffatt (W.) Land and Work; Depression, Agricultural and
Commercial. Crown 8vo, 5s.

Mohammed Benani: A Story of To-day. 8vo, 10s. 6d.

Mollett (J. W.) Illustrated Dictionary of Words used in Art and
Archæology. Illustrated, small 4to, 15s.

Moore (J. M.) New Zealand for Emigant, Invalid and Tourist.
Cr. 8vo.

Morley (Henry) English Literature in the Reign of Victoria.
2000th volume of the Tauchnitz Collection of Authors. 18mo, 2s. 6d.

Mormonism. See STENHOUSE.

Morse (E. S.) Japanese Homes and their Surroundings. With
more than 300 Illustrations. Re-issue, 10s. 6d.

Morten (Honnor) Sketches of Hospital Life. Cr. 8vo, sewed, 1s.

Morwood. Our Gipsies in City, Tent, and Van. 8vo, 18s.

Moss (F. J.) Through Atolls and Islands of the great South Sea.
Illust., crown 8vo, 8s. 6d.

Moxon (Walter) Pilocereus Senilis.   Fcap. 8vo, gilt top, 3s. 6d.
Muller (E.) Noble Words and Noble Deeds.   Illustrated, gilt
   edges, 3s. 6d.; plainer binding, 2s. 6d.
Musgrave (Mrs.) Miriam.   Crown 8vo, 6s.
Music.   See "Great Musicians."

NETHERCOTE (C. B.) Pytchley Hunt.   New Ed., cr. 8vo,
   8s. 6d.
New Zealand.   See BRADSHAW and WHITE (J.).
New Zealand Rulers and Statesmen.   See GISBORNE.
Nicholls (J. H. Kerry) The King Country: Explorations in
   New Zealand.   Many Illustrations and Map.   New Edition, 8vo, 21s.
Nordhoff (C.) California, for Health, Pleasure, and Residence.
   New Edition, 8vo, with Maps and Illustrations, 12s. 6d.
Norman (C. B.) Corsairs of France.   With Portraits.   8vo, 18s.
North (W.; M.A.) Roman Fever: an Inquiry during three
   years' residence.   Illust., 8vo, 25s.
Northbrook Gallery.   Edited by LORD RONALD GOWER.   36 Per-
   manent Photographs.   Imperial 4to, 63s.; large paper, 105s.
Nott (Major) Wild Animals Photographed and Described.   35s.
Nursery Playmates (Prince of).   217 Coloured Pictures for
   Children by eminent Artists.   Folio, in col. bds., 6s.; new ed., 2s. 6d.
Nursing Record.   Yearly, 8s.; half-yearly, 4s. 6d.; quarterly,
   2s. 6d; weekly, 2d.

O'BRIEN (R. B.) Fifty Years of Concessions to Ireland.
   With a Portrait of T. Drummond.   Vol. I., 16s., II., 16s.
Orient Line Guide.   New edition re-written; by W. J. LOFTIE.
   Maps and Plans, 2s. 6d.
Orvis (C. F.) Fishing with the Fly.   Illustrated.   8vo, 12s. 6d.
Osborne (Duffield) Spell of Ashtaroth.   Crown 8vo, 5s.
Our Little Ones in Heaven.   Edited by the Rev. H. ROBBINS.
   With Frontispiece after Sir JOSHUA REYNOLDS.   New Edition, 5s.

PALGRAVE (R. F. D.) Oliver Cromwell and his Protec-
   torate.   Crown 8vo.
Pall ser (Mrs.) A History of Lace.   New Edition, with additional cuts and text.   8vo, 21s.
   ——— *The China Collector's Pocket Companion.*   With upwards of 1000 Illustrations of Marks and Monograms.   Small 8vo, 5s.
Panton (J. E.) Homes of Taste.   Hints on Furniture and Deco-
   ration.   Crown 8vo, 2s. 6d.
Parsons (James; A.M.) Exposition of the Principles of Partner-
   ship.   8vo, 31s. 6d.

Pennell (H. Cholmondeley) Sporting Fish of Great Britain
15*s.*; large paper, 30*s.*

—— *Modern Improvements in Fishing-tackle.* Crown 8vo, 2*s.*

Perelaer (M. T. H.) Ran Away from the Dutch; Borneo, &c.
Illustrated, square 8vo, 7*s.* 6 ; new ed., 2*s.* 6*d.*

Perry (J. J. M.) Edlingham Burglary, or Circumstantial Evi-
dence. Crown 8vo, 3*s.* 6*d.*

Phelps (Elizabeth Stuart) Struggle for Immortality. Cr. 8vo, 5*s.*

Phillips' Dictionary of Biographical Reference. New edition,
royal 8vo, 25*s.*

Philpot (H. J.) Diabetes Mellitus. Crown 8vo, 5*s.*

—— *Diet System.* Tables. I. Diabetes; II. Gout;
III. Dyspepsia; IV. Corpulence. In cases, 1*s.* each.

Plunkett (Major G. T.) Primer of Orthographic Projection.
Elementary Solid Geometry. With Problems and Exercises. 2*s.* 6*d.*

Poe (E. A.) The Raven. Illustr. by DORÉ. Imperial folio, 63*s.*

Poems of the Inner Life. Chiefly Modern. Small 8vo, 5*s.*

Poetry of the Anti-Jacobin. New ed., by CHARLES EDMONDS.
Cr. 8vo, 7*s.* 6*d.*; large paper, 21*s.*

Porcher (A.) Juvenile French Plays. With Notes and a
Vocabulary. 18mo, 1*s.*

Porter (Admiral David D.) Naval History of Civil War.
Portraits, Plans, &c. 4to, 25*s.*

Portraits of Celebrated Race-horses of the Past and Present
Centuries, with Pedigrees and Performances. 4 vols., 4to, 126*s.*

Powles (L. D.) Land of the Pink Pearl: Life in the Bahamas.
8vo, 10*s.* 6*d.*

Poynter (Edward J., R.A.). See " Illustrated Text-books."

Prince Maskiloff: a Romance of Modern Oxford. By ROY
TELLET. Crown 8vo, 10*s.* 6*d.*

Prince of Nursery Playmates. Col. plates, new ed., 2*s.* 6*d.*

Pritt (T. E.) North Country Flies. Illustrated from the
Author's Drawings. 10*s.* 6*d.*

Publishers' Circular (The), and General Record of British and
Foreign Literature. Published on the 1st and 15th of every Month, 3*d.*

Pyle (Howard) Otto of the Silver Hand. Illustrated by the
Author. 8vo, 8*s.* 6*d.*

QUEEN'S Prime Ministers. A series. Edited by S. J. REID.
Cr. 8vo, 2*s.* 6*d.* per vol.

RAMBAUD. History of Russia. New Edition, Illustrated.
3 vols., 8vo, 21*s.*

Reber.   History of Mediæval Art.   Translated by CLARKE.
422 Illustrations and Glossary. 8vo,   .

Redford (G.) Ancient Sculpture. New Ed. Crown 8vo, 10s. 6d.

Redgrave (G. R.) Century of Painters of the English School
Crown 8vo, 10s. 6d.

Reed (Sir E. J., M.P.) and Simpson.   Modern Ships of War.
Illust., royal 8vo, 10s. 6d.

Reed (Talbot B.) Sir Ludar: a Tale of the Days of good Queen
Bess. Crown 8vo, 6s.

Remarkable Bindings in the British Museum.   India paper,
94s. 6d. ; sewed 73s. 6d. and 63s.

Reminiscences of a Boyhood in the early part of the Century: a
Story. Crown 8vo, 6s.

Ricci (J. H. de) Fisheries Dispute, and the Annexation of
Canada. Crown 8vo, 6s.

Richards (W.) Aluminium: its History, Occurrence, &c.
Illustrated, crown 8vo, 12s. 6d.

Richter (Dr. Jean Paul) Italian Art in the National Gallery.
4to. Illustrated. Cloth gilt, £2 2s.; half-morocco, uncut, £2 12s. 6d.

—— See also LEONARDO DA VINCI.

Riddell (Mrs. J. H.) See Low's STANDARD NOVELS.

Roberts (W.) Earlier History of English Bookselling. Crown
8vo, 7s. 6d.

Robertson (T. W.) Principal Dramatic Works, with Portraits
in photogravure. 2 vols., 21s.

Robin Hood; Merry Adventures of. Written and illustrated
by HOWARD PYLE. Imperial 8vo, 15s.

Robinson (Phil.) In my Indian Garden. New Edition, 16mo,
limp cloth, 2s.

—— *Noah's Ark. Unnatural History.* Sm. post 8vo, 12s. 6d.

—— *Sinners and Saints : a Tour across the United States of*
America, and Round them. Crown 8vo, 10s. 6d.

—— *Under the Punkah.* New Ed., cr. 8vo, limp cloth, 2s.

Rockstro (W. S.) History of Music. New Edition. 8vo, 14s.

Roe (E. P.) Nature's Serial Story. Illust. New ed. 3s. 6d.

Roland, The Story of. Crown 8vo, illustrated, 6s.

Rose (F.) Complete Practical Machinist. New Ed., 12mo, 12s. 6d.

—— *Key to Engines and Engine-running.* Crown 8vo, 8s. 6d.

—— *Mechanical Drawing.* Illustrated, small 4to, 16s.

—— *Modern Steam Engines.* Illustrated. 31s. 6d.

—— *Steam Boilers.   Boiler Construction and Examination.*
Illust., 8vo, 12s. 6d.

Rose Library. Each volume, 1*s*. Many are illustrated—

Little Women. By LOUISA M. ALCOTT.

Little Women Wedded. Forming a Sequel to " Little Women.

Little Women and Little Women Wedded. 1 vol., cloth gilt, 3*s*. 6*d*.

Little Men. By L. M. ALCOTT. Double vol., 2*s*.; cloth gilt, 3*s*. 6*d*.

An Old-Fashioned Girl. By LOUISA M. ALCOTT. 2*s*.; cloth, 3*s*. 6*d*.

Work. A Story of Experience. By L. M. ALCOTT. 3*s*. 6*d*.; 2 vols., 1*s*. each.

Stowe (Mrs. H. B.) The Pearl of Orr's Island.

———— **The Minister's Wooing.**

———— **We and our Neighbours.** 2*s*.; cloth gilt, 6*s*.

———— **My Wife and I.** 2*s*.

Hans Brinker; or, the Silver Skates. By Mrs. DODGE. Also 2*s*.6*d*.

My Study Windows. By J. R. LÒWELL.

The Guardian Angel. By OLIVER WENDELL HOLMES. Cloth, 2*s*.

My Summer in a Garden. By C. D. WARNER.

Dred. By Mrs. BEECHER STOWE. 2*s*.; cloth gilt, 3*s*. 6*d*.

City Ballads. New Ed. 16mo. By WILL CARLETON.

Farm Ballads. By WILL CARLETON. ⎫

Farm Festivals. By WILL CARLETON. ⎬ 1 vol., cl., gilt ed., 3*s*. 6*d*.

Farm Legends. By WILL CARLETON. ⎭

The Rose in Bloom. By L. M. ALCOTT. 2*s*.; cloth gilt, 3*s*. 6*d*.

Eight Cousins. By L. M. ALCOTT. 2*s*.; cloth gilt, 3*s*. 6*d*.

Under the Lilacs. By L. M. ALCOTT. 2*s*.; also 3*s*. 6*d*.

Undiscovered Country. By W. D. HOWELLS.

Clients of Dr. Bernagius. By L. BIART. 2 parts.

Silver Pitchers. By LOUISA M. ALCOTT. Cloth, 3*s*. 6*d*.

Jimmy's Cruise in the "Pinafore," and other Tales. By LOUISA M. ALCOTT. 2*s*.; cloth gilt, 3*s*. 6*d*.

Jack and Jill. By LOUISA M. ALCOTT. 2*s*.; Illustrated, 5*s*.

Hitherto. By the Author of the "Gayworthys." 2 vols., 1*s*. each; 1 vol., cloth gilt, 3*s*. 6*d*.

A Gentleman of Leisure. A Novel. By EDGAR FAWCETT. 1*s*.

See also LOW'S STANDARD SERIES.

Ross (Mars) and Stonehewer Cooper. Highlands of Cantabria ; or, Three Days from England. Illustrations and Map, 8vo, 21*s*.

Rothschilds, the Financial Rulers of Nations. By JOHN REEVES. Crown 8vo, 7*s*. 6*d*.

Rousselet (Louis) Son of the Constable of France. Small post 8vo, numerous Illustrations, gilt edges, 3*s*. 6*d*.; plainer, 2*s*. 6*d*.

———— *King of the Tigers : a Story of Central India.* Illustrated. Small post 8vo, gilt, 3*s*. 6*d*.; plainer, 2*s*. 6*d*.

———— *Drummer Boy.* Illustrated. Small post 8vo, gilt edges, 3*s*. 6*d*.; plainer, 2*s*. 6*d*.

Russell (Dora) Strange Message. 3 vols., crown 8vo, 31*s*. 6*d*.

Russell (W. Clark) Betwixt the Forelands. Illust., crown 8vo, 10*s*. 6*d*.

Russell (W. Clark) English Channel Ports and the Estate of the East and West India Dock Company. Crown 8vo, 1*s*.

———— *Sailor's Language.* Illustrated Crown 8vo, 3*s*. 6*d*.

———— *Wreck of the Grosvenor.* 4to, sewed, 6*d*.

———— See also " Low's Standard Novels," " Sea Stories."

SAINTS and their Symbols: A Companion in the Churches and Picture Galleries of Europe. Illustrated. Royal 16mo, 3*s*. 6*d*.

Samuels (Capt. J. S.) From Forecastle to Cabin : Autobiography. Illustrated. Crown 8vo, 8*s*. 6*d*.; also with fewer Illustrations, cloth, 2*s*.; paper, 1*s*.

Saunders (A.) Our Domestic Birds : Poultry in England and New Zealand. Crown 8vo, 6*s*.

———— *Our Horses : the Best Muscles controlled by the Best* Brains. 6*s*.

Scherr (Prof. J.) History of English Literature. Cr. 8vo, 8*s*. 6*d*.

Schuyler (Eugène) American Diplomacy and the Furtherance of Commerce. 12*s*. 6*d*.

———— *The Life of Peter the Great.* 2 vols., 8vo, 32*s*.

Schweinfurth (Georg) Heart of Africa. 2 vols., crown 8vo, 15*s*.

Scott (Leader) Renaissance of Art in Italy. 4to, 31*s*. 6*d*.

———— *Sculpture, Renaissance and Modern.* 5*s*.

Sea Stories. By W. CLARK RUSSELL. New ed. Cr. 8vo, leather back, top edge gilt, per vol., 3*s*. 6*d*.

Frozen Pirate.	Sea Queen.
Jack's Courtship.	Strange Voyage.
John Holdsworth.	The Lady Maud.
Little Loo.	Watch Below.
Ocean Free Lance.	Wreck of the *Grosvenor*.
Sailor's Sweetheart.	

Semmes (Adm. Raphael) Service Afloat : The " Sumter " and the " Alabama." Illustrated. Royal 8vo, 16*s*.

Senior (W.) Near and Far : an Angler's Sketches of Home Sport and Colonial Life. Crown 8vo, 6*s*.; new edit., 2*s*.

———— *Waterside Sketches.* Imp. 32mo, 1*s*. 6*d*.; boards, 1*s*.

Shakespeare. Edited by R. GRANT WHITE. 3 vols., crown 8vo, gilt top, 36*s*.; *édition de luxe*, 6 vols., 8vo, cloth extra, 63*s*.

Shakespeare's Heroines : Studies by Living English Painters. 105*s*.; artists' proofs, 630*s*.

———— *Macbeth.* With Etchings on Copper, by J. MOYR SMITH. 105*s*. and 52*s*. 6*d*.

———— *Songs and Sonnets.* Illust. by Sir JOHN GILBERT, R.A. 4to, boards, 5*s*.

———— See also CUNDALL, DETHRONING, DONNELLY, MACKAY, and WHITE (R. GRANT).

Sharpe (R. Bowdler) Birds in Nature. 39 coloured plates and text. 4to, 63*s*

Sheridan. Rivals. Reproductions of Water-colour, &c. 52*s*.6*d*.; artists proofs, 105*s*. nett.

Shields (C. W.) Philosophia ultima ; from Harmony of Science and Religion. 2 vols. 8vo, 24*s*.

Shields (G. O.) Cruisings in the Cascades; Hunting, Photography, Fishing. 8vo, 10*s*. 6*d*.

Sidney (Sir Philip) Arcadia. New Edition, 3*s*. 6*d*.

Siegfried, The Story of. Illustrated, crown 8vo, cloth, 6*s*.

Simon. China : its Social Life. Crown 8vo, 6*s*.

Simson (A.) Wilds of Ecuador and Exploration of the Putumayor · River. Crown 8vo, 8*s*. 6*d*.

Sinclair (Mrs.) Indigenous Flowers of the Hawaiian Islands. 44 Plates in Colour. Imp. folio, extra binding, gilt edges, 31*s*. 6*d*.

Sloane (T. O.) Home Experiments in Science for Old and Young. Crown 8vo, 6*s*.

Smith (G.) Assyrian Explorations. Illust. New Ed., 8vo, 18*s*.

———— *The Chaldean Account of Genesis.* With many Illustrations. 16*s*. New Ed. By PROFESSOR SAYCE. 8vo, 18*s*.

Smith (G. Barnett) William I. and the German Empire. New Ed., 8vo, 3*s*. 6*d*.

Smith (Sydney) Life and Times. By STUART J. REID. Illustrated. 8vo, 21*s*.

Spiers' French Dictionary. 29th Edition, remodelled. 2 vols., 8vo, 18*s*.; half bound, 21*s*.

Spry (W. J. J., R.N., F.R.G.S.) Cruise of H.M.S." Challenger." With Illustrations. 8vo, 18*s*. Cheap Edit., crown 8vo, 7*s*. 6*d*.

Stanley (H. M.) Congo, and Founding its Free State. Illustrated, 2 vols., 8vo, 42*s*. ; re-issue, 2 vols. 8vo, 21*s*

———— *How I Found Livingstone.* 8vo, 10*s*. 6*d*. ; cr. 8vo, 7*s*. 6*d*.

———— *Through the Dark Continent.* Crown 8vo, 12*s*. 6*d*.

Start (J. W. K.) Junior Mensuration Exercises. 8*d*.

Stenhouse (Mrs.) Tyranny of Mormonism. An Englishwoman in Utah. New ed., cr. 8vo, cloth elegant, 3*s*. 6*d*.

Sterry (J. Ashby) Cucumber Chronicles. 5*s*.

Stevens (E. W.) Fly-Fishing in Maine Lakes. 8*s*. 6*d*.

Stevens (T.) Around the World on a Bicycle. Vol. II. 8vo. 16*s*.

Stockton (Frank R.) Rudder Grange. 3*s*. 6*d*.

———— *Bee-Man of Orn, and other Fanciful Tales.* Cr. 8vo, 5*s*.

———— *Personally conducted.* Crown 8vo, 7*s*. 6*d*.

———— *The Casting Away of Mrs. Lecks and Mrs. Aleshine.* 1*s*.

———— *The Dusantes.* Sequel to the above. Sewed, 1*s*.; this and the preceding book in one volume, cloth, 2*s*. 6*d*.

Stockton (Frank R.) The Hundredth Man. Small post 8vo, 6s.
—————— *The Late Mrs. Null.* Small post 8vo, 6s.
—————— *The Story of Viteau.* Illust. Cr. 8vo, 5s.
—————— See also LOW'S STANDARD NOVELS.
Stowe (Mrs. Beecher) Dred. Cloth, gilt edges, 3s. 6d.; cloth, 2s.
—————— *Flowers and Fruit from her Writings.* Sm. post 8vo, 3s. 6d.
—————— *Life, in her own Words . . . with Letters and Original* Compositions. 10s. 6d.
—————— *Little Foxes.* Cheap Ed., 1s.; Library Edition, 4s. 6d.
—————— *My Wife and I.* Cloth, 2s.
—————— *Old Town Folk.* 6s.
—————— *We and our Neighbours.* 2s.
—————— *Poganuc People.* 6s.
—————— See also ROSE LIBRARY.
Strachan (J.) Explorations and Adventures in New Guinea. Illust., crown 8vo, 12s.
Stranahan (C. H.) History of French Painting, the Academy, Salons, Schools, &c. 21s.
Stutfield (Hugh E. M.) El Maghreb: 1200 Miles' Ride through Marocco. 8s. 6d.
Sullivan (A. M.) Nutshell History of Ireland. Paper boards, 6d.
Sylvanus Redivivus, Rev. J. Mitford, with a Memoir of E. Jesse. Crown 8vo, 10s. 6d.

TAINE (H. A.) " Origines." Translated by JOHN DURAND.
  I.   **The Ancient Regime.** Demy 8vo, cloth, 16s.
  II. **The French Revolution.** Vol. 1. do.
  III. **Do.** **do.** Vol. 2. do.
  IV. **Do.** **do.** Vol. 3. do.
Tauchnitz's English Editions of German Authors. Each volume, cloth flexible, 2s.; or sewed, 1s. 6d. (Catalogues post free.)
Tauchnitz (B.) German Dictionary. 2s.; paper, 1s. 6d.; roan, 2s. 6d.
—————— *French Dictionary.* 2s.; paper, 1s. 6d.; roan, 2s. 6d.
—————— *Italian Dictionary.* 2s.; paper, 1s. 6d.; roan, 2s. 6d.
—————— *Latin Dictionary.* 2s.; paper, 1s. 6d.; roan, 2s. 6d.
—————— *Spanish and English.* 2s.; paper, 1s. 6d.; roan, 2s. 6d.
—————— *Spanish and French.* 2s.; paper, 1s. 6d.; roan, 2s. 6d.
Taylor (R. L.) Chemical Analysis Tables. 1s.
—————— *Chemistry for Beginners.* Small 8vo, 1s. 6d.
Techno-Chemical Receipt Book. With additions by BRANNT and WAHL. 10s. 6d.

Technological Diction try. See TOLHAUSEN.
Thausing (Prof.) Malt and the Fabrication of Beer. 8vo, 45*s.*
Theakston (M.) British Angling Flies. Illustrated. Cr. 8vo, 5*s.*
Thomson (Jos.) Central African Lakes. New edition, 2 vols.
 in one, crown 8vo, 7*s.* 6*d.*
———— *Through Masai Land.* Illust. 21*s.*; new edition, 7*s.* 6*d.*
———— *and Miss Harris-Smith. Ulu: an African Romance.*
 crown 8vo, 6*s.*
Thomson (W.) Algebra for Colleges and Schools. With Answers,
 5*s.*; without, 4*s.* 6*d.*; Answers separate, 1*s.* 6*d.*
Th rnton (L. D.) Story of a Poodle. By Himself and his
 Mistress. Illust., crown 4to, 2*s.* 6*d.*
Thorrodsen, Lad and Lass. Translated from the Icelandic by
 A. M. REEVES. Crown 8vo.
Tissandier (G.) Eiffel Tower. Illust., and letter of M. Eiffel
 in facsimile. Fcap. 8vo, 1*s.*
Tolhausen. Technological German, English, and French Dic-
 tionary. Vols. I., II., with Supplement, 12*s.* 6*d.* each; III., 9*s.*;
 Supplement, cr. 8vo, 3*s.* 6*d.*
Topmkins (E. S. de G.) Through David's Realm. Illust. by
 the Author. 8vo, 10*s.* 6*d.*
Tucker (W. J.) Life and Society in Eastern Europe. 15*s.*
Tuckerman (B. Life of General Lafayette. 2 vols., cr. 8vo, 12*s.*
Tupper (Martin Farquhar) My Life as an Author. 14*s.*; new
 edition, 7*s.* 6*d.*
Tytler (Sarah) Duchess Frances: a Novel. 2 vols., 21*s.*

*U*PTON (*H.) Manual of Practical Dairy Farming.* Cr.
 8vo, 2*s.*

*V*AN DAM. *Land of Rubens; a companion for visitors to*
 Belgium. Crown 8vo, 3*s.* 6*d.*
Vane (Young Sir Harry). By Prof. JAMES K. HOSMER.
 8vo, 18*s.*
Veres. Biography of Sir Francis Vere and Lord Vere, leading
 Generals in the Netherlands. By CLEMENTS R. MARKHAM. 8vo, 18*s.*
Verne (Jules) Celebrated Travels and Travellers. 3 vols. 8vo,
 7*s.* 6*d.* each; extra gilt, 9*s.*
Victoria (Queen) Life of. By GRACE GREENWOOD. Illust. 6*s.*
Vincent (Mrs. Howard) Forty Thousand Miles over Land and
 Water. With Illustrations. New Edit., 3*s.* 6*d.*
Viollet-le-Duc (E.) Lectures on Architecture. Translated by
 BENJAMIN BUCKNALL, Architect. 2 vols., super-royal 8vo, £3 3*s.*

BOOKS BY JULES VERNE.

LARGE CROWN 8vo. WORKS.	Containing 350 to 600 pp. and from 50 to 100 full-page illustrations.				Containing the whole of the text with some illustrations.			
	In very handsome cloth binding, gilt edges.		In, plainer binding, plain edges.		In cloth binding, gilt edges, smaller type.		Coloured boards, or cloth.	
	s.	d.	s.	d.	s.	d.		
20,000 Leagues under the Sea. Parts I. and II.	10	6	5	0	3	6	2 vols., 1s. each.	
Hector Servadac	10	6	5	0	3	6	2 vols., 1s. each.	
The Fur Country	10	6	5	0	3	6	2 vols., 1s. each.	
The Earth to the Moon and a Trip round it	10	6	5	0	{ 2 vols., 2s. ea. }		2 vols., 1s. each.	
Michael Strogoff	10	6	5	0	3	6	2 vols., 1s. each.	
Dick Sands, the Boy Captain	10	6	5	0	3	6	2 vols., 1s. each.	
Five Weeks in a Balloon	7	6	3	6	2	0	1s. 0d.	
Adventures of Three Englishmen and Three Russians	7	6	3	6	2	0	1	0
Round the World in Eighty Days	7	6	3	6	2	0	1	0
A Floating City	7	6	3	6	2	0	1	0
The Blockade Runners					2	0	1	0
Dr. Ox's Experiment	—		—		2	0	1	0
A Winter amid the Ice	—		—		2	0	1	0
Survivors of the "Chancellor"	7	6	3	6	3	6·	2 vols., 1s. each.	
Martin Paz					2	0	1s. 0d.	
The Mysterious Island, 3 vols. :—	22	6	10	6	6	0	3	0
I. Dropped from the Clouds	7	6	3	6	2	0	1	0
II. Abandoned	7	6	3	6	2	0	1	0
III. Secret of the Island	7	6	3	6	2	0	1	0
The Child of the Cavern	7	6	3	6	2	0	1	0
The Begum's Fortune	7	6	3	6	2	0	1	0
The Tribulations of a Chinaman	7	6	3	6	2	0	1	0
The Steam House, 2 vols. :—								
I. Demon of Cawnpore	7	6	3	6	2	0	1	0
II. Tigers and Traitors	7	6	3	6	2	0	1	0
The Giant Raft, 2 vols. :—								
I. 800 Leagues on the Amazon	7	6	3	6	2	0	1	0
II. The Cryptogram	7	6	3	6	2	0	1	0
The Green Ray	6	0	5	0	—		1	0
Godfrey Morgan	7	6	3	6	2	0	1	0
Kéraban the Inflexible:—								
I. Captain of the "Guidara"	7	6	3	6	2	0	1	0
II. Scarpante the Spy	7	6	3	6	2	0	1	0
The Archipelago on Fire	7	6	3	6	2	0	1	0
The Vanished Diamond	7	6	3	6	2	0	1	0
Mathias Sandorf	10	6	5	0	3	6	2 vols., 1s. each.	
The Lottery Ticket	7	6	3	6				
The Clipper of the Clouds	7	6	3	6				
North against South	7	6						
Adrift in the Pacific	7	6						
Flight to France	7	6						

WALFORD (Mrs. L. B.) Her Great Idea, and other Stories.
Cr. 8vo, 10s. 6d.; also new ed., 6s.

Wallace (L.) Ben Hur: A Tale of the Christ. New Edition,
crown 8vo, 6s.; cheaper edition, 2s.

Wallack (L.) Memories of 50 Years; with many Portraits, and
Facsimiles. Small 4to, 63s. nett; ordinary edition 7s. 6d.

Waller (Rev. C.H.) Adoption and the Covenant. On Confirmation. 2s. 6d.

—————— *Silver Sockets; and other Shadows of Redemption.*
Sermons at Christ Church, Hampstead. Small post 8vo, 6s.

—————— *The Names on the Gates of Pearl, and other Stu..ies.*
New Edition. Crown 8vo, cloth extra, 3s. 6d.

—————— *Words in the Greek Testament.* Part I. Grammar.
Small post 8vo, cloth, 2s. 6d. Part II. Vocabulary, 2s. 6d.

Walsh(A.S.) Mary, Queen of the House of David. 8vo, 3s. 6d.

Walton (Iz.) Wallet Book, CIↃIↃLXXXV. Crown 8vo, half
vellum, 21s.; large paper, 42s.

—————— *Compleat Angler.* Lea and Dove Edition. Ed. by R. B.
MARSTON. With full-page Photogravures on India paper, and the
Woodcuts on India paper from blocks. 4to, half-morocco, 105s.;
large paper, royal 4to, full dark green morocco, gilt top, 210s.

Walton (T. H.) Coal Mining. With Illustrations. 4to, 25s.

War Scare in Europe. Crown 8vo, 2s. 6d.

Warner (C. D.) My Summer in a Garden. Boards, 1s.;
leatherette, 1s. 6d.; cloth, 2s.

—————— *Their Pilgrimage.* Illustrated by C. S. REINHART.
8vo, 7s. 6d.

Warren (W. F.) Paradise Found; the North Pole the Cradle
of the Human Race. Illustrated. Crown 8vo, 12s. 6d.

Washington Irving's Little Britain. Square crown 8vo, 6s.

Watson (P. B.) Swedish Revolution under Gustavus Vasa. 8vo.

Wells (H. P.) American Salmon Fisherman. 6s.

—————— *Fly Rods and Fly Tackle.* Illustrated. 10s. 6d.

Wells (J. W.) Three Thousand Miles through Brazil. Illustrated from Original Sketches. 2 vols. 8vo, 32s.

Wenzel (O.) Directory of Chemical Products of the German
Empire. 8vo, 25s.

Westgarth (W.) Half-century of Australasian Progress. Personal
retrospect. 8vo, 12s.

Wheatley (H. B.) Remarkable Bindings in the British Museum.
Reproductions in Colour, 94s. 6d., 73s. 6d., and 63s.

White (J.) Ancient History of the Maori; Mythology, &c.
Vols. I.-IV. 8vo, 10s. 6d. each.

White (R. Grant) England Without and Within. Crown 8vo,
10s. 6d.

—————— *Every-day English.* 10s. 6d.

White (R. Grant) Fate of Mansfield Humphreys,&c.   Cr. 8vo, 6s.
———— *Studies in Shakespeare.*   10s. 6d.
———— *Words and their Uses.*   New Edit., crown 8vo, 5s.
Whitney (Mrs.) The Other Girls.   A Sequel to "We Girls."
  New ed.   12mo, 2s.
———— *We Girls.*   New Edition.   2s.
Whittier (J. G.) The King's Missive, and later Poems.   18mo,
  choice parchment cover, 3s. 6d.
———— *St. Gregory's Guest, &c.*   Recent Poems.   5s.
William I. and the German Empire.   By G. BARNETT SMITH.
  New Edition, 3s. 6d.
Willis-Bund (J.) Salmon Problems.   3s. 6d.; boards, 2s. 6d.
Wills (Dr. C. J.) Persia as it is.   Crown 8vo, 8s. 6d.
Wills, A Few Hints on Proving, without Professional Assistance.
  By a PROBATE COURT OFFICIAL.   8th Edition, revised, with Forms
  of Wills, Residuary Accounts, &c.   Fcap. 8vo, cloth limp, 1s.
Wilmot (A.) Poetry of South Africa Collected.   8vo, 6s.
Wilmot-Buxton (Ethel M.) Wee Folk, Good Folk: a Fantasy.
  Illust., fcap. 4to, 5s.
Winder (Frederick Horatio) Lost in Africa: a Yarn of Adven-
  ture.   Illust., cr. 8vo, 6s.
Winsor (Justin) Narrative and Critical History of America.
  8 vols., 30s. each; large paper, per vol., 63s.
Woolsey.   Introduction to International Law.   5th Ed., 18s.
Woolson (Constance F.)   See "Low's Standard Novels."
Wright (H.) Friendship of God.   Portrait, &c.   Crown 8vo, 6s.
Wright (T.) Town of Cowper, Olney, &c.   6s.
Wrigley (M.) Algiers Illustrated.   100 Views in Photogravure.
  Royal 4to, 45s.
Written to Order; the Journeyings of an Irresponsible Egotist.
  By the Author of "A Day of my Life at Eton."   Crown 8vo, 6s.

YRIARTE (Charles) Florence: its History.   Translated by
  C. B. PITMAN.   Illustrated with 500 Engravings.   Large imperial
  4to, extra binding, gilt edges, 63s.; or 12 Parts, 5s. each.

ZILLMAN (J. H. L.) Past and Present Australian Life.
  With Stories.   Crown 8vo, 2s.

London:

SAMPSON LOW, MARSTON, SEARLE, & RIVINGTON, LD.,

St. Dunstan's House,

FETTER LANE, FLEET STREET, E.C.

Gilbert and Rivington, Ld., St. John's House, Clerkenwell Road, E.C.